Praise for Lexi Blake and Masters and Mercenaries...

"I can always trust Lexi Blake's Dominants to leave me breathless... and in love. If you want sensual, exciting BDSM wrapped in an awesome love story, then look for a Lexi Blake book."

~ *New York Times* bestselling author Cherise Sinclair

"A master at sexy, thrilling romance."

~ *New York Times* bestselling author Jennifer Probst

"Lexi Blake can do no wrong!"

~ *New York Times* bestselling author Carly Phillips

"Lexi Blake has set up show on the intersection of suspenseful and sexy, and I never want to leave."

~ *New York Times* bestselling author Laurelin Paige

"Smart, savvy, clever, and always entertaining."

~ *New York Times* bestselling author Steve Berry

"Lexi Blake's MASTERS AND MERCENARIES series is beautifully written and deliciously hot. She's got a real way with both action and sex. I also love the way Blake writes her gorgeous Dom heroes--they make me want to do bad, bad things. Her heroines are intelligent and gutsy ladies whose taste for submission definitely does not make them dish rags. Can't wait for the next book!"

~ *New York Times* bestselling author Angela Knight

"Ms. Blake's writing draws you in and will keep you riveted from the first chapter to the last."

~ Erin, Thelma and Louise Book Blog

"I can't get enough of the Masters and Mercenaries Series! Love and Let Die is Lexi Blake at her best! She writes erotic romantic suspense like no other, and I am always extremely excited when she has something new for us! Intense, heart pounding, and erotically fulfilling, I could not put this book down."

~ Shayna Renee, Shayna Renee's Spicy Reads

Love and Let Spy

Other Books by Lexi Blake

ROMANTIC SUSPENSE

Masters and Mercenaries
The Dom Who Loved Me
The Men With The Golden Cuffs
A Dom is Forever
On Her Master's Secret Service
Sanctum: A Masters and Mercenaries Novella
Love and Let Die
Unconditional: A Masters and Mercenaries Novella
Dungeon Royale
Dungeon Games: A Masters and Mercenaries Novella
A View to a Thrill
Cherished: A Masters and Mercenaries Novella
You Only Love Twice
Luscious: Masters and Mercenaries~Topped
Adored: A Masters and Mercenaries Novella
Master No
Just One Taste: Masters and Mercenaries~Topped 2
From Sanctum with Love
Devoted: A Masters and Mercenaries Novella
Dominance Never Dies
Submission is Not Enough
Master Bits and Mercenary Bites~The Secret Recipes of Topped
Perfectly Paired: Masters and Mercenaries~Topped 3
For His Eyes Only
Arranged: A Masters and Mercenaries Novella
Love Another Day
At Your Service: Masters and Mercenaries~Topped 4
Master Bits and Mercenary Bites~Girls Night
Nobody Does It Better
Close Cover
Protected: A Masters and Mercenaries Novella
Enchanted: A Masters and Mercenaries Novella
Charmed: A Masters and Mercenaries Novella
Taggart Family Values
Treasured: A Masters and Mercenaries Novella
Delighted: A Masters and Mercenaries Novella
Tempted: A Masters and Mercenaries Novella

Masters and Mercenaries: The Forgotten
Lost Hearts (Memento Mori)
Lost and Found
Lost in You
Long Lost
No Love Lost

Masters and Mercenaries: Reloaded
Submission Impossible
The Dom Identity
The Man from Sanctum
No Time to Lie
The Dom Who Came in from the Cold

Masters and Mercenaries: New Recruits
Love the Way You Spy
Live, Love, Spy
Sweet Little Spies
The Bodyguard and the Bombshell: A Masters and Mercenaries New Recruits Novella
No More Spies
Spy With Me
Love and Let Spy

Butterfly Bayou
Butterfly Bayou
Bayou Baby
Bayou Dreaming
Bayou Beauty
Bayou Sweetheart
Bayou Beloved

Park Avenue Promise
Start Us Up
My Royal Showmance
Built to Last

Lawless
Ruthless
Satisfaction
Revenge

Courting Justice
Order of Protection
Evidence of Desire

Masters Of Ménage (by Shayla Black and Lexi Blake)
Their Virgin Captive
Their Virgin's Secret
Their Virgin Concubine
Their Virgin Princess
Their Virgin Hostage
Their Virgin Secretary
Their Virgin Mistress

The Perfect Gentlemen (by Shayla Black and Lexi Blake)
Scandal Never Sleeps
Seduction in Session
Big Easy Temptation
Smoke and Sin
At the Pleasure of the President

URBAN FANTASY

Thieves
Steal the Light
Steal the Day
Steal the Moon
Steal the Sun
Steal the Night
Ripper
Addict
Sleeper
Outcast
Stealing Summer
The Rebel Queen
The Rebel Guardian
The Rebel Witch
The Rebel Seer

LEXI BLAKE WRITING AS SOPHIE OAK

Texas Sirens
Small Town Siren
Siren in the City

Siren Enslaved
Siren Beloved
Siren in Waiting
Siren in Bloom
Siren Unleashed
Siren Reborn
The Accidental Siren
The Reluctant Siren

Nights in Bliss, Colorado
Three to Ride
Two to Love
One to Keep
Lost in Bliss
Found in Bliss
Pure Bliss
Chasing Bliss
Once Upon a Time in Bliss
Back in Bliss
Sirens in Bliss
Happily Ever After in Bliss
Far from Bliss
Unexpected Bliss
Wild Bliss
Brooke's Bliss

A Faery Story
Bound
Beast
Beauty

Standalone
Away From Me
Snowed In

Love and Let Spy

Masters and Mercenaries
New Recruits, Book 6

Lexi Blake

Love and Let Spy
Masters and Mercenaries: New Recruits, Book 6
Lexi Blake

Published by DLZ Entertainment LLC

Edited by Chloe Vale
ISBN: 978-1-963890-33-4

Sign up for Lexi Blake's newsletter
and be entered to win a $25 gift certificate
to the bookseller of your choice.

Join us for news, fun, and exclusive content
including free Thieves short stories.

There's a new contest every month!

Go to www.LexiBlake.net to subscribe.

Family Trees

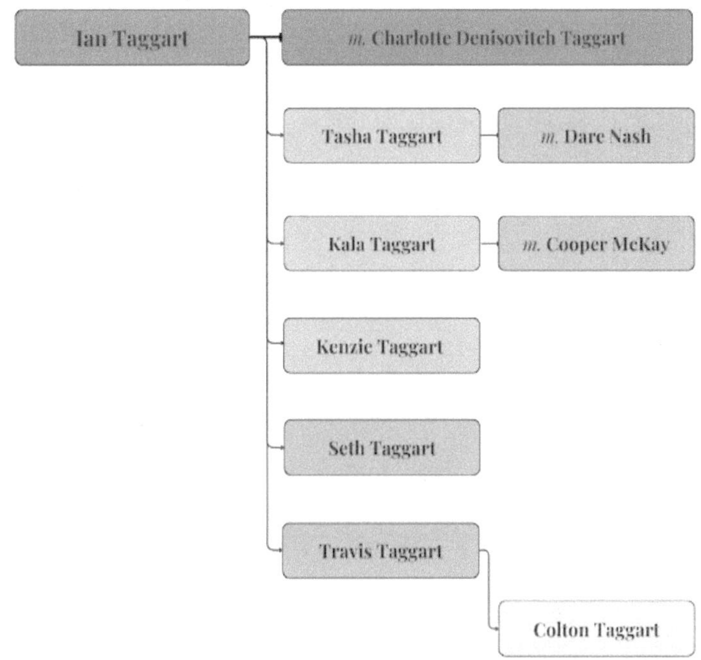

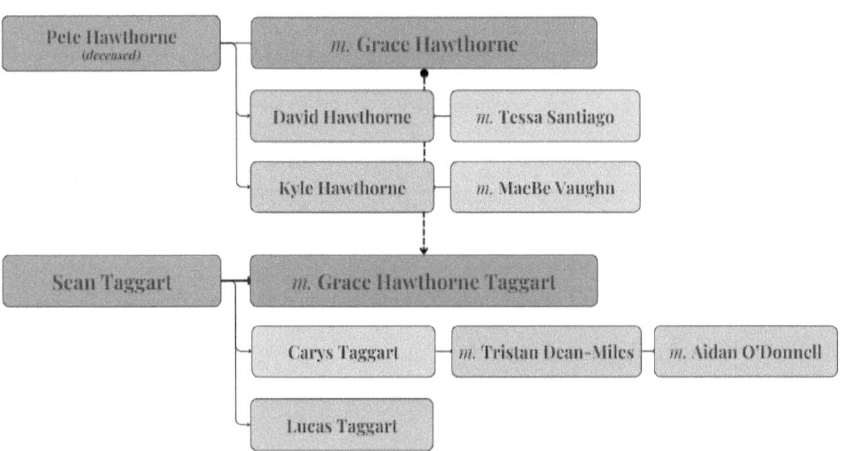

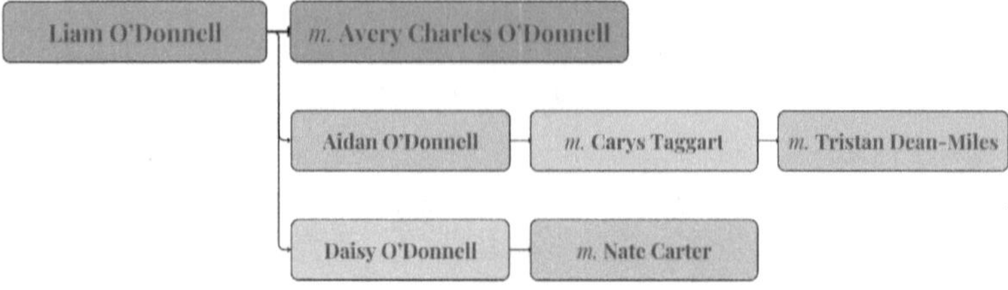
Liam O'Donnell
m. Avery Charles O'Donnell
Aidan O'Donnell
m. Carys Taggart
m. Tristan Dean-Miles
Daisy O'Donnell
m. Nate Carter

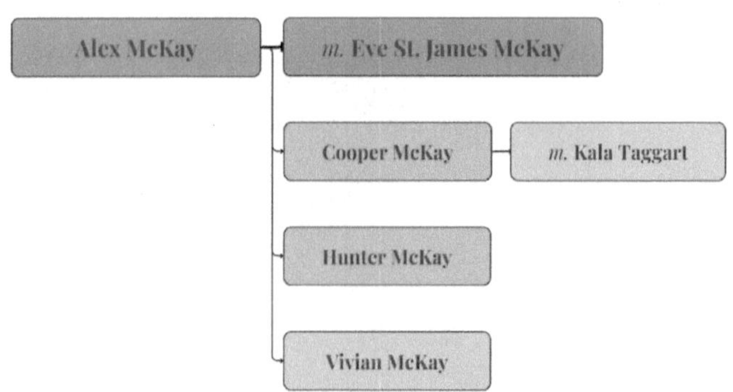
Alex McKay
m. Eve St. James McKay
Cooper McKay
m. Kala Taggart
Hunter McKay
Vivian McKay

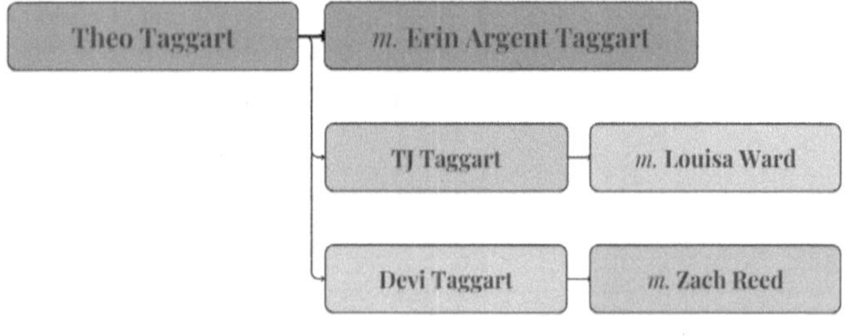
Theo Taggart
m. Erin Argent Taggart
TJ Taggart
m. Louisa Ward
Devi Taggart
m. Zach Reed

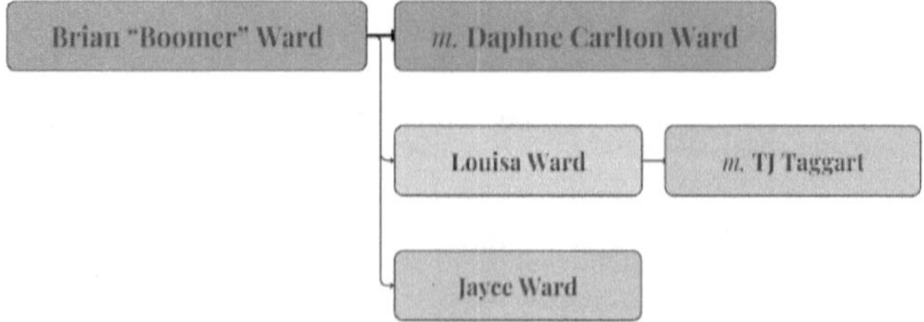
Brian "Boomer" Ward
m. Daphne Carlton Ward
Louisa Ward
m. TJ Taggart
Jayce Ward

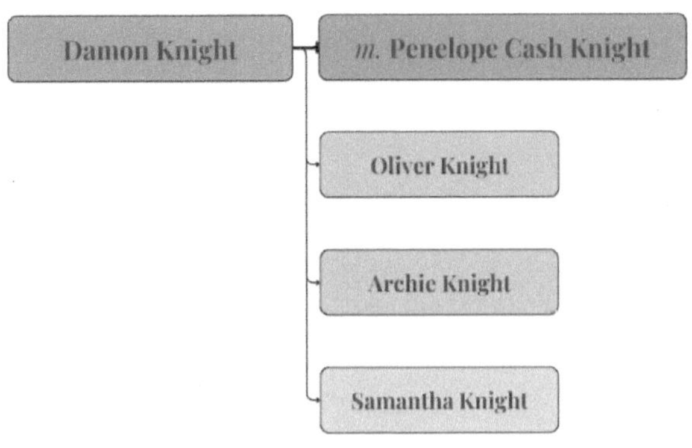
Damon Knight
m. Penelope Cash Knight
Oliver Knight
Archie Knight
Samantha Knight

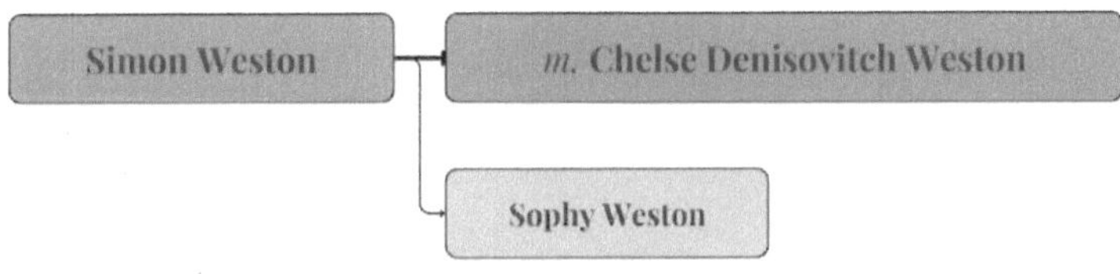
Simon Weston
m. Chelse Denisovitch Weston
Sophy Weston

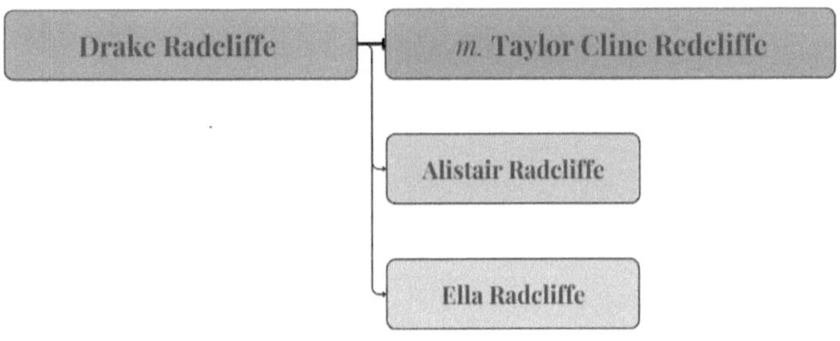
Drake Radcliffe
m. Taylor Cline Redcliffe
Alistair Radcliffe
Ella Radcliffe

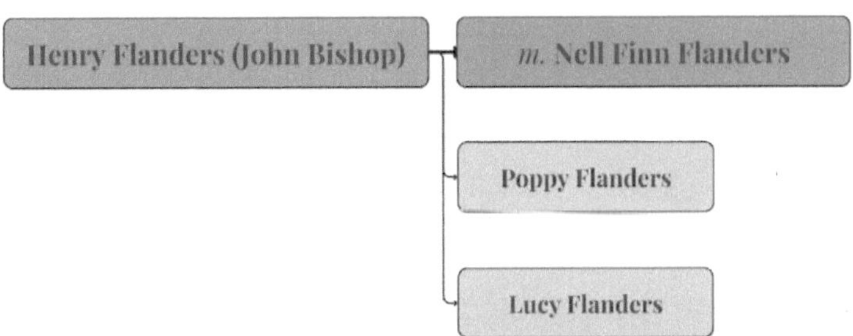
Henry Flanders (John Bishop)
m. Nell Finn Flanders
Poppy Flanders
Lucy Flanders

Acknowledgments

It's hard to believe we're here at the end of the first cycle of the legacy series. Not the end since my characters like to have lots and lots of babies. So we'll be moving to the London team soon, but it feels like closing yet another chapter to have Tag's twins find their happily ever afters. I can't thank you enough for continuing to support and love this weird world I created that lives in our minds.

Even when you're mad at me. Or think I made a terrible mistake. Or just have horrific taste in…say covers.

Let me tell you a story, one that would have gone very differently had it happened at the beginning of my career rather than this one. I'm excited about releasing the cover for this book. I thought my cover artist did a fabulous job with the twins. Put some money into it through a publicist. It goes out. There's excitement. And then I get an email. Now I'm not giving out names and don't want some flame war on the internet because you fans can ride at dawn hard for authors. I open this email and was accused of ruining the series because the cover of *Love and Let Spy* was a crappy Bratz doll trying to seduce a Louise Bay hero. Pretty sure it's a stock photo. Happens all the time. Once I would have cried and tried to figure out if I could change the cover. This time I sat back and laughed. I mean, she's not necessarily wrong. I'm glad she feels so passionately about the books that she would take the time to write to me. I did not write back. I don't respond to negative emails because most of the time they're not about me. Readers sometimes need a place to put their feelings and I'm pretty safe because I no longer take it personally. Are you even an author if you don't have at least one major review saying you've written the worst book ever?

And it was funny. I like funny. I sometimes like funny so much I put it in the book. Sosa didn't actually exist until that email. A few weeks after I started thinking about how to make that Bratz doll comment a running gag in the book, and Sosa and her sisters were born. And the Bratz doll became something more than a joke. It became a metaphor.

So I want to sincerely thank cranky Internet reader. For the time you took to write to me. For giving me a great idea. I hope you don't give up on me because of a cover and that you read this book and know you contributed in a way that makes me joyous.

To the authors, look for inspiration in all things. To Readers, I love you. You are the energy that fuels my worlds. Even when you don't agree with me.

Prologue

Ben Parker felt the cold press of stone against his face and his gut churned as he forced himself to sit up.

Why was it so dark? Where the hell was he?

Something dripped down his face, and he reached up. Blood. His eyes were starting to adjust to the low light of the…? Cage? Was he in a cage?

His heart raced. His gut knotted. He was better than this. He had to calm the fuck down. He was a damn spy, and he knew panic was the real enemy.

Well, panic and Manny. Fuck. What had happened? Manny had done something. He'd been with… He couldn't think about her now. He couldn't think about the look on her face. He'd tried to save them all but the cost…the cost had been more than he could imagine.

Lou. She'd been the cost. He had to think about Lou. Was she here? He had to find a way to get Lou out because he knew exactly how badly things could go for her.

He moved along the floor until he managed to find a corner, his gut wrenching, likely because some asshole used experimental drugs on him. Or it could be plain sedatives, but he doubted it since Manny liked to play. He wouldn't put anything past him. After all, he'd nearly killed

Kenzie's twin twice. Ben had carried her out one time himself. He'd held her thinking she was Kenzie, held her close and gave her to her family and walked away.

Kenzie.

Kenzie was never going to forgive him. Never. Not if Lou was hurt or if she…

"Benjamin, you don't seem to be taking to my new drugs," a silky voice said. It floated through the air, coming at him from seemingly all angles. Like the voice of a cruel god. "Such a shame. It did work, though. How were your dreams? It does contain a bit of a psychotropic. The other patients have described the effects as nightmarish."

The dreams. They welled inside him, shadows he didn't want to catch, but they still came. They flooded back, each devastating image.

His head ached at the thought of the shadow world he'd been in.

In his dreams he was in the car again. He was in the accident that took his fiancée when they were in college. It had been the day he'd discovered her affair with the man who was supposed to be his best friend. Ben had been in that car, and he realized the brakes were gone and he was hydroplaning, the rain and thunder forming a soundtrack to what was almost certainly the last moments of his life.

Except this time it wasn't Deanna in the seat beside him.

This time it was Kenzie Taggart. The love of his freaking life. The woman he'd chased across five continents and given himself to wholly. The one he was planning to marry and have a real life with.

He wished he'd told her.

It was Kenzie's body that was thrown from the car, that he'd dragged himself through the mud to get to, that he found face down in shallow water, her face ruined by glass and branches and stone. Her beautiful face a mottled mess, but he'd tried. Even as his own body was failing he tried to bring her back.

In the never-ending nightmare of the last few hours, it had been Kenzie who coughed and came back and cursed him. Who told him she hated him and would always hate him.

It was Kenzie who died on the operating table, and her family who wouldn't even let him see her, wouldn't let him hold her.

He'd been devastated by Deanna's death, but it was nothing compared to knowing Kenzie wasn't in the world. He'd been hollowed out and ready to do whatever it took to find her again.

It had been so real.

"Did you dream about her?" Manny sounded curious, a hint of sympathy in his voice.

Manny was a sociopath. Any sympathy was performative. He was excellent at hiding the fact that he was a monster who wanted to eat the world.

Starting with Ben Parker.

"Where is Lou?" It was the only thing that mattered. Finding Lou. Getting Lou back, because if he didn't Kenzie would never forgive him. Never.

What had he done?

"Rest assured, Louisa Ward is in good health. For now," Manny replied. "We'll see how intransigent she can be before deciding how much influence she'll require to do the job. Don't worry. I already have plans in place."

The bombs. He'd used a couple in the last few months, destroying lives for fun and profit, building his new world order by decimating the current one.

He wanted Lou to build more. He needed her brilliance, and Ben had been the one to give it to him.

He lost Lou. It was his fault, and the family he'd been hoping to be a part of would never have him now.

"I'm the one you want. You have me." He knew it was a stretch, but he had to try. "If you let Lou go, I won't fight you. I'll lay down on the table and become your next experiment."

A low chuckle moved through the room. It was some kind of speaker. Manny wasn't in the room with him, but he likely had the whole place on CCTV. Ben started to make his way around, feeling the cool stone under his hands to figure out how much space he had.

"I'm sure we'll get there, but unfortunately I care more about my work than hurting you. Don't you find that interesting, Benjamin? You spend all of your life trying to chase me down and stop me and you are…a secondary concern to me. How the tables have turned. I was the boy who always wanted your attention, and now I don't even care."

Sure, he didn't care. That was why Ben was in this… Yup, it was a cage. His hands found the bars. He could see something of a hallway. How long had he been out? Was he even still in England? Manny could move a person easily and quickly. A couple billion dollars and having politicians in his back pockets tended to work in his favor. "I'm not dead, Manny. It would have been easy for you to kill me but you didn't."

Another chuckle. It was fucking good to know someone found the situation amusing. "Well, I didn't say I don't care at all. I think it will be fun for us to get to know each other again, Benjamin. I only wish my father and grandfather were alive so they could see how far the golden boy has fallen."

It was so hard to believe this was his damn life. And all because Manny Huisman couldn't handle the fact his dad and grandfather liked Ben. Sort of. He supposed they hadn't liked him all that much, but they'd thought he acted normal where Manny had been a quiet, insecure child. "We were friends."

"No, I was the sad boy who begged for the scraps of your friendship." Manny was excellent at rewriting history and quite good at ignoring his own psychosis. "Do you think I don't remember how many times I was compared to you? Me, a genius. You can't begin to compare to my intellect. You're nothing, Ben Parker, and I'm going to make you see that. I can't quite figure out what to do with you. Shall I cut off your limbs one by one? I would allow you to heal each time, to begin to adjust, and then I'll take another until you're nothing but a torso in a box. Or I could use certain training techniques on you. I could train you to be my slave. That could be fun. Or I could force you to watch as I take another woman from you. I've been thinking about Kala Taggart. Such a fun female to break."

"You didn't break her." Nothing broke Kala.

He caught sight of a tiny red dot. A camera. Manny was watching him. Like he was some kind of entertainment.

"Oh, didn't I? The little bitch doesn't go in the field much anymore. She's learned her place, so I think I should move my attentions to her twin."

The threat was an actual ache in his heart. "Stay away from her."

"Yes," Huisman's voice purred over the speakers. "I will spend some time developing techniques to test on the other Ms. Taggart. I've avoided it because her father can be formidable, but I have my second wind now. I've joined a group more powerful than you can imagine. I'm going to assassinate the fucker and put his head on my wall. So he can watch while I violate his daughter. She would give me strong boys,

I suppose."

The thought made him nearly blind with rage because he knew Manny wasn't above it. "I will kill you."

He should have done it ages ago. He should have done it that night, but he'd told himself he had to be better.

Now his weakness was going to cost him everything.

"I'm sure you will try," Manny replied with a long-suffering sigh. "I have to go. Our scientist is awake, and it's time for her to begin her work. You'll stay in my prison until such time as I have use for you. Don't worry. There are a couple of guards to see to your basic needs. Try not to die from cold, and I hope you enjoy the vermin you'll be sharing with. By the time you see the light of day again, I'll have taken out everyone you care about. Again. Good night, Benjamin."

He heard the call cut out and fought the urge to rush the bars and attempt to tear them apart like he was the fucking Hulk or something.

How was he here? Where was Kenzie? Was she out there cursing his name?

He sat in the darkness, trying to breathe, to find a way out.

And that was when he heard it. Such a small sound. A ping, and he glanced up.

The camera was off.

Somehow, he didn't think that was Manny's doing.

Ben struggled to his feet. What was going on? He still couldn't see much, and his legs were shaky.

"Hello, lover. Want to tell me why Lou is gone but your mistress is still all happy and whole?"

Kenzie was here, and she was holding a gun on him. And he couldn't blame her.

He loved her. He loved her so much.

He dropped to his knees, the pain clanging through his body, but so much less than the way it twisted in his heart.

He leaned over, holding onto the bars so he could feel the press of the silencer against his skin.

"Do it." It would be better than living without her.

He closed his eyes, and his life flashed before him. Well, the parts that mattered.

His life with her.

Part One

Chapter One

Australia
One year before

Kenzie Taggart looked at herself in the mirror.

"She's going to kill you." Louisa Ward stood in the doorway that led from the bathroom out to the big hall where the medical conference was currently in full swing.

Kenzie wrinkled her nose and finished the last of her makeup. She looked good, if she did say so herself. She looked like Kara Trent, a pharmaceutical rep from Sydney, Australia. Normally she would have done her hair and makeup from the comfort of the safe house, but the quarters were tight with the whole team hanging out. Hopefully, if all went well today, Tasha wouldn't be going back to the safe house. "Is Tasha ready?"

She ignored the other part. Kala would be pissed that she'd snuck out before dawn and left her to get stuck in the safe house all day, but she would survive it. It was one of the pitfalls that came with being a spy. More specifically, one of the pitfalls of being a spy when one shared the spy identity with her twin sister and no one was supposed to know there were two of them, even the hottest man she'd ever seen.

Kala couldn't appreciate Brian Peters. No matter how many times her twin told her she was asexual and hated all peoples far too much to touch anyone, much less let one in her lady space, she was in love with Cooper McKay and legit didn't see anyone beyond him. So beautiful Brian was absolutely wasted on her, and it was Kenzie time.

If Lou was here it was because Tash was, too. Louisa Ward had been part of her girl gang since they were kids. It had been her and her sisters Tash and Kala and their cousins for as long as she could remember. They'd stuck together through everything. Through every teen drama and college despair. Through all the broken hearts and exploration that ended with them founding their own sex club—as one did—her girls had been by her side. It was kind of the same as high school except now they were a CIA team and had way more access to guns, and the enemies were more impressive than mean girls who called her a slut.

She wanted to be a slut for Brian.

Damn, it had been a long time, and her sexuality wasn't tied up in one dude. She had an itch, and she was worried the hot guy who worked with their target was the only one who could scratch it.

"Tash is nervous," Lou admitted, leaning against the sink. "She's worried he's going to reject her, and I'm worried that will hurt her in a way that has nothing to do with the mission. Is this a good idea? I think she really likes this guy. He's the first man she's slept with since that asshole man-douche."

Kenzie managed not to spit. Barely. It was an instinct when she thought about Chet Whittington, the asshole who broke her big sister's heart. Why hadn't her mom assassinated the fucker yet? Oh, yeah. Tash said no. But accidents happened, and Chet was a CIA operative so he could get in a fight where his insides came outside and die and no one would think much of it.

Sometimes she thought she probably needed therapy.

But then she remembered that all the violence was part of her sunny disposition. And it wasn't like she visited trauma on the undeserving. She was like karma but with good lip gloss.

"I have a feeling about those two." She gave herself one more glance, ensuring her magenta hair was soft around her face. Her dad had argued they should go to a more natural color for this assignment, but she'd started talking about the patriarchy, and when that didn't work how much her period hurt and voila, she kept her favorite color.

"Dare seems like a great guy."

"You're not worried about his divorce? Tris seemed to be," Lou said.

Tris hadn't met the man. "You know I have a sixth sense about these things. I am an excellent matchmaker. Like Emma from Jane Austen."

"Uh, I don't think you actually read that book," Lou countered.

She hadn't. One of the great things about having a twin was halving the homework. Mostly. Kala had read that one, and Kenz had taken on *The Great Gatsby*, which had like a lot of great literary merit and stuff. Sigh. It could have used some murders and definitely needed some spicy scenes. Maybe some horny fairies. "Anyway, I think Dare is Tasha's match, and the fact that he's suddenly become our target is the universe's way of telling her this is the path to take. Like me and Brian."

A brow arched over Lou's glasses. "There was nothing fateful about you sneaking out of bed to take Kala's place. You're supposed to be backup on this assignment. I know you two have the whole twins, we-can-switch-out-at-any-time thing down, but it's better if one of you does most of the work."

It was how they functioned. One twin took the majority of the op, with the other as backup because no matter how careful they were about reporting back on what happened, there were always mistakes to be made. They could be tripped up by the smallest things.

But it wasn't fair that Kala got to work the hottest guy she'd ever seen. Kala wouldn't even flirt with him. Unless one counted evil stares, sighs that reeked of disdain, and a lecture on proper torture techniques flirting. That was how Kala's meeting with Brian had gone. Kenzie should know because she'd watched the whole thing through Lou's spy glasses.

And the guy had totally seemed into her. Was he into her twin? Would he find her boring and docile? Though he'd also seemed frustrated with Kala's attitude. "This guy is a good way to get close to Dare Nash."

"I thought Tasha was the way to get close to Dare," Lou challenged.

"And someone needs to back her up, and that's going to be easier to do if we can move around as a foursome. Kala didn't set that up properly," Kenzie pointed out.

"Uhm, Kala thought Tash was blowing off steam with some random hottie. She didn't know he would become the target. She certainly didn't know the guy who came on so strong would end up being important." Lou's arms had crossed under her breasts, her intelligent eyes narrowing.

Lou might technically be her sister's bestie, but she was more like a fourth sister. She'd been with them since they were kids, and she didn't play. But the good news? Kenzie was excellent at justification. She nodded Lou's way like she made her point and was deeply grateful for it. "Yes, and now we know which twin should take the lead with our gorgeous best friend of the target. Me."

"She's going to kill you," Lou said with a sigh.

It was time to get serious. "Do you honestly think Kala made a connection with Brian?"

If she had, then Kenz would have to think about stepping back. There was still time. She glanced down at her watch. The opening breakfast was about to begin. She was sure Kala was awake and ready to punch her in the face. She could get over here and take Kenzie's place quickly.

Lou sighed. "No. Of course she didn't. She found him deeply annoying because he's not Cooper McKay, who she claims to find deeply annoying as well." Lou checked her hair in the mirror and fixed her glasses. "But he liked her. I think that was all about the gorgeous bombshell thing you both have going. He might not have noticed the daggers she was shooting him, and I managed to make sure those were all verbal, thank you."

"Do you really think she's the best person to work Brian?" She had Lou in a corner with that question.

"I will admit you'll probably be able to get more out of him." Lou pulled her cell and her fingers ran over the keys as she spoke. "Kala didn't like him, but I think some of that is the tension between her and Coop. It's going to explode at some point."

Kenzie felt a bright smile cross her face. She loved a love story, and her twin was in the middle of an epic one. Kala and Coop had loved each other for a long time, but Coop had been a dumbass kid and he'd hurt Kala and Kala had been…she'd been Kala and had not taken it well. Her twin wasn't one to forgive easily, and she never, ever forgot. Which was why it had been great to throw them together on a CIA team and let them work out their issues while they all saved the world and got to do cool things. Well, when their parents let them.

Sometimes she thought the whole I'm-a-spy thing would be cooler if her handler wasn't her dad.

"It's going to explode into a beautiful wave of love and passion," Kenzie said confidently. Manifestation was a real thing. Positive thoughts led to positive actions. It was how she handled her life. Rise above the fray. Well, until she needed to kick a little ass, and then she manifested that, too. "You watch. They'll be married in a year or two. It's why I was so enthusiastic about bringing him on the team. I knew when she said we should consider Coop that she was coming out of her tiff with him."

"Tiff?" Lou settled her bag over her shoulder. "It's been twelve years. I know everyone says you're like your mom, but there's a whole lot of Big Tag in there, too. But seriously, we need to talk about how you're going to handle Brian. You can't go in and be one hundred percent Kenz."

She started out the door. It was time. "I know that. I'm never one hundred percent me when I'm working. I'm Kara. I'm the operative. I'm not looking for true love. I say that shit because it makes Dad and Kala vomit. I wouldn't mind a couple of wild nights, though. I thought the whole spy thing would be way more interesting. James Bond gets all the sex, and when I find a hottie who I could seduce intel out of, my dad always finds another way. It's sad."

Lou stopped and faced her. "Kara, you're my cousin and I adore you, but I think you should be more careful."

Yep. She should since she now saw what Lou had seen. Brian Peters was standing right there in all his golden god gorgeousness. He had on a suit that looked like it had been tailored to fit his big body to perfection. He was talking to someone. A woman, and though Kenzie couldn't see her face, it was evident she was attracted to him since she kept leaning in and putting her hand on his arm.

She might have some competition. She tamped down the urge to walk over and tell the woman to take her hands off her man because that was an utterly ridiculous impulse. He wasn't hers and wouldn't be. Despite her teasing, this wasn't a love match. It was an op. He was an op but one she wanted to enjoy fully.

It had been a long time since she felt this kind of flashfire instant attraction. Though it had been Kala physically there the night they met, through the magic of Lou's glasses she'd been there for it all. They had cameras and sent back all kinds of data, but what she'd mostly gotten was how much Brian Peters called to her. He was charming and funny, and she'd been alone for a long time. Not even a slutty one-night stand because she worked all the time, and when she wasn't working she was at her home club, and those men were friends and brothers.

She belonged to a whole-ass sex club she'd helped to found and she'd never once had sex at The Hideout.

According to Tash—who did have a gloriously slutty night with Dare—the target was a Dom. Like used to be in the lifestyle Dom. Apparently, he no longer went to clubs after his ex-wife used it against him in their divorce, but Tash had said he hadn't missed a step.

Was Brian a top, too? Even if he wasn't formally a Dom, he had the dominance thing down.

There was the sound of a throat clearing. It contained no small amount of impatience.

Lou. Lou was still here and likely pissed that she'd walked out in the open still talking like they were besties without a care in the world. Nope. She had to be Kara now, and Kara had rejected this man once. She couldn't walk up and say *hey, want to see my boobs?*

She had to play this carefully because the truth of the matter was her sister would be Kara again at some point. No matter how much they wanted to be the exact same person, Kala had some skills Kenzie didn't, and vice versa. They would need to get Dare Nash's laptop, and Kala was better with a computer. So she had to ride a line with him.

"I'm going to be careful. You should go and make sure Tash is ready in case this goes well." If all went the way it should, Tasha was going to see Dare today. Her sister had thought she would never see the man again, but now she was going to be close to him. Physically.

Forced proximity. She loved that trope.

She wondered if Brian's room was a king or two queens because only one bed was also a fave.

"I'll try to handle your twin," Lou whispered, and then she was gone with Brian never seeing her.

But in that moment his eyes came up and he did see Kenzie. Those baby blues took on a distinctly predatory gaze, the kind that let a woman know a man was beyond interested.

Damn, but that was a feeling. Arousal. Desire. Longing.

No matter what happened she knew this mission would change everything.

* * * *

Ben Parker stared at the gorgeous woman across from him and wished he'd picked a better alias. What had he been thinking? Brian Peters sounded like a dude who sat in his cubicle and did boring work no one could quite describe as more than paper pushing.

Oh, yeah, that was his cover, and Tim had actually selected the name since he'd been the one to do Ben's cover. So it wasn't his fault at all.

He was having a talk with Tim. No more Brians and Johnnys, and he absolutely did not look like a Harold no matter what that shit said.

"Sorry about the other night. I'm afraid I was a bit on edge. I was worried about Tash, you see." Kara Trent had an accent that matched her background. Straight out of Sydney. There was some working class in there, but then he'd read the dossier on her and she came by it honestly.

When she'd walked into the bar a couple of nights ago, Ben hadn't been able to take his eyes off her. He knew he should have sat back and let Dare have his pick—after all, Dare was the boss and Brian Peters was his happy friend.

Damn it. He was Dare's friend. He hadn't meant to be, but Dare's goodness had truly won him over. Spending months and months watching the man try to survive his father and all the darkness around him so he could save his siblings had proven to Ben that not everyone was terrible. Not everyone turned on him.

Shitty long-term assignment. He was getting in too deep, but it was almost over. The American CIA team was coming in to help facilitate finding the intel he needed to prove to the world that Dr. Emmanuel Huisman was a monster.

Kara Trent was nothing but a distraction, and one he should ignore. And he couldn't. He'd looked up all her socials, found out she was going to be at the conference, and made damn sure he'd been in the breakfast meant for pharmaceutical reps this morning.

Because if there was a chance of spending even a night in her bed, he would take it.

Although he did actually come to Australia quite a bit. There wasn't any reason he couldn't check in on her from time to time.

He never thought that way. He had a mission, and women were lovely to spend time with but never for long and never exclusively.

He rather thought Kara Trent would demand more than he was willing to give.

And yet he couldn't make himself walk away.

Although now he was worried. The last thing he needed was a couple of women to watch after while he finished up this op. He was on thin ice with his boss, and it would get way thinner if civilians got hurt. It was precisely why he'd convinced Dare not to look for Tasha after she disappeared the morning after their one-night stand.

Which would be a good reason to be a jerk to her cousin so Tasha stayed away.

Every time he opened his mouth to be an asshole, he closed it because she was heartbreakingly beautiful. She was somehow both delicate and strong. Both deeply feminine and yet he got the feeling she could handle herself in a fight.

Why did that do something for him?

"Dare's a good guy. I think they had a nice time, but he needs to concentrate on this conference. I was surprised to see you here." He was happy at the steady state of his voice since his every instinct told him to roll out all his moves.

Except his moves hadn't worked on her that first night. She'd been surly and more than a bit rude. At some point he'd given up because he wasn't a masochist. She was stunning and he kept up the conversation because by then it was clear Dare was into Kara's cousin Tasha. He'd enjoyed the banter and talking to the other cousin…something with an L…but he'd given up on getting into Kara's bed no matter what he'd told Dare.

But here he was jumping right back in at the first sign she wasn't entirely dedicated to cutting his balls off.

"Oh, I've been gearing up for this for months. This is one of the biggest conferences of the year." She toyed with her cup of coffee, which she'd taken black with one sugar when she found out she couldn't get a flat white. "I wish it hadn't been the only time my cousins could come in. I was planning on sending them out to the Blue Mountains for a couple of days, but Tash changed her mind. Now I'm worried Lou's stuck at my place watching daytime telly. Not exactly the holiday she wanted."

Lou. Louisa. That was the name of the sweet-looking young woman with glasses and intelligent eyes. "Why wouldn't Tash be with her?"

Kara's gorgeous face turned impish. "Well, now that I've seen you again I'm hoping you'll talk to Dare. Let him know she's still interested. I think if he was interested, too, she would be up here in a heartbeat." She reached out and touched his arm. "But maybe you could make her not seem so eager. I shouldn't have put it like that. Maybe you could say you ran into me and I mentioned my cousin talked about him. Could you keep that a secret? She wants it to be a surprise. Well, I think what she really wants is to see how he feels. If you tell him…"

"He can prepare a reaction." She had no idea how good he could be at keeping secrets. And he understood. After all, once he'd made a surprise visit to see his fiancée so he could judge whether or not she was having an affair with his best friend.

The fucker.

Manny had no reaction at all. He'd stood there in the hospital, and for the first time Ben had seen him for what he truly was.

He took a long breath and released it because the last thing he wanted was for this woman to catch his anger. It wasn't directed at her, but it also never seemed to go away. For the last several years of his life he'd had one goal. Expose Dr. Emmanual Huisman for the fraud he was. And he was so close.

So close he should ignore the pull he felt for this woman. Two nights ago he would have told anyone who asked that it would be fairly easy. While she was gorgeous, he wasn't an animal, and it had been obvious she wasn't that into him.

Except maybe she was.

Something felt different this time. Maybe she was having a bad night when they met. Maybe she hadn't felt good. It didn't matter because it seemed like nothing mattered. His brain had already gone through all the reasons this was a terrible idea, and his dick wasn't listening. Even to the part about her cousin climbing back into Dare's bed and potentially distracting the hell out of him.

He had a couple of days. The head of the CIA team wouldn't be in Australia until then, so he was on his own. What would it matter if he chased after her a few days more? He might actually catch her.

"I'm hoping she can see on his face if he honestly wants her or not," Kara admitted. Her tongue moved briefly over that plump bottom lip of hers, and he felt it in his cock.

More than that, he felt a tug. Like a string connected them and wanted them closer.

He hadn't felt it the other night. This was deeper. This was dangerous.

It took a lot to stay on his side of the table. "I'll tell him I ran into you and ask if it's okay to give you his number. I know he'll want her, but I'm not sure it's a good idea for him to take her."

A brow rose over her eyes. "Why not? Are you worried she's a gold digger?"

There she was. She'd been so sweet, slightly shy, but there was her edge. It was almost as though the woman he'd met the other night and the one who asked him to join her for coffee were two completely different women, but now he wondered if they weren't both personas she presented to the world. The angry goddess and the sweet professional. He wished it turned him off, didn't make him want to figure out who the real Kara Trent was.

What he had to remember was no matter her real personality, she could never know him, could never have a place in his life because his life was dangerous and filled with secrets.

"Not at all. I'm just worried she's a nice lady, and Dare has a life back in Toronto. Honestly, I'm worried about Dare, too. He's not the kind of guy who goes through women like candy."

"He didn't seem to be," she replied, that brow arching in a deeply judgmental way. "Unlike you."

Oh, she wanted to play? "What makes you think that?"

Her eyes rolled slightly, and she gestured his way. "All of you, mate. Every inch of you screams lothario."

He laughed at the thought. It was good to know she liked how he looked, but she was wrong about a couple of things. "No. I haven't had some string of random women sharing my bed." He winced as he realized the truth. "I think it's been over six months since I had sex. I probably shouldn't have admitted that."

His last encounter had been with another CSIS operative. They'd been on a weekend op, and she'd asked if he didn't mind helping her with stress relief. He hadn't. The sex had been good, but there hadn't been this wild desire like he felt for the woman in front of him.

He hadn't been tempted to tie her up and keep her that way until he knew every inch of her body, until he had the taste of her on his tongue, her scent surrounding him. Dare had accused him of acting like a caveman and he hadn't been wrong, but his friend didn't understand how odd it was. He was a good-time guy.

Because he had a mission and he couldn't get too close. After all, look what happened to the last woman who got in Manny Huisman's way.

She shrugged and took a sip of coffee. "It's been a while for me, too. Life gets in the way. I broke it off with my last boyfriend eight months ago and have been in a bit of a hole since. Tash went through a bad breakup last year. Do you think Dare's capable of being kind to her?"

So she was finding her groove again. He could understand that. And it would give Dare someone to go to the party with. It wasn't like Ben could go. That was the one thing that blew all to hell when he realized Manny was actually attending. Ben was supposed to be Dare's friend who tagged along to the billionaire's party cabin in the mountains where he would find a way to get on Auggie Oakley's private system to prove the man was colluding with Huisman in a secret organization to disrupt the world's systems. Except now he suspected Manny would be there, and there was zero chance he didn't recognize Ben.

So he had to find another way, but now that he thought about it, Tash going with Dare meant he didn't need an excuse and he could confer with Whittington—the American operative backing him up—about how to get someone on the inside.

Then maybe he could invite Kara to the mountains with him, and she didn't have to know she was cover.

Damn, but he was excellent at bargaining with himself when he wanted something. And he wanted her. He'd fooled himself.

She'd asked him a question. Could Dare be kind to her cousin?

Could she be kind to him? Could she see through all his walls to the man he wanted to be?

"Dare wouldn't know how to be unkind," he admitted quietly, and every word made him feel his guilt. "He's been through a lot but he's solid. The trouble Dare will have is letting her go."

"Well, she has to return home eventually," Kara conceded. "We all do at some point. It's still nice to get to know someone. Does every relationship have to last forever?"

Oh, she was saying all the right things, and it kind of annoyed him. It was perverse but he wanted her to challenge him, to talk about true freaking love.

Which was weird, and maybe he was coming down with something. He didn't actually believe in love.

"What's Dare been through?" She sat back, considering him. "Was he married? I didn't get much of a chance to talk to the bloke. Tash had him cornered most of the night."

She was polite enough to lie. Dare had been the one to corner Tasha at the bar. Ben had taken Dare out that night specifically to see if he could get the guy laid. He was being a good wingman and then Ms. Pink Hair had walked in and he'd felt the damn earth shake and lost all sight of what he was trying to do.

"He's divorced. It was an ugly breakup," he admitted because he would do almost anything to keep her talking.

Kara nodded. "Tash told me he wasn't comfortable with his… needs. Normally I would tell her to run as fast as she can, but apparently they got through it."

"She told you that?"

Kara shrugged like it wasn't a big deal. "Of course. Look, the worst thing a sub can do is find a top who hates the fact that he's a top. Most of the time it's because he or she has been through a ton of trauma with people telling them their sexual needs are perverted. It's ridiculous. Sexual needs should always be somewhat perverted. Where's the fun in non-perverted sex?"

She was going to kill him. He looked around, trying to make sure no one was listening.

Her eyes were narrowed when he turned back to her. "Ah, you, too, huh?"

What? "Having some amount of delicacy doesn't mean I'm sexually suppressed. Dare's into some stuff that could get him in trouble with his family if he's not discreet."

"He's into D/s." Kara stated it flatly, like it was normal.

Dominance and submission. The words made his cock tighten. The idea of this woman being submissive made him want to throw her over his shoulder and run away with her.

He was back to caveman.

"Yes, and some bondage." Ben kept his voice low. "It's why his wife divorced him."

She frowned. "She didn't like sex? Why the hell did she get married then?"

"I think it was one of those rich people things." He was pretty sure Dare's whole life was about his family name. It seemed to be an awful way to live, but then Ben's whole life was about justice against one man, so who was he to judge?

Dare was getting a respite with Tasha. He wouldn't turn her down. If she showed up and offered herself to Dare, he would go with it. He would take everything she was willing to give him.

What would Kara Trent offer Ben? Was she into the same lifestyle as her cousin?

Her nose wrinkled. "That's sad. Anyway, I should get going."

She started to pull away, but he put a hand on her wrist. "Your first meeting isn't for another hour."

Her eyes widened, but she didn't move away. "How would you know that?"

Honesty. He used it like the weapon it could be at times. "Because you put your schedule on social media."

"You looked at my socials? Why?"

He stared at her.

She softened a bit. "If you thought it wasn't a good idea for Tash and Dare, why would it be better for us?"

He loosened his grip, turning her hand over so he could envelop it in both of his. "Kara, you feel it, too, right? I can't be the only one to feel this pull."

She sighed, and her expression held a longing he was almost certain they shared. "I'm like my cousin, and while it seems to be working out for her and Dare, I don't play with tops who shrink back when I talk about sex. I've found that's an excellent way to get myself in trouble."

"I wasn't shrinking back." He huffed. "Maybe I was. I was thinking about what it cost my friend. Look, if Dare's hanging out with Tash, then we're going to be around each other. You want to talk about sex. I can do it. I'd like to lay you out and run my tongue over every inch of your body before I spread your legs wide and force my cock inside you. If you prefer I did that while you're tied up and vulnerable and helpless to me, I'm more than happy to oblige. If you want to show me that pretty ass and let me spank it before I shove a plug up it to get you ready for anal, I'm willing to do that as well."

He thought she would blush, but no. Not Kara Trent. Her lips curled up, and she leaned back as though giving the prospect serious consideration.

"Well, that gives me something to think about, doesn't it?" She slid off the barstool. "I will see you later, Brian, and don't think that scenario won't be running through my head while I sit in on the lecture about the new uses for GLP1s. It should make for an interesting session. Until we meet again, Mr. Peters."

So smooth and silky. She walked away, her hips swinging.

Yeah, he was going to have to do something about her. Likely something deeply perverted.

He watched her until she disappeared down the hall.

He would protect her from Manny. Manny never had to know she existed. She was formidable, but a woman like her would be nothing but a toy to Manny, and he would use her to punish Ben.

He wouldn't let it happen.

She never had to know the man she was going to sleep with was a spy.

Ben took a deep breath as his cell rang and he saw the code name for the US operative he was working with. Chet. Douchebag, but what would one expect from a dude who thought he was James Bond?

Still, he answered. It was time to get this mission going. If he could catch Manny, he might be able to settle into an easier job.

No matter what, Kara Trent would be hearing from him again.

Chapter Two

Split, Croatia
Six months later

Naturally they sent her.

Ms. Magenta. Maggie. Kara freaking Trent, though he knew none of those were her name. He'd tried to figure out who she was in real life, but the Americans knew how to hide an identity.

"Hello, Ben." She looked good, but then she always did. It was hard to look bad when you were a nearly six-foot bombshell, with curves for days and a face that could be on any fashion magazine.

She was his fucking wet dream, and didn't that prove that he could use a whole lot of therapy.

"Maggie." He'd taken to calling her that after the shit show of an op in Sydney had torn off all their masks.

His sweet, hot, sometimes mean-as-hell pharmaceutical rep turned out to be a CIA plant, and that hadn't been what put him off her. There had been a piece of him that thrilled at the idea she was in the business. If she was a spy, he didn't have to be careful with her. She would understand his world. She would know the risks.

The idea of having a woman like that at his side had brought him a hope he hadn't imagined he could feel.

And then he watched her with her boyfriend.

"How's your boyfriend?"

Her eyes rolled. "I told you Coop isn't my boyfriend. I have never in my life so much as held that man's hand."

But he remembered how comfortable she'd been with the guy when they were in an actual sex club. Oh, he hadn't even seen them together in fet wear. He'd been tied to a spanking bench during that part of the op, but there was zero way those two hadn't gotten down.

And it burned a hole in his gut.

She wasn't technically wearing fet wear this evening, but it could be. The evening gown had a plunging neckline and clung to her every curve. The sapphire color made her eyes more blue, her hair more electric.

He'd seen her with pretty much every hair color since they'd identified her as the mysterious Ms. Magenta, but she always seemed to come back to her eponymous color. Pink. Magenta. Hence, Maggie.

Since meeting in Australia, he'd tangled with her a couple of times, and he never knew what to expect. Was this the woman who shoved him off a plane over Mongolia or the one who saved his ass in a back alley in Bangkok?

He rather thought she did it on purpose. Always keeping him on a string, never letting him hate her or love her. Constantly keeping him in this weird place where he both hoped he would see her and dreaded the idea of working with her.

She stared at him for a moment, and the soft look in her eyes made him think she was going for seduction rather than violence tonight. "You look good, Ben."

He looked like he hadn't slept in days. Which he hadn't. Prepping for this op had been exhausting. He'd spent weeks identifying the man who would receive the dead drop this evening. Then naturally the Americans glommed on. He'd done all the work, but she'd secured the invitation they needed to get into the gala where the drop was taking place. "You're talking to me again?"

She frowned. "I'm just remembering how you used one of my closest friends to prove a point? Lou could have died, you know."

He felt his jaw tighten. It hadn't been one of his finer moments. He'd seen a chance to prove Manny was behind the kidnapping of TJ

Taggart and he'd taken it. He hadn't meant to put Louisa Ward in danger, but he'd been there to protect her. "Somehow I think you and Cooper wouldn't have allowed that to happen."

She flinched slightly but covered it well. "You could have told us. You were right there in Dallas. We would have… It doesn't matter now."

It shouldn't, but he still found himself moving closer. "It did matter. You didn't believe me about Huisman. No one does."

Manny had done an excellent job of masking his intentions. He'd "helped" Maggie's boss and seemed like a perfectly reasonable man while Ben looked like a raging lunatic.

One slender shoulder shrugged. "Well, we believe you now, and we'll take care of it."

She was so fucking gorgeous standing there in the middle of Old Town. They were meeting in front of his hotel, and she seemed to light up the night around them. And he felt the white hot blaze of anger. "You think you can cut me out?"

She sighed. "I think I can't trust you. I think I've spent months mooning over a man who would use one of my closest friends to prove a point."

"I didn't mean to." She was being unfair. "And you're not exactly an angel, or have you forgotten Mongolia?"

She flushed, the first sign that she felt anything about what happened that day. "I didn't mean for you to get hurt."

It was his turn to roll his eyes. "Then why did you kick me out of a plane at twenty thousand feet?"

"I didn't kick you out." Her arms folded under her breasts, making them even more glorious than normal. She regained her confidence and looked him in the eyes. "I simply took the last parachute. I fully expected you to follow me. Which you did."

It had been the single most frightening experience of his fucking life, and that was saying something. He'd followed her out because the only other option had been hanging around so the bad guys could torture him before murdering him. He'd leapt out of that plane and turned his body into a bullet headed straight for her.

When he'd caught her, he'd wrapped his body around hers, looking desperately for the connection he sometimes felt when she was around. He'd clung to her and she'd…seemed to tolerate him.

It was her thing. She was hot and cold, and that was how she manipulated him.

He was taking the bait. Again.

He took a long breath as the car rolled up. Tim was in the driver's seat. His long-time tech gave him a grin. "Hey, boss. Looks like we got the invite. Ms. Magenta, good to see you."

She frowned Tim's way. "You, too, dude I do not know."

Tim hopped out. He was dressed in a suit and tie, looking to all the world like a professional driver. He opened the door for her, and she moved with elegance and grace.

Ben opened his own damn door and sat beside her. "Are you going to screw me out of this intel, too?"

She stared out the window as Tim took off, making his way on the narrow streets. "I'll make sure you get a copy. Lou is hanging out waiting to do exactly that. Hopefully you don't try to murder her."

His chest felt too tight. "I didn't try to kill her then." He let a moment go. "Why the hell are you here if you hate me? Somehow I think there are other women operatives who could do this job."

"And yet you got me," she shot back, still not looking his way.

"I'd like an answer, Maggie. I'd like to know how thoroughly you intend to fuck me over."

She finally turned, and her blue-eyed gaze burned through him. "I intended to fuck you in numerous ways, Benjamin Parker. I was going to ride that hot bod until I couldn't see straight and we began a truly epic love story. Like one for the ages. Like my mom and dad, but you turned out to be one more ruthless asshole who's willing to sacrifice whoever you need to in order to complete your mission."

What the hell? Epic love story? Her mom and dad? She'd never talked about them, and they'd talked. Sometimes. When she was in the right mood, he could talk to her about anything. "I wasn't going to let Lou get hurt."

"I bet you said that about whatever that dude's name is, too."

Whatever that dude's name is? It struck him for the one thousandth time that Terry was dead and it was his fault. He was the one who sent him in. Terry had infiltrated the group that kidnapped TJ Taggart thinking young Mr. Taggart was the international arms dealer known as The Jester. The German-based group had been working with Huisman to find the bombmaker. Ben had known it was his only shot at getting

Huisman's name to come out of the bad guy's mouth in front of the American team, so he'd set Lou Ward up to be the one to get the message. Lou and the rest of the American team had been safe, but Terry had taken a fatal bullet in the middle of the battle.

He would live with that guilt for the rest of his life.

He sat back, his soul threatening to sag. How was he this tired at the age of thirty? How was this his life? He should be working at some Toronto office, married with three kids and a mortgage he couldn't afford.

For years he'd seen Deanna when he thought of that life. Not because he wanted her. Not at all. She'd cheated on him with his best friend, but the guilt was still there.

The trouble now was whenever he thought of that life he could have had, it was the woman beside him who was the wife of his dreams. Which proved he was fucked in the head because his dream wife shouldn't steal the last parachute and nearly kill him.

"I shouldn't have said that." Her voice was softer now. "There's a part of me that understands why you did what you did. We were on the fence about Huisman. Now I think I'm getting a real idea of how dangerous the man is. Look, Ben, I've made calls, too. Not quite like that but I've put other operatives in what felt like a necessary line of fire, and it's not easy. It's certainly not easy when that person is someone you care about."

She belonged to an odd team. Ben worked with different teams, but he was always the guy on the ground, with Tim backing him up. Maggie worked with one team, including military backing in the form of Cooper McKay, Tristan Dean-Miles, Zach Reed, and now TJ Taggart. From what he could tell only Maggie herself, Tasha, and Lou were actually Agency. And that big guy who handled the team. Mr. Lemon was kind of an asshole, but he brought out all of Ben's instincts to please his freaking dad. Who couldn't care less about him since he'd gotten dragged into the middle of his war with Manny.

"Well, I assure you I won't do it again."

"Yes, you will, and so will I, and one day I won't be so lucky and I'll have that on my soul for the rest of my life," she said with a sigh.

"Somehow, I think you'll be fine. You've got a good team." He needed to focus on the op. She would be gone tomorrow, and then he might never see her again. They ran in the same circles but that didn't guarantee they would work together. She could get reassigned. He could get reassigned.

She could die.

He could die.

"What's our cover?" Ben asked, desperate to change the subject. Since the Americans had done the work of getting the invite, he'd let them pick the cover.

She stared for a moment like she didn't want to let go of the conversation and then sighed and sat back, crossing one long leg over the other. The high slit in the evening gown she wore showed off toned legs and perfect skin. "We're recently married. You're a tech investor and I'm your trophy wife. Easy peasy. I included a hefty check in the envelope with your ID and papers."

Naturally, she'd put him in a position where he had to have his hands on her. "You didn't think work colleagues was a good way to go?"

He opened the envelope and there was the invitation and all his papers, including a check written out to the foundation holding the gala this evening. The European Children's Fund was supposed to help children in war-torn parts of the world, but they were in bed with another organization. Manny's organization.

"I think recently married is something people will buy," she replied. "We have a certain chemistry, you and I."

She wasn't wrong about that. "And Cooper doesn't mind?"

An enigmatic smile crossed her lips. "Cooper genuinely doesn't care what I do with my body since I've never touched the man. Would never touch the man." She frowned, suddenly seeming to catch on something. "I mean outside of an op. Obviously we needed to look like a D/s couple in Australia. I should point out that you wouldn't know about that if you hadn't been running around with that fucker Whittington."

"I wasn't running around with him." That time had been a clusterfuck of a situation. Her team hadn't known he was Canadian intelligence. His team had no idea there was another Agency team on the ground. And that was how he ended up tied to a spanking bench in an Australian sex club. "He was literally assigned to help me with an important operation. I work for CSIS. The agency doesn't send us work rosters, you know."

She shrugged slightly, the diamond necklace around her throat sparkling in the low light. "Surprise, Ben. They don't send them to us either. Look, if it had been up to me, I would have sat you down and talked to you. I knew you weren't mob."

"They thought I was mafia?" It was ridiculous.

"My team can be suspicious," she admitted. "But I knew you were intelligence. I knew you were one of the… I want to say good guys. I guess what I should say is one of the guys we can work with. Sometimes what we do doesn't feel like good."

It was in the long run. At least it was supposed to be, and he needed to hang on to that fact. He needed to focus on that and what the intel tonight could produce if they played their cards right.

Her hand suddenly ran over his, and he practically jumped away from her.

A brow arched over her eyes. "Benjamin Parker, how are we going to pose as a married couple if you can't stand my touch?"

"Maybe we're one of those arranged marriage couples who actually hate each other but stay together for the family."

There was no way to miss the hurt in her eyes. "You hate me?"

This was what she did. She drove him insane pushing him away, and then she went all soft and he got gooey. He was fucking gooey on the inside for this woman. "No. I don't, but I sometimes think I should."

"But only half the time, right?"

She was weird. "I'm talking about the incidents when you fuck me over, and not in a physical way, although leaving me in that rice paddy was a dick move."

She turned all that charm on him, and he felt an actual dick move. His own. She smelled like citrus and sunshine, and the smile she gave him threatened to rock his whole world. "I made sure you were face up." She scooted over, and her voice went low. "Ben, I'm sorry. I sometimes get way too involved in an op and forget how to be polite. I think you should understand that. How about we call a truce? You're so uptight right now I'm worried about you."

He wasn't… His shoulders were up around his damn ears, and every muscle was tense because she was here. "I'll be fine."

"He won't," a voice came over the intercom. "He's not great when he's all pent up and shit, and he hasn't had sex in like a year or something, so it's a lot."

Tim was a fucking asshole. Ben reached down and shut off the intercom.

She was looking at him with the sexiest smile. "Ben, we need to get comfortable with each other. I know this is a big gala, but the head of the organization is known for being a stickler about who comes to his parties."

"I would think that check would be enough."

"And yet it won't be." She stared for a moment. "Is it so horrible to touch me?"

She wanted to play this way? He reached over and hauled her across his lap, his arm going around her waist to keep her there. "For the mission. This doesn't mean anything, Maggie."

She relaxed in his arms, her hand coming up to stroke his face. "It certainly doesn't mean I'm not still mad at you."

Her nearness was a fucking drug. He couldn't help but breathe her in, let the soft silk of her hair brush against his cheek. She felt right sitting on his lap. He liked that she wasn't some waifish supermodel. She was stunningly gorgeous, but she was solidly built, with hips and curves and breasts he wanted to see more than he wanted his next breath.

He'd thought Deanna had ripped him apart. What would this woman do to him? He hadn't been able to keep a normal woman satisfied, much less a freaking goddess.

"Ben, talk to me," she whispered, her cheek against his. "Not about the op. We know the op. Talk to me about your life."

"I don't have a life outside of work." He should set her back in her seat and concentrate on the op, but she was right about one thing. He was a mess. He needed to calm down or he would fuck up, and this job was all he had. "How are Tasha and Dare doing? Do you ever see him?"

Her smile turned… How to describe it? Bouncy? Happy? Like a flower opening to the sun. "They're doing so well. Dare found a job at a security company and the Agency is open to letting him come with Tash when he would be good cover for her. Not anything dangerous, of course, but Tash is mostly logistics and gathering intel."

When she got like this all he could think about was what a happy wife she would be. What a happy life he could share with her. When his day was shitty, Maggie could smile at him with that sunny expression and it wouldn't be so bad anymore. "I heard they got engaged."

She clapped her hands, and she wasn't a deadly agent. She was a teenaged girl at a boy band concert. "I'm a bridesmaid. It's so exciting. Let me tell you everything."

He let his chin rest on her shoulder and listened, wishing this could be his life.

* * * *

The gala was in full swing as Kenzie walked into the glittering ballroom, her hand in Ben Parker's.

If only they were here to enjoy the beauty of Croatia, the elegance of a ball. He looked like Prince Charming in his tailored tuxedo. She'd already straightened his perfectly placed bowtie just so she could feel like they were connected.

Her twin sister was a menace. Poor Ben. He was traumatized, and he didn't even realize she wasn't the one who'd done it. He likely thought she was some weirdo with a split personality.

"Mr. and Mrs. Packson?" The guard looked down at the invitation. "Can I see some identification?"

Ben pulled out his Agency-approved passport that showed he was an American from California. If anyone looked, he had a nice place right in the middle of Silicon Valley where his latest start-up was located. "Of course."

The guard studied it and handed it back with a solemn nod. "I apologize for the delay, but we can't be too careful these days. My employer would like to welcome you to the gala. Please enjoy yourselves."

Ben brought her hand up to his mouth, kissing her with what seemed like great affection. "We will. Thank you."

He had his full American accent on, and she missed the Canadian one. She wanted to get him to say *eh* or *sorry* so she could hear those sweet, rounded vowels. Maybe if she got him talking about hockey…

"Well, you seem to have put him in a good mood," a sarcastic voice said in her ear. She wore a small communications device that connected her to her team. Ben wore one that connected him to Tim. But that hadn't been the voice she'd expected to hear.

She frowned and glanced up at Ben, though he couldn't hear what was being said in her ear. "I thought Lou was running this one."

She kept her voice low, but they would be able to hear her. She couldn't simply come out and ask why the hell her twin was watching when she was supposed to be back at the safe house, far away from here so there was no chance of Ben finding out there were two of her.

"Lou is at the site. I busted into the feeds," Kala admitted. "You had comms off in the car. Did you forget what that asshole did to Lou? Are your girl parts in charge tonight?"

She thought seriously about turning them off again. She kept her face a careful blank.

Ben wrapped an arm around her, his voice barely a whisper. "Is it Tash? Does she have anything?"

Well, she couldn't say no, it was her asshole twin who had a burr up her butt about the Canadian. Like didn't her sister want her to be happy? If she ever got her shit together with Cooper, Kenz would be thrilled.

Of course, Cooper had never placed her sister's best friend in danger.

Kenzie had never actually had a friend like Lou. For a long time that friend had been Kala, but after they met Lou, so much of her twin's energy and affection went to her. And Kenzie never complained, never tried to oust Lou because she knew Kala needed her.

She just wished Kala needed her sister, too.

"It's Tash," Kenzie lied. "She's watching. She's not saying anything of importance right now. We should get a glass of champagne."

The event was being held at a castle that was usually a museum, but tonight it was decked out, and she wondered how it would have looked when the king was in residence. Did Croatia have a king? Now that she thought about it, Croatia might not have existed back then. She thought it might have been Yugoslavia then, but that wasn't the point. The point was she could see all those medieval ladies and gentlemen dancing and feasting and falling in love.

And having dysentery and no human rights and stuff, but again, not the point.

Ben would have been a king, and she would be the lovely servant girl who caught his eye. The good girl who was saving herself for marriage and a family. But he would take one look at her and claim *droit de seigneur*. The right of the lord. The one that meant any medieval lord could claim a night of sexual rights over one of his servants.

Of course, he would end up falling madly in love with her and they would have an epic love story that crossed continents and set the world on fire, and he would defy society and his family to make her his lady.

"Maggie?" Ben asked. "You okay?"

"Kenzie, I swear to god if you are writing some kind of romance novel in your head because you're in a romantic castle with lover boy, I'm going to punch you right in the face when you get back," her sister vowed. "Hey…"

"Sorry." It was Lou's voice that came over the line now. "I cut her off. It'll take her at least half an hour to figure out what I did, so let's get this op going. The target checked in earlier, and I have eyes on two men who could potentially be the meet-up. They're both in the ballroom."

It was time to work. She was sure she would catch hell from her twin when she got back, so she should concentrate on the job and get through this.

"We should dance. You promised me you would dance with me," she said like a good trophy wife should. With a pout that proved how indulged and coddled she was by this man.

Except she wasn't indulged or coddled by anyone. She was supposed to be tough and competent, and sometimes it was so exhausting.

He stared down at her for a moment. So few men could tower over her. She found it intoxicating. "What were you thinking about? Don't tell me the op. I know what your face looks like when you're concentrating on work. This was different."

He knew what Kala's expression looked like. It rankled that she had to share this, too. She loved her sister. Loved her like she was a part of her own body, and they had their strengths and weaknesses. Kala would lay her life down for Kenzie, but she'd never had to share the way Kenz did. Kala was broody and dark and often uncompromising. It hadn't endeared her to other kids. So Kenzie shared her friends. Kenzie lost friends when Kala got annoyed with them. Kenzie always included her sister no matter how much it hurt.

She didn't want to share Ben. Not even a little. Not even when she was mad at him and sure it could never, ever work, she hated the idea that half the time they'd "spent" together had been with Kala.

"I was thinking about how fun it would be to role-play here. You could be the lord of the manor and declare sexual rights over me, your lovely but lowly serving girl." She took a breath and turned to the ballroom where a stringed quartet was playing. "We should dance."

He tugged on her hand, and when she looked back his jaw was slightly open. He stared for a moment and then took the lead. "We should dance."

It was only an op. It wasn't more. It wasn't the culmination of her girlish dreams to find a man she loved more than life itself. Nope.

Sometimes it was hard to be the wide-eyed dreamer in a family full of spies and military men and women.

A waltz started up, and Ben brought her hands into the proper position. "Is he here?"

The question was asked on a whisper, his lips barely moving in case anyone was watching on the cams. Of which there were many.

She squeezed his arm once. Once for yes. Twice for no.

"On the dance floor?" Ben asked as he started to lead.

One squeeze.

"You're going to be the death of me, Maggie," Ben whispered, the hand on her waist tightening. "Were you really thinking about role-playing?"

She shrugged. He probably thought she was a complete pervert. Or that she was trying to manipulate him with sex. She'd had a boyfriend who told her that. When she'd explained she was only trying to get an orgasm, he'd gone to the she-was-a-complete-pervert argument.

"I was. It's a beautiful place, and I enjoy role-playing. It takes me out of my head and lets me unleash the parts of myself that don't get let out often." While she was talking softly to Ben, she was also keeping up with her steps and looking around to get eyes on the target.

"What parts, Maggie?" Ben asked. "What parts don't get to play?"

The man could dance. She felt light in his arms, like this was where she belonged. "My submissive parts. On your left."

His eyes moved with the practiced subtlety of a man who'd played spy games for years. She could see the moment he clocked the target moving with his partner. "Submissive? I rather thought you preferred to be the top."

So he'd been reading up. She was fairly certain the man had been mostly vanilla. Oh, she knew from Dare that Ben claimed he'd studied a bit for a woman he was seeing, but she didn't think he had any real training. And naturally his read on her was completely wrong. Kala was the one who felt the need to top a partner. Not lover. She wasn't sure her sister had ever had a lover.

She had to consider the idea that Ben was attracted to her twin more than her. It would be her luck and her eternal curse. To seem to be the sunny, bright one, and to always be relegated to her sister's shadow.

"It doesn't matter," she replied.

"I think our secondary is on the edge of the ballroom," Lou said in her ear, and there was no small amount of sympathy in her tone. Probably because Lou had heard the longing in those dismissive words. Lou was smart about tech, but she was no dummy when it came to emotional intelligence either. "Did I mention how gorgeous you look tonight?"

She felt a ghost of a smile cross her face. "Thanks. I think it's time to move."

Ben started to maneuver her toward the edge of the dance floor. "That's him. I recognize him from the reports. He works directly for Huisman. And he's nervous. His hand is in his pocket. I think that dumbass is playing with the thumb drive."

Sure enough, there was a pasty-faced man in an ill-fitting tux openly looking for his target. Like no subtlety there.

The man approaching him wasn't technically a spy either. Not the government kind. He worked for a multinational conglomerate, and this was apparently how Huisman liked to move information around without leaving a trail that could lead back to him.

If they were right, there was some nasty intelligence on that thumb drive. Huisman was working on some form of weaponized anthrax he'd stolen from Dare's father's company. They wouldn't be able to stop his research, but at least they'd be able to see what he had.

If she could do her job.

She smiled brightly at her fake husband. "Could you get me a drink?"

Ben frowned but played his part, leaving her alone.

She watched as the exchange was made, the corporate spy sliding Huisman's drive into his pocket.

One thing they'd learned about this man was his weakness for lovely women. The target didn't see women as anything but servants and sluts. He was married but kept at least two mistresses around and couldn't even stay faithful to them.

Kenzie positioned herself perfectly so the man would have to brush past her.

As he was approaching, she dropped her small handbag.

"Perfectly done," Lou said in her ear. "He's looking and he's practically drooling. Careful. He's moving in."

She bit her bottom lip and started to bend over, but there he was, leaning down to grip her tiny bag.

"Here you go," he said with what she was sure he thought was a charming smile. He was roughly her height, and he wasn't looking at her face.

Well, there was a reason the girls were on generous display. She gave him a smile and reached for the bag, her hand lingering one second too long. "Thanks. I was worried about bending over. I guess my dress is on the tight side."

"Your dress is perfect." He was taking in every inch of her, and it was clear he liked what he saw. "Like the rest of you."

"The car that's supposed to pick him up is incoming. You don't have much time," Lou warned. "Also, I've got a great camera angle on Ben, and let's have a long talk with him about resting murder face because that's what he has right now. Luckily that dude only has eyes for your boobs."

She didn't want to make anything of it. Ben had a murdery vibe to him a lot of the time. It was one of the things she found most attractive about him. He was all dangerous and seriously fucked up, so she could fix him with her love. Had she at times seen herself in a pretty sundress on a farm her family had never owned running toward her father with the wind in her hair screaming *but daddy I love him* as a Taylor Swift song surged in the background?

Yes. Yes, she had.

"Thanks." She gave the target a soft smile and then a little frown. "I wish my husband thought so."

There were times when she wouldn't mention another man's claim on her, but she rather thought this one would view it as a challenge. A man's ego and libido were the smart spy's keys to the kingdom.

"Your husband's an idiot." He glanced around. "Where is he?"

"Reel him in, sister," Lou encouraged.

She shrugged and let the hint of tears pierce her eyes. It was easy. When she needed to cry she thought about her dog and that someday she would lose Bud Two the way she'd lost Bud One and… Nope. Only a hint of tears. She didn't do dripping wet sobs. That would defeat the point. Men wanted her to cry pretty, not see her soul. Even Ben. "I think he's talking to someone on the gala team. A woman. He didn't even dance with me."

A brow rose, and she saw the calculation in his eyes. "Well, why don't I step in for him and then maybe I'll whisk you away? Wouldn't that teach him a lesson?"

Yeah, that was a way to get herself raped, but he didn't have to know that she could kill him fifteen different ways. Instead, she smiled tremulously and took his hand.

From there it was simple. She was charmingly graceless and bumped against him, looking at him with breathless anticipation so he was watching her lips while her hands slipped inside his pocket and she transferred the thumb drive to the hidden pocket in her evening gown. She would have to tell her cousin Devi how well it worked in the field. Lou was their gadget guru, but Devi designed and made clothes, and there was nothing wrong with that.

"Why don't we…" the target began.

"And here comes the drama," Lou advised.

Ben was right there as though he'd been watching and waiting for the chance to extract her. Or he simply wanted to get it all over with. "Maggie, what the hell are you doing? I told you to wait for me. I didn't tell you to plaster yourself all over another man."

There were suddenly eyes on them, and the target stepped back, disappearing into the crowd. Coward. She hoped he got his ass kicked for losing those files.

Ben's hand was on her elbow as he led her off the floor. "You okay?"

"Perfect," she whispered back. "My team is one block over. I'll meet you at your hotel."

He huffed as they walked past the line waiting to get in. "Not on your life. You don't leave my sight until I have a copy. Do you think I forgot how you walked off with the Mongolian intel?"

Again, that was her sister, but she couldn't point that out. "Fine, but we should move."

They made it outside and started walking toward the small building a block away where they were set up. The townhouse was a CIA safe house complete with all the gadgets Lou could ever want to play with.

And a lonely twin bed for Kenzie to sleep in. She didn't even have Bud Two to cuddle while she was here.

"You're safe. I've got her in lockdown since you're bringing the boy back after your date," Lou promised. "She's locked up good and tight if you want to bring him upstairs."

She wasn't about to do that because while her sister might hide, her father wouldn't. He would be right there with judgmental eyes and sharper than a stiletto sarcasm. "Meet me in the lobby and I'll pass it off."

"Or I could come up to your room," Ben replied, his eyes on the cobblestone street in front of them.

It was a warm night, and the tourists were out in droves. There was soft lights and music coming from the cafés and clubs around them, but they simply moved as quickly and quietly as they could.

"I don't think my handler wants you up there."

"I don't think I care what your handler wants," he shot back, his face in a deep frown. "Maggie, we should talk. This is bullshit."

She took him around to the garden entrance. It looked all perfect and normal unless one caught the signs that there were like twelve cameras on them. It didn't matter. She needed to get through the next couple of minutes and he would go away and she would be alone again with her righteous anger.

The evening hadn't gone the way she'd hoped.

What had she hoped for?

The gate closed behind him, and she saw the shadow of Lou moving from one of the upper floors toward them.

"Tell me what I'm missing, Maggie."

He was half hidden in shadows, the willow tree behind him and the moon above.

Damn, but she should have taken him to the front porch. It was bland. It didn't look like a place where the hero and heroine of her latest romantasy obsession would talk about their dragons or the vampire nation rising. "It doesn't matter."

She turned, and he caught her elbow. "It does to me. Maggie, tell me one true thing."

Her heart constricted. "I've told you lots of true things, Ben."

"And have you lied?"

"Of course I have. We're spies, and we don't work for the same agency. We've both lied and we'll continue to lie." Which is why it would never work no matter how much her heart wanted him. They might be able to have a brief affair, maybe hook up when they were working together… Except that half the time he was working with Kala, and wouldn't her twin lose her shit if Ben reached out and grabbed a boob because he thought she would respond to him?

Kala would respond with a bullet.

Why the hell couldn't she fall for one of the guys at The Hideout?

Lou appeared and seemed to feel the gravity between them. She gave Ben a nod and a half smile and took the thumb drive. "I'll be back with a copy."

She turned and walked in the house.

How many people were watching them now?

She moved behind the willow, pulling him to a spot where she knew the cameras wouldn't catch them. "What do you think you're missing?"

"I want to know what you mean when you talk about your submissive part." His jaw was tight as he said the words. The moon-light caressed him, the shadows painting his gorgeous face in stark lines. "All I've seen is the part that wants to tell a man what to do."

Kala. Though that wasn't what she was trying to do. Kala needed control. Kenzie required something else. "It doesn't matter whether you believe me or not, but I've never topped a man. There's a part of me that longs to submit, to find a lover I trust so much I'll kneel at his feet and let him treat me like a sweet fuck toy."

She heard him groan.

"I dream about having hours and hours where I don't have to be in control, where I don't have to worry about anything but making my Master happy." She could hear the stupid longing in her own words. "Where I can be naked and never once worry he'll use it against me because I'm his and he would never allow anyone to hurt me. Not even him. That's what I wish I could get, but I'm starting to think it's nothing more than a pipedream."

"I don't know." The words came out gravelly, as though he had to force himself to speak. "You said Dare and Tash are happy."

"They aren't us," she replied with a bittersweet sigh. It felt good to be here with him in the moonlight, but they had such little time and he was… She wouldn't call him the enemy, but he couldn't feel the same way about her and do what he'd done to Lou.

Her father was right.

"You think we don't get a happy ending?" Ben asked.

"Not with each other."

His hand found her wrist, and he drew her in. "I don't know that I accept that. Fuck all, Maggie. Half the time I want to murder you and the other half all I want to do is lay you out and feast on you. I want to get into bed with you, and I don't think I'll ever get out. Tell me you don't love Cooper McKay."

Every word went straight to the wistful girl part of her that longed for him. "I don't love Cooper. Not the way you mean."

He was so close. He towered over her, and she was wearing heels. "I don't want to never know, Maggie. I can't never know."

Her breath caught as she realized he was leaning over. He was going to kiss her. He was going to plant his lips on hers, and then she would know, too. She would know if there was any way this could work. Even for a little while. Even if they had to keep it secret.

Just one secret that could be hers and hers alone.

She could feel the warmth of his breath and…

"Here's your copy. Tell Joseph I said hello."

Her father. She stepped back, the moment broken.

Ben stepped away, though the frown on his face let her know he wasn't happy about the interruption. He took the new drive. "I hope it's all here."

Her father's brows drew together. "I'll give you that one because of what's happened in the past, but I would also suggest if you don't trust my team, perhaps you should find another to work with. You've done it before."

"Yes, and we know how that worked out," Ben said enigmatically. He glanced over at her. "Why don't you go change and I'll take you out for a late supper? I think we should talk more."

It was everything she wanted. And nothing she could have. She couldn't simply date the man. She'd figured out a long time ago that she could have stolen moments with him or she could be all in, and there was nothing in between. That was wrong. There was this thing they had now. Purgatory. This was her sexual purgatory. Always close but never once getting properly dicked down. Hell, half the time her twin was actively trying to separate this man from his penis. So maybe she should throw herself into being his booty call. Wouldn't that be better than this awful place they found themselves in? At least they would know.

Before she could open her mouth to turn him down her father was speaking again.

"The team is moving to London tonight," her dad said. "We pull out of here in thirty. Good luck, Parker."

Ben turned and walked away without another word.

Kenzie took a long breath and forced herself to go numb.

It didn't matter. Nothing mattered except the mission. She'd signed up for this, and she wasn't going to cry about it now.

"I'm sorry, sweetheart. I know it hurts, but as long as you're in the field with your sister, it's not smart to spend even a night with him."

She forced a brittle smile on her face. "Of course. I was making sure he didn't cause a scene. I've found flirting keeps him from going over the top."

Her dad sighed. "Sure you were. I was serious about leaving, though. We need to be in London by morning."

Kenzie strode into the townhouse, ready to deal with her twin, who would likely have an enormous amount of opinions on how she'd handled things.

Kala was in the kitchen, a tub of ice cream and a bottle of vodka in front of her. "Hey, I already packed. I left some sweats out for you to change in to, but I thought you could use some comfort food. And vodka. Are we in a Ben sucks mood tonight or the world sucks because I can't be with that douchebag Canadian? I'm prepared for either."

"Kala," Lou admonished.

But it was just the way her sister was. She'd basically told Kenz she loved her. "I'm in an I need a hug mood."

Her twin—who was not touchy feely in any way—opened her arms. "I'm sorry it was shitty. I know it's partially my fault. Come here."

She hugged her sister and hoped this stupid feeling would go away.

Chapter Three

Ben stood outside the swanky restaurant. Top. He wondered what it meant. His brain had gone straight to the sexual meaning, but then it always did when he was thinking about Ms. Magenta.

He'd kissed her.

He'd finally kissed her and it…

Maybe it was because they had loads of pent-up sexual frustration between them, and it couldn't possibly be as good as he built it up in his head.

It had felt…wrong.

He'd been a dick. She'd come all the way to Toronto to give him a debrief on the possible attempted assassination of Dr. Rebecca Walsh. Her car had blown up outside her home in Sweden, and everyone knew she had connections to Manny since it had been Manny's father's kidnapping of the good doctor that had led to his death. While Manny pretended to admire the famous neurosurgeon, Ben knew the truth. Manny hated her.

So that intel was important, and he'd known she would be the one coming after she'd kissed him in the hospital months before.

He didn't count that as their first kiss since she'd done it because he'd saved her.

He could still see her body on that fucking table.

He'd come to apologize to her and he'd known exactly where to go. While he might not know where she laid her head at night, he knew where she spent her time. The Hideout. He'd been to the place before, and Maggie's team treated it like their clubhouse. They played in the club and did not mind having classified meetings in the conference room.

The first time he'd come she'd been sitting waiting for him in an electric blue corset that made his eyes damn near bulge out of his head. And he'd wondered if she'd been playing with Cooper McKay.

So when he went looking for her this time, he'd gone straight for the club.

He'd found her there and after kissing her she'd asked him to meet her here.

Should he leave? Did he have the answer he needed in that one kiss?

"Ben?"

He turned and she was there. She'd changed from athleisure wear to a cocktail dress that clung to her every curve. Her magenta hair curled around her shoulders like sweet candy he wanted to sink his hands into.

But that kiss…

That fucking kiss. "Was it weird for you the way it was for me?"

Her head tilted slightly. "What are you talking about? The fact that you saved my life and Cooper made a big scene? I was unconscious, you know. I couldn't control how he reacted."

She was referring to the time he couldn't forget. "We should probably talk about that, but it wasn't what I meant. I was talking about the kiss. I kissed you an hour ago and I'm worried it was forgettable enough that you've already put it out of your mind."

Her lips curled up in a secretive smile. "So it wasn't a good kiss for you?"

"It was awkward. It wasn't… I suppose I've built it up in my head."

She moved into his space, and his dick responded immediately. "It was rushed, Ben. And it was awkward because I knew Cooper was there and could see us." She put a hand up. "I don't love Cooper. I didn't run after him. I got ready to come and see you, but I couldn't have this discussion at the club. I can't ask him to leave."

Cooper had been there at the end. Cursing him and telling Ben that he wished him luck with her.

She was right. It had been rushed and awkward, and it bothered him that it was their first kiss because he was done playing. He wanted her. He was going to have her, and he didn't care about the potential fallout.

He'd seen her die. He'd held her body that day in Toronto when Manny kidnapped Maggie and a woman named Carys and her fiancé, Tristan Dean-Miles, and Captain Zach Reed. When the bullets went flying, Manny set off a fail-safe—a bomb meant to take the house down around them. And Ben knew he couldn't leave Maggie behind.

"Maggie, I want to forget all the reasons why this can't work."

She went on her toes and brought her lips close to his, hovering. "Then maybe you're ready. Kiss me, Ben. See how it feels this time. See how it feels when it's the right time and the right place and the absolute right woman for you."

This was what he'd expected. This heady, almost drugged feeling he got when he was close to her, when their bodies brushed together and he could feel her warmth. When he could smell the citrus of her shampoo and her pink hair caressed his cheek.

He followed his instincts, which had gone haywire when they'd kissed earlier, but they were right back online now. He felt electric when his mouth touched hers. He moved this time instead of standing there. He took control because it felt right to do it. She wanted a dominant lover, and damn, but she brought it out in him. One kiss and he was ready to strip her bare and place his mark on her.

His tongue slipped inside her mouth and stroked over hers, and it took everything he had not to come in his freaking slacks.

He stepped back because they were standing right on the street, and no matter how much he wished it wasn't true, they were still targets for his psycho ex-friend. "Let's go inside."

She pulled on his hand when he started leading her in. "Ben, was it different? Was it good?"

Was it good? It was beyond, and he had to deal with it because he was through pretending she wasn't the be-all, end-all of his existence. "It was perfect." He leaned over and kissed her again. "It was everything I wanted it to be. Needed it to be, and we need to talk."

There was the sweetest flush to her face. "Yes, we should talk."

He led her into the restaurant, hope in his heart for the first time in a long time.

An hour later, Ben wasn't sure how they'd stayed apart. He felt magnetized around her.

"I don't remember what happened," she said, and there was the slightest flush to her cheeks. Like she was embarrassed. Or telling a bit of an untruth. "I woke up in the hospital. I'm still not entirely sure what that man put my body through."

She was talking about what Manny had done to her mere weeks before. He could still remember seeing her on that fucking medical bed, an IV in her arm and attached to various wires that would give Manny data about her pain. "It was an experimental drug. I think a bit of it survived." He wasn't doing this to her. "Maggie, I know some of it survived the fire. That room he held you in wasn't completely destroyed."

She seemed to take that news in stride. "So CSIS has it."

"I'll do what I can to get you information about it," he promised.

Her head shook. "Don't get in trouble. I'll let my handler know. He's still got some ties in your world. Ben, if this is going to work, we have to understand that there's a wall when it comes to our jobs."

"You don't want to work with me?" He didn't like the idea of a wall between them. He wanted nothing between them. Despite the fact that he knew she was being practical, he didn't want to acknowledge that their agencies, while somewhat friendly, had issues with each other. Relations with the States had frayed years before and were still touchy.

Her hand came out and moved over his. "Of course, I do, and I will whenever possible. But we have to deal with the fact that it might be hard for us to be together. What are you thinking? I'll be honest, I started off with the deep belief that we would have a couple of filthy, glorious one-night stands and then I would be able to move on. I don't think I can move on from you."

He got such a sense of peace when she touched him and spoke sweet words. He felt her caring. Or she was an excellent actress and she was still playing him and he was the dumbest asshole in the history of time because hadn't he been through this before?

Her hand moved on his forearm, the motion soothing, like he was a predator and she was going to stroke him down from his emotional turn.

"You're thinking about him," she said quietly.

"He nearly killed you." He had some things to admit to her. "I tried to get your medical records."

"Tristan would have gone in and erased them." She sat back with a glass of Pinot Noir in her hands. She looked comfortable in the space, like she'd been here many times, and she probably had since the staff had put them in a private dining room. It was one more mystery to solve when it came to the most mysterious woman he'd ever met. "I'm fine. It was terrible and I have some new scars, but I'm okay. I'm cleared for field work and everything."

"Baby, you need to understand that he knows how I feel about you. I have no idea how." He was getting paranoid about it, looking for cameras or people hanging around to listen in. It felt like Manny was everywhere.

"He's very likely excellent at reading your signs and signals." Maggie offered another possibility. "He finds me interesting, and he likes to take apart the things that interest him. Literally."

She needed to understand. Manny wouldn't stop. It was one of the reasons this was a bad idea in the beginning, but she was on his radar now. It was better that they were together. Better that he could protect her.

Except he wouldn't be with her most of the time.

He was going to have to tell his shitty tale. He was almost certain she knew a little of it. "When we were in Australia and Manny came to Dare's hotel suite, he told Tasha and your handler about a woman named Deanna."

She nodded, and there was suddenly a sheen of tears in her eyes. Sometimes she was so emotional. Others almost completely shut down. It was probably about work. There was the professional Maggie and the real one. This one. If she sometimes seemed like she was two different people it was because she had to be. "Yes, Tasha gave us all a report. She was your fiancée, and she had an affair with Huisman."

"I think she was young, and he was richer than me. He could offer her more. She tried to tell me it was all a mistake, but I think she just figured out what being with Manny was really like." He took a long breath. He didn't like to think about what Deanna might have gone through. Time had lent him some perspective. "Manny hates women."

A sardonic look hit her eyes. "You don't have to tell me that. I've recently gotten some clear evidence of his misogyny."

The thought turned his stomach, but he forced himself to take a long swallow of the ridiculously expensive Scotch she'd ordered. Had the CIA become a bit like the mob and they now had whole establishments as cover? "Yeah, I'm aware. He stopped your heart. I carried your body out, and I was almost certain you were dead."

She stared at him for a moment and then stood, and for a second he thought she was going to walk away. Instead, she moved to his space. "I think we should have this talk while I'm sitting on your lap, Benjamin. I think I'll feel safer and more secure if your arms are around me."

He didn't hesitate. He pushed his chair back and found himself with a lapful of the most gorgeous woman he'd ever seen. Fuck, she'd been right. The minute they were close, he felt like he could breathe again, think straight again. He let her scent wash over him as she stroked a hand over his hair. "This feels nice. We're going to shock the staff."

She chuckled, a sound that went straight to his dick. "Oh, we would have to do so much more to shock this staff."

Top. Of course. "This place isn't connected to the Agency. It's connected to a club. Is the chef a Dom?"

Her body relaxed, and one arm drifted around his shoulders. "Pretty much everyone. I think maybe one of the line chefs isn't, but it's most of them. There are three clubs in Dallas that are somewhat connected, so they don't all play at The Hideout. Some of the younger workers do, but most of the married ones play at either Sanctum or The Club. So don't worry that they'll be surprised."

He rubbed his cheek against her hair and realized she'd done this for him. She'd done this to make it easier for him to talk.

He was fucking falling for this woman. "I met Deanna in high school. The same one Manny went to. I was there on a scholarship. Well, I thought I was. I later found out the scholarship fund was supported by the Huisman Foundation."

"His family paid for your school? And they didn't tell you?"

"I suppose somewhere deep down I knew. I certainly knew I didn't get an academic scholarship. I wasn't that great in school, though I learned later on how to take a test. I got serious in college, but in high school I was all about two things—sports and girls."

"I played volleyball and basketball," she admitted. "It was fun. I've always liked being a team member. So you met Deanna there?"

He wanted to ask about her high school. He had so many questions, but he needed to give her this story. For her own safety. If she was smart, she would listen to what happened to Deanna and walk away from him.

He didn't think for a second that she would, which was why he needed to stop being suspicious of her. He trusted her on a base level. And hey, she hadn't tried to kill him in months. "Yes. She was an actual scholarship kid. She was on Manny's study team. Yeah, he was the kid who formed study teams, as he called them. He was serious about test taking. If he didn't make a hundred, his grandfather would punish him. He would tell him that all he had was his brain since the family looks and charms had skipped a generation."

"Oh," she said with a sad huff. "That's mean. He was a kid."

"I don't know if Manny was ever a kid." He was tired of talking about Manny, tired of his life revolving around a mistake he made when he was barely eight. The mistake had been being friends with a neighborhood boy. "But I mention the abuse he suffered because I saw it. I don't think his grandfather ever physically abused him, but he certainly humiliated him. He never measured up to his father."

"The same father who kidnapped Dr. Walsh? He was trying to steal her research, if I recall. From what I can tell, Huisman's obsession with my handler comes from that moment in time."

"I don't know as much about it as I should. Manny was good at hiding his dark side from me. He tended to play the victim around me, and I bought it all."

"He can be a victim and a bad guy," Maggie corrected. "Sometimes it's precisely how people slide into their villain era. I've often wondered if I could do that."

"You?" This soft woman in his arms could never be a villain. "Never."

She snorted. A bratty sound. "Hello, Mongolia?"

Funny how now it seemed like a cute story. "I forgive you for Mongolia. After all, you did let me hold on, and you got a squeeze in there. Tell me something, did you like how my ass felt in your hands?"

"Excus…" She'd gone stiff but then laid back again. "I suppose I had forgotten that part. Sorry, but you're making my point. We were about to die and I copped a feel, and I should get a real talking to about that. There should be some serious repercussions. That was completely unprofessional of…me."

She was adorable when she was embarrassed. And he needed to consider the fact that after two seconds of her being affectionate with him, he was tossing out all the bad shit she'd done. But he wasn't thinking that way tonight.

"Uhm, I think I'll forgive you for that, too." He liked cuddling her. He could absolutely get used to this. "If you go into your villain era, then be ready to have a boyfriend who helps you. Let's keep it to the cool villainy though. Maybe we can assassinate a couple of tyrants and free some people."

The smile on her face did things to his cock that she could probably feel. But she sobered and let her head drift to his shoulder. "Tell me what really happened."

Guilt gnawed at him. "Manny… Our relationship is complex. We knew each other from a young age. He was so much smarter than everyone else. He was also slightly younger because his father pushed him so hard academically. I didn't like how the other kids treated him, so I became his only friend. I liked him back then. He was kind and ridiculously smart. His father hated me. Said I was a waste of time, but Manny actually stood up to him when it came to me. And then his father was killed and he went to live with his grandfather. When we met again it was high school, and he was broken somehow. He'd gotten very dark."

"From the profiles our team has been given, it's highly likely there was a lot of abuse in his grandfather's home, and the fact that his mother abandoned him probably led to his misogyny."

"He truly loathes his mother. Loathed. She was killed during a robbery in Paris. I've often wondered if he arranged that," Ben explained. "But I didn't see that back then. I saw an old friend who could use some help. We got close again. Unlike his father, his grandfather did approve of our friendship. To the point that he constantly criticized Manny for not being more like me. I became the golden child of a family I didn't belong to. To a brother who wasn't mine. But he was excellent at hiding his darkness. He wrapped himself in this calm, peaceful doctor persona. Even in high school. He would cause trouble and then step in to fix it, and everyone looked up to him. Everyone except his grandfather."

"Who died conveniently after Manny graduated. I was surprised he refused an autopsy."

Ben had thought this through long ago. "Why would he? Anyone who held stock in the company was gone, and surprise, all of that stock found its way back to Manny. So no, he didn't care why his grandfather died. He might have done it himself."

"What happened with Deanna? You got together with her before college, right?"

"We started dating during our sophomore year of high school, and I was comfortable with her. She was smart and funny, and she and Manny got along. She wanted to be a doctor, so they had several classes together. I wasn't surprised when she announced she was going to the same college that Manny had gotten into."

"How did you feel about that?"

There was nothing to do but tell her the truth. "I was happy about it. Happy that she was getting what she wanted. Happy that she would have a friend there."

"And you were also relieved."

Well, no one said she wasn't smart. "I was. I was never in love with her, and she'd started talking about us getting married. She wanted me to come with her, but I had a baseball scholarship. I wanted to see the world, to party and have fun. I tried to break up with her but she was so fragile. Her mother had recently died from cancer. There was never a good time to break things off, so we tried long distance."

"She wasn't your responsibility. You were a kid."

"So was she, and we made some adult choices, so yeah, I felt she was my responsibility."

She shifted. "So you took her virginity and felt responsible for her even though she made the same choice and didn't think about what you would need when it came to college. She thought you would follow her because she was smarter than you. Because she needed it more than you did."

That summed things up nicely. "She was smarter than me. It was pointed out on more than one occasion that she had more to give to the world than I did."

"Ohhh, let me guess. That was Huisman."

"It was. He encouraged me to follow them. On more than one occasion he discussed the fact that I was never going to play pro baseball, so why didn't I take some business classes and learn how to run parts of the foundation for him. He and Deanna would be the brilliant doctors, and I would handle the business."

"You would be the staff," she corrected.

"I didn't view it that way at the time, but now I wonder. I wouldn't give up my place, and I remember Manny staring at me and saying so be it. I didn't know what he meant at the time. I liked being away from home, being on my own. Deanna and I talked a couple of times a week, and things seemed to be going well. I kept up with Manny, too. He came up to see me and we would have a good time. And then I got the call."

"Was it during your freshman year?"

He shook his head. "It was the start of junior year."

"You stayed with her for two years?"

"I did, although we didn't spend much time together. A couple of weekends here and there, a month during the summers, but the last time she'd avoided going home. She spent the summer at Manny's. I thought they were hooking up, and honestly, I was okay with it. Her father had passed by that point. Suicide, although now I wonder."

"So she had some tragedy happen every time you were pulling away? It sounds like a Huisman thing to do. Play on your empathy." She frowned his way. "You're surprised I believe you? Babe, I've seen what the man can do. It doesn't surprise me at all. I wonder why he didn't go after your parents, though."

"He saved that for later." Ben didn't like to think about his parents. "It was after Deanna died and I declared war that he tried to hurt my parents. You should know they blame me. They were forced into hiding, but not before my father told me I wasn't his son anymore. I don't know why I told you that. I was talking about Deanna."

"I'm willing to listen if you want to tell about them," Maggie offered in a soft tone.

He shook his head. "No. Not now. Where was I?"

"She called you?" Maggie prompted.

He didn't like to think about the day. "She begged me to come see her. I didn't want to go but she cried and told me I owed her. So I went, but I was planning on ending things. She told me she'd been seeing Manny but it was all a huge mistake and she was scared of him now. She said she'd always loved me but Manny had manipulated her into a relationship."

She took a long breath. "I'm so sorry that happened to her."

"I didn't know what to believe. I confronted Manny, who told me she was trying to cover up the fact that they'd been having an affair and he'd broken it off. He gave me evidence, and for a moment I was confused. He showed me text messages and pictures of them. I was angry."

"Of course you were. He was running a psy-op on you. You get that, right?"

"I do now, but at the time it felt like betrayal. I got in my car. Which had been sitting in Manny's garage for a day. I was leaving, and she got in before I could keep her out and my brakes failed."

"Manny tried to kill you." It didn't seem like a question.

"I think he would have been happy if I'd been injured and he could step in and help. I've come to realize it was all to put me in a corner so I couldn't leave him. But Deanna paid the price. She wasn't wearing a seatbelt when we went over the side of the road. She died on the operating table. I still wonder if Manny didn't have something to do with that, too."

"It was not your fault."

"I didn't love her. I know Manny didn't love her. She got in the middle of this fucked-up rivalry and she died." He needed to say the words, needed for her to acknowledge the danger even though she'd already had a visceral example of how Manny could treat a woman. Especially a woman connected to Ben.

"I'm not Deanna. I'm trained and I have a team."

It hadn't helped. "And yet you almost died. He still got you on that table and experimented on you."

"That wasn't your fault either." She shifted so she could look him in the eyes. "Ben, there's a lot I need to tell you, but the most important thing is I'm not afraid of Emmanuel Huisman. That doesn't mean I don't take the threat seriously, but I'm not going to hide. I'm not going to let him ruin my life. I'm going to catch him. I hope you'll work with me on that."

Such a brat. "Uh, I think you'll be working with me."

"We'll see about that," she vowed and leaned over, brushing her lips against his.

There was a rustling sound, and he realized they were no longer alone. A man in a chef's jacket walked in with two servers. The man looked to be in his mid-twenties, and he probably got all the ladies he wanted. Or all the guys. The man could likely get whoever he wanted in bed, and Ben felt a well of jealousy.

"Good evening, special guests," the chef said with a knowing smirk. "I've got an amuse-bouche before your first course. Are you enjoying the Scotch? Ke… Ms. Trent told me to send you nothing but the best."

Maggie slid off his lap and resettled herself. "Tell your dad I'll pay him back." She looked his way. "This is Luke. He's my cousin. I live here in Dallas, and we should talk about my name."

Her name? A cousin? He knew Dallas was her base and that her team was different from other Agency teams, but other than that he'd been able to find nothing. Was she about to tell him the truth?

Luke's eyes went wide. "Wait? We're doing this here? Because if we are, I should make some calls."

"This is not a spectator sport, Luke," Maggie replied, rolling her eyes.

"Oh, but there are so many bets on this," Luke shot back, and now it was easy to see how comfortable they were with each other. Like they'd grown up together. Actually, he could see some resemblance between them. Right in the eyes and the shape of the jaw.

How different was her team?

"Nope," Maggie said, waving her cousin off. "No bets. If all goes well, you can tell everyone that we'll be at The Hideout later tonight."

The club. Fuck. The idea of getting her in that club made his cock twitch. She'd taken him through once and they'd watched scenes, and ever since he'd been studying. Because he'd known he wanted to be more than her boyfriend. He wanted to be her Dom.

The server placed a small dish in front of him.

"Caviar vol au vents," Luke explained, going back into professional mode. "You'll find my cousin here has some expensive tastes and is picky when it comes to both caviar and vodka."

Two tall shot glasses of chilly vodka were placed next to the small, caviar-covered pastries.

Maggie downed hers with the grace of a pro. "I simply like what I like." She smiled Ben's way. "And I like you."

She was going to kill him. When was the last time he had a good relationship with a woman? A normal relationship where they dated and talked and enjoyed each other's company without him worried she was a plant from Manny.

The doors to the private dining room opened again and Tasha and Dare were there.

For a moment he thought Tash and his former friend were there to save Maggie from him.

"Hey, Kara," Tash began. "I'm afraid I need to talk to you. I'm sorry to interrupt, but we have a situation."

Ben stood. Situation?

Maggie joined Tash, while Dare moved into Maggie's now empty seat.

"Hey, it's work. It's nothing to worry about, but Kara needs to deal with it. I thought we should talk since it looks like we're going to be something like family." Dare sat back. "We were friends, right? I know I've pushed you away, but I need…either some closure or to forgive you."

Ben felt his heart clench. What he'd done to Dare… Well, he regretted it deeply. "We were friends."

"I'm sorry, but I need to go," Maggie said.

"You okay?" He wouldn't make a big deal. He understood what it meant to work in intelligence.

"Something's come up with Zach," she replied.

Ah, Zach Reed. He'd gotten some intel on the man. Zach had walked away from his team during the same mission in Toronto that had caused Maggie so much pain. "Go. We'll talk later. I'm in town for a couple of days."

She gave him a smile. "Have fun with Dare."

She walked away, but Ben was feeling lighter than before.

* * * *

She was going to have a seriously long talk with her sister.

Kenzie followed Tasha out of the private dining room. "Is Kala at The Hideout? I know Mom and Dad are worried, but she'll be there.

She's hiding from Cooper and probably pissed at me since Ben showed up and she had to handle him. Did you know she cupped his ass? Next time I see Coop, I'm planting my hand right on his butt."

See how she handled that.

Of course, Kala had made a major sacrifice for her today. She'd allowed Ben to kiss her and that had likely set her twin off on a desperate attempt to get rid of the cooties. Hopefully someone had found the bottle of vodka they left in the bar. It was a good antiseptic.

It was like her mother said.

Vodka reshayet vse problemy.

Then she remembered how worried he'd been. Because the kiss hadn't been good. He'd known. Deep down, his soul had known the woman he was kissing wasn't his.

His mate. They were like fated mates in a werewolf story. Ben would be such a hot werewolf. He would look amazingly sexy with his clothes ripped off and his pure predator form unleashed. And he would know his mate.

Tash turned, her face paler than before. "I was lying about Zach. I had to get you out of there because I couldn't tell you that Kala's been taken. The shrink the Agency sent was working for Huisman. He's got Kala and Devi."

Well, that made all thoughts of Ben Parker as a hot werewolf flee. "What the hell? She was at The Hideout and Devi has a bodyguard. Fuck. Tell me Landon's okay. Is he dead? Does Dad know?"

Tasha took her hand. "Landon's fine. Devi got away from him. She intentionally snuck away, and Dr. Gallagher caught her and used her to get Kala to give herself up. She shot Aunt Eve."

Tears filled Kenzie's eyes, but she felt resolve harden inside her.

It was time. Time to take down Huisman and finish this, and then she could go after her man.

She followed her sister, ready for battle.

Chapter Four

Nepal
Four weeks later

Kenzie stepped into the hallway that—according to the reports she'd studied—led to Dr. Huisman's personal office. The one she now had the code to because while Huisman was super evil and wanted to blow up the world, it wasn't like the dude was picking up after himself. And surprise, he also didn't pay well which is why that keycard was in her pocket.

"Did you find it?" Lou was in her ear. She was in a safe spot working to try to gain control of this mountain base of Huisman's.

And Ben was here.

It seemed like forever since the last time she saw him. Last time she'd kissed him and sat on his lap and made the decision to be with him even if it was only once.

That night she'd flown to Virginia and with the help of Zach, they'd managed to save Kala and Devi. Well, Zach had sort of, kind of kidnapped Devi. That girl was racking up points on her bingo card. Kidnapped three times now, if one counted the Zach encounter. Which Kenzie didn't because according to Kala, their cousin had been playing some serious kinky games with Zach in a barn.

Not how she would have gone, but good for Devi.

"It's ahead of me. It looks like the outer door is already open," she replied.

"Comms are in and out," Lou said, her voice crackling a bit over the connection. "Be careful. I'm looking at this system, and I think he's got traps everywhere. I'm worried, Kenz."

"I'll be fine. I'll get the key to Ben and circle back to help find Devi." She moved down the hall, the sounds of gunfire in the distance. "I take it we're already at work."

"It's chaos," Lou said and then the comm went dead.

"Lou?" She touched her earpiece. "Kala? Anyone?"

Dead air. She was on her own.

Well, that was what happened when an evil villain decided to put his lair in the side of a mountain in the middle of the Himalayas. Where the Internet was sketchy. It was annoying. She would bet they had electricity problems, too. And it was cold. If only she was…

Ben was here and she was not feeling like the cool, competent agent she should be because they hadn't seen each other since that day at Top. She'd called but they'd had work stuff. Ben and his tech Tim had stumbled into an op being run by Henry Flanders and his daughter, Lucy Brooke. Or LB, as Kenz called her. Or Lucifer, as Kala called her. LB answered to a lot of names.

Deep breath. She looked good. She was in Lou's latest, a snowy white winter uniform made entirely of nanites so it could adapt as she needed it to. It fit perfectly and could double as body armor.

Also, she could make it go away with the push of a button. She could literally melt her clothes off if Ben looked at her in a panting, melting way.

Damn it. Her father was right. She was a mess when it came to this man. Deep breath. It was time. She stepped into the antechamber. If the reports were accurate, this space served as Huisman's office, research center, and private rooms.

And there was Ben. Tall and gorgeous in all white, too. He and Tim had come up the hard way, but he looked fresh as a daisy, not like a man who'd climbed a twenty K mountain and squeezed through air ducts to get here.

He stared at her and for a moment she hesitated. He looked cold.

As cold as the air around them. Huisman liked it chilly.

Maybe he'd rethought his position. If he had, then she better get through this.

"Ben, I'm sorry I'm late." Kenzie pulled back the hood of her parka as she approached him. "We had trouble with the helo, but it looks like you handled everything with your usual aplomb. That was a lot of bodies out there, buddy."

He studied her for a moment, his eyes taking her in, and not as cold as they'd been. "I didn't realize you were late because you're not supposed to be here at all."

What kind of game was he playing? "You know we were responsible for getting the code. How did you think I would get it to you?"

"Text works." Yep, he was upset with her.

Maybe he hadn't felt what she had that night.

Her heart threatened to break. Somehow she'd thought this would be a happy reunion. They both worked in a job where they couldn't be available all the time. He had to know she'd tried to contact him the only way she could, so this was his answer. She was going to have to admit to everyone that she'd been wrong and this man wasn't the be all, end all of her existence. Professional. She could find a little of that. "You need this along with the code. I took it off one of Huisman's men last night at a bar. He's still sleeping it off, so I doubt he'll miss it. Now, if you don't mind, I'll open that door and we can be home in time for dinner."

He stopped her before she could get to the door. "Did you get the vaccine?"

Well, at least he didn't want her to die. They knew Huisman was working on a weaponized version of inhalation anthrax. Or he was hoping she wasn't prepared so he could leave her behind. He was about to find out that even if he didn't want her anymore, he wasn't getting rid of her. Not when it was her cousin in this facility.

She rolled her eyes, something she never would have done if he'd been even halfway nice to her. If he had, she likely would have knelt at his feet. Because she was a dumb girl. "Of course. Do you think I have a death wish?"

He seemed to consider the problem for a moment, and Kenzie worried she might have to fight him.

All in all, not how she thought this would go.

"All right, I'm going first," he finally said. "I don't know if Huisman is behind that door or not. According to our intelligence, he hasn't left the base in a week, but he sent home the rest of the non-security employees a few days ago. Be careful, eh? He might be a doctor, but he gave up on his Hippocratic oath a long time ago. He will be armed, and he won't hesitate to kill you. Stay behind me."

She moved to the door, using the key card and punching in a five-digit code. If he was going to be cool and casual about this, so could she. "You know I love it when you say 'eh.' And hey, if you want to get murdered first, who am I to stop you? What's wrong with the comms? I can't get my team on the line."

Ben stared at the door. "Apparently the storm is wreaking havoc on our electronics. Stay behind me."

Kenzie gripped her SIG, taking a long breath and trying to shove the drama out of her head. It would be okay. She could get through this. Finding Devi was the important thing. Finding Devi and getting rid of Huisman.

When they got rid of Huisman she wouldn't have to see Ben again. She could move on.

The light came on and Ben glanced around the anteroom. "According to the plans we stole, this is where Huisman works."

"This outer section is part of his office. The lab is in the back. It's a level-four biosafety lab, so we'll have to change if we go in there." Did he think she didn't read the reports?

A brow rose over his eyes, his annoyed look. Now that she thought about it, he sent her that look a lot. "Yes, I got that intel. And we don't have to change at all. I'll deal with it, and you'll stay out here and watch for any stragglers. And Huisman. I haven't found him yet. He's got to be here somewhere."

Who the fuck did he think she was? At least up until now he'd respected her professionally. "I'm not going to sit out here like a good girl and wait for you. I can bet what would happen. You would go in and the formula would mysteriously disappear."

He simply turned and started down the hall.

He wanted to ignore her? Oh, she wouldn't let that happen. "If you think I'm going to allow something that deadly to fall into your country's hands, you don't know me."

They made it through the fairly utilitarian outer office to the more private part of the space. If she was right, the door to the left led to the lab. There was a green light blinking above. Why the hell wasn't it locked? Huisman's office was on the other side. It didn't have the same elaborate security setup the lab had. This felt like a trap.

"I don't know you at all, sweetheart. I don't even know your real name. The only thing I know is that you'll do anything for your country, including turning over a weapon of mass destruction when you would be better off destroying the formula." He strode down the hallway. "And don't even talk to me about our countries. Let's see which one is known for being involved in every war it can send its troops into, and which one is known for maple syrup and delicious donuts."

She followed him. "We have excellent donuts, too. And maple syrup. Have you never been to Vermont? Name me one thing Canada has that America doesn't. Face facts. You're nothing but America North, buddy."

He chuckled, but it wasn't an amused sound. "You know what we have that you don't, baby? It's called common sense. Sweet, sane common sense. Which is precisely why you're not stealing this formula."

Ben stopped at the doorway to the office, and something about how still he went had her getting the SIG ready.

Then she realized she didn't need it. Not for Huisman.

"Is he dead?" Kenzie walked in and stared at the body on the floor. Yep. That was Dr. Emmanuel Huisman, and he had a bullet hole in his left temple.

Ben kicked the revolver away from the doctor's hand, but he didn't touch the body.

"He must have decided to kill himself rather than face the Agency." Her dad was going to be so upset. He'd wanted to murder that asshole in very medieval ways.

"Maybe he knew he was facing CFI."

Canadian Foreign Intelligence. It was an offshoot of CSIS.

Were they comparing dicks? It wasn't how she thought he would use his dick on her. "You've been around for five years, buddy. You're not known for being particularly ferocious when it comes to dealing with prisoners. You do tend to give them donuts and hope they like you enough to talk."

Where was the Ben she knew better than her own heart? Why

could she hear her sister vomiting even though she'd only said the words in her mind and Kala wasn't even here?

Huisman was dead. They should be celebrating, but Ben seemed shut down. As though that wasn't truly the outcome he wanted.

Ben stared at the desk in front of them, avoiding looking at Huisman. This was obviously the man's private office. The rest of the place was Spartan, with only utilitarian features, but this was luxurious. She counted three separate laptops and a desktop she would need to figure out how to download. She would take the laptops with her.

Would he fight her over them or agree to come back to her hotel so they could share the intel? A couple of minutes before she'd had a scene in her head. She and Ben entwined on that big bed, naked and sated and talking about all the intel they were finding.

Ben stood by a monitor and held up a sad sticky note.

Play Me

That was a terrible idea. Huisman liked games, and the only way to win was to ignore them all.

"I don't think we should go down that rabbit hole. Let's get into the lab and get out of here. If he wanted to monologue like a good villain, he should have stayed alive."

He set the note down and moved to the door that led further into the apartments.

Kenzie felt her jaw drop. This wasn't the lab. It was a decadent bedroom with cream-colored walls and a massive four-poster bed.

And some paintings that were supposed to have been lost during World War II. She was almost sure there was a Picasso on one of the walls, but her attention was now firmly fixed on the big-ass piece of equipment with wires flowing all around and a…damn it. That was a timer on the top.

"What is that?" She asked the question even though she was pretty sure of the answer.

Before he could reply, there was a hissing sound and she realized the door behind them had closed and likely locked. In horror she watched as the clock came online.

1:00:00

0:59:59

0:59:58

Well, she'd known. "Shit. It's a bomb."

Ben tried to open the door. It didn't budge. "Try the key card."

She knew it wouldn't do a lick of good. They were caught, and now she wished she'd put a bullet in that asshole's brain. Damn it. Her father was going to kill her. Her sister would never let her live this down. She tried the security card but all she got was a red light.

There was the sound of something shifting above them as a monitor slid down from the ceiling. It looked like Huisman liked to watch TV in bed.

She bit back a groan as Huisman's face showed up. Fucker was going to get his monologue no matter what.

It was taped, not live. There was still a shot that Huisman was dead outside, but she wasn't holding out much hope.

"Welcome, Benjamin. I figured you wouldn't follow my very reasonable orders, so I had to set a bit of a trap to get you to hear me out. If you are not Benjamin Parker of Canadian intelligence, I apologize. But I think it will be you. You and the American girl. I seem to find you together so often. Welcome. You finally found me. I applaud you, and you've managed to catch me at a delicate time. Even now you're at work in the outside perimeter, taking out my soldiers. I went cheap on the mercenaries. I suppose thrift was my downfall. The good news is the bomb you are currently sharing space with is not cheap. It's quite expensive, filled with all the best uranium China could get to me. It's certainly enough to blow the top off this mountain. And it will be enough to send my enriched and hearty anthrax all over the country of Nepal."

"What the fuck did Nepal do to him?" She wasn't sure if she believed him. The good doctor was known to lie. Oh, she believed the asshole was going to blow them all to hell, but if he already had the right bomb, why did he need Zach Reed's mom?

"Why do I care about Nepal, you might ask?" Huisman mused. "I don't, but the Chinese want it destroyed and they paid me an enormous amount of money to do it. The explosion will destabilize this part of the world. In addition to blowing off the top of this mountain, I've rigged something special up there. When my new anthrax hits the upper atmosphere, it will breed and form clouds. It will rain down on the people of this region. Imagine that. Not acid rain. Anthrax rain that only the Chinese and their select friends will be immune to. It will seep into the soil. Perhaps my new bacteria will continue to breed. It will be a brave new world, my friends. Unfortunately, you and I will not live to see it. I think I'll go out on a high note, but I wanted to leave you a bit of time to contemplate the end of your existence. This is my final gift to you, Benjamin. I give you the gift of time. What will you do with the final hour of your life? I think you will be like a rat on a sinking ship, scratching and panicking to save your own pathetic life. You see, there are worse things than dying. *Au revoir, mon ami.*"

She wanted to throw up. He was a monster and now he would be the end of her team. She let go of her petty worries about Ben and slipped her hand in his.

41:34

The clock kept ticking.

She was trying to stay as calm as possible. Her dad was out there, and he would figure this out. Or he would realize he had to save the rest of the team. "I think we should cut the blue wire. The only problem is I'm fairly certain this sucker has a couple of land mines attached. I don't mean that literally, of course, but I think bad crap could happen if I clip the wrong wire. The red wire goes to something that looks like it's empty, so it's probably a gas."

"I wouldn't put it past him to release some sarin on us if we did something wrong."

Kenzie sat up, pushing her hair out of her face. She was down to her white jumpsuit. "I could use some optimism."

"I don't have any when it comes to that bomb. I think we should try to work on the comms. Neither one of us is a bomb expert." Ben had tried everything he could to get that damn door open. It wasn't budging, and he'd nearly killed them both trying to shoot the locking mechanism. Now he was playing around with the tablet he'd taken out of his backpack. A satisfied grin crossed his face. "I'm in his computer system."

Lou hadn't been able to bring the comms back online, so she'd been worried the whole system was down. "How did you manage that? Can you get the door open?"

"The TV is a smart screen. It should be able to connect to any system with a signal. Huisman sprang for the best. The satellite connection is still working. It looks like he's shut down electrical to all the doors. No one can get in or out."

"Send out a message before his handlers decide to shut down the satellite."

His fingers flew across the tablet before passing it to her.

"Thanks," she said, turning away slightly. "At least I can warn my team."

"Where are they?"

"They're somewhere in the building, though I know there will be a couple who stay behind in the docks," she said. "My partner was worried about losing the bird. It's brand new and it's capable of getting up to almost thirty thousand feet, but it struggled with the storm. Langley will murder us if we crash that chopper. It's their baby, and we might or might not have had permission to take it out for this op."

His brows rose. "You stole a helo?"

She finished typing, hit send, and hoped the message made it out. "I think they will discover that we were simply mistaken about which helo we were supposed to take. It was early, and that requisition form can be hard to read before I've had a cup of coffee."

"Let me see if I can affect this bomb from here." He took the tablet from her and started poking around the system. "I have no idea how you get away with that shit. If I did it, I would be fired."

"It helps to have friends. We work with some of the best Special Ops teams in the world, and I happen to have grown up with some of those guys. I'm sure if times weren't what they are, those relationships would cost me plenty, but I'm incredibly valuable for them now. My helo pilot used to steal cookies from my mom's cookie jar."

"Yeah, well my childhood friend is about to blow up a good portion of Asia," he replied, his voice dull.

"Hey, it's okay." Kenzie put her hands on his shoulders. "None of this is your fault. Unless Huisman was your secret lover and you cheated on him and that's why he hates the world."

It was a joke, though she acknowledged that it often felt like Huisman was the third point in their triangle.

Ben snorted. "Not my type. I'm starting to wonder if I have a type."

"Oh, I'm you're type. Don't get me wrong, Ben. I can be arrogant, but I'm self-aware, too. I know perfectly well that I'm not every man's type. I'm a brat of the highest order, and I was probably raised to have ridiculously high standards, but we're alike, you and I. I'm your natural mate."

"Then why the fuck do you keep leaving me?"

"I didn't leave you. I had to go to work. My…team needed me." She wanted to tell him everything, but they were right back to their corners, and it didn't matter now. "We've talked in the last few weeks. I told you what I could about the Wales mission."

"I was working, too. You know maybe I wouldn't have gotten dragged down by that old dude if you'd been more open," he said, his voice tight.

Henry Flanders had been posing as a Welsh vet to support LB's mission. From the reports that "old dude" had gotten the jump on both Ben and Tim. "I don't know the complete workings of the Agency any more than you do yours. Can't we… It was never going to work, was it?"

The lights went out all of the sudden and they were plunged into darkness, only the red light of the timer providing any illumination.

Ben found her hand. "Maggie?"

"I'm here." She moved close to him, bumping up against his chest, and she let her arms go around him. "I don't want to lose you. I can't see a thing."

"Is the timer still ticking down?"

She let her head rest against his shoulder. "Yes. It's on some kind of battery, but if I try to clip it, it looks like it triggers the system."

Naturally.

"And the sensor that connects it to the bomb on top of the mountain is probably battery operated, too."

"I think I can see enough to get around now." Kenzie moved, her eyes adjusting to the low light. She tried the door again. It was worth a shot. "Damn it. Well, the power going out didn't kill the security system. That door is not budging."

Was Huisman up and moving again? Somehow she didn't think he'd planned all this out and then actually killed himself. He'd counted on Ben's squeamishness and her need to not have Ben watch her make entirely sure his childhood bestie was dead.

She hoped her father found him.

And she remembered she had a pen light. Lou had designed the nanite program with many pockets. She pulled it out and a single stream of light cut through the darkness. They needed to take inventory of their assets.

She opened the drawer of the bedside table. "Oh, look. The good doctor believed in safe sex. And a shocking amount of lube. Who needs that much lube? Ah, there we go."

She'd found matches. She set down the small flashlight and struck a match. Lucky for them whoever had decorated this space liked candles.

"Do you think he used this place as his pleasure palace?" Somehow she didn't see Huisman being much of a ladies' man.

Ben hadn't moved. Not an inch.

She looked at him, the soft light of the candles doing nothing to take away his stark masculinity. "You okay?"

"No."

Despite the fact that he was angry with her, she couldn't let him stir in his own misery. She was in love with him and it might never work, but it was real for her. "You need to have a little faith. We're stuck. There's nothing we can do, but our people know what's going on. They won't let this happen."

"But there's no way for them to stop the bomb that's five feet away from us."

She'd already accepted this. "No. I don't think they can, and they know what their priorities are. I've already assessed this and the most likely outcome is that my team takes out the big bomb and we die in here anyway."

"Yes, I think you're right." He touched her, his hand moving over her hair. "I wish you weren't here with me."

"That's funny because I was thinking that there was no place I would rather be." She stepped in closer, tilting her head slightly up. "I've thought of nothing but that night at Top for weeks. I wish you had picked up on my signals long ago. I wish we'd had more time."

His fingers tightened, and she knew he'd made some kind of decision. "Your signals suck, baby. All you ever had to do was this."

He lowered his head and brushed his lips over hers. Fire sparked through her, but it was a warm, loving thing. There was passion in his kiss, but longing, too. A longing that matched her own.

Somewhere in the back of her head she knew the clock was still counting down, but time stopped for her. They hadn't gotten the white picket fence and two point five kids. They hadn't had a big wedding. They wouldn't get to watch each other grow old and face it all together.

But they could have this.

One moment. One perfect moment where they were together.

When his tongue swept across her lips, she welcomed him inside, her hands going to his hips. A long, satisfied sigh came from her chest as he deepened the kiss. She wrapped her arms around him, giving herself up to the moment. To this one bit of joy in all the hours of horror. This was the way she wanted to go out. With him. Finally with him.

Somewhere out there her sisters were working, saving the world. They would never know the gift they gave her. Knowing her team would get the job done meant she could spend this precious time with him. She would be able to feel him inside her just once.

She could love him in the time they had left.

"Don't cry, baby. You know I'm crazy about you. If this is all we get…" he began.

She rubbed her cheek against his. "We'll take it. I want to be with you. Just once."

"Maggie, I'm crazy about you. I've wanted to touch you since the moment I saw you. Well, most of the time," he whispered against her mouth. He dragged his tongue across her lower lip, and she shuddered in his arms. "Sometimes it's like you're a different person."

Because she was a different person those times, and her twin could be a lot. "Don't think about that. That was all work. This is different, Ben. I want you so badly sometimes I can't stand it. My friends know it, too. They know you're the reason I haven't had a damn boyfriend in forever."

He kissed her over and over, drugging her with his closeness. They'd never tangled their bodies together before, and the rest of the world seemed to fall away. Nothing mattered except this moment with him. Her parents would want her to try to get out, but she knew there was no getting out of this. This was fate.

His hands roamed over her back and down to cup her ass, pulling her against his body and letting her feel exactly what he was offering her. "Do you have any idea how hard it is to work with you? I get this way any time you're around."

She did not like the thought of him getting hard around Kala. She loved her sister, but Ben was the one thing she wanted for herself. Kala…she was happy. She had Cooper and Lou and Tash and she would be okay. They would all be okay. "Even when I'm busting your balls?"

"There are times when you seem more pissed off than others. I often wonder who hurt you."

She let her hands find his chest. "One day I'll explain everything, but for now, please kiss me again, Ben."

There wouldn't be time for explanations. Their bodies would do the talking, but she had faith that he would understand. When it was over and they were wherever spies went, he would know everything—including the fact that he was half of her soul.

He kissed his way from her mouth to her cheek and down her neck, each caress lighting up her skin.

"Baby, I want to see you." There was a pleading frustration to his tone that let her know how on the edge he was. "I want to touch you. I know we don't have much time, but I want to spend every single second we have left getting inside you. It's all I want now."

She could handle that.

"You know we have all the best toys." She turned slowly, showing him there wasn't a zipper anywhere and yet it fit perfectly. "Nanites. They conform to whoever's wearing them. They're also resistant to bullets and weapons. Oh, push hard enough and you can still get a knife through there, but it gives me some protection."

He did not look impressed. At least not with the tech. His eyes were on her breasts. "How do I get it off you?"

"It's easy," she said. "It's voice activated. Undress."

The nanites flowed down her body like a metallic wave, the sensation oddly soothing. Even her boots joined the group of mems. It was what Lou called the collective. Apparently it stood for micro-electo mechanical systems. She liked to call it Bob. She reached down, picked up the clothes she wouldn't need again, and placed it on the nightstand. "Cute, huh?"

"I take it that voice control is only for you. Because I could find a definite use for that. Damn, but you're gorgeous. Come here. It's cold and I don't want you to feel the chill for even a second."

"I didn't notice. I'm perfectly warm." Somehow it was easy to forget the fact that they were going to be blown all to hell. It felt right to finally be here with him. "And I would never give you that code. I know what you would do with it."

She was lying. If he was her top, she would wear those nanites like fet wear and give her Master the keys to unlock the kingdom.

The life they could have had…

He gave her a gentle smile, one that told her he knew what she was thinking. "I don't have clothes that undress themselves. I think I need you to help me."

She pulled his shirt free from the tactical pants he wore. She eased her hands under the sweater and thermals he was wearing underneath. Ben bit back a moan the minute he felt her hands on his flesh. She slid them up, running along his abs and up to his chest.

He was perfect. She loved the feel of his skin under her palm. "I should have known you would be needy. Lucky for you, I don't mind a little work."

"I should have kissed you the first time we met. I should have taken you into my arms in that bar in Sydney and not looked back," he whispered.

That would have been a mistake because Kala would have murdered him and left his body in a dumpster.

She dragged the layers over his head and tossed them to the side. She let her hands drift over him, getting to know the valleys and plains of his body. Pure need pulsed through her as she kissed his neck and let his scent wash over her. Naked. She was naked with him, and it felt like the most natural thing she'd ever done. Her nipples were tight nubs as she rubbed them against his chest before kissing her way down his torso. She knew exactly what she wanted. They had so little time, but she wanted this. She wanted to know how this man tasted on her tongue. She stopped briefly at the scar on his left shoulder, the bullet wound now raised and white.

"So sorry about that, babe." She kissed the scar and then ran her tongue around it before continuing down, not explaining that she was apologizing for her sister.

She did that a lot.

She dropped to her knees, the soft carpet cushioning the fall. He wouldn't know what she was doing when she spread her legs wide and placed her hands, palms up on her thighs. He wouldn't understand that she was greeting her true Dom for the first and last time. After a moment, she reached up and unbuckled his belt and eased down the heavy fabric of his slacks and thermals. Then his cock came free and she licked her lips. "I knew you would be beautiful, Ben. I win that bet."

She leaned forward and gripped his cock in her hand, loving the feel of it, the power she had as she began to serve him. She tongued his cockhead and he gasped, his hands sinking into her hair.

She was surrounded by him. She worked her tongue over every inch of his cock. His taste, his heat and smell, the way he tugged on her hair in just the right way. He was everything in that moment, and she found the sweetest sense of contentment. It was joy mixed with lust, stirred with a bittersweet sense of what could have been. She sucked him hard, wanting to give this man everything she had.

"Take more." He pushed his hips forward, forcing that big cock deeper.

She loved the sensation. If they had time, she would let him fuck her mouth, treat her like a fuck toy that was all his to use. She would do it because it was fantasy and safe because he would never see her that way. He would love her.

"You have no idea what that deep voice does to me. I wish we had a chance to have a long talk about my personal kinks, but for now just know that I can take orders. I want to please you." They'd never talked about a contract, never gone over hard and soft limits.

He stroked her hair as she settled in to finish the job. "You please me in every single way, baby. Now take me. Suck me hard and fast and don't stop until I tell you to."

The order sent a thrill down her spine, and she could already feel her pussy was wet and wanting. She licked her lips and settled back down, sucking him in long passes. After a moment she felt the hold on her hair shift from soft to a hard twist as he took control.

It was everything she wanted. He used her mouth for a moment, fucking his cock in and out before he tugged hard on her hair and stepped away.

She sat back on her heels, waiting for his command. It was nothing she would ever want in real life. She wouldn't have a man telling her what to do. Well, not one who wasn't her boss and happened to be her father, and even then it was a fifty-fifty shot that she obeyed.

But she would obey Ben here.

"Get on the bed and spread your legs for me. I want to see that pretty pussy before I eat it like a starving man."

Yeah, she wasn't going to argue with that order. Her whole body was humming with anticipation as she climbed on the bed and spread her legs for him.

He watched her, his eyes seeming to burn with lust in the low light. "Touch yourself. I want you to rub your clit and get it hot and ready for me. I want that pussy wet. I want to lick that pussy and get cream all over my tongue. Do you understand me?"

"You're killing me." She drew her hand down her body until she found her pussy and brushed her fingers over the pearl of her clitoris.

Ben stepped out of his pants and stroked his cock as he looked down at her. He was the sexiest thing she'd ever seen. So masculine and perfect. She even loved his scars. They marked him as a warrior. As her mate.

He climbed on the bed, looking like a sexy predator ready for his feast. "Give me a taste."

She offered up her fingers, the ones that were coated in her cream. He brought them to his lips, sucking them inside. Pure heat flashed through her, and she bit back a groan.

"You taste perfect, but I'm going to need more." He covered her body with his, leaning down to kiss her, and she tasted herself on his tongue.

She gripped the covers as he moved down her body. He sucked one nipple into his mouth and then the other, laving them with his affection. Every tug of his mouth made a straight line to her pussy.

"Please, Ben." The words came out of her mouth on a low moan as she spread her legs even further.

She watched as he lowered his mouth and covered her pussy. Sparks. She could feel damn sparks hitting her body. His tongue was motherfucking magical. She could barely breathe. He'd just started in, and she could feel the orgasm building. She was out of control, and it was all right because he was here. She didn't need control. All that mattered was him. She sank her fingers into his hair. It was the tiniest bit long and so silky.

She swore she saw stars as he eased a big finger inside her and his tongue ground over her clitoris. That finger curled inside her, finding her sweet spot, and she went over the edge.

The orgasm made her stiffen and then relax, pleasure flooding her system.

Ben got to his knees, stroking his cock. She watched as he picked up one of the condoms and rolled it on. She could have told him he didn't need to, but her breath caught and he moved over her, settling himself between her legs.

She loved his weight on top of her, loved the feel of his muscular back under her palms. She definitely loved the way he worked that big cock of his into her. She groaned as he stretched her with every thrust of his hips, sending him deeper and deeper.

It was beyond anything she'd felt before. This was what making love meant. She'd had sex before, good sex, but this was something more. This was what singers wrote songs about. This was love.

His hair fell over his forehead in the sweetest curl, but his expression was all arousal. He fucked her hard, making her eyes widen with every thrust. All the while Ben held eye contact with her. He watched her, giving her his every expression. He opened himself to her and she found a home she hadn't expected.

Then her whole body was awash in sensation as the second orgasm hit. She clutched him, her nails digging in lightly, but she didn't care. She wanted to mark him, then he could mark her. She wanted a physical sign that they had been together. Even if no one would ever see it.

She felt the moment of his orgasm. He tensed and held himself hard against her, his breath heaving in and out and making that beautiful chest move.

When he let his body fall on hers, she wrapped her arms around him.

She held him for a moment before the chill hit her skin and she couldn't hold back the shiver that went through her. Tears threatened, but she blinked them back. How long did they have?

"Baby, let's get under the covers. I want to hold you." His voice was so tender.

No panicking. Just peace. It was not a bad way to go. She kissed him and gave him a smile. "I can get with that. But go and get rid of that condom first. I do not want that slipping off and going everywhere. Sticky is not the new black."

His lips curled up before he brushed their lips together again. "I'll be right back. Get under the covers. I want you warm."

She loved it when he got bossy. "Yes, Sir."

He walked off and she did as he asked. She slid under the covers, trying to avoid the red light across the room. She didn't want to look at it. Didn't want to know how little time she had left. And yet she caught sight of it.

3:10

She was in love with him. She'd known it for a long time. Likely since the minute she'd seen him through those glasses of Lou's. She wished so much she'd been the one with Tash in that bar that day and she'd had this time with him. Maybe if she'd been there, they wouldn't be here.

Except Huisman would always have come between them.

He might think he won because they were both about to die, but they were going together, and that wasn't a loss.

She stared at the clock, her life running through her mind. It had been good. So good. Her parents were weird, and she loved them for it. She'd had such good brothers and sisters. Such a loving home. And she'd gotten to meet her nephew. She would never joke about Travis wearing a condom again. It was one more blessing the universe had given her.

Like this one.

2:37

Ben strode out and she drew back the covers, welcoming him. He immediately pulled her into his arms.

"I hate that I wasted all this time," he whispered, kissing her forehead. "I should have made a move, should have told you that first time that I thought you were the most gorgeous thing I'd ever seen, but you seemed so cold."

"About that." She could tell him anything now. She rubbed her cheek against his chest seeking his warmth and affection. "I'm glad you didn't because it would have been awkward."

"I tried to kiss you in Croatia, but Mr. Lemon showed up. Do you remember? I still hold a grudge. It was like he was your dad or something."

She smiled against his chest. "I remember. You danced with me. I wish we'd danced more."

"You were wearing that ridiculous dress that had every man in the room panting after you."

She'd dressed for him. "Including you?"

His hand smoothed over her hair. "Oh, so including me. I was jealous of the target. That was when I knew I wanted you. You were distant before and then we clicked."

She suddenly needed him to know. She rolled to her side so she could look at him. "I should explain that. Why I seemed like two different people at times. Ben, I want to be honest with you."

The clock caught her gaze.

1:10

No time. No time at all. Seventy seconds of life left. She laid back down and wrapped her arms around him. "It doesn't matter. Just know that I always wanted you. I knew it from the moment I saw you. I knew you were the one for me and even though it was complicated, I was always going to end up right here. With you. This is how we end, Ben Parker. We end together."

He held on to her and found her lips with his. He kissed her again and again, but there was no expectations of anything this time. This was love and affection with no other reason than they loved each other. With no other goal but to die in his arms.

It was almost time. She wrapped her arms around him and held on.

For way longer than a minute.

Like she could lose track of time, but this was a bit much.

Kenzie sat up and looked at the clock.

"What's happening?" Ben sat up beside her.

What the hell was going on? She glanced over and the clock read *0:00*.

It held for one second and then another.

"It didn't go off." Ben started to get out of bed. "What the hell? Fuck. Manny did this."

"Uh, I don't think we should be upset that the bomb didn't kill us." He was having an odd reaction.

Ben stood in front of the bomb. "This was a trick. He did something. I don't know what, but I'll find out. He's obviously not fucking dead. He planned this."

He changed so fast. One minute he was her sweet lover and the next… He hated Manny Huisman, and that felt like all that mattered.

She was about to ask him to come back to bed when she was

startled by a clanging on the outer door.

"I'm coming in. Dear god, please cover up and don't be doing something that will make me vomit," a familiar voice said.

"Oh, shit." Well, she wasn't going to have to tell Ben. He was about to meet her sister. For real this time.

Ben went for his gun.

"Don't. She's friendly," Kenzie explained. "I mean that in the secondary usage of the word. She's actually mostly rude, and she's going to be very familiar to you. Ben, I'm so sorry."

The door came open and Ben was left facing… Well, he was facing a second her.

Kala winced as she looked at Ben. "Dude, way more than I wanted to see." She turned back to Kenzie. "Okay, sis, there's good news and bad news."

Kenzie reached for the mems cube, though Kala wasn't at all affected by her nudity. They didn't have a lot of boundaries when it came to that, though she didn't like her sister getting a look at Ben. She was nervous again. Moments before, everything seemed perfect. Besides the whole "we're about to get blown to bits and scattered across Asia" thing. But she and Ben had felt done. Ready. Settled. Now the ground was shaking again. She could feel his eyes on her, and they were narrowed with seeming irritation. Or rage. She had lied to him, and the proof was standing in front of him. "I take it the good news is that we didn't blow up, and that's awesome. How did you manage to shut down the bombs?"

"Lou did," Kala replied. "With some help from the Canadian dude. He's not a complete moron, though his British accent is shit. I can't believe Devi fell for it. Also, we've got Devi. She's cool but we need to move."

"I don't understand." Ben said the words calmly, but there was a hard undercurrent.

Kala sighed and turned his way. "Twins, buddy. I would have thought that was clear now. I'm the one who did all the fun stuff like shooting at you and leaving you behind on a plane with a bunch of killers. She's the one who flirts and sighs and signs your name in her journal and shit. Also, thank god now we can be clear. I'm married to Cooper. Please don't kiss me again."

He stood there wearing nothing but his pants, his arms over his chest as he watched them. "I meant the mission. How the hell did Lou and Tim handle the bomb? Everything is down—Internet, electricity, comms. Or it was. Do you think we didn't try to get a message out?"

He sounded so cold. Shouldn't he ask her about the elephant in the room?

She'd waited too long, and now he wouldn't forgive her.

Kala huffed. "We got the messages. How do you think we knew to send Lou and Tim after that bomb? Devi saw Huisman, by the way. How did he get by you?"

"He faked his death," Kenzie admitted, knowing damn well what came next.

"And you didn't put a couple of bullets in him?" Kala asked, all the judgment in the world in those words.

"I thought he was dead." She wasn't going to tell her sister she hadn't done her job because she hadn't wanted Ben to see her do that to a corpse.

Her sister's glare told her they would talk about this later.

"He was convincing. I won't make the same mistake again. I've learned appearance can be extremely deceiving," Ben said. "When did the damn comms come back online? You know there's a system in here. You could have contacted us. You didn't have to…"

His voice trailed off, and she realized he was talking about the sex. He wished he hadn't had sex with her.

She was not going to cry.

The question came from Ben, but Kala turned Kenzie's way. "The comm problem was totally one way. We could hear everything, and also, there are cameras that fed out even after the power went off, so way to make a sex tape, sis. Dad's trying to bleach his eyeballs." She finally addressed Ben. "He's going to kill you, dude."

"Your father?" At least he'd lost the angry look. It had been replaced with pure shock. "Maggie, is your father your handler?"

She forced a smile on her face. She might have made a sex tape, but honestly, who hadn't at this point. It might be her only souvenir of her entire relationship with Ben. She hoped Lou had kept it. "It's Kenzie. Kenzie Taggart. My father is the man you know as Ian or Mr. Lemon, which I've told him is cringe but he's like totally Gen X and does not care."

Ben's head shook. "Mr. Lemon is fucking Ian Taggart? The single, scariest dude in the whole of the intelligence agency? He's a legend. And he's your father? What the fuck else do I not know?"

Kala had a hand on her. "You're a spy, dude. Figure it out. We've got to go. Tim's waiting for you. Byeee."

Kenzie pulled back. "I need to…"

Kala leaned in, whispering. "We have to go. We have Zach's mom, and if we wait around someone will show up for her. Dad's letting Henry take her to Bliss. We're going to hide her, but we need to go and not let the Canadians know."

Naturally her job fucked them over again. She turned back to Ben. "Can we talk later? Maybe you could come to Dallas for a debrief."

Kala's grin was slightly sinister. "Come for family dinner, dude. I'm sure my dad would love a word."

Ben ignored the taunt. "We need to find Manny. And get all the data we can."

Kala pulled her toward the doorway. "Already have it. Well, we have what Lou managed to get before Huisman's protocols went into effect. We'll go through it back home. I believe you're wanted in a debrief in a couple of hours, and then our agencies are going to form a team. That should be fun now that little sister scratched her itch."

Kenzie frowned her sister's way. "He wasn't an itch. You know that, Kala."

Kala sent her a sad smile. "I know. But we have to move. We have to get that helo back or Coop will be in trouble." Kala winked at him. "And nice package, Parker. I'm glad I didn't wreck it."

Kenzie stopped at the door. "Ben…"

He shook his head. "I guess I'll see you next time. Good-bye, Maggie."

There was nothing to do but follow her sister. And leave her dreams of Ben behind.

Part Two

Now

Chapter Five

Ben Parker sat at the conference table staring at his mentor. Joseph Caulder was in his late forties and had been working intelligence for twenty years. So long that there was almost no way he didn't know who Mr. Lemon was. "How long have you known?"

Joseph looked up from his notes. "Parker? You're still here? Do you have a problem with the new assignment?"

It had been three weeks since that day in Nepal, and he hadn't spent a single second thinking about anything but Mag…Kenzie Taggart.

His whole body felt alive when he thought about those minutes they'd spent together. He'd made a mistake. He shouldn't have allowed her to walk away. He should have thrown her over his shoulder and forced her to come with him. He'd seen it in his head. He could find a nice cell for her and she could serve him until she'd made up for lying and making him look like a fool.

Then he thought about the hollow look in her eyes, and he wanted to call her, to ease her and soothe her.

Which was exactly what she wanted.

"I think I should be the one to go to Dallas. Now answer my question."

Joseph stared at him for a moment. "How long have I known what?"

"That our American contact was Ian Taggart." He'd spent every spare moment he had learning everything he could about the Taggarts. On paper they were a family of five with an adopted eldest daughter, Tasha, and two sons, Seth and Travis, and one grandson, Colton Taggart.

On paper Kenzie Taggart and her twin didn't exist.

Joseph sat up and took his glasses off. "I've known Ian for a long time. Most of my career, actually. I got involved in a case that revolved around his nephew many years ago. I was a field agent then." He sighed. "I suppose this is about Ms. Magenta."

"So you know she's his daughter." The betrayal cut through him.

"I suspected, and I suspect she's not the only one. If I recall he had twins. Two girls who looked an awful lot like their mother," Joseph said softly, as though remembering. "If you look today there is no mention of the twins. Given that I know for a fact the young woman who runs the team and coordinates with base for them is his oldest kid, I did think it was more than possible Ms. Magenta was Ian's as well. The whole team is something of a family. TJ is his youngest brother's son. Cooper McKay is his best friend's kid, and Tristan Dean-Miles belongs to a family Ian's worked with forever. So yes, I suspected."

"And you didn't think to mention it to me?"

"Well, I don't gossip about other agents, Ben." He took a long breath as though considering the situation. "I know you've had trouble with her and you suspected her of keeping intel, but Ian always made sure we got it. He's a valuable asset to our agency. I know things are touchy with the Americans, but he's solid. So no, I didn't give up his secrets because you didn't need to know them, and before you say something you shouldn't, fucking another operative in the field is not enough to make me cause a rift between our team and Ian's. Though I think you've managed to do exactly that."

"What is that supposed to mean?"

"It means we have data the Americans don't have and when I suggested you go down and debrief the team, they requested another operative," Joseph replied.

A wave of anger surged through Ben. She thought she could fuck him over? "If they want the data, they can get it from me or they don't get it at all."

Joseph groaned. "And then we don't get their data. For fuck's sake,

Ben, I thought you wanted me to take Huisman seriously. Well, here I am. Taking him seriously, and you're the one screwing around. Literally. Can you think with your actual brain for ten minutes?"

Not when it came to her. He'd proven that time and time again.

What made him ache was how peaceful he'd felt with her in his arms. He'd lain there and known he was going to die and it was okay because she was with him. She'd been everything in that moment, and she never bothered to tell him she was two different people.

Gaslighting. He was pretty sure this was a textbook case of gaslighting since he'd mentioned several times it felt like she was two different people and she'd blown him off saying it was a work persona.

"You kept important intel from me, Joe."

A brow arched over icy eyes. "So you needed to know which twin you were dealing with when all you were supposed to do was work with her? Did you need to know which twin you were passing intel to? Or did you want to know which one you were hitting on? Tell me—did you sleep with both of them or just one?"

"I'm pretty sure it was only the one." Tim walked in, carrying a folder. "You see, boss, there was a good Maggie and a pretty evil but still hot Maggie. I think he liked the sweet one. I've thought about this a lot and I think the one Huisman tortured is the mean one."

Yes, he'd come to the same conclusion. He'd spent days and days going over every op he'd been on with the Americans, and he'd split up the times he'd dealt with Kenzie's twin. Kala. That was her name. Kala Taggart. Well, Kala McKay, if what she'd told him was true.

"Is there a point, Tim?" He didn't need input.

"Many," Tim said with a sigh and turned to Joe. "I've tried to talk to him. He's got this thing going where he thinks the twins have been like laughing behind his back or something, but Lou says Kenzie's been crying for weeks and that she's listened to something called her sad-girl mix, which from what I can tell is a lot of sad songs about how guys are assholes."

She'd been crying? "When did you talk to Lou?"

That felt like a betrayal too. Tim had been talking to the Americans behind his back? Was he working for another team? Damn it. Could he find a single person who was loyal to him?

Tim handed over the folder to Joe. "We've been working through the data. Not all of it. Rest easy, friend. We're all still holding out on each other, but I think we have enough that we should work with them. I know you're going to be mad, but I'm going to Dallas with the new girl."

Hannah Hayes, a long-term operative who'd been working in Europe for the last several years. She sometimes worked with MI6. The same MI6 team Ben had worked with when TJ Taggart was kidnapped. She was good, but she didn't know Huisman. "So I'm out. I do all the work and I'm out because your relationship with Taggart is more important than taking down Huisman. Am I being benched? Should I start looking for another job?"

"The only reason I'm benching you is your attitude. And honestly, your professionalism. I get it," Joe explained. "She's a beautiful woman. Are you done with her? I'll rethink everything if you can promise me you're not going to take some kind of revenge on her. She had a job to do, too. It's actually brilliant, if you think about it. They managed to have an operative who could literally be in two places at once if they needed her to be."

"He won't be able to do that," Tim said quietly. "He's in love with her."

He hated that word. "I am not. I don't even know who she is."

Tim sighed. "Then it's best you leave her alone and let her heal, man. I worked with them, too. And now that I know what I know, I do feel like I can tell them apart, and Kenzie was always fair with me. She was always nice. I know Kala was rough, but I think that's just who she is."

"She left me to die," Ben pointed out.

"And caught you and took you down with her when you jumped," Tim replied. "She could have fought you off, could have let you fall, but she didn't. And I know you're pissed because she was in love with Cooper, but she isn't Kenzie. So Kenzie didn't lie to you."

"Oh, she lied." She lied about everything. Her name. Who she was half the time.

And yet he could see how brilliant a play it was. One of them could be out in public while the other worked in the shadows and no one would question her.

He fucking missed her. That was the worst part.

"So did you." Tim frowned his way. It sucked because often Tim was the only one in his life who seemed to be in a good mood. "Do you think I forgot the Australian op just because you left me behind? You didn't walk in and tell her who you were. She thought you were Brian Peters. You didn't tell her who you truly are until you tried to kidnap her sister and they caught you."

Not his finest moment. And he'd only had questions for Tasha. He wasn't really trying to kidnap her. Still, Tim had a point. "All right, I'll give that to you. I didn't intend to ever tell her my real name. But after…"

"She works for another Agency. She had a secret. If you don't want a woman with a couple of secrets, hop on a dating app and put *no spies* as one of your requirements," Joe said with a long sigh. "Maybe it's for the best. I think you're too close to Huisman. He's escalating. We have reports that he's planning a strike somewhere in Asia. He managed to get out with one of the bombs and his formula for the anthrax. We have it, too, but he knows so he'll likely change it now. I need someone to go down and explain the situation to Big Tag. Thank god I can call him that again. I swear that asshole picked Mr. Lemon because he knew it sounds stupid. You should get ready for your new assignment."

"I'll quit before I leave this case," Ben announced. His brain was trying to wrap his mind around the problem. What if he could kill two birds with one stone? He could keep his place and get Kenzie Taggart out of his system. "Look, that team is angry with us. I should go and smooth things over."

Joe snorted.

But this could be the best way to handle things. "I can play nice. Look, you're all right. I overreacted. She's reached out several times, so I know she wants to talk. Maybe if we talk, we can work things out. Between our teams. You know they sometimes hold out on us."

"And we hold out on them when I think we should." Joe seemed determined to make his case. "This case is not one where our country can get ahead if I hold back some intel. This case is one where the world bleeds if I do it."

"But you know the Americans won't see it that way," Ben argued. "I can go down and talk to Kenzie and get on the inside. She's always eager to work with me. If she's upset with how we left things in Nepal, she'll want to please me."

Tim's eyes rolled. "I hope that somewhere in that brain of yours this is all justification because you can't handle the idea of not seeing her again. Because if it's not and you're seriously thinking about playing a woman who loves you, you're not the man I think you are. I watched that tape. She wasn't faking. She didn't try to run. She didn't fight for her life. She only wanted you. I can't tell you what I would do if I could get a woman to look at me the way she looks at you. I would be willing to put up with a slightly deranged twin and all the professional lies she would tell me. But that's me. I guess we don't have the same values."

The words hit him hard.

And then that voice started whispering.

What if she knew all along that Huisman was alive?

What if the whole thing was a setup to distract him while Huisman got away?

A flash of the look in her eyes when he reached for her hit him.

She'd softened, those eyes going wide like it was everything she'd hoped for and all that mattered was being with him. He'd felt more connected to her in that moment than he'd felt to anyone for years.

His parents had gone into witness protection when they realized Manny had hired someone to kill them. He hadn't seen them in years. All he had was this team.

Tim walked out without a backward glance.

Was she that great an actress? Now that he looked back he could easily tell which twin he'd been with every time they'd met. Even when he'd saved her, when he'd walked into Manny's old house in Toronto and found her lifeless on a medical table, it had felt off. Like he was touching something that wasn't his. Perhaps it was mere fancy, but when he'd made love to Kenzie he'd known she was his.

Joe looked grim. "Ben, I need to ask you a question. Do you honestly think she was playing you?"

"I don't know."

"You do, but your past is a wall between you and the truth. Huisman fucked you over. He's the boogeyman, and I am not making light of what he's done to you. It might be time to try to find a way to move on."

"I don't fucking want to move on from her." He realized what he'd said. "Damn it. You were talking about Manny."

There was an amused expression on Joe's face. "So Tim is right and you're fighting something that could be good for you personally.

Terrible for your career, though."

"It is not. We just need to have a wall up when we're not working together." Why had he said that? He'd thought it through a thousand times, but he hadn't meant for Joe to know.

"Allowances could be made, especially if we're working on mutual goals," Joe offered. "The truth of the matter is we've found some property lists and other information that could use your subject-matter expertise. You know the doctor in a way no one else does. What would you say if I offered to let you manage the data? I'll assign you your own team and you can work this from a desk. I will make sure that when we get boots on the ground, you'll be there."

"I quit." He hadn't meant to do that either. "I'm going to Dallas one way or another."

"To screw with Taggart's team?" Joe asked tightly.

"To figure out why I can't get her out of my head. To find some fucking peace when it comes to her. Maybe you're right. Maybe Tim's right. Maybe I'm letting what Manny has done to me affect my relationship with Kenzie. I won't know until I see her again." He thought about the invitation he'd received in the mail three days before. The crisp cream stationary had contained a request to attend the wedding of Natasha Taggart to Darren Nash in Dallas, Texas. This weekend. Five days from now the whole Taggart family was gathering, and if he walked into that wedding he would know everything. All their personal secrets. He would be on the inside.

He could be one of them. Like Dare. He could have a family.

He shoved that idea aside.

There had been a handwritten note slid in.

Hope you can be there. Kenzie misses you, and honestly, so do I. Dare

What had been his first thought? That Dare was in on it, too.

He was fucked up. He needed a damn therapist.

He needed her.

"I have to see her. Even if it means stepping away from the only thing I have." His job. His mission. There was a sense of shame that ran through him. He was picking a woman who had lied to him over justice for Deanna. Over the peace and safety of the world.

And yet he wasn't going to take the threat back because this was the first time in weeks that he felt better. The decision to go to Dallas and…confront her? Accuse her?

Try with her?

He would know when he saw her. He would know when he got close to her again. He wouldn't let Manny's cruelty force his hand. He would figure her out and only then would he let her truly in.

But they would have a chance.

Joe stared at him for a moment. "I think this is a mistake."

There it was. He was in a corner, and he didn't even hesitate. "You'll have my resignation before I leave."

He wasn't going to sit behind a desk. He'd had his childish tantrum, and he was going to see her. He would find out the truth no matter what.

And he would have her again. But this time, there would be no time limit, and they would do things her way. Which meant taking control. It also meant he had to be prepared.

"Ben," Joe called out.

He stopped, his hand on the door. He should walk on, but he owed Joe and he needed to stop letting his confusion and anger turn him into a massive asshole. "I'm sorry, Joe. I have to know."

"I understand." Joe stood. "If this is about her and not some kind of revenge, then I refuse your resignation and I'll need to fully brief you on what we've found. We can call Tim back in."

Well, at least he wasn't fired. He wanted both. He wanted to know the truth about her and wanted to take down Manny for every evil deed he'd done. He also wanted his friend back. His friends. He wanted Tim back and he wanted Dare. He wanted to be in that damn circle.

He hated that he wanted it so badly.

"Can we call out for Thai?" It was time to get to work. "Tim can be bribed with food. If we get some root beer, he'll forget we ever fought."

"I can get you a new tech," Joe offered.

Ben shook his head, walking back to the table. "No. He's the best, and he's been good to me over the years. I've been a dick since we got back from Nepal. They left us, and it would have been easy to give us a lift back down. She chose not to, and I've been trying to figure out why. My head goes to dark places."

"I believe you'll find that Shannon Reed is missing again," Joe said quietly. "She was supposed to be handed over when they reached the States, but she got away."

"The bombmaker is out there? They let the bombmaker go?"

Joe passed a file to him. "This is a picture from a CCTV cam of Shannon Reed coming into Canada. She came in under a false passport and was escorted by a woman she called her niece. They flew into Winnipeg, and I believe there was a vehicle waiting for them. Likely driven by this woman's father or mother."

He stared down at the grainy photo taken from CCTV. Lucy Brooke Flanders. Oh, most people wouldn't recognize her because she knew how to hide, but he'd spent time with the woman. She was an Agency operative with ties to Kenzie and the Taggarts. Her father was quite scary. Not as scary as Ian Taggart, but right up there since that old man had taken both him and Tim down. "So they were involved in letting a dangerous criminal go?"

"I believe she's in a town called Bliss. Have you read her file? What she went through?"

"She built bombs," Ben replied.

"It's not always so simple, and I believe Taggart settled her in a place where she can find something beyond mere survival in her last years." Joe's voice was calm, like he approved of what Taggart had done. "I suspect if she'd been placed in the hands of the Agency, she would be pressured to build bombs for the US, and I don't think she wanted to do that. I suspect she wanted to spend time with her son and his new girlfriend. With the son she lost and his new wife."

Cooper McKay. He was talking about Cooper and Kala. Had Kala asked her sister to leave so she could save the woman who gave birth to her husband? He knew Cooper considered Alex and Eve McKay his parents, but did the man feel something for the woman who gave him away to try to save him?

It was more complicated than he was making it.

The door came open again and Tim was there. He gave Ben a suspicious look before turning to Joseph. "You texted?"

"Ben is going to Dallas and would like you to accompany him. He's going to spend the next couple of days going over the data so he's ready to brief the American team next Monday," Joe said. "I do believe he intends to have serious talks with Kenzie Taggart about how to make things work between them."

Tim put a hand to his heart. "Thank god. Lou said she's slipping into some serious depression. Like she's mourning Ben. She's wearing a lot of black and listening to way too much Lana Del Rey. She's worried."

"Don't tell her I'm coming. I need to see how she reacts," Ben warned. "Tim, I'm sorry. I know I've been hard to deal with, but I'm going to figure this out. Now let's get you some pad thai and some mango sticky rice and talk. I also need to call Dare. I think I need to do some research before I get to Dallas."

Some serious research, and a crash course in BDSM.

Because that was where he would get her. He would learn her language, figure out how to give her what she claimed she needed, and he would find the truth there.

He would risk everything to know if they could work.

"All right. I'll keep my mouth shut."

"And pack a tux." Ben sat down, calmer than he'd been since the last time he'd held her.

Tim frowned. "Uh, I don't actually have one of those."

Ben ignored him. "We're going to a wedding."

And he would decide if he was going to join the Taggart family.

Or take them down.

* * * *

The sweet sounds of Beyonce's "Halo" played in the bridal suite.

Ben had practically had a halo the last time Kenzie had seen him. He'd been damn near angelic, with his hair curling around his ears and his eyes bright with passion. For her. It might be the closest to heaven she would ever get.

And now she was in purgatory.

Wearing a lovely rose gold matte corset bodice with a matching floor-length skirt. Devi had designed it. Devi, who was happily settling in with Zach Reed. Devi, who had designed the gowns as both bridesmaid and fet wear since if one lost the skirt, the bridesmaid would be down to a corset and thong and ridiculous heels.

She was pretty sure Kala had already had sex in it.

She was never going to have sex again.

The song ended. She looked up at Lou, who was probably looking forward to being violated by TJ at some point in the wedding. "Could you put on 'Cornelia Street'?"

Lou's whole body sagged. "No. No 'Cornelia Street.' And while we're at it, no more Lana Del Rey. If you want more Bey, it's going to be *Lemonade*. How about Florence and the Machine?"

"Early Flo," Kala suggested, walking in and straightening her skirt. Her twin looked calm and cool, relaxed in a way she hadn't been before getting properly dicked down by a pilot. "*Lungs*. You know I love 'Girl with One Eye.' We can rechristen it 'Spy with One Eye' and dedicate it to Ben."

Just hearing his name made her heart ache.

She'd spent weeks sitting in her surprisingly lonely house since Kala had moved into Cooper's place, and they now shared it with Devi and Zach. Lou and TJ had their own apartment, a place close to Lou's cover job with 4L Software's development lab. Tasha and Dare were in the same building.

Now it was just her and Brianna, who had been attending a week-long writer retreat before returning last night for the wedding. So Kenz had spent that time eating cookies she baked, listening to sad-girl music, and switching between cursing Ben's name and wishing he was there.

She might be fading like the Fae did.

She laid back on the chaise lounge. They were at a luxurious downtown hotel that must have cost a shit ton of money. She should be happy.

Everyone was happy. She was happy for them. She was. She was also sad for herself.

"You look like you're trying to fade. Like some faery queen who lost her only love." Kala stood over her, arms crossed under her chest. She was in a matching dress except hers was a dark green. Lou was in a sunny yellow version. "Are you going to perk up when Tash comes out or should I prepare her for your funeral?"

"Hey, you know she's sad." Lou moved in, bringing Kala a glass of champagne. "Watching Tash and Dare get married has to stir up old memories."

"They're not old memories. I know my sister can paint a patina of tortured romance over anything, but it was only a couple of weeks ago and she'll probably see him again and probably make the poor choice of sleeping with him again." Kala's eyes narrowed. "Unless you've actually given up. Lou, do we have an 'I just broke up and I'm going to run through some dick' playlist? Because there are a bunch of Canadians out there. I can catch one for you. Dare's relatives aren't half bad, and you won't have to run into them in a professional setting. Also, I think some of the Bliss guys are here. I can get you two of those."

"Hey, I think this is the part where I point out that those are men and they have feelings," Lou began.

"Yes, in their penises. Which is the only thing I'm worried about right now," Kala shot back.

It wasn't like she hadn't thought about it. She'd thought about going to Bliss and standing in the middle of town until she was claimed by two hot men and lived the rest of her life chasing aliens and finding new ways to make beets edible. It seemed nice. Simple. And there were lots of animals.

Ben probably liked animals. Like Canadian animals. Beavers and stuff.

A tear slipped from her eye. She missed Ben.

"You have to rally," Kala announced. "This is Tasha's day. I can't have you fainting while you're walking down the aisle. I've told Seth if you do, he's supposed to drag you."

Well, that felt rude. She forced herself to sit up and frown her twin's way. "I'm not going to ruin Tasha's wedding. I'll be fine. I'm excellent at hiding how I feel. I keep calm and carry on."

Now Lou was staring at her like she'd said something dumb.

She could. She hadn't felt the need to around her friends and family. "You know I don't think it's good to bottle things up. When you do you end up with those frown lines Kala's getting. Thank the universe we're not pretending to be each other anymore and I can go back to a proper skincare regimen."

Kala groaned but sat down beside her, putting a hand over hers. "I'm sorry he turned out to be an asshole."

"I lied to him." She could still see his beautiful face…and body. He had such a hot bod.

"We're spies. He should expect some…subterfuge," Kala allowed.

Before she could reply the door came open and her father walked through. And he wasn't alone.

Kala stood and Kenzie was right behind her because their unrufflable dad looked extremely ruffled.

Shit.

"Another attempt?" Kala asked, looking him over.

It had been a week. Things seemed quiet for about two weeks after they returned from Nepal, and then someone had taken a shot at her dad. He'd been in Deep Ellum at the time, so he'd chalked it up to angry hipsters—which did not track in any way. It was after a second attempt outside his office that her dad started to take things seriously.

Aunt Chelsea had been surprisingly peppy about reporting the news that there was a bounty on Ian Taggart's head.

The person he had with him looked young. Maybe twenty or so. Maybe younger. She wore all black, though not tactical wear. She was in a black velvet jogging suit with the hoodie pulled up over her light blonde hair. Her mascara was running like she'd cried briefly but sucked it up. It gave her some raccoon eyes. She was pretty but hard. So hard for someone young.

"She tried to blow up my car. I just paid that fucker off," her dad announced. "Alex is coming to take her back to the club where I will have a great time interrogating a child."

"I am not child, and I was doing you favor, old man. That car is junk," she said in a familiar accent.

Her twin's eyes rolled. "Naturally, she's Russian."

"Ona chto, iz mafii? Iz kakogo sindikata?" Kenzie found herself surprisingly excited about dealing with a young Russian mob assassin. It gave a girl something to look forward to.

The young woman rolled her eyes. "Speak English. Your Russian is worse than this man's."

"She's a delight," her father announced.

"Is not. My Russian is perfect." Kenzie had been speaking Russian for…as long as she could remember. Her mother hadn't wanted to lose the language she'd fought hard to learn, so Russian was spoken often in their home.

"Sure. Perfect," the woman said with a sneer. "I don't belong to a syndicate. I'm college student. Here to soak in all the freedoms. This man is pervert. He tries to make me his sex slave."

"Sure. I always go trolling the parking lots of luxury hotels to find infants to enslave," her father said with a sigh. "Kala, sweetie, do you have some sedatives on you? I don't think she's going to go quietly. I don't want to interrupt the wedding. Dare's relatives are already freaked out since someone took a shot at me at the rehearsal dinner."

She'd been there. They were Canadian. It was fairly easy to convince them it was nothing more than a rando Friday night in the US.

"Uh, no, Dad," Kala said. "I do not carry around sedatives."

"I do," Lou said, grabbing her bag.

The young woman backed away. *"Ne nado."*

Don't. It was the first time she looked even slightly frightened.

"I can shut her up without putting her under." She walked right over to the lovely buffet the hotel had set up. It had coffee and champagne and many, many pastries. Kenzie selected one. A big-ass croissant. She walked over to the assassin and shoved it right in her mouth. "See, now she can't talk. But she'll know we didn't do anything to her."

Kala sent her a grateful look. "Yes, she'll remember."

Their father sighed and hauled his quarry over to the chaise lounge that had so recently been the site of Kenzie's brood. "Sorry, daughter. I didn't think about that."

Kala had lost an enormous amount of time wondering what happened to her when she was fifteen and drugged by a group of mercenaries. Not knowing had nearly killed her. She wouldn't put anyone else through that if she didn't have to.

The young woman sat, her hands tied behind her back. She didn't want to know why her dad had been walking around with rope in his pocket. Nope. That was better left to the wind. She noticed their captive had started chewing her way around the croissant, and her eyes closed briefly. Like she was struggling. Or enjoying it. Could be either.

"She had a bomb," her father complained. "She was on the ground trying to put it behind my wheel. How long has your mother been in there with Tasha?"

"Over an hour," Kala replied. "Devi's in there, too. Problem with the hem. She's working on it but she could be out any minute, and you know she told you no blood on the carpet. I'll go get the tarp."

"You are not going to kill me." The young woman was good.

She'd gotten through that croissant in record time. Surely someone had a ball gag. Like half the wedding guests were lifestylers. If one needed to restrain a suspect, this was the place to do it.

"I can cut your tongue out," Kala offered. "Look, I get the whole waking up and trying to figure out what happened to your body thing.

Been there. Done that. No sedatives as long as you're calm, but I can do other things."

Gray eyes rolled. She was actually quite pretty even if she was a little on the thin side. The thin side could be lovely if it was natural, but Kenz got the feeling this girl didn't get much of a chance to eat. "I think that the… What is word. *Keks*. The *keks* would work. The one with the berries."

Muffin? "You want a muffin?"

"I don't get carbs where I come from. They're serious about fitness," she explained. "That croissant… Death might be worth it. I don't suppose you could gag me with champagne. I have never been allowed alcohol."

"Sure you haven't," her dad said, pacing and looking down at his phone.

"It is terrible where I come from." It was clear the girl had decided to change tactics. "I am taken from home at young age and forced to go to France."

"Are you serious?" Her dad was suddenly interested. "That is terrible."

"They make me change name. I was Olga and now I am Sosa, which is short for Solene. Which is stupid name but apparently Olga is not sexy. I was eight. I did not want to be sexy," she said quietly.

Kala groaned. "That is not going to work. I liked you better when you were spitting bile."

"I mean, I do feel bad she had to go to France," her dad replied.

Olga/Sosa nodded as though accepting all of the sympathy she could get.

Her dad could be an asshole. France was amazing. She wanted to go to Paris with Ben. They always ended up in Nepal or some other place like it, and while beautiful there weren't a whole bunch of five-star restaurants and world-class shopping. Every time they got to go somewhere romantic, work got in the way.

Was that where they'd gone wrong? They should have found ways to need to work in more romantic places. Maybe Ben needed a soothing space to find his emotional center.

"Is something wrong with her?" Sosa asked, and it took Kenzie a moment to realize she was talking about her. The would-be assassin looked to Kala. "Did you get all the brain parts? I hear this can happen with twins. Not enough to go around. She obviously got the boobs."

Kenzie growled. Their boobs were the same. Mostly. Sometimes she thought Kala's nipples were a bit out of alignment, but no one was perfect and Coop seemed fine with them.

"She's going through… Are we calling it a breakup?" Kala seemed amused. "They weren't technically together, but my sister is always looking for an epic love story. If I had to guess she was thinking about what she would have worn in Paris when she met Ben beneath the Eiffel Tower."

Kenzie picked up the massive blueberry muffin and stuffed it into Sosa's mouth before looking to her sister. "Do you want one, too?"

Kala squared off with her. "Am I wrong?"

Oh, she could do this. Maybe this was exactly what she needed. "Fight club."

Sosa nodded, her eyes lighting with glee as she managed to somehow start eating that muffin.

Lou turned to the only man in the room. "I don't know what to do. I left the spray bottle at home because Devi told me if I ruined Kala's dress, she'd be upset. She's making my wedding dress. I have to be cool with her, but I don't think Tasha wants a fight club on her wedding day."

"Fight club?" a feminine voice said, and Kenzie realized the doors to the portion of the suite they were using to get dressed had opened. Her big sister stood there looking like an angel in her white wedding dress with a veil and a sweetheart neckline, and Kenzie was never getting married because Ben was a total asshole. "We are not having fight club."

"Shit," her father cursed.

"Ian." Yep, her mom was right behind Tash, and her eyes had gone straight to the chick with the muffin in her mouth. She simply stared.

There were women in the world who would wonder why their husband dragged a young woman to his daughter's wedding. It could be the start of a tale as old as time—older man, young hot girl… Yeah, her mom did not go there.

"Tell me they're not sending little girls to take you out." Her mother looked fabulous in her emerald green floor-length gown that hugged her every curve.

"Not little girl. Haven't been for long time." Sosa had finished her muffin. She eyed Charlotte Taggart, and Kenzie saw the minute she decided she could cause some turmoil. Her expression changed, and she managed a couple of actual tears. "I'm so sorry, ma'am. He tells me he is divorced and when I tell him I'm having his baby, he freak out. I didn't know."

Kala snorted. Lou shook her head.

Her dad simply stepped back, obviously leaving her to fate. Fate was named Charlotte in this case. Her dad shook his head and leaned against the door. "Sorry, baby. You know how much I love super-young people with their weird words like *skibidi*, and I don't even know what *Ohio* means in their language. I only know it does not mean Ohio. I couldn't resist her charms. And if Alex had gotten here earlier, you would never have known."

They had such a beautiful love. Her mom and dad. It brought tears to her eyes. Her father was perfectly comfortable joking because Mom trusted him so much. Because they were meant to be.

She could have had that love with Ben.

"Uhm, should I get the tarp now?" Lou asked. "I actually brought one because I know Lucy was invited and said she couldn't come, but you never know."

Lucy Brooke Flanders. Kenzie liked her. She was a lot like Kala. Which was probably why her twin viewed the slightly younger woman as her nemesis.

Charlotte went to stand in front of the girl, towering over her in her Louboutins. She stared at her and said nothing. Sosa kept crying.

"I was hungry. He was kind to me," she insisted. "Please not to be hurting my baby."

"Mom, don't kill her," Tasha said. "It's got to be bad luck on my wedding day."

"She's not going to kill her." Kala sank down to the chaise, obviously ready for the drama. "But we might need that tarp."

There was a brief knock on the door, and her Uncle Alex appeared. He was in a tux, like most of the men, and had a harried look on his face. He glanced around the room and winced. "Sorry. I got caught helping Li after Dai… Well, it's all good now. No damages. Why is there a strange girl covered in cake tied up in the bridal suite?"

"She's having my baby," her father replied simply.

"Shit. She's the one who's been trying to kill you?" Alex asked, reaching the obvious conclusion as to why her father would threaten to disrupt his eldest daughter's wedding.

"I don't know." Kala always had to poke the bear. "Dad does like a Russian mob princess."

Her mother snorted. "*Ona ne printsessa. Ona obuchennaya ulichnaya krysa.*"

That was harsh. "I don't think she's a street rat. Rude, much, Mom? And I don't know how trained she is since she thought it would be smart to plant a bomb on Dad's Nav in broad daylight."

"Also, she impugned the reputation of said car," Kala pointed out.

Her mom glanced over at Alex. "Could you please have a few of the bodyguards escort our friend here to the club? I'll deal with her after the wedding. For now, I'm going to watch my daughter marry the man of her dreams and have some champagne. I'll be in a better mood later, but we need to figure out what's going on."

Kenzie knew. "Huisman's done playing around. I know the hackers haven't settled on who put out that hit, but we know it's Huisman." She looked back at her sister, who was marrying the man of her dreams. "You look gorgeous. Don't worry about this. You'll be on your honeymoon soon, and Kala will have a new chew toy."

Everyone looked to her twin, who simply shrugged. "That's fair."

Kala was pretty self-aware. It was time to get this thing moving. And by *thing* Kenzie meant life. Her life.

Her sister looked stunning and she was about to start her marriage, and her other sister was married to the man she'd been in love with since she was a kid, and Lou was happy with TJ and they'd gotten a rescue dog, and her parents were still happy pervs after all these years. So happy they would never believe the other would cheat. Because they wouldn't.

And Kenzie was lying around all sad and shit. So sad she was a bit worried Bud Two had caught her depression.

She wasn't going to let one man bust her life down.

"I don't think I like sound of this," Sosa said. "I will not to be going anywhere with you. Call the police."

But Uncle Alex worked fast now that he wasn't solving whatever disaster her cousin Daisy had caused. Probably a fire. Or a lightning strike. Once Daisy managed to accidently let a snake out of its cage and they had an extra party guest.

Landon Vail and Ross Brighton walked in. Landon was the son of one of Uncle Sean's partners, Eric Vail, and his wife, Deena. Ross was the son of Dallas Police Assistant Chief in charge of Investigations, Derek Brighton, and his wife Karina, who was a kick-ass private investigator. While Ross worked with his dad and not at McKay-Taggart, the man would know how to not let a potential suspect go.

But also, it was handy since Sosa had offered. "There you go. He's a police detective. Ross, I know it's hard to believe but this is a trained, paid assassin who probably works for a group who will murder her if she hits the county jail. She would like you to bring her in."

Her mom winked her way. "Well played, baby girl. If she's with a syndicate, they don't like it when you hit the local jail system."

Sosa had gone a pasty white. Well, pastier than she had been. Girl could use some sun. "Fine. I'll go with your thugs."

"Hurtful," Landon said, a hand on his chest. "Also, it sucks that I'm going to miss this. I was told there's an open bar."

"Not for us, buddy," Ross said, helping Sosa up. "Let's get her to the club. I don't suppose you want me to get professionally involved."

"No. This is unfortunately Agency business, and she probably would get whacked in jail. I suspect there's more of her out there," her father explained.

"We have police presence," Ross reassured them. "The wedding is safe. I'll let my dad know where I am and that he needs to keep an eye out in case she has friends."

"Oh, she has friends. I assure you," her father said with a sigh. "It's like a John Wick movie out there. When I get my hands on Huisman, I'm pulling his balls off his body and shoving them down his throat. But as for this one, be careful with her. She might try to hurt herself."

Landon and Ross nodded and walked Sosa out.

"That was weirdly kind of you." Kala sounded disappointed. "Any particular reason why you're playing nice with an assassin?"

Her mom moved into her dad's space and wrapped her arms around him. "Thank you."

Sometimes Kala didn't understand nuance, but Kenzie did. "She's young and Russian and likely trained against her will."

Very much like their mother, and her father obviously saw the parallels.

"I've got some intel about a couple of groups in Europe and Asia recruiting young women for training," Tasha explained, her eyes on the door.

"And by recruiting we mean trafficking," Lou continued. "And there have always been rumors of a group who uses young orphans—girls from the old Eastern Bloc states and Russia—as operatives and thieves. They run a bit like a syndicate. I like to call them Black Widow groups."

Her mom stepped back, holding her hands up. "We will deal with this later. Right now, we're going to celebrate. Now Kala, your cousin is waiting to steam the skirt of your dress because it's obvious you have already played around with your groomsman."

Kala groaned and stood since she totally had and her skirt bore some wrinkles. "Fine. And we're not doing fight club."

"No, we're not." Kenzie had an announcement, too. It had been too long. She hadn't even looked at another man since the moment she saw stupid Ben Parker, who didn't deserve her in any way. It was past time to get right back on that horse. "Lou, let's put on some Rhianna and talk about which Bliss boys I'll be riding tonight."

"Whoa." Her father's hands went to his ears. "That turned so fast."

It was time for her bad bitch era to begin. Sad girl was out. Boss babe was taking over. She was done being down bad for that man. New beginnings.

She would start over. She would live for her job and her family, and have righteous sex whenever she wanted because she was giving into the spy life. Her sister's heart condition wouldn't let her go into the field anymore. Not for anything other than an emergency with a full backup team. So it was up to Kenzie. She was the operative now, and she had to be everything.

She would stand tall. She would take Huisman down, and she would do it in style. Ben Parker would rue the day he decided to walk away from her. He would come crawling back and she wouldn't be there for him. She would be the queen. It was like Halsey said. If she couldn't have love, she would take all the power and take out her enemies while enjoying herself with whatever man caught her eye.

"She's going into what I like to call wronged queen mode," Kala said with a nod as though she approved. "The playlists are about to get really girl powery, and we should prepare for some slutty times, my sisters."

"I should have let the bomb take me," her father whispered.

"It's a good thing," she heard her mom whisper. "She needs to let that asshole go."

Cool. They were reaching the insult-the-guy stage. She could do that. It was like immersion therapy. She would immerse herself into the world where she hated Benjamin Parker and cursed his name and wished she'd never met him and… Oh, no…she was tearing up again.

Everyone was watching. Like they were all waiting for that tear to fall and they would know she wasn't ready.

Kenzie sucked it the fuck up because she *was* ready. Ready to live again. Ready to leave Ben behind. Ready to stand in her own glory, needing no man.

"Kenzie," a deep voice said. "I was hoping we could talk before we walk down the aisle together. If you let me walk you down the aisle…"

Ben stood in the doorway wearing the sexiest tuxedo she'd ever seen. It fit him like a glove. And his face. She'd missed his gorgeous face. He was here.

"It was supposed to be a surprise. Dare asked him to be part of the wedding party. Seth is willing to step down so you can walk with Ben," Tasha whispered. "Unless you're determined to make your own ménage."

She practically tripped running to him. He was here. He was just slow. It was okay. She could deal with slowness. What she couldn't deal with was never seeing him again.

He caught her and his face lit with the sweetest smile. "So we're okay?"

She wrapped herself around him, feeling more at peace than she had since that moment in Nepal when she thought she'd lost him. "No, but we will be. We need to talk."

His hands stroked over her back, and she felt him kiss her temple. "We will, but first we've got an aisle to walk down."

He shifted back and the room was in motion again. Devi had stepped out of the side room and was dragging Kala back to what she called the steamer. Lou helped Tash into her shoes. Her mom took pictures and tried hard not to ruin her makeup. The aunties showed up. Grace and Avery and Serena and Erin and Eve.

Her family. And Ben was here.

"By the way, I hope you don't mind but I didn't get a hotel," he whispered, his arm still around her waist. "You look fucking gorgeous, and now that the two of you are in a room together, I can't believe I thought you were the same person."

No one could tell when they wanted to play the other. Not even her parents, but she would give this to him.

Because he was here. "You can stay with me. We can get your things after the wedding, but you should know I might have to work some this evening."

A brow rose over those intelligent eyes of his as he stared down at her. "I suspect you've discovered Manny put out a hit on your dad. I have some thoughts. And, baby, my things are already in your room. I broke in. I thought you would think it's sexy that I can get through any security system you want to put between us. You should understand that everything changes tonight. I won't let anything come between us." He kissed her forehead. "And your dog is sweet. I'm going to go check on Dare. See you soon, baby. Kenzie. I like calling you Kenzie. I'm going to like whispering your name when I order you on your knees. When I tell you to serve your Master."

A shiver went through her. It was everything she wanted.

She watched as he walked away.

Her epic love story was totally back on.

Chapter Six

Ben watched Kenzie with the group of bridesmaids. They were hovering around Tasha, making toasts and dancing in a circle. The whole ceremony had been filled with love and family, and he was so fucking confused.

There had been a piece of him that thought her light, that part of her that was warm and loving and offered such comfort, was nothing but a performance. As if Kara had two personas and she shifted between them, deciding which would work best.

Now he knew the truth, but wrapping his head around the idea that she could truly be that sweet and bubbly was hard.

"You okay?" a familiar voice asked.

Dare. His friend looked like a million bucks in his tux. It fit him perfectly, and he looked like he belonged in this ridiculously luxurious hotel. There had been a lot of talk about what would happen if an armed militia group tried to take over, but it was done in a jokey way that Ben couldn't tell if they were serious or simply sarcastic.

He didn't understand her family at all.

Still, he gave Dare his smoothest smile. "I'm great. Thank you for letting me come at the last minute."

Dare put a hand on his shoulder. "The more the merrier. How are things going with Kenz? That's what I meant. We haven't had a lot of chance to talk since the last time you were in Dallas."

"The wedding took up a lot of your time," Ben murmured, his eyes still on her.

He felt different than he thought he would. He thought he could treat this like any other mission. He was gathering intelligence. He had to since his own boss hadn't bothered to tell him important details.

But then she'd jumped into his arms. Like his presence had lit up her world. In that moment when he'd wrapped his arms around her, because she would have fallen if he didn't, and wouldn't that give up his game?

Damn it. He had to try to be honest with himself. He'd felt better and bigger and more important than he had in forever the minute she'd jumped toward him. As if it never occurred to her that he might not catch her.

Of course it was her openness that had drawn him in, but no one seemed surprised.

"Buddy, I'm trying to ask you how you're handling the whole Kenzie thing," Dare said with a smile.

Like they were friends. Of course he was likely in on it. Whatever "it" was. Sometimes he worried he was paranoid, then he remembered his own history. The thing that annoyed him was he thought he was over this. Over the need to form bonds. He'd told himself he gave up those notions when his own parents—crappy as they had been—rejected him. Or maybe it was when he'd brought Deanna into his world and her life had ended.

"When did you find out?" They had talked that day at Top, but they'd been pretty careful about certain subjects.

Dare flushed slightly but didn't hesitate and didn't pretend to misunderstand him. "I found out when we were at The Station."

So he'd known early on. The Station was a club in Sydney. The one he'd been taken to after Tasha drugged him. In her defense, he'd been trying to take her in for questioning. He'd figured out she wasn't exactly what she said she was and had made the decision to extract her to find out more information, but she'd been smarter than him.

He was pretty sure everyone was smarter than him.

The news hit him hard, but he simply nodded.

"Ian brought me in because he thought offering me his most

closely held secret would prove how serious the whole family was about supporting Tasha's love for me. I mean he put it in terms I could understand at the time," Dare explained.

Of course he had. Ian Taggart was a tricky bastard. "So he told you a secret to get you to trust him. I believe at the time he was trying to get information from your father's business. So he gave up his secret to keep you from walking out. And you thought it was about Tash?"

Dare's brows had risen. "Yes. Ian wouldn't have sold out his daughters to get a couple of reports he could likely have gotten on his own. He told me why he was doing it and then also gave me language I could accept at the time. I was angry."

"Because she lied to you." Intellectually, Ben knew Tasha hadn't meant to lie. Meeting Dare was supposed to be some fun before her op began. It had gotten incredibly tangled, and Dare hadn't been the only one caught in that web.

"I was angry at you, too," Dare said quietly. "I've come to understand that you didn't mean to hurt me. I've come to believe we can be friends. I hope you can acknowledge that doesn't happen without Ian. I know you're mad at him."

He shook his head. "He was doing what a good handler always does. He protected his operatives."

"But that's not what a truly good handler does, is it?" Dare asked. "A good handler protects the op, not the operative. Ian is something of a maverick at the Agency. There isn't another team like it. I've heard there's an MI6 team that's similar, but nothing in the States. They're controversial, and the truth is the only reason Ian went back into this line of work was to make sure his girls didn't get killed. He loves them. I know you're pissed at all of them, but he's sincerely one of the best men I've ever met."

"Well, he doesn't like me much." It was fucking great that Dare found his perfect family. But then Dare hadn't fucked up the way Ben had. As far as he knew, Dare had saved the people he loved, as evidenced by his half siblings in attendance. Even his damn stepmom was here, telling everyone how much she adored Tash and how she was thrilled to be part of this new family.

"You can win him over," Dare assured him. "Treat Kenzie right and he'll forget about the past. You're okay with her, right? You know why she had to keep that secret? She wasn't trying to fool anyone. She was trying to protect her sister and her team. The same way you did in the beginning."

"I'm not holding on to grudges," Ben said, and he didn't think he was lying. He was trying to figure out what was real and what wasn't. He wanted to believe Kenzie cared about him, but it was hard.

Did he want that? Or did it feel like too big a leap? Like putting himself right back into the fire he'd barely survived the first time. He hadn't loved Deanna. He was pretty sure if he was capable of love, Kenzie was the woman who could bring that out in him.

"I doubt that, but it's okay for a little while." Dare smiled as Tasha and her sisters danced to some happy, bouncy pop song. Tasha looked his way and waved to her new husband even as she danced.

The love between them was so fucking real he could practically feel it.

Did he want to love someone that much? Did he want to be part of the men who were joking around, talking about sports and their jobs and their families? Did he want to get invited to barbecues and go on vacations with his wife's family?

Could he even marry her? How would it work between two operatives from different agencies?

Was he thinking about marrying her? If he did, he could keep an eye on her. When he thought about it, marriage might be the best way to actually handle his mission. She couldn't get into too much trouble if she was underneath him all the time. If he got her pregnant, she might even pull back from going into the field, so it could be considered taking one for the team. The team being his country, of course.

Damn she was pretty, and she danced like no one was watching, like she was in the middle of the best movie.

"Let's make some time when Tash and I get back from Loa Mali," Dare offered. "We can hang out or maybe go up to the lake house and fish and catch up."

That sounded so normal. Like something regular people did when they had friends. Was Dare softening him up? It wouldn't be the first time he'd been used to cover for Kenzie. After all, Dare had been the one to keep him company when Kenzie went to Virginia to save her sister. Ben could have helped, could have been extra hands, would have done anything to help her.

"Sure. That sounds great." He would have to be careful around

Dare. The same way he would be careful around all of Kenzie's male relatives. The women, too. He'd already had several conversations with Cooper and TJ about being good to Kenzie. And he'd gotten cornered by her brothers, who swore even though they weren't military men, they could fuck a guy up if said guy hurt their sister. Seth had promised something called a diss track to end all diss tracks, and Travis sounded lawyerly in his threats of physical violence.

He'd still kind of liked them.

The man they called Big Tag walked up, beer in his hand. He'd ditched the bowtie of his tux and the jacket, rolling up the sleeves. "Dare, the wedding planner tells me she's about to call for your first dance."

Dare nodded. "Then I should go get ready. See you soon, Ben."

He strode off to grab his jacket for the pictures.

"I hope my boys weren't too rough on you." Taggart's eyes were on the dance floor. "They love their sisters."

Ben nodded Taggart's way. "They were fine. They made it plain all the horrible things that will happen if I hurt their sister."

And then they'd told him a bunch of stories about their childhood and how Kenzie took care of them. She was apparently the best storyteller of the group.

"Are you planning on hurting her?" Taggart asked the question casually.

"Of course not." He was investigating her. He didn't mean to hurt her. She'd told him time and time again that she hadn't meant to hurt him, so she should understand. It was a job in the end.

If he were honest with himself, he would acknowledge that he didn't have any real idea what he was doing. He only knew he couldn't stay away from her.

"I would understand the inclination, though I would try to stop you. I'm afraid Kenzie wouldn't let me. That's the hardest part about having kids. Knowing the mistakes they're going to make and being utterly unable to stop them. They put these tiny humans in your hands and for a while you can protect them from the world, but then they grow up and you have to realize there are some heartaches that are necessary," Taggart said, tipping back his beer. "I know this is going to come as a surprise to you, but my Charlie lied to me and for similar reasons. She was protecting her sister. The one who's now happily married and thriving and has become important to my whole family. The family that honestly doesn't exist without her. There were days I resented her, but it's funny how time changes us. How simply living and being family blurs those edges that once seemed so sharp."

"Kenzie has mentioned what she calls your epic love story." He hadn't known she was talking about her handler at the time. He thought she'd been talking about her parents, who had nothing to do with her job.

"She can be a bit over the top," Taggart acknowledged. "Sometimes I'm certain those two share a soul. Kala got all the dark stuff, but the truth of the matter is people take her seriously. Kenzie got the bubbly, happy personality that everyone marginalizes. She also got the deep need for drama. I worry she got that from me. I do like some drama, especially if I'm not actually involved in it."

"I'm trying to be drama free, sir," he promised Taggart.

"That's what I'm telling you. She likes some over-the-top shit." Taggart straightened up as a woman approached the microphone. "Just remember a little drama can be fun. I think I should probably get back into my jacket because I'm pretty sure I'm going to get to dance with my daughter. Maybe you should do the same. And Ben, don't let the bad stuff keep you from finding the good stuff, but it's okay to need some time. I understand how you could see this as a massive betrayal. I've found that the thing we need most is time and patience."

The woman with the microphone invited Tasha and Dare to have their first dance as a married couple.

He was going to dance with Kenzie. He was going to hold her in his arms while surrounded by her family.

Wasn't this the life he wanted once? The life he thought he would have before Manny took it all away?

What if he pretended he was normal for a night? What if he was here to support his friend and be with his girl? What if he could fit in? It wouldn't hurt to spend one night pretending.

Kenzie walked up, and suddenly her hand was in his. "Aren't they the cutest?"

He wouldn't say Dare was cute. He liked her hand in his. He threaded their fingers together. "They are definitely in love. I like your family."

Her nose wrinkled sweetly. "I'm sure my brothers were lovely.

Don't worry about them. They get paid to try to drive off potential suitors. I'm serious. They used to scare off my boyfriends and Dad would give them bounties. Travis talked a lot about his own poop. Seth would ask incredibly invasive questions and then he would write songs about the answers."

He didn't want to find her whole family fascinating. He was going to suggest they take a walk when his cell buzzed. He pulled it out of his pocket. Unknown. Tim used a lot of burners. "I need to take this. I'll be right back. Don't dance without me or I'll be a jealous ass. I'm good at that."

Her lips quirked up like he'd said the exact right thing. Drama. Her dad wasn't wrong about that.

He waited until he got to the door to the ballroom to accept the call and put the phone to his ear. "Hey, Tim, what's going on? You hear something?"

"Oh, Benjamin, I hear everything."

Ben stopped, the silky slide of that familiar voice a snake threatening to strike.

"How the hell did you get this number, Manny?" His whole body tightened, going into survival mode at the mere sound of his voice.

A low chuckle came over the line. "I have friends who own businesses that can get any information I need. The world is so beautifully connected now, isn't it? Or perhaps I have some of your friends on the payroll and one of them didn't mind sharing your number."

His gut tightened. It wasn't the first time Manny had suggested that he was surrounded by his people. And it wasn't like he hadn't managed to get people into positions of power, as Kala Taggart had recently learned. "What do you want, Manny?"

He was too smart to hang up. Manny didn't like being ignored. He tended to give Ben a reason to pay attention, and it usually cost someone their life.

He'd read the reports about how Manny had disrupted one Taggart wedding already.

"I wanted to know if you're enjoying the wedding," Manny said smoothly.

He forced himself to not look around for the cameras that were obviously all throughout the hotel. It would be easy for Manny to find a way in. "It's going great. You going to send a mercenary team in to give

Taggart a jolt of adrenaline?"

"Oh, I suspect that's coming." There was a deep chuckle in Manny's tone. A certain arrogance Ben had studied over the years.

He didn't know. Maybe he wasn't in the hotel's security system. If he was, he would know Taggart had caught his teenaged assassin and he would have asked different questions.

It would be easy to figure out Tasha Taggart was getting married. Lots of people got invitations, and Tasha had social media. Her existence hadn't been scrubbed clean, so there was no reason she couldn't post a million pictures.

None of which included her sisters.

How hard was that on someone like Kenzie?

"I ask again. What do you want, Manny?"

"I was lonely. I wanted to talk to my oldest friend. Is that so strange?"

"You try to kill me on a regular basis."

"No, I don't. I could have killed you many times now. I simply kill the things you love. Tell me, how is my sweet Kara? How is her heart?"

Ben had to take a long breath. Staying calm was of the utmost importance. Manny was pushing buttons, trying to see which one would set him off. Manny had tortured the woman he knew as Kara Trent. Manny was well aware of his affection for Ms. Magenta. He'd taunted him with it time and time again. He had no idea that the Kara he'd tortured and damaged was Kala and not Kenzie. "She's fine. I don't think your drugs work the way you think they do."

A chuckle, self-satisfied and arrogant, filled the miles between them. "Oh, I suspect they work better than you realize. They still aren't letting you in, are they? You're always going to be on the outside, Benjamin. I find it incredibly ironic since I spent so much of my young life being told to be more like Benjamin. *Manny, why can't you be charming like your friend? Why can't you get the girls your friend does?*"

If there was one thing he was certain of, he wasn't responsible for Manny's grandfather's obsession with him. "Maybe because the girls I hung out with were smart enough to sense a predator was in their midst."

"Oh, I've found for the most part women are dumb animals who are simply looking for some man to protect them. When are you going to understand that they are only truly necessary when it comes to breeding? Otherwise, a man's life is far more peaceful without the bleating of those sheep." The casual misogyny was part of Manny's core personality.

"Sure. Because you're going to raise the next generation on your own. You're going to be right in there changing diapers and feeding your young." He used the term since any of Manny's kids would be treated like lions, taught to take as much as they could.

Except for the girls. He would likely throw them away as useless.

Or place them in a situation where they would be trained to make him money.

"I suppose not. I guess I have to keep a few around to cook and clean, but they're nothing to get upset over. You know she's your weakness. The way Deanna was your weakness."

Ah, now he understood why Manny had called. He'd figured out things might be getting serious with the gorgeous operative. But how? Lou and Tim had promised him the sex tape they'd made had been obliterated from the system. Tim had ensured him that Lou had deleted everything from that mission before anyone could have downloaded the content, and then after they'd gotten everything they could, the system had self-destructed. There was no backup.

So the secret about Kara was safe, but they'd been reckless. If Manny knew…

"I think Kara can take care of herself in a way Deanna couldn't." He was pleased with how calm his voice was. Just the thought of Deanna and his brain replaced her still body with Kenzie's.

No matter how she'd lied, he couldn't let that happen. He couldn't allow her to be hurt. Couldn't think of a world she wasn't in.

Even if she was playing him for all she was worth.

"Yes, she can. Benjamin, how do you think I know your number?" The question was a knife made of pure suspicion meant to infect him.

"I think you own a couple of telecom companies. I never said you weren't capable, Manny. I never said you weren't powerful. I said you were evil."

A long-suffering sigh came over the line. "Such a bourgeois word. And naïve. Every dollar, euro, yen, peso, it's all the same. It's all blood money, and money is the only thing the world understands. We've become overpopulated. It takes a true king of men to see it and do something about it. I am doing what I need to do to fulfill my legacy."

"He's dead, you know. They're all dead. You don't have to prove anything to your grandfather or your father."

The silence felt like a threat.

"Yes, believe me I understand my father is dead and you're currently celebrating with the man who started that line of dominoes that ended in my father dying," Manny pointed out.

"Your dad was trying to steal another doctor's work. He was literally in league with the bad guys." It was useless, but he felt the desperate need to point out the truth. "It was a rogue CIA agent who killed him, not Ian."

"It's Ian now, is it? Has he brought you in? Made you one of his boys?" Manny asked. "I wonder how much truth he's told you. I wonder if I know more than you do. Wouldn't that be delicious? Or perhaps we know the same, but my timing is so much better than yours. I was going to, perhaps, come up with some surprise for Tasha and her new husband, but I think I should let things play out. I think they'll hurt you far more than I can, and then perhaps you'll be willing to talk to me. Perhaps you'll be able to see the light when you realize how much this one has betrayed you and for how long she's been doing it. Tell Taggart if this one fails, I'll send another. Or don't tell him. I suspect your life would seem easier without your whore's pimp around all the time."

He hung up.

How the fuck had he gotten the number? Despite what he'd said, this wasn't a phone he'd gone to the local strip mall to sign a contract on. It was straight from his agency. No one except the people he gave the number to should be able to figure it out.

So it was people from his team, including Tim and Joseph and the support staff, and Kenzie Taggart. She was the only one outside of his highly vetted group who had the number. It was precisely how she'd gotten hold of him and sent him to Wales. He'd been the one to tip her off as to where Zach and Devi were hiding.

Now he wondered who he'd dealt with. Did Kala have his number? Probably. Kenzie would have passed it around if she thought it was good intel.

"Hey, they're dancing. Like everyone, and the song's slow, so I was thinking… What happened?" Kenzie pulled her hand away. She'd seemed to be ready to touch him but then he'd turned and she'd seen the look on his face.

The one he always got when he talked to Manny.

She'd gone stiff. He didn't want to talk about this. He needed to think. It wouldn't be the first time Manny had dangled some truth in front of him. Manny had ruined and wrecked every relationship he had in some way. Small injections of poison that over time killed the trust between Ben and…everyone.

"Just work," he said and took her hand. If he started asking questions, she would want to know why. "Joseph. I updated him on the assassin situation. He's looking into a couple of groups she could belong to. He'll send us what he finds in the morning, but for now, I'd love to dance with you."

Her shoulders came down and a brilliant smile crossed her face. "I was hoping you would say that."

He led her back into the ballroom, his mind working overtime.

* * * *

Kenzie brought out the shoes Tasha was changing into in anticipation of her leaving for Loa Mali. The small jet was ready to take her and her brand-new hubs to the island paradise for days of sex and beach walking and dinners for two.

She wouldn't be surprised at all if Tasha had a baby in the next year or two.

"Are we not going to talk about it?" Kala stood at the doorway to the bridal suite, her arms crossed over her chest.

Devi moved in, taking a look at the hem of Tasha's sleeves. The honeymoon dress was perfectly tailored and sweetly sexy. If Dare didn't do her sister in the limo, she would be shocked. "Which *it* are we talking about? The way Chloe Lodge stared at Seth like he was a piece of cake and she'd been on a no-sugar diet for years? Or the way Nate managed to save the punch bowl when Daisy nearly took a header into it?"

"I do believe she's talking about Ben." Lou sat on the sofa, a glass of wine in her hand. "She's been worried about him all night."

Well, of course her twin was worried. And she knew exactly what was going through Kala's mind. "She thinks he's here for revenge."

The truth was Kenzie was a little worried about that, too.

"I don't know if he's here for revenge." Kala paced. It was a thing she'd done since childhood. When she was worried, her feet started to move.

And Kenzie tended to get still. "But you're worried about his intentions."

"I think we fucked him over. We didn't mean to. Well, Kenzie didn't mean to," Kala admitted. "I only know that he didn't call right after he found out the truth. He waited weeks. I know what I would have done with those weeks if I felt betrayed."

Her twin would have used that time to plot an elaborate revenge, but then she sometimes did that for fun. Ben wasn't Kala.

"He needed time to process." It had been awful waiting around, watching her phone, hoping he would call. She'd spent days wondering if she'd made the wrong choice. She'd told Kala it was time to let Ben know. Her father and mother had given her the go. Even her Agency handlers had agreed it was time for Ben Parker to know he was dealing with twins. "I should have waited. I should have done it when we weren't working."

Kala's brows rose. "I'm the one who went to get you. I could have sent Lou."

Lou's head shook. "I was busy trying to ensure there was no way Huisman got hold of that sex tape. Not that it wasn't beautiful. And Kenz, your butt looked great. Seriously, nice glute work. But she really couldn't have sent me and by that time Tim knew, so it would have been weird to be like 'hey, Tim, your best friend in the world is dating a woman who happens to be a twin, and could you not mention that to him?'"

Put like that she was right. They'd been in a corner and there had only been one way out. Her twin was pragmatic, but Kenzie could own up to her mistakes. "I should have stayed and talked to him. I could have made my way back. He would have taken care of me."

"We don't know that," Kala replied. "I saw him. He was pissed."

What he'd been was emotional. They'd genuinely thought they were dying and then they weren't and he was faced with the fact that the woman he'd clung to in what he believed were his last moments of life had been lying to him the whole time. Would she have forgiven him instantly? Probably, but she was pretty sure Ben hadn't grown up on rom coms and epic romances that played out in front of him.

"He was rightfully upset." Tasha allowed Devi to adjust the cuff of her sleeve. Her eldest sister had handled the whole day with beauty and grace, but that was Tash. She would never be in this position. Well, not exactly this position. She'd lied to Dare but not for as long, and it wasn't like she'd had a secret twin who pretended to be her some of the time.

"We're spies," Kala argued. "It wasn't like he walked up and told us who he was."

Lou sent her a look.

Kala sighed. "I get it, but I also don't. Apparently that doesn't mean anything and I am supposed to be supportive. But I can't not point out the fact that Ben showed up without a call and suddenly everything is okay except he's bad at hiding his true feelings because I watch him when he's watching you."

"He looks like he wants to eat her up," Devi pointed out as she stepped back, obviously happy with her work.

"He also looks like a dude who's trying something, if you know what I mean," Kala said.

"No one knows what you mean, sweetie." Her mom walked in, stopping to stare at Tash for a moment. She'd been crying off and on all day, but her mom cried pretty, offering her emotions to her family without reserve. "You look beautiful."

"She does." Aunt Chelsea was with her. "She's so beautiful, and Dare looked amazing. I'm so happy for you, sweetie." She moved in, hugging Tasha before she stepped back. "You're going to have a fabulous time in Loa Mali." She moved over to stand next to Kala. "You know this is what you could have had."

Kala had gotten married in a small ceremony that had come together in three weeks, unlike the year it had taken to put together Tasha's extravaganza. "I could have had weeks of sitting around picking flowers and having Devi poke me with needles only for it to all culminate in a bunch of people watching me? Pass."

Aunt Chelsea sighed. "Put like that, I would pass, too. So are we warning Kenzie that the hot Canadian is probably here for revenge and possibly working with the enemy?"

"He is not." No matter what reason he was here, he wasn't working with Huisman. "I know that asshole tried to put the idea in everyone's head, but he's not. Ben would never help Manny."

"I know you think you know him," Chelsea began.

"Dare knows him," Tasha added. "Dare's known him for a long

time and he believes in Ben."

"He thinks Ben's come here for purely nice purposes?" Her mother's question held a bit of challenge.

Tasha's lips pursed. "He thinks Ben needs time to come to terms with things. Unfortunately, he's not going to get much."

"He's had weeks," Kala pointed out. "Weeks where he ignored her. He never called. He showed up, and I know it was romantic and shit, but it's also convenient since we've got all the data unlocked now. The meeting is tomorrow. We knew CSIS was sending someone. We didn't know who. One would think Ben could give us a heads up."

"Or he wanted to surprise her," Lou suggested, always the optimist. "What if he's been thinking all this time and he needed to see how she would react. Without preparation. Now he knows that she'll leap into his arms. I'm honestly surprised he didn't propose tonight."

Kenzie held a hand up. "Oh, we're not there, and I would not allow that to happen at my sister's wedding."

But it would happen. She hoped it would happen. Maybe in Europe. She would say yes. She would make that leap because when she'd known she was going to die the only thing she wanted was a few more minutes with him. They were meant to be, but she couldn't force that on him.

"Kenz, I love you. I know you've been waiting for this guy for a long time, but he's damaged. Like seriously damaged," Kala said.

Chelsea cleared her throat.

Kala shrugged. "Yeah, I know. Super damaged, and guess what, Aunt? Like knows like. Ben is in a bad place. He's wrapped in guilt over what happened to his high school girlfriend. He's pretty much lost everything to Manny Huisman. Even the car accident where Deanna Fisher died affected him physically. He was being scouted by major league teams for his pitching skill. After that accident, he didn't play again. He finished up his degree, joined CSIS, and started working on taking down Huisman."

"Which is a good and productive thing to do." Kenzie wasn't sure why she was arguing since she thought the same thing, but she couldn't leave it. She felt the deep need to defend her lover. "He's trying to stop that man from ruining the world. The same way we are."

"Ah, but we're not obsessed with him," Kala replied. "We don't think about him night and day. Look, Huisman did spend time trying to sow dissent and suspicion between our team and the Canadians. Do you honestly think he's not working Ben the same way?"

She couldn't help but think about that phone call he'd taken. He'd told her it was work, but she'd seen that look on his face before. It was rage and cold calculation, and there was no small amount of guilt in there. She'd known who had been in his ear, but he hadn't wanted to talk about it.

So she'd held his hand and led him to the dance floor. He would talk to her when he was ready, and honestly, given their jobs, he might not talk to her about it at all. She had to make peace with the fact that there would be a wall between them when they weren't straight up working together. She would have to keep things from him, too.

Could this work?

At least when she'd danced with him he'd seemed to relax. He'd swayed to the music with her, and she'd felt him kiss the top of her head like she was precious. They'd stayed on that dance floor for the longest time, simply existing in each other's space. Their space. Making a new place where they were together.

That was all that mattered, after all.

Was she being naïve?

"I think he'll handle it the same way we do. No one bought what Huisman was selling." Even Kala had rolled her eyes and said Ben was way too bad at acting to pull that off.

Would he be good at role-play? Since the day she'd met him she'd dreamed of some fantasy role-play.

She should probably keep her mind on the conversation at hand since if her sister truly thought she was in danger of getting her heart broken, she might try to take said danger out.

Kala's expression softened. "I'm worried he's not coming from the same place we are. He's had a shit ton of betrayal in his life, and it colors how he looks at things. I worry the right words will plant suspicion in Ben's head because the truth is he's been waiting for you to do exactly that. He's waiting for you to betray him, and that can be a self-fulfilling prophecy."

Aunt Chelsea's jaw dropped. "I thought the therapist was evil."

Lou grinned. "Oh, she was, but that doesn't mean she didn't say some things that were super true. Also, Kala's been seeing a good therapist to get over the fact that the last one tried to murder her."

Kenzie had made that happen. "She lost at poker. She was so sure she had me but she was out of cash, so I suggested she meet with Willow once a week for the next two months."

"I'm almost sure she cheated," Kala said, eyes narrowed.

She'd totally cheated. A girl had to keep her skills up, and cheating at cards came up a lot in her line of business. It was weird, but she was good at it. And in this case it was for a good cause because Willow Madden was doing a great job at the Ferguson Clinic, and Kala did seem to be dealing with her shit now. "I had good cards that night. I certainly wouldn't cheat."

"She wouldn't." Lou had been in on it, and it was good to know her sister's bestie was solid when it came to a plot for Kala's own good.

Sometimes her sister didn't listen to good advice and needed to be led to happiness by any means necessary.

Maybe Ben was the same way. Maybe Ben needed to be led to happiness because his tortured past had taught him not to trust joy.

"Well, I don't care how it happened," her mother admitted. "I'm happy my baby is happy and that she has someone she can talk to. It's important."

Her mother would know. So would her aunt. They'd both been through extensive therapy and both were still deeply involved in their women's support group.

Devi gave Tasha a long hug. "I was there. I kind of think she cheated, too, but I'm smart enough to stay out of a Taggart twins showdown. I have to go. Love you, Cousin." She turned to Kenzie. "You be careful with Ben, and watch each other's backs. I'm going to need you guys because I'm pretty sure I'm getting married next year. I think Zach is going to pop the question soon."

She blew the group a kiss and walked out. Kenzie was sure there was a bodyguard waiting to escort her cousin to the airport.

Lou stood, straightening her skirt. "She's right. Zach already asked Theo and Erin for permission. It'll be interesting to watch Zach let Devi dress him. I don't think he knows what he's in for. I'll go make sure everyone is ready to pelt you with birdseed."

Tasha frowned. "Maybe I should sneak out the back."

Her mom took Tash's hand. "Nope. The photographer is waiting. I want all the pictures, and you should prepare Dare for what's waiting in Loa Mali. Yas promised to give you a couple of days, but she's going to want at least a girls afternoon."

Princess Yasmine, the future queen of Loa Mali, had been a playmate when they were young, and no one did a girls day like a real princess. It made Kenzie wish she was going to Loa Mali, but no, she would be running around looking for Huisman.

At least she would be with Ben.

Tasha moved in, putting her hands on Kenzie's shoulders. "Be patient with him. He's hurt and he might lash out, but that doesn't mean he doesn't need you. It doesn't mean he doesn't love you and that you won't be right here in a year or so."

"She's right," her mother agreed. "Patience, and you'll probably want to punch him a couple of times."

"But I shouldn't."

Her mom's strawberry blonde hair shook. "Oh, no. Punch away if he crosses a line. It's how your father knew I loved him. I'm sort of joking. Your dad was pissed when I came back. I'll give you the same advice I gave Tash. Be patient and show him how good life can be with you."

Kala made a vomiting sound. "That is not the advice you gave me."

"You don't take advice. Ever. Also, you were the one who was hurt, sweetie. Like your aunt here. You are the ones who needed patience from the men who loved you," her mom pointed out.

"Did not," Aunt Chelsea said under her breath.

But she had, and what her mom said was true. Patience and understanding would win her man.

And an enormous amount of generous, filthy sex.

Tasha stepped to the door, glowing and happy. Chelsea and her mom followed her.

Kala caught her arm and pulled her in for a hug.

Which was meaningful because Kala wasn't generally affectionate, so Kenzie hugged her hard.

"I know you cheated, Kenz," Kala whispered. "But I like Willow and I know sometimes you have to play dirty to help the ones you love."

Kenzie pulled back but before she could argue, Kala leaned in again. "So don't be surprised at the lengths I'll go to for you."

Kala kissed her cheek and strode away.

Kenzie prayed she could survive her sister's "protection."

Chapter Seven

Ben sat on Kenzie's bed and let the events of the evening wash over him.

He was here. In her room. She was feeding her dog and talking to her roommate. She would be a little while, and her laptop and phone were right there, but was he doing his job and trying to figure out all of Kenzie Taggart's secrets? No. He was studying the pictures on her wall. Her room was painted a cheery yellow, and it was so feminine it hurt. And comfortable.

It made him think about the apartment he kept in Toronto. It was bland and dull, with Spartan furniture because he was almost never there. His fridge was always empty for the same reason. If he was "home" he ate takeout.

Kenzie had a plate of cookies under a cover. The roommate had happily noshed down on one as they talked.

Kenzie had a life, and it was seemingly warm and open.

One whole wall was covered in pictures and posters. In some, Kenzie was young and surrounded by other kids. There were pictures of her family standing in front of a cabin in what looked like the mountains. It was easy now to pick her out from her twin. Kala rarely smiled in pictures, but Kenzie glowed like the sun.

He glanced over to her desk. There was a stack of books, and not a one of them looked like material she was reading for work. Unless their next mission had something to do with dragons.

She was bold and bright and not insecure. She was everything he needed in his life.

Could he keep her for any amount of time?

If he did find something, would he even use it?

Walking down the aisle with her…

It felt right. He thought he would get here, look at her, and remember all the bad shit she'd done. That was not what had happened. He'd looked at her, and something fell into place. Something that had been missing for a long time. He wasn't even certain he could explain it properly, but being with Kenzie Taggart when they weren't working was the most peace he felt in a long time.

And that was dangerous. He had to find a way to put up a wall between them—one Kenzie wouldn't be able to sense—while he decided which way this would go.

"Hey." She stood in the doorway, still in that dress. He was certain some women would look nice in a dress like that, but on Kenzie it should be fucking illegal. She was the sweetest treat, with her breasts offered up like fruit by the corset-like bodice, and those long legs highlighted by the high slit in the gown.

"Hey." His cock was already hard as a rock, and they'd barely gotten back to her place. "Is your roommate okay with me staying?"

A brilliant smile crossed her face. She'd been a bouncy ball of sunshine all night. She'd held his hand and introduced him to all her friends and family, and his lonely ass had soaked it all in. Had been stunned that she could be this open and happy after what she did for her job.

But then maybe the difference was why they did the job. She seemed to do it because she believed.

He had joined up to take down Manny Huisman.

Where the hell would he be if he managed to do it? What would the rest of his life look like?

He shoved the questions aside because Kenzie joined him, sitting down next to him so close their hips touched.

"Bri? She's cool, though you should be prepared to get grilled in the morning. She's already got a list of questions for you. Just so you know she is not super into the whole 'it's classified and I can't talk about it' excuse."

"Uhm, why does she want to question me?"

"She's an author. Well, she'll tell you she's trying to be an author, but she's written a couple of books so I say she's already an author." Her expression turned serious. "Are we going to talk about it?"

He didn't want to talk. "How about we chalk up the whole lying to me thing to a professional problem and move on."

Her eyes narrowed. "Just like that?"

He shrugged. "Just like that."

She'd see it as proof that he wanted her.

Her eyes closed and she sniffled. When she opened them again, she stood up. "Then you're not really here for me."

"What are you talking about? This has all been about you." What was she trying to do? Manipulate him, almost certainly.

She stared at him for a moment, and Ben realized she had a hell of a dumbass-said-what face. "Let's see if I can get this right. I've been thinking about it all night, and there's a piece of me that wants to ignore it and be happy you're here and be in love for a while."

He would argue with the word *love*, but that was a battle he didn't want to fight tonight. "And you're choosing not to why? Was I not attentive enough? Did I not tell you what a goddess you are in that dress?"

"Yes, but you wouldn't listen when I wanted to talk about Nepal."

He stood and put his hands on her arms, staring down into that exquisite face of hers. "I want to move on. I don't want to argue. I want some peace between us."

She stepped back. "Then you've probably got the wrong girl and we're in the wrong line of work. You know I've considered it from time to time. I've considered quitting and seeing if that helped. I decided my job is nonnegotiable. I'll step down at some point, but not now."

"I never asked you to quit."

"What if I asked you to," she began.

"Why would you want that?"

"Because I worry this obsession with Dr. Huisman will kill you, and that will kill me, too."

He sighed and moved into her space again. He could save this. "I'll be fine because we're going to take him down together. I've got a whole plan laid out with the new intel we have from Nepal. I'm presenting it to your father tomorrow. We're going to deal with the situation and then we can talk about how to proceed. I will consider moving here, but I'm not quitting until Manny's in jail. Kenz, if you want me to tell you I'm mad at you, I am, but I'll get over it, and I'll get over it a hell of a lot faster if you kiss me. Way faster if you take off your clothes and let me spank your pretty ass."

She stared at him for a moment as though contemplating her next move.

Or trying to figure out if he was worth the risk.

"I'm going to need help with the corset." She turned and offered him her back.

"Just like that?" he parroted back to her.

Her shoulders shrugged. "Not really. I'm making a calculated move since I'm worried you're viewing this as a chess match rather than seeing if a relationship between us can work. I think you decided collaborating with my team is the best way to get Huisman, and we all know you'll do anything to achieve that particular goal."

He put his hands on her shoulders. Soft, warm skin. He loved touching her. He felt better when he had a hand on her. "Can't I do both? Can't I want you and want justice?"

She leaned back against him. "You can, but I worry if you're put in a position where you have to make a choice, it won't be me. But I suppose every woman has to take that chance. Not having sex with you won't make me happier, and it won't increase the chance that you might be able to love me. So I'm going to go with it for now, but I know you didn't just come here for me."

He wrapped an arm around her waist. "Then pretend. Pretend the only thing I think about is you." He breathed her in, loving the way she smelled, how she fit into his arms. "Pretend we met some other way. Pretend I saw you and couldn't stand the thought of not having you. You know I thought you were gorgeous, but what you don't know is I came onto you…your sister that first night in Sydney because I was worried Dare would get distracted by her."

Kenzie chuckled. "Well, he got distracted all right, but not by Kala. She wouldn't have gone for him, by the way. Kala never does the close work."

"What do you mean by that?"

"Flirting. Working a target who's male. It's all me, so even if we had been targeting Dare that night, he would have been safe."

He gently gripped her elbow and turned her around. "Your father sends you out on honey pot ops?"

Her lips curled up slightly, like she knew he was being a jealous ass and kind of liked it. "Not at all. He's against it, but you know how our business goes. Why fight for intel when I can seduce it out of a man?"

Yep. Volcanic rage. "I'm having a long talk with your father tomorrow."

"That should be interesting. Tell me something, Ben. Have you ever slept with a target for information? Or is it different because you're a man?"

He had, of course. He'd worked a target, but the idea of another man's hands on her…

This woman could drive him insane if he let her. He turned her around again and started unlacing the corset. "Well, I won't be doing it again. I can assure you of that. This isn't casual sex, Kenzie."

Her palms found the door, the position so submissive it nearly made him lose it. "My dad has sent my mom in to work a target before. I mean he's always watching so he can step in if she gets in trouble. She only flirts, but she says the sex afterward is incredible. Apparently my dad is better in bed when he's super jealous."

He managed to unlace the corset and get it over her head. She turned around and leaned back against the door. If she was concerned with the fact that she was half undressed and he was completely clothed, she didn't show it. This woman was comfortable with herself and her sexuality. "I am deeply disturbed that you know so much about your parents' sex life. Take off the skirt. I'm putting 'no fucking around even if it's for national security' in our contract. Am I going to have to run our contract by him?"

"Why, Benjamin, I had no idea you were in the lifestyle," she said as she slid the skirt off her hips and his jaw nearly dropped.

"You're not wearing underwear." Her gorgeous pussy was right there. He hadn't had a chance to really look at her before. They'd been far too emotional and hurried. He was taking his time now.

"Well, I was hoping to get lucky tonight. Always the bridesmaid, never the bride, so I find ways to ease my loneliness." There was a sparkle in her eyes. No one ever teased him the way she did. "I go to a lot of weddings these days."

"You are an incorrigible brat." She was going to be such a handful, but she'd given him a roadmap on how to handle her. D/s. "Is that how you greet me? As for being in the lifestyle, I wasn't until some gorgeous girl tied my unconscious body to a spanking bench."

She winced slightly. "That was actually Zach."

He shook his head. "I'm rewriting that particular history. It was all you. Kenzie, no matter what else you think I'm doing, know that I joined a club so I could learn how to give you what you need. No other reason. I've been studying for a while now, but I have never had sex with a sub. I've never touched one past what it took to teach me because you're the only sub I'll ever want, ever take. I was telling you a story before you poked the jealous ass who lives inside me. I didn't connect with you that first night. I thought you were gorgeous but cold. I wouldn't have slept with Kara that night even if she'd offered. But then we met again at the conference. That was you."

"That was me."

He put his hands on her hair, pulling out the elegant comb that held it in a twist. All that cotton-candy hair flowed around her shoulders down to her breasts. "I didn't connect with you until I was with you. I thought you were lovely and sexy, but I didn't fall for Kara until Kara was you. And every single time I fought with your twin I came back for more because I wasn't going to let your bad-girl side take away from all the sweetness I felt when I was with you."

She stepped back, and for a moment he worried he'd pushed too hard.

And then she dropped to the soft carpet, her knees going wide, her head down in the most exquisite offering of submission he could have imagined. Her hands were turned up on her thighs and her pussy was on display.

His cock pressed against his slacks. He'd never wanted any woman the way he wanted this one. It would be so much smarter to have let someone else handle this, but he couldn't. Even if they didn't get forever, he would at least save her from Huisman.

He put a hand on her head, accepting her submission. He wanted to be in a club, accepting it in front of her friends so they all knew she belonged to him, that he had the right to love and protect her.

The right to fuck her when and where he wanted.

"Unzip my pants," he ordered. "I don't want to wait. We can be kinky in the club. I need you now."

Her hands moved without hesitation, and she unbuttoned his slacks and undid the zipper. His tie and jacket had been discarded the minute they got to her place. Her place. Would she let him into her cozy world? Would she welcome him if she truly knew how guilty he was?

She tugged his boxers down and his cock sprung free.

He had to force himself to breathe as she took him in hand, that warm palm of hers enveloping him. Pure heat flashed through him, and his knees threatened to go weak.

"Kenzie," he began.

But her mouth was already on him. Her tongue whirled around his cockhead until he couldn't think straight a second longer. His whole body tightened as her tongue explored his cock. So good. The first time had been suffused with desperation, and there was a bit of it in there now.

Could he keep her?

Should he keep her?

Could he believe anything that came out of her hot as hell mouth?

But he had time now. A little. Maybe a lot.

He couldn't think with her mouth on him. Worshipping him.

He made a decision in that moment. A decision to leave the spy out of this space. To be what he'd promised her. Her lover. Her protector. Her Dom.

Only here. In the real world he had a job, a responsibility.

But here they wouldn't be Ms. Magenta and the Canadian.

Here they were Ben and Kenzie.

And Ben wanted her so badly he couldn't breathe, couldn't wait another damn second.

He tugged on her hair, and she rose in front of him. So graceful. Her mere presence was like a drug to him. He stared for a moment at her flushed face, her lips swollen, and then she licked her tongue across the bottom like she could taste him there.

If he didn't get inside her soon, he was going to die. He gripped the back of her neck, something savage and primal running through his veins. "You're mine. For as long as this mission lasts, you fucking belong to me. Say it."

Those glorious eyes of hers narrowed. "I'm yours as long as you're honest with me. I know I come off like some naïve romantic, but if you fuck me over, I won't walk off and cry."

No. She would come at him, and it would be war.

And then she would still be in his life. In that moment he knew he was fucked because he would take war from her over never seeing her again.

"Deal," he said before lifting her up and shoving her against the door. Somehow, he managed to get the condom out and on.

His cock was inside her a second later, and he didn't hold back. She wasn't some fragile thing. She gave every bit as good as she got. Her legs wound around him, and he could tell she wasn't afraid he would drop her or hurt her. She wanted it. Wanted his cock, wanted this thing between them that felt ancient and so warm it could hold him forever.

He kissed her as he moved inside her, all that silky heat threatening to overwhelm his every sense.

He wished he'd taken his damn shirt off because he wanted to feel her breasts against his chest, to know there was absolutely nothing between them, but the situation was too desperate.

He'd worried she would turn him away, but she'd opened her arms and her home and heart to him.

If he could trust her…

Her nails bit into his back. She'd gotten her hands under his shirt, touching him like she couldn't stop. She shuddered, and he felt her tighten around him as she came.

Then there was nothing to stop him. He thrust in again and again, as if he could brand himself on her flesh, could own her through sheer physical possession.

The orgasm slammed into him, and he fused their mouths together, needing to be as physically close to her as he could in that moment.

This was far more than sex. More than anything he'd felt before, and he couldn't be sure she wasn't the enemy.

And in that moment, when she held him close and whispered to him, he didn't care.

"I'm so glad you came back to me."

He eased her down but held her close to him, not ready to let her go.

He might never be ready.

* * * *

Kenzie closed the car door and prayed for patience.

Her mother waved from the front porch and then disappeared, likely to go help Travis pack.

They'd made the decision to send her brothers to Bliss for a couple of weeks until they figured out the whole assassin thing. Her mom was taking Colton and Travis and Seth to the airport later that day. They didn't want the younger men of the family caught in the crossfire.

Though there were apparently other reasons she was acting as her dad's personal chauffeur.

She turned on the car as Sosa kept talking.

"Then Miss Charlotte gives conditioner and shampoo, and it smells so good. Like the kind we get when we're going to have to sleep with target before we kill them." Sosa was a peach this morning.

"They don't let you bathe? Or is that a French thing." Her father sat next to her, claiming the seat before Ben could get in. He said something about his back and the seat heater.

She shouldn't have walked in. She should have honked at the end of the drive and forced her dad and his would-be murderer to walk out and take the seats that were left. But no, she'd driven all the way to the house and gone in.

The houses in this part of the city were big and had some serious land. If someone wanted to drive up to the Taggart house, it was a haul and with so many cameras.

She'd thought she would meet with a crying Russian assassin, but Sosa had been sitting in the kitchen devouring Kenzie's mother's strawberry waffles and making friends with her dad's Black Russian Terrier, though Kenzie had been pleased to see that her mom's Cavalier King Charles Spaniel had watched from a wary distance.

Apparently Sosa was giving them decent intel. Decent enough they hadn't buried her body in the backyard, and wasn't that a shame.

"Dad." Her father could be a massive ass sometimes. "Sorry, new friend, he's sarcastic, but you'll find out he's brutal with pretty much everyone. He'll tell you that's what being tolerant means, but he doesn't actually understand the definition of the words."

Sosa's head shook in the rearview mirror. It was obvious her mom had spent some time on the girl. She was wearing what looked like

Kala's old sweats and a McKay-Taggart hoodie, her hair in a ponytail, and with light makeup she looked even younger than before. "No, he's not wrong. I'm not saying all French men are terrible. They're not, but you should understand that I mostly assassinate mobsters and politicians and criminals. Surprisingly, it's usually the politicians that are…how you say…smelly like unwashed ass. See, my friend Astrid, she believe that if you're going to distract victim with sex before you murder you must allow them to finish and then slit the throat. She think it is good karma, but I usually get the killing done and say what a good time he has. Outcome is same, but with less scrubbing afterward for me. I find pretending to want to ride sweaty man like bull is excellent way to stab him in heart. What's your favorite way?"

First off, Kenz was pretty sure that wasn't how to ride a bull. Huh. Now that she thought about it, that wasn't an accurate representation of girl on top since one rode a bull or stallion's back, so it would be more like humping, though it would be a good position from which to slit a throat. Accuracy was important in her line of work.

She started to turn the car around, noticing there were no other cars in the drive. Her dad's and mom's were in the garage, but usually there were at least a couple parked out front.

"She doesn't have a favorite way," Ben said quickly.

"Kenzie is an afar assassin. She does it the classic way. With a long-range rifle from three-hundred feet away," her father explained.

Ben harrumphed from the backseat. There was a lot of judgment in that throat clearing.

This was not the way she'd expected the morning to go. She'd kind of thought it would be all sexy and cuddly, with brief respites where they ate muffins and had some coffee.

She hadn't even gotten a single cup since fucking Sosa had taken the last one claiming no caffeine was in her Black Widow training jail or some shit.

"Does someone want to explain why we're bringing her to the office?" She'd gotten the call way too early. She should have ignored it or turned off her cell. She could be macking down on Ben right now. "Also, why me? Kala lives closer. Or Seth could have given you a ride."

They'd decided to not let her dad drive in case someone tried to blow up his car again since there were apparently a whole lot more

Sosas out there.

A bright smile hit Sosa's face. "Your brother is delight. He comes this morning and has the breaking fast with us. We are not allow this in the training house and never have beautiful men around. They all look like pig."

Kenzie felt her eyes roll completely of their own accord. Because her eyes and her soul were in synch, and her brother was a manwhore. "Tell me he didn't already sleep with her." A thought hit her. They wouldn't. "Please tell me you didn't set my brother on her to get intel. Did you not hear the whole heart stabbing thing?"

Her dad waved that off. "Your brother doesn't have a heart. Or a brain, for that matter. That kid is all penis. I was once weirdly proud of that. Careful what you wish for. And no. Seth came by this morning to pick up Travis so they could get what they need for the cabin. His car's in the shop. Strangely, someone slashed his tires."

Sosa shrugged. "I did not know how delightful Travis is, too, though not as much fun as Seth since he has child. He should wear the condom. Honest? I thought his car would be yours. It's not very… uhm…it is not car of young, hot person, so I think it is yours."

Well, she'd figured out how to deal with Ian Taggart.

Who laughed long and hard. "They taught her all the best insults. I like her."

Sosa sobered slightly. "They did not, actually. They teach me to always be sweet. I don't like to be sweet. As to why you have to drive, the other Bratz doll tells Father she's busy with husband, and he did not wish to hear. She tells him to call you. When she could get words out…"

"I failed on every level as a father," her dad grumbled.

Had her twin picked up the call mid-bang? Why hadn't she thought of that? It was brilliant. Completely would throw off…wait… "What did you call me?"

"Oh, I call you…" She seemed to think for a moment. "You see in our business when very nice, attractive man comes on to well, to Bratz doll, we assume he's trying to get information from her. We call this the *medovaya lovushka*."

Honey pot. But that wasn't the problem.

Kenzie felt her blood begin to simmer. "Bratz doll?"

"Sweetie, I mean…" her dad said with a shrug as though it was all amusing.

She was only wearing the thigh-high leather boots with a mini skirt because they were comfortable. She'd kicked many an ass in this outfit. It did not have to be all camo and athleisure wear.

"I am not a Bratz doll. I'm an intelligent and highly professional Barbie, obviously," Kenzie argued. Did this woman believe she hadn't taken every "what doll am I" quiz on the Internet? Also, she was obviously the good twin from *Sweet Valley High*. Mostly. Elizabeth, but with a violent streak. "I'm Spy Barbie. I don't think Bratz dolls had careers."

"Oh, they have work. Lots of work with many men," Sosa said under her breath.

"What does *medovaya lovushka* mean?" Ben asked. "Sorry. I'm the only one here who doesn't speak Russian."

Her dad's hands clapped together like he was enjoying the chaos. Which he probably was. Her father was often compared to the dude who played Thor in *Marvel* movies, but he was actually Loki. He was god of impish chaos. "That's Russian for honey pot, buddy. I do believe our gentle Sosa is trying to imply you're fucking my daughter for intel. Or was it the other way around, because I might be able to live with that."

Ben was not using her.

Except she was kind of worried he was. Or that he was at the very least trying to get her out of his system. The night before had been beautiful and soul moving for her. But there was still a careful distance between them.

He would always pick Huisman. Always.

She wasn't lowering herself to Sosa's level. Nope. She knew exactly what Sosa was doing. The Russian was needling her to see what she could get. To control whatever she could. The young Russian had figured out Ian Taggart responded to sarcasm and brutal honesty. She was playing to Ben's ego with the attractive and nice man comments. She was poking Kenzie to get the higher ground, so Kenzie wasn't going to…

Damn it. "I am not a fucking Bratz doll. If anything I'm a Bratva doll. One whole side of my family is syndicate, you know."

Sosa shrugged, her eyes widening as though saying *thank you for making my point*. "Yes, that is where the Bratz dolls come from. Everyone in Russia knows this. They are dressed like the syndicate whor…

lovely women who take care of physical needs in exchange for many presents."

"I would like to talk to you about honey pots, Taggart," Ben said suddenly.

What?

She was rapidly losing control of this situation.

Kenzie stopped the car near the end of the drive. There was only one way to deal with Sosa and that was to beat the shit out of her. She felt for the young woman, but sometimes the pack hierarchy needed to be reenforced. She put the car in park in front of the gate. On either side was a line of trees so they had some privacy. "All right. It's time for fight club."

Her dad turned to her. "You know how much I love a fight club, but now is not the time. Also, have you considered that…" He glanced back at Sosa. "Are there dude Bratz dolls?"

Sosa shook her head and didn't seem deeply concerned that Kenzie was about to wrap her arm around her throat and squeeze. "Yes, but they are sad. They wear very…how do you say…bags of douches clothing. But our friend here is not like that. He is Canadian Ken doll. It's okay. Even if he be doing her for intel, it is probably polite. Like the donut."

Now the Russian brat didn't even make sense, but she did seem to know exactly what buttons to push. She could maybe even handle being compared to an obviously skanky doll, but no one was calling what happened last night polite. "It was kinky as fuck. That man had his filthy mouth on every part of my body for hours."

"Kenzie." Now her father was outraged.

"I am not honey potting my sub," Ben announced. "Why would you even think that?"

"Who is sub? Oh, is this sandwich thing?" Sosa seemed genuinely confused. "He makes meal of you. But he is probably doing this so he knows what your pickle knows."

Now they were venturing into the ridiculous. She didn't have a damn pickle.

He'd needed time to process the whole she-was-two-people thing.

But he'd called her his sub, and he knew what that meant to her. He certainly didn't have to go so far as to learn an entire lifestyle. She would have been happy to have vanilla sex with him. At least in the beginning.

"I am not trying to get information out of Kenzie. That's what debriefs are for," Ben explained.

"I mean, from what I can tell you did de her briefs," Sosa insisted.

Her father got out of the car. "I can't. I'm not going in today. I'll head to Colorado with the boys. I might actually retire and never come home."

She wasn't sure she was his sub yet. Not technically. Right now they were just playing around, but she kind of liked how he said it, and it made her less fight clubby. Also, her father was not thinking. "Dad, get back in the car. Have you forgotten there's a price on your head?"

It was precisely why she was here, and why her whole family was going to have to split up.

This was all part of Huisman's plan.

Chaos. Huisman loved it. Which made her worry he was planning something big. He was definitely a "look here while I do something much worse somewhere else" kind of villain. And that particular kind was moving up on her list after all this mess.

Ben shot out of the car and before Kenzie could move, he tackled her dad, both of their big bodies hitting the thankfully recently mowed lawn.

Which was weird because while her dad hadn't been particularly kind to him, it could have been so much worse. She'd kind of thought Ben was planning on winning her dad over. Honestly, sometimes the old guy did appreciate a good fight.

Then the reason was clear because a shot sounded out and Kenzie realized the chaos had found their home.

Chapter Eight

Ben saw the glint of metal coming from the trees a hundred feet away and shot out of the car. As much as Ian Taggart was a pain in his ass, he wasn't about to allow Kenzie's father to die on his ridiculously large front lawn.

Even as he tackled the mass of muscle, he admired the softness of the grass and how well kept that sucker was. He thanked the universe they weren't doing this on concrete outside the office building because while the guy was in good shape, there was a reason people his age talked endlessly about their hips and sciatica.

He hadn't expected Kenzie to come from wealth. He'd thought she would be one of those brilliant poor kids who had no family and a flexible moral character that all intelligence agencies preferred. But no, she had grown up on this beautiful compound with two loving parents and a family that rallied around her whenever she needed them.

Unlike his, who asked him not to contact them again. Who told him it was his fault they'd had to go into hiding.

He rolled with the big guy, who seemed to have figured out shit was going down.

"Dad, Ben, get behind the car," Kenzie called out. "Stay down."

Thank fuck Kenzie drove a solid SUV.

She would be out of the line of fire if she stayed on the driver's side. She would huddle down while he found a way to deal with the situation.

Taggart managed to get behind the car. "She wanted one of those clown cars. Like a two-seater that wouldn't fit most of the guys she's dated. Hey, sweetie, you're liking the Bronco now, aren't you?"

She was silent and Sosa was suddenly with them, and she was smiling like this was the best day. He hadn't actually seen her smile before. It was a bit creepy. "They think that I am dead. They would never send other girl if I am not dead."

She wasn't thinking straight. "Or they sent the other girl to clean up your mess, including killing you."

Where was Kenzie? She should have crawled back here by now.

Sosa's jaw dropped. "That is…"

She launched into a litany of what had to be Russian curses.

Taggart sighed and had his cell phone in hand. "Baby, we did not make it out. Yeah, they're making house calls now. She's in the trees. I might have mentioned the trees were a bad idea. But don't worry. Kenz is taking care of it. The last thing we need is you strapping our grandchild on your chest and climbing on the roof to snipe her." There was the sound of a bullet tearing through metal and then a hiss. "Damn it. There goes the tire. I swear to god I will take Manny Huisman's heart out and crap on it before I stuff it down his throat."

"You should take crap in his mouth before you take heart. He will be dead if you take heart and will not to be caring. Then all you get out of this is clean bowels," Sosa said like that was a fucking normal thing to say.

Also, what had Taggart said? Kenzie was doing what?

"Yeah, the kid's right. I need to up my fiber intake, baby," Taggart was saying.

He had been transported to Planet Surreal.

So yeah, Kenz had been raised in privilege, but she also had to put up with this. No wonder she ended up at the Agency.

Where the hell was Kenzie? Ben pulled the SIG from its place under his jacket and started to ease from behind the SUV. "Kenz?"

Sosa leaned back against the bumper. "She goes after other girl. She is fast in those boots. It's surprising."

She went after the sniper who had the higher ground? His heart rate ticked up. He was cold as ice. They literally called him the Ice Man, and here he was freaking out because his girl was trying to take down an assassin dressed in stripper boots and a mini skirt that barely covered her pretty ass.

"I'm going after her, but you should understand that we're going to have a long talk, Mr. Taggart," Ben said as he eased around Sosa. "You let her run wild, and that is not going to happen on my watch."

Taggart nodded, leaning back against the SUV. That was when Ben realized there was blood on Taggart's lower leg. "Yeah, buddy, you go for it. I have a couple of liability waivers I'd like you to sign. You should also know that I'm willing to send her in with ten goats and a couple of chickens and her gassy dog as her dowry."

"How bad is it?" Ben asked quietly since it seemed like everything had gone silent. He had to tamp down his panic because he had wounded.

"I mean you haven't been around that dog when he gets in the trash. Bud Two can clear a… Ah, you mean my leg. It grazed my calf. I'll survive, but I'll need help walking until I stabilize it," Taggart admitted.

"I will put pressure on." Sosa pulled the sweatshirt over her head, revealing a white T-shirt she wore. It had a logo on it. Top. The restaurant Kenzie had met him at. After her twin had sent him there.

Should he leave his maybe, probably future father-in-law with the chick who'd tried to blow up his car yesterday? Damn it. Kenzie was getting her ass smacked.

Could he spank her for essentially doing her job?

"It's fine," Ian assured him. "She's not a bad kid, and she knows I'm going to be more helpful to her personally alive than dead."

"I will not be hurting anyone," Sosa assured him. And then sat up straight. "Mr. Ian, do you still have cell phone?"

"Yours?" Kenzie's father pulled it out of his pocket. "You know I think it's a bad idea to call base. Right now they can't be sure you're not dead, although your friend in the trees will tell them."

She shook her head. "No base. I think I know who they will send, and she will not tell them. I am not supposed to know this number she uses, but I do. I have small group of friends. We try to make things not so bad for each other."

Taggart handed her the phone.

Ben eased his head around the left side of the SUV, trying to figure out where Kenzie had gone.

A bullet hit the ground not an inch from him.

So many spankings. How long could he go? He worked out. As exercises went, the motion was probably one he could keep up for a long time.

Sosa dialed a number and put the cell to her ear. Then dialed again. And a third time before someone picked up. "Gabby, it's Sosa. No, I am not dead. Like he could kill me. No, I find the target and he turns out to be nice man who wants to help us. Like we always talk about. He is spy with many contacts, and his wife is one of us. Not one of you because you are actually French, but she know about us and wants to help. Also, his daughter is Bratz doll, and she's stalking you now. Come out of tree. They have the Pop-Tarts and you can have all the bread you want, and they have many streaming channels."

Ben sighed. His life depended on traumatized girls who wanted to escape a low-carb diet and binge watch some shows.

"Hey, tell her I'll take her to Costco and she can buy out the bread section," Taggart snarked.

Sosa's eyes widened as though he'd offered her the world. "Yes, he say he has Costco card."

Then there was a scream and Ben no longer cared someone was going to shoot him. He stood and started running for the tree line. Kenzie couldn't be hurt. He wouldn't even think about her being dead.

Kenzie had someone on the ground and they were tussling. *"Zhalkiy gadyonysh. Lezhat', a to budet khuzhe."*

The other girl was on her belly, and there was a sniper rifle about three feet from her hands along with a backpack that had obviously fallen since it had spilled out across the grounds.

He was pretty sure Kenz had climbed up that tree and hauled her prey down.

Damn, she was hot when she was fighting. Also, he was pretty sure she still wasn't wearing underwear.

The young woman Sosa referred to as Gabby's head came up, and a flash of hope hit her eyes. "Mister, please help me. I was bird watching and this crazy Russian woman is trying to kill me. My friend Sosa is here. She will tell you."

Ben holstered his gun since it looked like Kenz had this one. "Her name is Gabby, babe, and I don't think she speaks Russian."

"No, she is not smart enough." Sosa was suddenly beside them, and she was allowing Taggart to balance against her shoulder. She'd tied her sweatshirt across his injured leg. "She only to be speaking French and English. Her Russian is not good. French is bullshit so we use English, which is also bullshit, but it wasn't English man who sells me out so here we are."

"They told me you were dead." Gabby's English was way better than Sosa's. "Could someone tell the Bratz doll not to kill me?"

Kenzie's eyes held a deeply enraged flame that he hoped never to see again. His baby could only be pushed so far. He needed to calm her down.

"You are not a Bratz doll, baby. You are the sexiest fuck toy ever created. You're Spy Barbie, and I will give up all my secrets if you let that one go," he said in a soothing tone. "Although you look hot like that. Damn, baby, you are fierce."

"Like a model?" Kenzie asked, her eyes narrow.

"Like a psycho," Gabby complained.

"Like you could be on *Vogue* right now," Ben replied. He was dealing with a gorgeous beast. He thought he'd seen this part of Kenzie before, but that had almost always been her twin. So much so he'd questioned if Kala was always the one to do the dirty work and Kenzie handled anything that needed a softer touch but no, here she was. There was a part of this woman who relished the kill when she thought it was justified. Which it wasn't here. She would feel bad later. "Baby, she's a kid."

Gabby frowned. "I am not a kid."

Ben pointed to one of the items that had fallen to the yard when their tussle had taken them out of the trees. "Then why do you carry around a teddy bear?"

Kenzie's head swiveled, and she caught sight of the sad-looking pink bear on the grass. Her hands loosened. There she was. The sweet side. It could be coaxed back out. "Oh, that's so cute."

Sosa shook her head. "It's good way to smuggle in the poisons."

Gabby took advantage and rolled out from under Kenzie, grabbing the bear. "I do not poison. That is Uma's job and she would… Well, she would poison me if I try. You know who gave this to me."

Sosa's expression softened. "I do. Gabby, he say he can help. He say he will help get our sisters out."

Gabby clutched that worn-out teddy, ignoring the guns and knives that had also fallen. "I don't simply want out."

"I will help you burn them all down," Taggart promised.

Kenzie sat back in the grass. "Damn it. Fine. But you have to stop trying to kill my dad."

Her dad frowned fiercely her way. "And you have to start wearing damn underwear. What the hell, Kenz? Like that skirt isn't short enough? Are you going to smother the poor girl with your vagina?"

Gabby clutched her bear.

A big dog lumbered up, stopping and staring around like he was trying to figure out who he needed to kill. He was huge and black, with curly fur and intelligent eyes.

Another dog ran up and started licking Kenzie's face. Pretty dog. Not a spark of real intelligence behind those eyes.

"What the hell," Charlotte Taggart had a baby in a sling and a semiautomatic in her hand. "Sosa, I told you…"

Sosa held her hands up. "It was not me. It was Gabby, but she does not know about the helping and the Costco. She only know about the job. Now she knows and will be helping like me."

Charlotte lowered the gun and sighed as she looked at her husband. "How the hell did she shoot you while you were in the Bronco? It's fortified. The bullets shouldn't have gotten through."

It was the first time he'd ever seen Taggart go pale. "Baby, I…"

Oh, he could throw Taggart's ass under the bus. Yes, he'd saved the man's life, but giving him a taste of hell wasn't something Ben could pass up. "He got out of the car after I started talking about how Kenzie's my sub. I think he was feeling a little nauseated. Now I wonder why since I've heard him talk about sex pretty openly."

He went over and offered Kenzie a hand up. He hauled her up and pulled her in, wrapping his free hand around her. And yes, he tugged her skirt down. "You okay?"

"Well, I won't wear these boots to climb a tree again," she groused but snuggled close.

"You got out of the car when there was clearly a hit out on you?" Charlotte's voice was dangerously low and her free hand was around her grandbaby, who seemed to be sleeping peacefully through it all.

Even the dogs seemed to back up from the sound of her voice.

"There was a lot of talk about mouths, and it was gross, baby," Ian tried to explain.

Sosa helped Gabby up. "It is to be being okay, G. I trust them."

"You do not trust anyone," Gabby said, eyes wide with obvious shock.

"I see her as my new mother, and while I did try to do that thing where I am having random man's baby to cause chaos between couple, he is my new and very mean to everyone else papa," Sosa said with a grave nod.

"Now, wait a minute," Ian said, going even paler.

"Ian, I am getting *Open Door* notifications," Charlotte complained. "They want to know who's shooting on the crazy guy's property. I do not want another HOA meeting where I have to explain away multiple gun fights."

Kenzie sighed as her parents started to argue and Gabby and Sosa talked about all the hot dogs and chicken bakes they could eat at the Costco food court.

He held her and kissed the top of her head, and somehow the chaos wasn't so bad.

* * * *

"You couldn't get him to a hospital?" Lou asked, looking inside the conference room where Kenzie's father was preparing to go through with his debrief despite the fact that Aidan O'Donnell was patching up his leg, where a bullet had apparently taken out a nice chunk of his calf.

Kenzie sighed. "You have no idea how stubborn he is. He and my mom had a massive fight over the HOA thinking we're some kind of criminal enterprise, and then they were on about the trees. Then I had to hold Colton while they made out."

Her parents had a beautiful marriage. There had been a lot of talk about spanking her mom for her sassy mouth.

Ben hadn't even threatened her with a good time and she'd run into gunfire and everything.

"But the trees are beautiful," Lou complained. "You won't have any privacy if you get rid of the trees."

"Drones." TJ rounded the corner carrying two coffees. He handed one to his fiancée. "I'll set up Uncle with a fleet of drones that patrol the tree line and he'll chill out. He'll have a lot of fun with it, and it'll give the HOA something to talk about that isn't gunfire."

Actually, that wasn't a terrible idea. She could distract her dad with drones. "Huh, I never thought of that."

TJ sighed as he gestured back toward the break room. "Well, I never thought our office would be taken over by youthful assassins. What exactly do we know about them?"

"Not enough to bring them in," Ben groused.

He was cranky, but then he'd had a day. Which would have been made better had he taken her into an office and smacked her ass silly and then fucked her until his eyes rolled to the back of his head and did that slump down on her like she was the best fuck toy in the world thing and then she would get them some tea and cookies.

When she'd suggested they talk in private he'd kissed her briefly and said he needed to call in. He spent half an hour calling his boss from a secure line and then joined them.

Like nothing had happened. Like this was just another day.

"What are we supposed to do with them?" Kenzie asked. If he was going to be professional, then she would be, too. "We need to figure out if they know anything about the person who hired them."

Kenzie was calmer about the two young women, who couldn't be much past twenty. Sosa was obnoxious as hell and Gabby could talk a mile a minute, but it was obvious that they were both traumatized. Gabby had held on to that stupid teddy bear like it was a lifeline, and Sosa had held on to Gabby.

"I already had my boss look into them. I sent your father what Joseph discovered," Ben admitted.

Kenzie cocked a brow. "And?"

"Hey, are you having a meeting without me?" Kala strode in and frowned at Ben. "Ben."

He frowned right back. "Chick who nearly deballed me for no reason."

They'd avoided each other at the wedding and would likely have continued to if they hadn't been called up here.

"Oh, I had reasons," Kala shot back and might have said more but Cooper chose that moment to slide an arm around her shoulders.

"Ben, my man." Her brother-in-law was as sunny as her sister was dark. He held out his free hand.

Ben shook it, but there was a reluctance. "Good to see you, Cooper."

"Nah, it's not," Cooper replied with a smile. "But it will be one day. So the old guy got shot by another Russian girl?"

"French," TJ said.

Cooper stepped back and laughed. "Perfect. And now he has to deal with… What are we calling them?"

"Benzie," Lou said after a long swallow. "TJ's right. It's the only way to go. Kenjamin sounds like someone got cute."

"I like it." It was fun. "It's way better than Kalper."

Ben's expression had gone all cute-boy confused. "What?"

Kenzie pointed to her cousin. "TJ likes couple names. Says it saves him time. So Tasha and Dare are Dasha. I like to call Lou and TJ Loot. We decided on Zevi for Zach and Devi. And we're obviously Benzie. Cute, huh?"

He did not look impressed.

"We are not calling us Kalper. It sounds like some equation from physics we're supposed to solve," Kala complained.

"Yes, that's why I like it," Lou shot back.

Eve McKay walked in from her office. She was casual today in jeans and a sweater, her blonde hair in a bun on her head. She winked her son's way. "Hey, sweetie. Where's your brother? The new one."

That was Aunt Eve. She found out her adopted son had a brother and she brought him right in. Zach had been going to family dinners with the McKays for weeks now.

"He and Devi headed to Colorado after the wedding," Cooper explained. "Charlotte is sending Seth and Travis out today. Zach is going to coordinate with the sheriff and Henry Flanders for their protection, and he wants to check in on his mom."

Who was also Cooper's bio mom, but he'd made it plain while he was open to a relationship with Shannon, Eve McKay was his momma.

Huisman would love to get his hands on Shannon Reed. She was the infamous bombmaker who'd designed the perfect system to deliver Huisman's anthrax, but she'd been smart enough to not let him learn how to make it. Keeping her safe was important.

She hoped her cousin didn't get all kidnapped and shit again. It was getting to be a real habit for Devi and one she wanted to break.

Eve sighed. "Yeah, I think your father and I are going to take a vacation for a week or so, too, just to be careful. Everyone needs to be careful. Right now they're after Ian, but when it becomes clear they can't get to him, they might start looking at the rest of us as a way to draw him out."

"I think we should fake his death," Kala said loud enough for their dad to hear them.

"I'm not faking my death," he shouted back. "Get in here. We have a plane to catch."

That was news to Kenzie. And not good news. If they got called into DC, she wasn't sure Ben could come with them. She strode into the conference room. "Uh, I'm going to the club tonight, Dad. Tell Drake we can do a Zoom."

She had plans, and they included getting her brand-new Dom on the dungeon floor and seeing if she could open him by allowing him to torture her in the sweetest way.

"We cannot do a Zoom because you're horny, Daughter," her father shot back and grimaced before looking down at his leg. "Aren't you done yet?"

Aidan O'Donnell's head came up, and he stared at her dad. "I would be if we were in a proper ED and you weren't such a stubborn asshole, Uncle. You know I never wanted to be some kind of mafia doctor. Oh, I know you're not mafia, but this feels like Bratva to me."

Aidan was a trauma surgeon, but for the last few months he'd also kind of been the team's on-call doc, along with his wife, Carys.

"He goes into the hospital, I assure you there's someone waiting for him," Ben said as he held out a chair for her.

He was a little standoffish, and she couldn't figure out if it was because he was upset with her or because this was how he was when he was working. She'd hoped he would warm up after they put their relationship on a good footing.

Were they on a good footing?

"Which is why I've got my family fleeing right now," her father explained. "Theo and Erin already agreed to join the boys for a trip to the cabin. I called Case to let him know to up his security. I've got bodyguards on Sean and Grace, and Aidan and Carys are staying at their house for a couple of weeks because Tris is going to be in DC with Drake and Taylor working on some project Taylor has going."

Drake and Taylor Radcliffe were technically their CIA handlers, though they were given an enormous amount of latitude.

"Is this about the thing Tim found?" Ben asked as she settled in beside him.

"Tim found something?" She had not been informed.

Kala sat across from her, one brow raised. "You didn't read the report? Ben's boss sent it two days ago."

She frowned and pulled out the phone she used for work. Sure enough, there were actually several emails that needed her attention. She gave her dad her best "sorry, Dad, but I'm still you're baby girl, right" wince. "Technically, I took a couple of vacation days."

Her father looked at her like she'd lost her mind. "There are no vacation days in the CIA."

He was forgetting some things. "Uh, tell that to my sister and her brand-new husband, who are currently enjoying a few weeks in Loa Mali."

"Keep looking at your email," he said as he hissed. "Hey, kid, gentle, please."

Aidan huffed but Kenzie was wincing again because this morning her newlywed sister had sent her several updates and new analysis of the data they'd taken from the Nepal site and some reports on the recent anthrax attacks they were attributing to Dr. Huisman.

Tasha was always perfect. Always. Now she couldn't even use the excuse of the wedding. But sometimes she needed a couple of days to figure things out. Some people did that in thoughtful meditation. Kenzie did it with sad-girl rock, Ben and Jerry's Tonight Dough, and whatever shitastic reality dating show had recently come out. She could always watch those and think at least she hadn't dated one of those assholes.

"You were brooding," her twin accused.

Yeah. That was pretty fair.

"Please read the files. We're going to forgo the debrief on the properties because Drake has asked us to work with another team to start investigating those, so I've asked Eve to talk to our new friends and tell me if they're lying and planning on killing us all," her dad said.

Aidan put his bag on the table as he got to his feet. "You're stitched up. Someone needs to change the dressing twice a day, and keep it clean and dry. Do you want to go to your office for the antibiotic? No, I am not writing a prescription because you won't take it. So I'm not leaving here until I shove this needle into your ass and push the plunger."

Kenzie breathed a sigh of relief. She might be able to get through a couple of Tasha's so important she wrote them on her honeymoon emails while Aidan was making sure her dad didn't go septic.

Except her dad simply stood on one leg and shoved his slacks down.

"Dad!" She and Kala managed that duo in-synch stereo thing they could do when they were truly outraged.

Her father merely leaned over and let Aidan adjust his boxers as he brought out the alcohol wipe. "Eve, the floor is yours. Did you get the material Ben sent over?"

Kenzie turned to her lover. "When the hell did you have time to work?"

She had obviously failed.

Ben looked entirely amused. "While you were making breakfast. And while you were asleep. I don't sleep much so I watched you for a while and then I gathered some intel we have on groups that the assassin twins could have come from."

He watched her when she slept? It was a little stalkery. Slightly creepy. Also hot.

Did she snore? Her sister said she did, but her sister could be an asshole. Surely she didn't snore. Right?

"Did her elephant sounds keep you up?" Kala asked.

Kenzie used the pen she had like a dart going straight for her sister's forehead. But Kala ducked, anticipating the move.

Cooper caught the pen midair. "Kala, you said you would be nice."

TJ held up a hand. "I do believe the deal was that she would be somewhat nice to Ben. Kenz was not involved in those negotiations at all. She can totally be mean to Kenz. I think she would call it sisterly love."

Aww. That was kind of sweet when she thought about it. "You promised to be nice to Ben?"

Kala shrugged. "I said I wouldn't take his balls, either literally or figuratively. I know he's a sensitive dude."

"I'm not," Ben argued.

Kala glanced his way. "I'm pretty sure your balls are, buddy, but those balls are now attached to my sister, so they are off limits by way of the Treaty of the Johnson High School Cafeteria, junior year."

Kenz had several high school boyfriends that Kala hadn't been fond of. A summit had been held. She'd given up a lot for those assholes since Kala had forbidden all girl-power pop from being played in the car on the way to school. Kenzie's whole senior year was heavy metal and goth rock.

"Thanks, kid," her father said as he redid his slacks and sat back down.

Aidan stared at him. "I will write you a prescription for pain killers. It's got to hurt since you wouldn't let me use anything but lidocaine."

Her dad simply held up a glass of amber liquor. "Got it covered."

A long sigh came from Aidan's chest. "All right. Cousins, good luck, and kill that motherfucker. He's not a doctor. He's a butcher."

Aidan had a run-in with Huisman, too.

Her dad held a hand out. "You wait for a bodyguard. I know it's obnoxious, but I called in Landon. He's with the psycho twins in the break room. God, I hope he isn't attracted to them."

Aidan chuckled as he started for the door. "I'll knock before I enter."

The door closed behind him, and Eve sat back. "I seriously doubt any sex those two young women engage in is for pleasure. I know I've only spent an hour with them, but I've seen this before in severely traumatized women. If they behave in an overly sexual way, it's the trauma talking."

"They did not seem traumatized when they were trying to murder me," her dad pointed out.

"Or calling me a Bratz doll." It still rankled.

Kala snorted. "I like her already."

Kenzie stared, gesturing at her twin. "Uh, samesies. How do you like being a Bratz doll?"

"Oh, I'm like the Halloween edition, and I accept that about myself," Kala countered.

Ben leaned over. "I find Bratz dolls sexy. Well, the adult, living, breathing version."

She turned because she loved it when he talked like that. So she followed her instincts and kissed him.

He seemed surprised at first and then his hands came out and he deepened the kiss. This. This was what she needed. He didn't get that it was perfectly fine to make out in the middle of a meeting. Her parents did it all the time. But Ben was Canadian and they probably were polite and stuff in all the meetings he had. Yeah, her whole body was relaxing under his lips and tongue and…

Something soft hit Kenzie's head, and she sat back.

"Lou, I need you to make me a water gun out of parts you can find in this building," her father said.

Lou opened her bag. "Oh, I have the sprayer ready."

"Do not give that to him," Kenzie warned. Her father was a terrible hypocrite.

Eve slapped at the desk. "Guys, I know you're used to playing around, but this is serious and we're on a timer. I wish I had weeks with them, but I think this is all the time I'll have."

"Why would you say that?" TJ asked. "We can keep them safe."

"I don't know if they'll let you. I don't think they'll hurt anyone here unless they feel threatened, but I also can't promise you that they're not biding their time until they can run," Eve countered. "Okay, the Canadians have been tracking a couple of groups that like to kidnap young women."

"There are thousands of traffickers," Kala pointed out. She looked down at her tablet, studying the reports they'd been sent. "Why is Joseph interested in these?"

Ben sat back up, looking more professional. He looked hot when he was being professional. Could an All-American Bratz doll and a Canadian Ken doll make it work? Their parts fit together perfectly. Would their hearts do the same?

"I don't know what you're thinking about, sis, but it's making me nauseous," Kala said without looking up.

She glared at her sister and thought lots of mushy things. They weren't the twins who could truly read each other's minds, but Kala was apparently sensitive when it came to perfectly normal romantic thoughts. Like when they made love, she was almost certain their heart-beats had been in synch and she could hear the music of the earth.

Kala went a shade of green.

Ben chose to ignore them. "Canada takes human trafficking seriously, but my team is studying a very specific type that we believe have a direct impact on national security and our intelligence-gathering operations. We've identified three separate groups that target young women."

"Because they're doing more than offering them up for wealthy men to rape," Kala said tonelessly.

Her twin was already thinking of who to kill. Kenzie didn't have to read the reports to know what came next. "They're being trained as assassins."

"They're being trained as spies," Eve corrected. "At least Sosa and Gabby are. Assassination is merely one of their jobs. What they truly are is information brokers. Well, they gather the information and secrets and place powerful people into compromising situations. Sosa talked about several corporate clients and gaining intel into certain governments her group considers either unfriendly or potential targets. Gabby recently got dirt on a politician in Asia, and I hate thinking about how she was forced to do it."

"So they are being used as prostitutes." Lou glanced out as though she could see them. "Didn't Sosa say she was eight when they took her?"

"She thinks," her father said. "If we can trust a word she says since she's been taught to lie."

"She's an adult now, right?" Cooper asked. "I understand she's been conditioned to obey, but we're offering her a way out."

Kenzie might not like the girl, but she understood her. "She's worried about what happens to her sisters. I don't have to read reports to know that one of the ways they would condition children is to hurt the people they care about. They need leverage over a kid, and teaching them they have to obey or they lose the only people in the world who matter is one way they do it. So they're teaching them criminal arts. I would bet she's also excellent at breaking and entering, safe cracking, and hacking."

Lou held up a hand. "Uhm, shouldn't we think about that since I watched Landon walk out with Aidan? It's Sunday. No one's here. There's a lot of confidential information in this building."

Her dad nodded. "Which is why I left a laptop and several folders in the break room. So far all they've done is flirt with Landon and demolish the chips Boomer left up here. I really do have to make a Costco run now. They're either smart enough to know I've got a camera on them or they want to snack down on a bunch of carbs and pretend to be normal."

"There's nothing normal about them," Eve said gravely. "The good news? I don't think they're lying about the group they belong to."

"Forced to be a part of." Words mattered, and they should use the right ones. Sosa hadn't made the choice. It hadn't been a cozy boarding school. She hadn't been a kid obsessed with gymnastics or trying to be the world's next figure skating icon. She looked to her dad. "Is that why you took her in? You wanted to see what she would try?"

"I took her in because if she's older than twenty, I'll eat my own shoe. And there's this thing called irony. Russian girl forced to assassinate people she doesn't know? Trying to save her sisters from pain? If someone had turned your mother in, none of you would be here," he replied with a solemnity she rarely saw in him.

"Remind me to ask about your mother's history," Ben whispered before leaning forward and addressing the group. "I think Sosa and Gabby both have important intelligence, though they might not know it. Being able to have either of them ID who hired the group would be helpful. I would also like to map the structure of the group and how it works."

"Why would they know who hired them?" Lou asked the pertinent question. "I can't imagine they would be involved in the decisions about who to take on as clients. Also, aren't we afraid they'll send someone else when they realize Uncle Ian isn't dead?" Her hand slapped across her mouth. "I called him uncle."

They'd been so careful up until now because they'd been actively hiding their family ties from Ben Parker. "It's okay now."

"I watched Gabby call back to base and explain that she'd wounded me but some asshole pushed me out of the way so she's trying again." Her father took another sip of the Scotch he would use to blunt the discomfort he had to be in. "According to her she's got forty-eight hours to complete the assignment, but they're wary because they can't confirm the injury. Which is why Tris is uploading Aidan's report. It will state that I was admitted to Parkland and spoke with police but have no idea what happened."

"Are we back to faking your death?" Kala asked with a hint of glee. "Because I have thoughts."

"She does," Lou agreed. "She has a notebook and everything. It's both inventive and disturbing."

Her dad sighed. "No. And while I know they aren't consulted on the clients, from what I can tell they're housed in the same places the other less targeted trained girls are."

"So they were kept in a brothel." Ben's hand came out, and he covered hers. "I would be interested in a client list. From what I've heard, this would be for men with money and power."

"I am not going to fuck this up," a quiet voice said.

Sosa stood in the doorway, Gabby behind her. "We saw the laptop and folders, and we are not foolish, Mr. Ian. We are not going to look at them and tell the people who hurt us. Was that what this was about? Did you lie when you said you would help? It's okay if you did, but we would like to know so we can choose our own way."

"I will not shoot you again, sir," Gabby promised. "I don't actually like shooting people. The only fun thing was being able to climb the tree, but then the Bratz doll pulled me out of it and now I have an ache in my backside. Oh, no, Sosa, there are two of them."

Sosa nodded. "I tell you. One of them is goth version."

Kala grinned. "Damn straight. Welcome, weirdoes."

It took everything she had to not roll her eyes. She turned and tried to remember that she was the lucky one with great parents and friends and a wonderful life where she wasn't forced to be an assassin. She'd chosen that all on her own. "Sosa, we had to test you."

She nodded. "I understand, and I know you will continue to. I know it will be hard to be trusting, but it is hard for me, too. I wouldn't trust at all if it weren't for Miss Charlotte. She understand. If she cannot help, then there is no help in all the world."

"She's going to help," her father said in a far more careful tone than he usually used. "The only reason she isn't here now is she needs to get our boys ready to travel. She'll join us. She wouldn't miss it. She wouldn't miss the chance to help out girls who were hurt like she was."

It was so shitty. Why couldn't she have her love story without a bunch of sad-sack, traumatized young adults hanging around? Kala hadn't had to deal with mini-moms. Lou hadn't been forced to handle sarcastic newbies. Still. She had to be who she was. Kind. Patient. Open. "I will help you as well. As soon as we finish the mission we're on, I'll help take down everyone who hurt you."

"Yeah, it'll be fun," Kala vowed.

"Then we will help you, too." Gabby stepped inside and smiled shyly Eve's way. "It was good to talk to you, Miss Eve. Even if you think we are crazy."

Eve's head shook. "Traumatized. Not crazy. There's nothing crazy about coping mechanisms, even when they're extreme. Can you tell us anything about who hired you? Where does the boss find clients?"

Sosa selected a seat across from Ben and sat down, Gabby in the one next to her. "Our house is run by woman, but her boss is man. What you should understand is the house does many tasks. Some girls are used sexually, and they bring in money that way. Others work on the Dark Web. They are good at scams."

"They get to eat the pizza." Gabby had a sullen look on her face. "I tried to tell them I should be hacker, but they don't believe me."

"Because you are terrible with them." Sosa looked to Kenzie's father. "She cannot remember how to reset password. Also, despite the fact that she works with scammers, she is easy to scam. Sometimes they let us use the computers to study, but she clicks on everything and gets all the viruses."

"I wanted to see the puppy videos," Gabby argued.

"You were telling us how they select clients," Ian encouraged.

"Yes. I watch when they don't think I do. I can make myself small," Sosa explained. "I've learned more since they trust me to be in the world. They think I am good girl. Probably because I always have been. I wait for right time. But until then I learn."

"And she teaches," Gabby said. "There are four of us. Milena and Claire are still there. Though Milena is often out on jobs since she's had specialized training. We have figured some things out. We hoped to eventually have enough we could go to police, but then we realized…"

Kenzie could guess. "The police are in on it. At least some of them, and that could make things difficult. So you need a higher power. Despite his sarcasm, my father has deep ties to European intelligence."

"And enough suspicion that I wouldn't go straight to them until we figure out the tangle," her father added. "Until then we'll document and investigate and try to get your friends out. Is there any way one of them could get a client list?"

"The whole network is involved with a group." Sosa seemed to think about how to describe them. "It is thing that seems fine on the outside. Like they seem to do good in the world. Charity. That is word."

She felt Ben stiffen beside her. Kenzie leaned forward. "Are you talking about a group known as Disrupt?"

Both Sosa and Gabby nodded.

Kala pulled out her tablet and turned it toward the young women. "Do you know this man?"

She had pulled up a picture of Emmanuel Huisman.

Sosa went a nice shade of green.

Gabby ran to the nearest trash can and threw up.

She was taking that as a yes.

Chapter Nine

"Hey, man, did I thank you for the ride?" Tim settled in beside Ben on the ridiculously extravagant jet that was currently flying over some part of America connected to the Mississippi River.

Tim wasn't talking to him.

"You did," Charlotte Taggart said with a gracious smile.

"Several times." Big Tag eyed Tim like he was a snake that might bite him since Tim had been super flirty with his wife.

Ben had known exactly who to talk to in order to not force Tim to fly commercial to London. Where they would be meeting with MI6 as a team. He was officially working with the Americans now, but he wanted his own tech with him. Lou would always prioritize her own team, so he needed Tim with him, watching out for their interests.

It also wouldn't hurt to have a reminder that he didn't belong in this weird-ass, comfortable family thing they had going on.

Tim had been more than happy to join since he'd been sitting in a La Quinta Inn for days waiting to be called in.

The annoying thing was when Tim showed up at the small private airfield, he'd walked in like he was one of them. He'd strode right up to Lou and given her a hug, but only after he'd handed TJ Taggart a bag from someplace called HEB that apparently had TJ's favorite snacks.

He'd joked with the twins like they hadn't lied to them. He'd joked with Cooper and said hi to Zach when Cooper had called him.

Tim fit in better than he did, and it rankled.

It also rankled that Kenzie was sitting with her twin at the front of the plane instead of in this living room-style setup with him. He'd rather expected her to follow him and try to get on his lap or make out in front of her parents, which he couldn't figure out if it was rebellion or real desire she couldn't control.

Well, she was controlling herself now.

His cell buzzed and he glanced down. Text.

From Dare.

Damn. He sat up straighter and moved to get the message on screen. Like he was a kid with one friend in the world.

He was pathetic at times, but one of the best things to happen to him was meeting Dare Nash. When he'd started this op, he'd begun by getting a job with the Nash group—a known business associate of Huisman's legitimate side. He'd spent months as Brian Peters, getting to know the guy, and he'd liked him.

Hey, what's going on with Kenz because she is talking to her sisters, if you know what I mean.

He did not. He wished he could call Dare. They hadn't had real time to talk since he'd been getting married and then going on his honeymoon. Ben didn't have anyone he could talk to about relationships since Tim's longest relationship was with his laptop. Dare had briefly been his go-to guy.

He could be again if he played his cards right.

I think we're fine. But maybe not. Look, we had an incident, and it's bugging me. She is running completely wild, but I don't know if I can or should discipline her.

He typed it out and then erased it.

We're good.

Bubbles appeared immediately.

You are not. Talk to Big Tag. He won't steer you wrong when it comes to his daughters. I'm serious, man. The emojis are coming in hot and heavy, and none of them are eggplants. Talk to him. Or Coop because Kenzie is questioning if your… What does *medovaya lovushka* mean? My Russian isn't great yet.

Damn it.

It's nothing. A little joke. I'll handle it.

Was Kenzie telling her sisters she thought he was playing her for information? Had Sosa gotten into her head?

"Something wrong?" Taggart asked, staring at him like he could read minds.

Charlotte took a deep breath. "Hey, Tim, can you come help me? I was going to make us some snacks."

TJ sat up from where it had looked like he was napping. "Oh, I could eat. I'll come help."

Charlotte rumpled his hair like he was a kid she liked. From what Ben had been able to put together, she'd probably been doing it since TJ was a boy since she was his aunt.

They were all related, from what he'd learned. By blood or something else. Something that made Ben… He didn't even know what to call it. When he thought about this team, some unnamed emotion welled inside him.

It might be longing.

"You stay here. I think your uncle is going to appreciate some backup," she said.

Tim glanced his way as if to ask if it was okay to follow the gorgeous woman who also happened to be old enough to be his mom.

Ben nodded and the minute Tim was gone, TJ Taggart was in his place and Cooper McKay was taking the fourth seat, the one Charlotte had abandoned.

And here he was. Surrounded by wolves. Lying wolves.

There was a part of him that accepted and understood why they'd done it. And a boy part who wished she'd trusted him from the start.

"Dude, what is going on because the women are all texting and they are silent, and that is never a good sign," Cooper announced. "When they go silent, you are in trouble."

"I assume they're on the group text," TJ said solemnly. "The one that if a man sees it, he turns straight to stone."

Ben was confused. "If you're trying to say I did something to hurt Kenzie, I don't know what it could be. I've been polite. I made sure she had what she needed. I thought I was saving her a seat until she didn't show up."

"And you didn't go get her," TJ said with a yawn.

"Rookie move," Cooper agreed.

Yep. Definitely confused. "I'm supposed to go haul her back here with me?"

"Yes," they said in unison.

"Look, you either go and get her and drag her back or you make a place for yourself," Cooper explained.

"He has to do it a lot of nights," TJ said with what seemed like a long-suffering sigh. "He ends up in bed with me most nights."

"New friends, buddy," Taggart complained.

"What is that supposed to mean?" He was deeply confused.

"She hasn't talked to you about how Kala sometimes has bad dreams and tends to get in bed with Lou?" Cooper was the one who seemed caught off guard. Like he'd expected Ben to know. When Ben gave him nothing, he continued his explanation. "The first time she did it when she was sleeping with me, I followed her. She needs the comfort after one of those dreams, so I chose to simply slip in bed beside her. I think Kenz needs to know you're willing to pick her up and carry her back to you."

TJ nodded. "In this case, she'll think it's romantic."

"What surprises me is that you told me off for letting her run wild, but you didn't even slap her ass for that stunt she pulled today. She didn't have cover when she ran for the trees. If Gabby had been aware of her perimeters, she would have taken Kenz out with one shot," her father declared. "She wasn't dressed for combat either, if you know what I mean. She should be wearing some damn panties. Combat panties, none of those thong things." He looked around like checking if anyone could hear him. "What the hell does the word Dom mean to you, son? Because to my mind you're acting like one of her damn high school boyfriends who let her walk all over them and do crazy shit that could kill her."

Ben sat back flummoxed, but Taggart had asked the right question for the clarification he needed. "I thought we all did that thing where we're the tops in the bedroom and our subs did what they wanted everywhere else. I do believe I got a lecture from the man who trained me on not taking more from my sub than she was willing to give, and then there was a bunch of conversations about honoring feminism and consent and stuff. Also, do you think I was fine with what happened today?" He was just getting going. Now that he thought about it, this was exactly the chance he'd been waiting for. "And while we're on the subject, this is all your fault. You could have shut this shit down a long time ago. She learned all of this from you and Charlotte. You know my sub might have done something dangerous today, but your wife came out when she knew there was a shooter, and she had a baby strapped to her chest."

"How is Colton going to learn if we never put him in the line of fire? She was watching the security cams. Charlotte knew it was safe," Big Tag shot back and then waved him off. "Did you decide to explore D/s and train because you figured out Kenzie was sexually submissive? Or because you wanted to understand my team so you can use us better?" Taggart asked.

He got the feeling if he lied, Taggart would know. "Can't I have done both? I'm going to be honest, I didn't start training after the Australia op. After that op, I believed Kara wasn't a woman I could have real chemistry with since she was very aggressive and also obviously in love with Cooper."

"Because she was Kala," Cooper allowed. "And she is becoming more and more of a switch, but only in certain cases."

"I do not need to hear this," Taggart complained.

TJ was having none of it. "Then go join Auntie in the galley, Uncle. You're the one who said we needed a man talk. Coop and I can handle this. We've both known Kenz for as long as we can remember, and we understand the complexities of her situation."

A brow rose over Taggart's icy blue eyes. "Really, so you know what the actual problem is?"

"He doesn't understand his role as her Dom," Cooper replied with pure confidence.

He understood it on an intellectual level.

"He's trying to figure out when the Dom takes over and when the operative respects his partner's choices," TJ added.

And they said TJ was mere muscle. Ben pointed his way. "That. That part. You see, how am I supposed to manage her behavior around danger when going into danger is her literal job? I can't tell her not to do her job."

"Oh, I assure you that you can, and you should if she does something that could get her killed. I've stopped my wife from doing things she considered her job, though I don't think you're there yet because you haven't even played. She's been crazy about you for a long time and you're both into forbidden fruit, but you haven't spent a damn lick of time actually getting to know each other." Taggart sat back and looked a lot like a king on his throne.

"We know each other." But did they?

"Oh, I'm sure you know each other in a biblical sense. I wish I wasn't. But how many dogs did she have when she was a kid? Did she like school? How close is she with her brothers? What's her nephew's name?" Taggart peppered him with questions.

Questions he couldn't answer. Even though he knew he'd heard the nephew's name. It started with a C, or was it a K like her and her twin? He was the son of one of her brothers, but he couldn't remember which one. He was the one who should have worn a condom. He could feel his face heating, but he needed to save this. "We've talked. We would have talked a lot longer that night at Top if you hadn't sent Dare in to distract me."

He watched Taggart to see if he would admit it.

The man simply shrugged. "She wasn't ready to tell you, and we had to save her sister."

"I would have helped," he insisted. Would he feel differently if she'd reached out for his hand that night and told him her secrets? Would he feel more certain of her? Would he look at these people without suspicion?

"She wasn't ready." Taggart's voice had gone soft. "Not then."

"What changed?" He was a little worried he knew the truth, and he wasn't sure how he felt about it. "Was it because Kala was injured and can't go into the field?"

"You have to understand how careful they've been," Cooper began. "How hard they've worked to get to this point."

TJ sighed, his muscular arms crossing over his equally muscular chest. "What you have to understand is that they've pretended to be the same person for so long, I'm not sure Kenz knows who she is. I mean she knows but she doesn't."

"You are both a little brainless and extremely aware, TJ." There was an odd approval in Taggart's eyes. "He's right. Look, Kenzie and Kala have always been these odd shadows of the other. They were completely different and also capable of shutting down and becoming one person. I know everyone views Kala as the more difficult of the two, the darker one."

Cooper's head shook. "Kala has always known who she is. Kenzie… I'm worried about her being out there without her sister. Kenzie is the bubbly one, the one everyone talks to."

"Talks at," TJ corrected. "Everyone unloads all their problems on Kenzie and almost no one knows what's happening in her life. She's that woman. The one who seems to be the center of everything but is actually lonely even when they're surrounded because no one asks the sun how it's doing. They simply expect her to shine. She doesn't have a Lou."

"She's never had a Lou," Taggart said quietly. "Kenzie has always had friends around her, but she's never once had the kind of connection Kala found with Louisa Ward, and don't think I don't praise the day Boomer brought that kid into our lives. I would trade all the friends Kenz had before for her to find one half as loyal and lovely as Lou. She's had her sisters, but she has to share them. I've always known Kenzie's best friend will be the man she falls in love with, but I worry she's struggling right now and won't be able to make proper choices and won't have that one friend who could change her mind."

He'd had a friend and it wrecked his whole fucking life.

Ben took a long breath. He wasn't going to let Manny in today. Not now. He wanted to understand the gorgeous woman he couldn't stop thinking about. "How is she struggling because she seemed competent earlier today. Hence me thinking I'm kind of an asshole for considering spanking her. She did take Gabby down, and she did it without harming her."

"And you can praise her while you spank her," Cooper explained. "Look, I would never tell anyone to discipline a woman or man who didn't enjoy and choose to be disciplined, but after an op, you need a debrief and not merely about the intel collected. If you're involved, you both need to come down from the adrenaline and talk about how it made you feel."

Scared. Proud. More than a little hot. Outraged at the chances she took.

He admired her. "It's hard for me to follow my instincts."

"Because they were so very wrong once," Taggart said slowly. "Because you didn't see the threat until it was far too late. Benjamin, don't let that man ruin your life. It's admirable that you want to hunt him down and bring him to justice. But it won't matter if you lose your soul while you do it. Don't sacrifice something that could be the best thing that ever happened to you. However, you need to actually get to know her. Spend time with her that doesn't involve national security."

"You need to watch dumb movies and go to restaurants and share food and sleep in all cuddled up," TJ said. "You need to know her."

"I'm worried if you don't know her, no one really will." Cooper took a long drag off the beer he held. "Ask about her scars. Ask how she got them. You'll be surprised, and it will tell you a lot about what she's willing to do when she believes in something. How far she'll go for her team."

Her scars? She had several. They didn't bother him at all. They were proof that she was smart and she'd survived. She was beautiful, and no marks on her body could make her less.

Was her father right? They'd fought and fucked and they had talked.

Shit. He'd talked. She'd asked him questions and he'd soaked up the attention. She knew what his favorite movie was. She knew he missed his mom's meatloaf and wished he'd had siblings because he felt alone sometimes.

She seemed so perfect, so well put together.

He'd had to talk her down this morning. She'd been damn near feral.

There was a lot of rage under her happy, shiny exterior. But there was a problem.

"We're on an op. An op that doesn't exactly have an end date. We're going to be stuck in some tiny safe house living on top of one another. How am I supposed to date her like that?" He wasn't sure there would be time after this op. They would likely have to go their separate ways. This was their best chance to see if it could work.

Taggart snorted. "Uh, you have your apartment."

"Dude, The Garden is massive." TJ looked enthusiastic again. "It's like fifteen stories in the middle of London."

"It's six, and it's not that amazing," Taggart countered. "It's barely even a club."

That got his attention. "It's a club?"

He didn't have to ask what kind of club. He knew. When they'd told him they were going to London since their portion of the mission would be based in Europe, he'd envisioned a cramped brownstone or a cluster of tiny flats they would all have to share. He should have known.

Taggart nodded. "Yes, it's a lifestyle club run by one of my business partners, a man named Damon Knight. Former MI6. And yes, I've already arranged for your Master rights. I might have already known where you trained and what your trainer thinks of you."

Of course he did. He had no secrets from these people, but they kept everything from him. "And what is that?"

"He told me you were a responsible top, if a bit cold," Taggart explained as though he hadn't blown right past all boundaries. "I have my theories as to why you didn't warm up to the subs."

"Because they weren't her," Ben admitted. He needed to be honest with the man. He would apparently find everything out anyway. "I don't know that I would have trained if I hadn't met her. It's not that it doesn't speak to me. It does. I was surprised how much it did. But I trained so I could give her what she needs. I won't take another sub. If this doesn't work out, I'll be vanilla the rest of my life."

"So do you want to game plan?" Cooper asked. "Use this chance to run a real scene with her whether it's private or public."

"Private at first, but I'm open to moving into the public sphere of the club if she likes it." He knew she did. She'd walked him through her club, The Hideout, one night. She'd worn a blue corset, and she'd looked so fucking delicious he couldn't stand it. Was she sad he hadn't slapped her ass silly? Had she been expecting it and he'd been remote because he couldn't stop thinking about the fact that she could have died? "I have my own room?"

"Yeah." Cooper ran logistics. He would know the layout and what they would need, and he would likely be the one to assign spaces. "All the couples are together. Kenzie offered to bunk down with… I'm not allowed to say her name out loud or Kala will appear, and it's a whole ritual. I've been told it's how Appalachian witches toss out demons. I'm worried that she knows that."

Ah, so they were going to be working with Lucy Brooke Flanders. He'd witnessed some of the way Kala interacted with the young woman she called her nemesis.

Taggart stood up. "You and me both, buddy. If you are going to discuss scenes, then it is my time to join my wife."

Taggart walked off and he was left with Cooper and TJ.

It was kind of nice to be one of the guys when the "guys" weren't psychopathic narcissists. He'd held back, but it might be better to play this straight. To be honest with them. Let them help him. It could make them trust him more.

Yeah, it didn't have anything to do with the fact that he liked these guys. Or he would if he let himself.

The same with really getting to know Kenzie Taggart. He should know the target.

"So how would you play it?" Ben asked.

"Well, I think she might appreciate the element of surprise," Cooper began.

Cooper leaned in and Ben listened.

* * * *

Damon Knight was an attractive man around her dad's age, and like her father, he could truly express his disappointment. Sometimes Kenzie wondered if they taught that particular look in the military. Or in Dad School. "Tag? Are you serious? Did you bring two wanted criminals into my club?"

Thank the universe. A shudder of relief went through Kenzie. She was worried she would spend the entire rest of the day focused on how Ben wasn't interested in her anymore. Now she could watch her dad and Damon go at it. They could be amusing. Of course, anything was more amusing than sitting in her own head right now.

Maybe the sex hadn't been as good for him as it was for her.

Maybe she'd misread him entirely and sleeping with her was nothing more than a conquest. A way to get back at her.

But damn it, that wasn't how it was supposed to go. He was supposed to be a good guy.

So she was deeply grateful for Damon's hissy fit.

"First off, from what I can tell they're not wanted. Their organization has been careful to keep them off the authorities' radar, and I didn't exactly call in the cops. So no Red Notices on the girls." Her dad gave him a grin. "And last time it was way more, buddy. Last time I dropped off five of them. You can't count Owen. He was yours already. Those two young women are way better at hiding their crimes than the Lost Boys. Hey, Pen. How's it going?"

"Good afternoon, Ian, Charlotte. Lovely to see you. Well, I can tell you that Sosa is definitely native Russian, but I would say she's not from a city." Penny Knight had been MI6, too. She'd was an expert in languages and codes. "And Gabby is French. Probably from one of the southern regions. It's hard to tell because they were taken so early, but some of their native accents remain. I'll know a bit more when we have extensive interviews tomorrow."

Damon looked down at his wife as though he'd expected way more support. "There are no interviews. Tag is not dumping them on me. Not this time. Nothing good came from the last time."

"Whoa. Rude, boss." Ariel Adisa Seeger walked in dressed for work in a pencil skirt and silk blouse that showed off her graceful curves. "I got a rather nice husband and two kids from that adventure. I won't mention this to your longest-term employee. You know Robert runs a good portion of your business now."

"Who is she?" Ben sat beside her. It was the first time he'd sat by her the whole way here. He hadn't even gotten in the same car when they'd made the transfer from the airfield to The Garden.

It had been a shitty flight where her sister told her to be patient. Well, Tash had. Tash had taken time out of her own honeymoon to give her advice. Kala told her to go get her man and tell him if he didn't do what she wanted, he could jump out of the plane again. He'd survived it the first time. Somehow, she didn't think reminding him that her twin had nearly gotten him killed would help the situation.

She'd taken neither way, trying to hold on to that kiss in the conference room. He'd been open then, but he'd shut down again.

Professional. Lou had offered up that explanation. Ben was being professional and it would be all right the minute they closed the doors and they were in private again.

He was not going to fit in if that was his excuse. There was no professional here. She was pretty sure her parents had a quickie in the bedroom on the plane and that TJ hauled Lou somewhere.

It was going to be a while until they had any privacy at all. If he even wanted privacy with her. She'd slept restlessly in her seat on the overnight to London, and now they were sitting in The Garden's conference room and her parents were right. She couldn't think straight because she was thinking about him.

She leaned his way, trying to be as professional as he was. "Her name is Dr. Adisa, though technically her last name is Seeger. She's married to one of Damon's investigators. Robert Seeger. Funny story. He was taken by a crazy doctor lady and had his memory wiped along with some other dudes and my dad hid them all here. They're mostly spread out across the globe now, but Robert stayed in London as Damon expanded this part of the company. He's in charge of all personal security. I don't think Damon wants a second round, though. I'm not sure how Sosa and Gabby would fit in here."

The Garden had changed over the years. She'd been coming here since she was a kid. Damon and Penny mostly lived in the country, though they kept a flat on the top floor of this space. Two of their kids had flats here. Oliver and Samantha Knight were active MI6 operatives based out of London, and Lucy Brooke Flanders had a place here when she was in Europe.

She'd had a perfectly nice flat in Liverpool, but Huisman had wrecked that. Naturally.

"She's a doctor?" Ben asked.

"She's a psychiatrist. Think of her as The Garden's Eve McKay. She's their profiler. I'm sure she'll spend a lot of time with Sosa and Gabby over the next few days. How was your flight?" The assassin girls were already moved into their own room. They'd been alternately wide eyed and in awe of everything, and then shut down like they were certain it would all go wrong and there was nothing they could do about it.

Like Bud Two had been when she'd picked him up from the shelter. He'd been adorable behind the cage but tentative when she and Kala first got him home. He'd bedded down in a corner, and it had been days of coaxing him before he gradually became the big, beloved goofball he was today.

Stupid empathy.

Ben sat back as the dads started arguing and Penny and Ariel talked about the new girls and how they would figure out if they could be trusted. "It was fine. Did you sleep? I did. The Agency takes care of your team. Tim and I usually get shoved in a military transport or we fly commercial."

It was nice to know he'd gotten good rest. "Oh, that's not the Agency. That's my dad. Technically we have access to two private jets. That was the big one. We share them with my Uncle Adam's company."

"He's the one who developed the facial recognition software, right?"

She nodded. He must have been talking to the guys. She'd notice him deep in conversation with Cooper and TJ before she'd tried to nap. "Yes."

"I find it so interesting that a rich girl ended up at the Agency," he murmured.

She didn't feel like a rich girl. Oh, she recognized her privilege. She'd grown up in a big house, never worried about where her next meal was coming from or if she'd have a place to stay. Her parents owned a couple of vacation houses, but they shared with the family. It was all a big family, and when one struggled the rest helped.

Maybe that was what truly made her a rich girl. But the way Ben said it gave her a bad feeling. She stared straight ahead as her dad and Damon kept arguing and her mom set up the presentation.

It was an actual physical ache in her chest that he wasn't who she thought he was. Or maybe that he didn't care about her the way she did him.

"Just bored, I guess." She took a sip of her tea and wished her older sister was here. Tasha could walk her through this. Tasha would tell her to be patient, that they'd put this man through a lot of confusion and he needed some time.

But no. She'd walked right into his arms without a single thought.

"I wasn't trying to offend you. I suppose I was surprised at your home life. Most of us don't go into the whole spy gig because our families are great and supportive," he whispered, staring straight forward as well. "But you know about my family. You know I haven't talked to them for years. You know they blame me for pretty much everything. Your father thinks I haven't tried to get to know you, and in some ways he's right. In some he's wrong. You wouldn't have told me the truth until recently."

"I would have told you as much as I could." She felt tired. Infinitely tired. "I didn't lie about things I liked or experiences I had."

"You didn't talk about yourself. You let me drone on and on."

"Because I was interested in who you were," she replied quietly. "You've had some time to think about things. I guess last night didn't mean the same to us."

"The night before. Last night was the flight here and we didn't talk, but I assure you it was meaningful." He sat up straighter as the door came open and a man and a woman walked through. The man was large and broad, dressed in a slick suit with movie star good looks and an arrogance that covered an actual heart and softness that Oliver Knight didn't like to admit existed inside him when he was in work persona. The trouble was he was always in work persona now.

And there was Sami. Samantha Knight was petite with a curvy body and the sweetest-looking face that belied her deep relationship with violence. Her blonde hair was a halo around her head. No one would call her a Bratz doll. Angelic. She was heavenly looking.

There were men who preferred that. Oh, she knew if Ben spent any time at all with Sami, she would show him how not angelic she was, but he was looking at her, and Kenz had to wonder if she was more his type.

His fiancée had been a delicate-looking blonde. She'd spent too much time staring at Deanna's picture.

Kenzie was well aware she was most men's type on a physical level. She had a banging bod and a pretty face. There was something wild about her that drew them in, but they didn't stay.

Because men didn't marry the Bratz doll. They all wanted a respectable Barbie. She was a Marilyn. Not a Jackie.

"She looks like the translator," Ben murmured.

"I'll send you dossiers." He should have them since they would be working together. Well, since he was on the team. She was starting to think it wasn't smart for them to actually be partners. Sami and Oliver knew Europe better than she did, so it might be best to split them up and pair them with members of her team.

And then she could figure out what the hell to do with her life.

Her sister was moving on. It was like she didn't even miss the field, and it was supposed to be their dream. Mostly hers.

Shit. Did she feel abandoned by her sister?

Kala had always had Lou, but there was a place for Kenzie. Now Cooper took that spot. Tasha had Dare.

Was she trying so desperately to find someone so she wouldn't be alone?

She needed a session.

Would she be the worst person in the world to call home and ask one of the Doms she worked with to fly all the way to London so he could spank her ass and she could cry and get the tiniest bit of clarity?

It wasn't like Gabriel Lodge had a nine-to-five job. He could even bring one of his "friends" and they could both top her since Gabe liked to keep a male switch around. He was a deeply fluid man in a sexual sense.

"I would rather hear it from you." Ben turned her way.

"Oh, god." Kala pushed back from the table, and her expression shifted to one of general horror. "It's coming. I can feel it."

Their father turned. "You are not performing another exorcism. Do you even remember you're not Catholic?"

"Kala, this is ridiculous," their mother complained.

"What's happening?" Tim asked, and then his face lit up from behind his laptop. He'd seemed to be working, politely ignoring the tension between Ben and Kenzie, but now he was animated and happy. "Is it the chick with all the goats? Kala hated her. I thought she was fun."

"I thought you looked nice tied up and ready for slaughter," Kala shot back.

Lou sighed. "I'll get the sprayer."

Kala pointed her best friend's way. "I melted down the sprayer. Both of the ones in your luggage and the one my dad snuck in. I kept one and I'm filling it with holy water so I can smoke her out when I need to."

"How should I handle her?" Ben asked.

Lucy. Lucy might be a good sounding board. Despite what her twin thought, Lucy was forthright and tended to be brutally honest about what she saw, though she never meant it unkindly. "Ignore her. Kala's always had a problem with Luce."

Kala hissed—actually hissed—as Lucy walked in and immediately rolled her deep brown eyes. She was in jeans and a sweater, her long dark hair in braids.

Kenzie stood and walked right up to her. "Hey. Missed you."

"I'm going to vomit," Kala muttered.

"No, you're not," her husband assured her. "Nor do you need to make the sign of the cross, love."

Oliver laughed as he settled into the seat on the other side of Kenzie. "I forgot. Those two are like oil and water. This is going to be fun. LB is so reasonable most of the time. It'll be fun to see the unflappable get flapped."

Sami sat down on the other side of Tim. "I hope you're the one assigned to escort them around. I'll take the Canadians."

She winked Ben's way.

Maybe Sami was the one who needed a damn exorcism.

Lucy hugged her tight. "Hey, Kenz. Missed you, too. I have so many stories to tell you, but don't lose your shit on Sami. She doesn't mean anything by it, and she's going through some things."

Kenzie took a deep breath and nodded. She kept her voice low. "Okay."

"Ladies, can the reunion wait? I've heard the younger crowd is planning on playing tonight. I'd like to get the assignments done so we all can get some rest," Damon said, taking his place at one end of the table.

"We'll talk tonight. We can order some curry and I'll tell you about my new Highland cows and about all the whacky shit Poppy's doing." Lucy gave her a big smile, the kind Kenzie rarely saw on her face.

Kala didn't realize Lucy was her mirror. Or maybe she did and it rankled.

Kenzie nodded and moved back to her seat.

Oliver winked her way. "You can share with me, love. It looks like we're short a chair."

If he wasn't such a heinous flirt, she would ask Oliver for a session. He was a good top, but he did like to get into his subs' panties, and she wasn't going there. Ever. She sank down into the seat beside Ben.

"Somehow I think the long-term D/s couples will work it out," she murmured. She noticed Ben looking Oliver's way, but he didn't say anything.

Lou was already on TJ's lap, her fiancé having snatched her up at the first mention of the missing seat. Lou simply reached over and grabbed her laptop. He grinned Cooper's way because Coop had been reaching for Kala. "You snooze you lose."

Lucy kept a careful distance between her and Kala, although she managed to shoot her the finger before she sat next to Ariel.

"Excellent," Damon began. "Charlotte, why don't you start?"

The lights dimmed, and she felt Ben move beside her, settling back.

Her gut twisted because he seemed so far away. Maybe this whole epic love story thing wasn't all it was cracked up to be. She didn't like this desperate feeling going through her body.

It pretty much sucked. Did she want to be the sad girl chasing after a man who couldn't forgive her?

No. No, she really didn't.

She was in love with this man but if he could shut her down so easily and so quickly, maybe her father was right and they needed time to think. They weren't on the same page. They weren't even in the same book. She was in some spy romance where everything ended in happily ever after and he was in a thriller where the hero probably died sacrificing himself for the good of the world and to assuage his guilt.

He would never choose her over what he considered to be his destiny.

"All right," her mom began. "I sent you some information, but this is what we found in broad strokes. One of the treasure troves we got out of the mission to Nepal was a lot of information on Disrupt's financials. Thank you, Lou and Tim. I genuinely don't believe he thought you could get to that information."

Kenzie took a deep breath as her mom started to go over all the myriad ways Disrupt made its money. Including a corporation located in France that Sosa had recently told her ran the organization she belonged to. Had been kidnapped by.

All in all it was a daunting report and showed what they were up against.

"They have billions?" Sami asked, obviously incredulous.

"Yes," Dad replied. "If you add up all the property, stock, cash, investments, it's considerable. Huisman won't have any trouble buying whatever he needs with one exception."

"The bombs." It was time to stop worrying about her love life and concentrate. "Shannon Reed managed to make the ones he's been using without giving up how she programs them. He can build them but he can't replicate the protocols for detonation that would make the bombs even deadlier. He has used them but not in the fashion he would like to."

"He didn't kill as many people as he wanted," Ben said flatly. "He's been experimenting since he lost Shannon's skills. He thought she'd properly primed those bombs, but she tricked him, and not even the couple he got out of her work the way he intended."

"She wasn't going to blow up half a country," Cooper pointed out. "Not even to save herself and her sons. My biological mother is done causing harm. She never meant to in the first place. If he caught her today, she would force him to kill her rather than work for him. The only reason she pretended to go along with him was to spare Devi."

Which was why it was a good thing she was in Colorado along with Kenzie's brothers and nephew and cousin. They could use Zach, but she understood the need to protect family.

Tim nodded, taking up his partner's explanation. "We believe the recent attacks on subways in Hanoi and the transportation systems in Kinshasa are all Disrupt."

"Kinshasa is the capitol of the Congo. It's a hub for minerals and gems coming out of Africa," Lucy said, her eyes on the folder in front of her. "From what I've learned, Disrupt wants to do what its name says. Disrupt established authority and in particular unsettle the economies of First World countries by decimating supply lines. On the surface they say they're doing it to make the world a more fair place, but it's quite the opposite. Vietnam has one of the world's largest deposits of rare earth metals, and they would like to disrupt those chains so their companies can buy them up and keep them for themselves."

Rare earth metals powered the batteries for electric vehicles and had many other high tech uses. A battle for control of them was already beginning.

"But the authorities managed to stop the worst of those attacks, though they did send several of the world's markets into a tailspin," her mother continued. "He's close to being able to destabilize whole parts of the global economy."

"Because he's stayed away from the First World," Oliver said. "He's able to grease the wheels in most of the places he's attacked."

Her father's head shook. "Don't be so arrogant to think he can't do it right here in the UK. As we all found out in Liverpool a couple of months ago. Or the States. We have plenty of assholes who would love to take Huisman's funds. I believe this is all a big play for money."

"You're wrong." Ben held up a hand as if asking for time to make his point. "I will give you that it's about money for his partners. They would love to tank the world economy and waltz in and buy up everything they can in the fire sale, but for Manny it's different."

"You believe Emmanual Huisman is a sociopath," Lucy said quietly.

"I agree with him." Ariel gave Ben a nod. "I've looked over his records and I believe he was always a sociopath, though one who is excellent at mirroring the people around him. He learned to hide his predilections. He's well aware that his thoughts and actions are not considered right in civilized society. I believe his fixation on Ian began when his father was murdered by Levi Green."

"If I could kill that motherfucker again, I would," Dad announced.

Ariel ignored the outburst. "He's fixated on Ian and all the people around him. He's fixated on Ben, but in a different fashion."

"I assure you he hates me every bit as much as he does Ian," Ben announced, and there was some offense in his tone.

Like he needed to be the one Huisman hated most.

"I don't know about that." Ariel sounded almost sympathetic. "I would like to know more, but from what I can tell he's had many chances to kill you."

"Manny enjoys playing with his victims," Ben insisted.

"Huisman is a violent misogynist," Ariel continued. "I actually liken him far more to a cult leader mentality, but he's also a bit of a misanthrope, which is why almost everyone around him is paid. You told me the girls had a violent reaction to seeing a picture of him."

"They did." Her mother had been deeply worried about the young women. "Sosa said he's an active client in all sides of the business. She's worked for him before and he's beaten the shit out of her. I don't like to think about what he does when he's in the brothel portion of the house."

Damon sighed. "Damn it. They're kidnapping young women and training them to be assassins or sex workers? Here in Europe?"

Penny reached over and patted her husband's hand. "They are, my love, which is why we're going to have a new challenge."

Damon's head fell back and he cursed.

"Dad, Sami, and I will handle the heavy lifting," Oliver explained. "Ariel and Mum will deal with Sosa and Gabby and the others when we figure out how many there are and what it's going to take to free them."

"Hey, I'm working on this, too," Lucy added. "I've got feelers out. I suspect between what the girls know and what I can discover, we can at the very least devise a plan to extract their friends. Also, from what I've discerned, it's not just assassins or rape victims. Don't call them sex workers. Sex workers choose their professions and provide something a lot of people need. They're rape victims. Slaves. Sosa was trained to be an assassin, but they are pretty much a one-stop criminal shop if you're looking for young women."

Tim held up a hand. "I would think they would want some dudes, too. No offense to the many deadly women in this room, but men are still better at killing. All the stats prove that."

"I would agree with you on a mass scale," her father began, "but they're not looking for some shooter. They have their weapons of mass destruction. I talked to Sosa on the plane. She admitted to a couple of her victims. All political or business enemies of the men who paid for her services. Every one of them needed surgical precision."

"Which is why I question the ham-handedness of how she handled you," Kala pointed out. "Dad, I understand what you're saying and I get why Mom wants to believe them, but blowing up your car in a public parking lot is not her usual MO. If we believe her, she's good with poisons. Two of those assassinations she's claiming were labeled natural deaths because she did such a good job. So why change it up and cause a massive scene?"

"Because the other thing she does is research on her targets," her mom said quietly and her hand covered her dad's. "I think she knew she might have a shot at getting Ian to listen to her. I think she wanted to get caught. She's worried about one of her sisters, worried she won't last much longer."

"You think this is all a play to get us involved?" Lou asked.

It was a smart one since there was no way they could ignore the situation. "I'm trying to see the advantage to Huisman planting Sosa here. I saw her. She wasn't playing. She's terrified of him."

"Or she's an excellent actress," Ben countered. "It would be exactly like Manny to embed someone with the group that's investigating him. And you should understand he would know exactly how to slip her in. He's never tried to kill Mr. Taggart before. He doesn't need to. We haven't really threatened him."

"I assure you the data we got in Nepal threatens him," her father replied. "I know Charlie thinks he can't know we have it, but I suspect he knows and this is all chaos to distract us from what he's hiding in one of these locations. And before you tell me he's likely looking for something, something either Sosa or Gabby could get from us, that's why we moved. I didn't want them around sensitive material, and The Garden has far better security than I can provide since I don't live in a club."

"We've got eyes on them at all times," Damon promised.

"And if I'm uncomfortable having an obvious spy around?" Ben asked.

Her father simply shrugged. "Then you probably picked the wrong business to be in, Benjamin. We are working with you, but you should understand I'm in charge of this operation. CSIS is more than welcome to conduct their own investigation if you don't appreciate how I'm handling it. You have the same intel. You can do this on your own."

Tim held up a hand. "I vote for sticking with the team. Like it's nice here. I totally believe this British dude can handle two young women."

Damon huffed. "Then you haven't met some of the women I've dealt with."

Ben's jaw had tightened. "I have my assignment, Mr. Taggart. I'll do my job and if you don't want my advice, I can keep my mouth shut, but you should understand that I won't allow the fact that you let Manny play on your emotions and your history to hurt me or mine."

"Agreed." The tension between her father and Ben was palpable.

Kala looked from one to the other. "Well, this is awkward." She looked to Cooper. "Dude, thanks for being cool with my dad. This whole marriage thing would be a lot if you two were always on the verge of punching each other."

"Did you seriously dude me?" But Cooper looked amused.

Kala was missing a couple of clues. "Then it's good there's no marriage thing. Mom, I think you should present a couple of the properties we've identified. It's why we're here. I'm with Damon. We should get our assignments and get some rest. Maybe we'll be in better moods then."

Her mother went back to discussing the properties they'd discovered and how they were going to split them up to investigate. There were sixteen sites they were particularly interested in, including one that Sosa claimed she remembered from her training days.

"You okay?" Oliver leaned over and whispered.

Not really. Her mother would tell her she needed to be patient and that she could handle some of his anger. Her mom would point out that she'd survived her father's wrath and they'd had so many sweet years together.

But her father hadn't been obsessed with Emmanuel Huisman. Her father would have given up revenge or even justice if it meant keeping her mom safe, and Ben had proven time and time again he would risk anything for a chance to take down his white whale.

Maybe it wasn't an epic love story. Maybe it was a tragic one.

Maybe it was time to grow up and stop insisting that fairy tales were real.

Love wasn't something she could force.

Her mother handed out assignments. Cooper and Kala would go with Sami. Lou and TJ would be with Lucy, and Ben and Kenzie would have Oliver as their European escort. They were going to Scotland where Huisman kept a small castle that might be where he stored his records.

"I think Tim should accompany Ben." She wasn't a masochist.

"Oh, I'll come, too," Tim said in his normal cheery fashion.

"I wouldn't go without Tim," Ben said. "Though I think we would be more comfortable with Lucy."

Not what she'd meant. "I was thinking I would stay here. I would like to continue interviewing Sosa and Gabby and prep a possible mission to get their friends out."

Ben suddenly decided she was worth looking at. "No."

She felt her eyes widen. "What is that supposed to mean?"

His face was a gorgeous cold mask. "It means I agreed to work with you, not with MI6."

"Cool," Kala said. "You can come with me then."

Ben didn't even look back at her. "No."

"I think I'll take the assignment I was given," Oliver interjected. "It's been forever since I got to work with my cutest American cousin. Though that's what we call each other. No blood between us, right, gorgeous?"

She rolled her eyes and got ready to give Oliver an earful, but Ben stood up.

"We could ditch the Canadian and work on our own," Oliver suggested.

Ben gripped the back of his suit and hauled him up bodily.

It was violent. It was sexy in a way it should not be. In a way that was dangerous since the man had spent the last twenty-four hours ignoring her. So why the hell was he jealous?

"Hey," Oliver began.

Ben punched him in the face and then let him drop. He turned to her father. "I'm not taking that asshole with me. He'll be far too busy hitting on my sub to protect her. We'll take Lucy with us. And Kenzie will be coming with me."

Oliver turned and started to throw a punch, but Ben simply put out an arm and blocked it then swept out with one leg and put Oliver on the ground. He stood over him.

"Mine," Ben said, his voice dark and deep. "You look at her again and I won't hold back."

It was exactly the kind of thing that should have her panting after him, but she couldn't forget the coldness he'd wrapped himself in after taking all her warmth.

She was a prize, something he could toy with for a while before he decided if she was worth keeping around.

Or he was planning some revenge on her. She could see that, too.

Her father stood. "Well, on that note, I'll take my wife and settle in. We'll meet again tomorrow morning to talk logistics. Kenz, figure out what you want to do."

"She's coming with me," Ben insisted, stepping back and letting Oliver up.

Oliver straightened his suit. "I don't think this is going to work. I never realized Canadians were so humorless. Fine, then. I'll go with Louisa. I've always appreciated a smart bird."

"I will kill you," TJ vowed.

"Or I could stay back and help out around The Garden," Oliver offered. "The club is open for the younger set tonight since we'll be out of my father's hair in a day or two."

Damon sighed and agreed. "I think Tag and I should talk anyway. We'll head out to dinner and discuss the situation with his assassins. I'm afraid the younger set is a bit too much drama for me."

Her father stood and held a hand out for her mother. "Ben, that was the smartest thing you've done since I met you. Ollie's a menace. Kenzie, let me know where you think you can best benefit this team."

Her mom hesitated. "Maybe we should talk, Kenzie and I."

Lucy stood, holding her laptop to her chest. "I'll take care of her. I'll get her settled in and we can spend the evening watching Netflix and drinking some truly delicious wine. My mom brought it back from New Zealand. It's completely ethically sourced."

Yep, that was probably her night.

"She's staying with me," Ben declared. "I already had her things moved. Tim can use your spare room."

Lucy frowned. "Uhm…"

Tim held up a hand. "I already found one of the privacy rooms. It's cool. I don't mind sleeping with a bunch of sex toys and a spectacular amount of lube. The bed's nice."

Oh, well that was lovely. He'd ignored her all day and then expected her to comply with his wishes?

Who the fuck did he think she was?

Kala stood, Cooper beside her as everyone seemed to understand the conference was over. "You got this, sis, or should I take out the trash? I told you I thought you needed to make yourself plain. Canada there can be thick headed."

Kenzie stood as well. It was time to have a chat with her very confused crush.

Chapter Ten

Staying away from her had likely been a mistake, but he'd needed space.

The fact that Kenzie's father still wouldn't listen to him when it came to Huisman rankled in a way it shouldn't.

And then that English fucker flirted with her like he had some kind of right.

The door closed behind Kala, who had given him a look that could freeze fire. Lucy Brooke had done the same before walking away.

If they united against him, would it be a miracle or the beginning of the apocalypse?

He turned and stared at her. Kenzie looked tired. Gorgeous. She was always the most stunning woman in any room, but there was a weariness to her that pulled at him. "You're still tired. Let's go back to our room and you can take a nap."

Her head shook. "I'm not sharing a room with you, Ben. You've made yourself plain over the last twenty-four hours. I understand. I'm not going to argue with you or try to sway you. I think it would be best if we worked separately. I have some pretty big feelings when it comes to you, and I need some time to process and start letting go."

He had no fucking intention of being let go. "What is that supposed to mean?"

She didn't control this.

"It means you're not ready to have a relationship with me, and maybe I'm not ready either." Her voice was a quiet monotone. "I think I've made this more than it really is. My sisters and friends are all getting married and you're the first man I've ever been…intense about."

"I doubt that." She was an intense person. She was weird and emotional, and he was trying to figure out how to handle her.

Because it was important to handle her. He'd needed some space and he was still angry with her, but he couldn't stand the thought of her walking away. She wasn't going to walk away from him. He wouldn't allow it. He realized suddenly that he would take her away if he had to.

She made him volatile. Vulnerable.

"Well, I'm a liar, right? It's what I do."

He was confused. He stared at her across the table. He'd moved when he'd taken that British ass down. "What is this about?"

A brow rose over her eyes. "You haven't been avoiding me? You didn't ask me to sit with you on the plane. I would have, you know."

He had avoided her because he needed a plan. He needed space. And if she gave it to him, he would hate it. He would reject it. "Kenzie, I wanted to talk to your dad. I'm afraid I'm not an experienced top and I'm trying to figure out how to handle you."

"You don't have to handle me. You can talk to me. You could ask me, but instead you chose to ignore me."

He could never ignore her. The whole time they were in the air, he'd been deeply aware of where she was. "I didn't ignore you. I needed space."

Her eyes closed, and he saw her fists clench. She took a deep breath.

He wanted so much to know what she was thinking.

She told him to ask.

"What's going through your brain right now? I don't think I would like it."

Her eyes came open and her chin tilted up as she stood. "I am attempting to not play to my baser instincts, Benjamin Parker. They tell me I should tell you to take all the space you like and storm out and go down to the dungeon tonight and find a hot Dom to play with."

He moved quickly, getting into her space and making sure she didn't follow through on those bad instincts. If she walked out, he wasn't sure he wouldn't follow, throw her over his shoulder and take her right out of this glorious building that had been built for work and more importantly, for pleasure. It didn't matter that she'd lied or maybe it did. Maybe some of this was pure revenge.

It didn't feel like revenge.

It felt necessary. Like if she walked away, he wouldn't be able to breathe.

He reached out and gently but firmly gripped the back of her neck. "You are not going anywhere."

"Don't think you can handle me the way you handled Oliver," she shot back. "That was unnecessary, by the way. I grew up with him. He's teasing me."

"Have you ever played with him?" Jealousy was a real thing, and it thudded in his chest. The thought of Kenzie with that overly privileged player made him damn near see red.

"No," she replied. "This show of jealousy doesn't make a lot of sense."

"I think it makes perfect sense, princess," he shot back.

She shook her head and broke his hold with a twist of her body, reminding him she was well trained. "Don't call me that."

"You are a princess," he replied.

"You don't mean it in a nice way. I get it. I hurt you and you're getting a little of your own back, but I'm not going to comply because I feel bad."

She was supposed to be the easy one, but there was a lot of complexity that got missed when compared to her far more difficult sister. "Do you? Feel bad?"

"I hate that it hurt you, but this is the job. I didn't exactly meet Ben Parker in that bar in Sydney."

"Oh, you didn't meet me at all, baby. Your twin did." He had more questions. It was odd. Now that they were alone again, he felt more himself. It was impossible to shut down when he was alone with her. When all the stress of her family and their jobs melted away, he felt for her. She was the only person in the world who genuinely made him feel again, and he wasn't sure if he loved her for it or hated her. "Why did you come the second day? Did you switch off days?"

She crossed her arms over her chest, a defensive move. "Not at all. She was supposed to play Kara for the entire Australian op. I tried to steal the role any time I knew you would be there. I watched you through Lou's glasses and I wanted to be near you. It was pretty much love at first sight for me, but I get it now. It was always a job for you."

He sighed, genuinely confused. "Baby, I was trying to be professional around your dad. I honestly don't know how to deal with this. I was so fucking angry with you for running into the line of fire. I wanted to pull your pants down right then and there and slap your ass silly, but how can I punish you for doing your job? Honestly, I worry about using the word punishment at all."

Her shoulders relaxed slightly. "It would have been better to do that than ignore me."

"I can't ignore you, Kenz. How can I ignore someone I think about twenty-four seven? All day. You're in my head. At night you're in my dreams. The good ones. The bad ones. You're there and you have been since that day at the hotel."

"I don't know if I can trust you," she said quietly.

He took a deep breath and tried to figure out how his younger self would handle her. He'd been confident once. He'd been the guy who could get any girl, though he hadn't tried. He'd genuinely been happier in a relationship than he had when he played the field. It's just that the most important relationships of his life went so very wrong.

So when he'd met a woman he thought was extraordinary, he'd basked in her attention and gave her nothing of himself.

He'd been more open with actual targets of a mission than he'd been with this woman who seemed to be the center of his world for the last year or so.

He reached for her hand, and this time she didn't step back. He'd gone from professional mode, since her father had been sitting there, to violent, jealous asshole mode and given her none of his tenderness. None of his charm.

He was still reeling but he needed to get his ass under control. She was important to this delicate state of his mission.

She was important to him.

Could he find that part of himself? Would looking for it make some kind of a difference because he was starting to wonder if anything would matter at the end of this op if he didn't come out of it with her.

He let his whole body soften. "You can trust me not to hurt you. I never have and I never would."

"I was hurt today," she insisted.

He pulled her into his arms. "I'm sorry. I didn't mean to. I'm struggling to figure out how to handle this. I care about you. I'm still upset that you lied to me, but I'm wrapping my head around why. I can't stay away from you, but I also can't toss out everything that happened between us. Can we take a day or two and try to figure out how to be together?"

"I can't if you're going to go cold on me any time you're confused or feel vulnerable." She held herself apart.

He didn't like the space between them. "I don't remember how to be comfortable being vulnerable. I'm not even all that close to Tim. I call him my friend, but we don't hang out. We don't tell each other anything important. The closest I've come in years to a real friend is Dare."

"Dare is your friend." She softened and her arms went around him.

He could smell her shampoo and feel the warmth of her skin. If she was playing him in that moment, he didn't want to know. He wanted her comfort to be real. "He was Brian Peters' friend. I'm afraid he's just starting to know me. If I even know who the fuck I am anymore."

Her head on his shoulder felt right. "We can lose ourselves so easily."

"We don't have to be in Scotland for a few days. Can we take some time to be you and me for a while? Can I feel out how we're going to be together while we're also working together?"

Her head came up. "We should have a contract. I think that would help. I can have someone from The Hideout send over a basic contract and we can add what we need."

He liked a contract. "Is it going to include me getting to spank your ass red when you scare the fuck out of me?"

Those lips curled up ever so slightly, and he knew he had her. "Don't threaten me with a good time." She sobered a bit. "You should understand that withdrawing affection is a hard limit for me. If you go cold again and won't talk to me, I will walk."

"You didn't ask me to talk," he pointed out.

"Would you have?"

In this he would be completely honest with her. "Yes. If I had known how much it hurt you, I would have put aside my discomfort and talked to you. I've been alone for a long time. I don't turn to other people when I'm down because I can't trust them."

"No, you can trust some of us. You haven't figured out how to manage the trauma you've been through. Right now the only way you handle it is to put up walls, but that's not a life, Ben."

She wasn't wrong, but he also wasn't sure what else to do except take these days with her. "Did you sleep on the plane?"

"Not well."

At least he could start proving to her that he could take care of her. He leaned over and scooped her up. "Then we're taking a nap and we'll talk about a contract and tonight we're going to play. And you're coming with me. I'm not going to be able to think straight if you're not with me on this. I'm sure as fuck not letting you run around Scotland with that massive ass."

She didn't fight him at all, simply let him carry her. "He's a childhood friend."

"I don't care," he admitted as he managed to get the door open. "I don't like the way he looks at you. You might see him as a childhood friend, but he doesn't feel the same."

She yawned and rubbed her head against his shoulder. "He does, but he's got a whole lot of baggage. It's all right. I shall keep him at arm's length. Ben, I don't want anyone else. I haven't for a long time, which is why I'm asking you not to break my heart."

The soft voice, the vulnerability…it threatened to break his heart, and he'd been so sure he no longer had one. He'd been certain he'd cut it out and tossed it away. She was supposed to be safe. She was beautiful and sexy and had this part of herself he could never accept, so it was okay to lust after her.

This woman in his arms had none of her twin's darkness. She was all light, a light that could lead him somewhere.

She could break him utterly.

"I won't." He hoped it wasn't a lie.

He hoped when whatever happened, she wouldn't break his, too.

* * * *

"Okay, I now understand." Sosa looked around the luxurious dressing room. She was wearing a T-shirt that was too big for her and sweats

Kenzie was certain were tied a couple of times around her too-thin waist. "You are all the perverts. I expect this of the Bratz doll, but you seem so normal."

She was going to have to deal with Sosa.

Was there any way Ben was right? Was Sosa a snake Huisman had sent in to bite them all? Or a victim who thought she might have found a way out?

She could be the woman who brought Sosa to justice. Or take on a big sister role. Either way the comments were going to stop.

She kind of wished Kala hadn't destroyed all those spray bottles.

Kenzie walked into the dressing room and saw who she was talking to.

Both whos. Sophy Weston and Vivian McKay were seated at adjoining mirrors. Sophy was straightening her dark hair while Vivi finished polishing her makeup.

"I am happy with my pervertedness," Sophy explained with a shrug. "Though it does make my dad go green, and he doesn't do that often. You would think the amount of times the poor man's had to clean me up that he wouldn't care anymore, but no, the sight of me in a corset makes him ill."

"I'm not a pervert." Vivi put a hand to her chest like she was delicate and might faint. "I'm hurt."

She was not. Vivi was kind of a badass. She'd been in England for the last couple of years going to grad school where she was following in her mother's footsteps and studying psychology. She worked at McKay-Taggart and Knight part time and shared a flat with Kenzie's cousin Sophy.

Who looked…healthy, and that felt like a miracle.

"Don't listen to her, Sosa." Kala walked in behind Kenzie. "She's a happy pervert. You've got a terrible relationship with sex because of the whole 'kidnapped as a child and forced to grow up in a brothel' thing. It's fine. You'll find the right dick and it will be miraculous."

Vivi's jaw dropped. "Kala. Seriously?"

Kala looked to their cousin with a shrug like she didn't see the problem. "Or pussy. I've heard pussies can be magical, too. Honestly, or a vibe. Lou used to cuddle with hers when the nights got lonely, but then she got together with TJ and now they're happy. But TJ does still cuddle a hot dog. He gets hungry at night. It's weird."

"Kala, new friends." Kenz wasn't sure they were friends at all.

But then she also wasn't certain Ben Parker wasn't playing her for all she was worth.

It hadn't felt that way. The afternoon had been lovely. He'd taken her straight to bed, but he hadn't stripped her and spread her wide for himself. He'd cuddled her and asked her about her family. He'd listened to her stories until she'd fallen asleep, and he'd still been holding her when he'd woken her and told her it was time for dinner.

He'd sat beside her as they'd talked with Cooper and Kala and Lou and TJ. Oliver had kept his distance, sitting with Lucy and Sami and Tim.

It felt good to sit there with a Ben who paid attention to her, who was polite to her family and seemed to want to be there.

Of course, she'd told him exactly how to play her.

Sosa shrugged and found one of the comfy seats. "She is not wrong. She is very smart Bratz doll. I don't know about other one."

"I swear if you call me a Bratz doll one more time, I'm going to show you that I held back with your friend yesterday," Kenzie snarled. "I know my mother is being nice to you and I want to be nice as well, but I can be mean."

Kala snorted and sank down in front of one of the free mirrors. "She can be. She's one of those lovely souls who is sweet as pie until she's done and then she will throw down, and she does not mind pulling out large portions of hair. If you aren't attached to it or you've been wanting to try something different, try her, man."

Sosa looked her up and down as though assessing. "Fine. But just because I do not say thing does not mean it isn't true."

"And just because I let you live doesn't mean I like you," Kenzie returned. And then immediately felt guilty, but she wasn't taking it back. She turned to her cousin. She'd seen Vivi earlier. Vivian had been waiting to greet them when they'd gotten to the building, but Sophy didn't work here. She only came in for club nights. "Soph, it's so good to see you. I am not going to ask the question."

The question Sophy had been asked since she was thirteen years old and diagnosed with cancer.

Her cousin gave her a brilliant smile. "I'm fine. All my checkups are good. Still in complete remission."

Her port scar had faded, but the evidence would always be with her in that thin line on her chest. Kenzie hugged her tight and tried not to get emotional. Cancer ran in Uncle Simon's family line, and though Sophy had come through it like a champ, it still almost wrecked them all.

Kenzie took a step back and smiled brightly. "I'm glad to hear it. How is your uncle doing?"

"The duke is quite well, thank you for asking," she replied. "Don't I sound like a proper British aristocrat? Uncle Clive's been giving me lessons. We're handling a bunch of renovations out at Norsely right now, so I'm in full-on Downton Abbey mode. Except we don't have all the servants and stuff because my uncle's on the solitary side."

"Your uncle is named Duke?" Sosa asked since she seemed to be such a curious girl.

"My uncle is the Duke of Norsely," Sophy replied. "My father is his heir right now, and I am here in England learning as much as I can about my family."

"And breathing, since her mom and dad are helicopter parents," Kala quipped.

Vivi's head shook. "I forgot how bad she is at the whole civilized-conversation thing."

"She's not wrong," Sophy admitted. "I'm afraid a long fight with cancer for their only child made them a bit overprotective, and the truth of the matter is they were both something of spies when they were younger, and also they run a company that literally finds missing people. You can imagine I did not get to do a bunch of teenage rebellion things since the one time I snuck out to go to a party, my mom showed up and insisted on taking my temperature and making sure everyone around me had their flu shots. I was not popular in high school. Or college, really. So I needed some space. My dad showed up at my apartment in Dallas when I had a boyfriend over and I walked out to find them discussing my diet and exercise program. That poor man who I kept around for his large dick was sitting there listening to a lecture about how to keep my blood count where it needs to be. So here I am in England, and my uncle doesn't ask about my doctors' appointments."

It had been a hard time for her family, but she knew it had been devastating for Uncle Simon. They were fine now but he still worried, and letting Sophy out into the world had been difficult for him.

"You were sick?" Sosa looked her up and down as though it was hard to see the sick child in the healthy woman.

"I was, but I'm good now. I've been in remission for a long time and I take care of myself," Sophy said and then wrinkled her nose a bit. "Mostly."

"And I watch out for her, and it has nothing to do with the fact that I get to stay in this fabulous flat right here in Chelsea," Vivi proclaimed. "I'm not joking. Uncle Si bought this ridiculous penthouse. I bring my broke-ass grad student friends up there and they think I'm some kind of billionaire. I have to tell them no, that is my best friend. Ooo, Kenz. Did I tell you we've been talking about getting a dog to go with the cats? Soph and I are settling into our spinster era. It's kind of fun."

Sophy's eyes rolled. "She went through a shitty breakup. It's nothing."

Kala leaned back, eyeing Sophy and Vivi. "Hey, is one of you doing Ollie? Because the moms are super worried."

Vivi snorted. "No. That's ridiculous. Ollie is fun and I adore him, but we're too smart to ever fall for him. He is the ultimate player."

Sophy nodded. "Yep. He's a massive ass when it comes to women."

But Kenzie got the feeling there was something Sophy was hiding.

She was going to have to figure that out.

"How is your guy?" Vivi asked. "I didn't get a chance to spend much time with him. He is stunning. Like my jaw dropped when he walked into the room. How is that man not a model?"

"The spy thing is a whole gig," Kala quipped. "We're not allowed side hustles unless they help the Agency. And even then sometimes it goes wrong. Like the time they decided we could get some serious intel by becoming ride share drivers. You would be surprised what people will say to a driver."

Kenz sat down and started checking her makeup. "We were targeting a particular set of hackers, and not a one of them drove. The problem was to make it look good we had to actually accept real rides, and turns out my sister isn't great at customer service."

"Hey, it was Malibu jail. I even got a gift bag," Kala retorted.

It hadn't been the first time her twin had been arrested. Probably wouldn't be the last. After all, their dad got hauled in by cops a weird amount of times. He had jail stories from around the world.

"Ben was planning on being a professional baseball player." She'd learned pretty much everything she could about the man she was obsessed with. Obsession, it turned out, was a lot easier than actual love. A lot less scary than love. "He went to college on a scholarship and was being scouted. He was what we call a south paw."

Kala's eyes rolled. "She only knows that because she's an obsessive bitch. Trust me. She knows nothing about sportsball."

"I do, too. Well, now." Cooper had given her a whole class on the finer points of baseball. He and TJ knew all the sportsballs.

"How did he become a spy?" Sophy asked. "I would think left-handed pitcher would be far more lucrative and less dangerous."

"He is Canadian." Sosa was listening intently. "Do they really have spies? Or do they just want to be included? I mean how dangerous can Canada be?"

Kala gave her a thumbs-up. "About as scary as France, am I right?"

Kala might have found a fucking soulmate. "You two try to survive winter there and we'll see."

They both looked at her.

"I am Russian," Sosa said.

"Dude, Russian genes," Kala added.

She was going to ignore them both. For now. She stared at herself in the mirror. Ben had kissed her nose earlier. He'd told her how cute she was when she slept. "He got in an accident and he couldn't pitch anymore. So that's how he ended up in CSIS."

"Yep," Kala agreed. "That's how he became a pain in my ass."

They wouldn't talk about Huisman right now. They had no idea how much Sosa knew about Huisman. It was best to play their cards close to the vest.

"Well, I'm surprised he didn't go into acting or something," Vivi admitted. "That man is hot. Are the two of you playing tonight?"

"Yes, but he got a privacy room. We haven't played together before. Not in a formal way. We signed our contract very recently," Kenzie explained.

"Oh, the girls in other part of house, they sign contracts sometimes, too," Sosa began.

And she was done with Sosa.

Kenzie stood.

Kala grinned. "Cool. This is one of my favorite things in the world."

"Uhm, Ariel kind of told us we needed to be gentle around the new girls," Sophy pointed out.

Gentle hadn't worked on Sosa and wouldn't.

Kenzie strode up to the younger woman, who had a look of general annoyance on her face. Like she didn't believe for a second Kenzie could take her.

"Do you seriously think you can take me out, Bratz doll?" Sosa asked.

"I think I have at least twenty pounds of muscle and six inches on you, petite baby doll. I think you like to shoot people and blow them up and you keep your distance. You kill people from afar. I've done it up close. Do you know what it feels like to slide a stiletto between the third and fourth ribs? It requires far more pressure than you would think. The movies make that shit look easy. But you have to go through skin and tissue and muscle to get to that heart. Which I did. It's funny because if you leave the knife in, there's no blood. I know exactly when to step back so I don't get blood on my clothes because when that dumb motherfucker pulls it out—and he always pulls it out—it's a fountain that washes everything red."

"Are we sure she's not Kala?" Sophy whispered.

Vivi nodded. "Kala wouldn't be talking. She would stab her and get it over with. Also, I don't think she'd care about her clothes."

"That's why I got Devi making me a new set of killing clothes. Easy to clean," Kala agreed. "No, this is my sister when she's been pushed way too far. I'm betting they don't train Sosa in anything but what she's supposed to be good at. If she was able to fight, she might be able to get away. So this isn't even a contest."

Sosa's chin went firm and she stood, like she wasn't intimidated at all. Like she could handle this.

Her arm pulled back slightly and Kenzie sighed. She was terrible. She projected her moves. Completely untrained. Kenzie caught the fist that was going for her face. That would have ruined her carefully done makeup. She simply caught it and didn't let it go.

Sosa's eyes went wide and she tried to pull back, but Kenz had a point to make. She squeezed slightly, not enough to hurt the other woman but enough to let her know she wasn't going anywhere.

Sosa cursed under her breath. She had quite the potty mouth. She kicked out, which gave Kenz the perfect chance to sweep her legs out from under her and set Sosa on her ass.

Kenzie straddled her, wrapping a hand around her throat. "So, this is how it's going to go. You get to make the decision. I can be your friend and we can start training because I think my sister is correct and they keep you weak in everything but the one thing they need you to do. You only snipe people and blow them up."

"I am good with poison, too," Sosa spat back.

She probably wouldn't be eating anything Sosa gave her. "Again, not very physically difficult to do. You are brutal with that mouth of yours. Wouldn't it be good to know how to defend yourself? So you can take the fight to the fuckers who did this to you. Or you're here because someone sent you and you'll do their bidding and slink back into your cage because you're too much of a coward to turn yourself into what you need to become."

Sosa's eyes were bright with unshed tears. "I did not want to be this thing they made me."

"Then be something else." Kenz stood, looming over the young woman on the floor. "Fight. You're not eight years old anymore. You're strong and you've survived, and now it's time to let them know what a fucking mistake they made when they took you. Now it's time to burn it all to the ground and dance in the ashes."

"That is what he say. I hear him when he talks to the boss. He say he will rule the ashes," Sosa replied.

"Not the same thing." Kala was suddenly at her side. "Huisman wants to burn the world down. All you want to do is torch the place that tortured you and will torture other girls in the future. He's an asshole, and you're doing the world a major favor. But you do need training. That was pathetic."

Sosa lay there for a moment and then held up a hand. Kala reached down but Sosa shook her head. "This is between me and her."

Kenzie helped her up.

Sosa straightened her clothes. "When they take me, I only have one toy. It is still at the base. It was Bratz doll. Sometime she was my only friend, the only piece of me from before. I'll take your training. I think you might be good person to have on my side. So you should know, I have seen your man before. Not in person. He doesn't come to the castle. But when the bad man comes, he has a room. They set it up for him. One of the things he keeps with him is a picture of your man. The girls he abuses say he always sets up the picture like he wants the man to watch what he does."

The thought sent a chill through Kenzie.

She knew Ben had an obsession with Huisman and it was wrapped in guilt and fear and anger, but somehow she'd thought it was one sided. Like Ben was nothing more than a fly to swat in Huisman's eyes.

But there was something sick and twisted, like a love affair with the darkest intentions, and she was either Ben's way out or perhaps his final sacrifice to the relationship that had truly defined his life.

Or Sosa was lying.

There was only one way to find out. Spend time with her. Train her. Analyze her.

All while watching her back.

Sosa started to walk toward the door. "I think I'll go and check on Gabby. She's having trouble being away from home. Isn't it weird? I feel like I can breathe for first time and she's crying."

Kenzie looked to Vivi, who usually loved to spend her time explaining how feelings were normal and we should accept them.

Vivi simply shrugged. "Yeah, weird."

Oh. She'd been given a mission. So she was more comfortable here than she let on. Vivi always said she did nothing but answer the phones.

"Tomorrow morning. There's a gym on the fourth floor. Meet me there before breakfast. And Sosa, was there really a doll?"

Sosa stopped, her hand on the door. She didn't look back. "Maybe there was. Maybe there wasn't. In the end, none of it matters."

She walked out and the door closed quietly behind her.

Kala nodded, her lips curling up in a smile. "I like her."

Kenzie rolled her eyes and turned to Vivi. "All right, what's up with you? That should have turned into a session."

Sophy joined her roomie, standing side by side with her. "She doesn't know us. She thinks we're nothing more than a receptionist and a rich girl working with her even wealthier uncle, and I'm not going to disabuse her of the notion. You know I love to use the airhead, rich-girl thing."

"So Ariel wants the two of you to watch them?" Kenzie asked.

"I was going to if Ariel didn't," Kala admitted. "They'll be on their guard around us."

"They'll be on their guard around everyone." Vivi's pretty face had lost its careless expression, and she was the hawk Kenzie knew. "But they might slip up, and they don't know how much Russian we understand."

"I've already caught them talking about whether they can trust your parents." Sophy's Russian was every bit as solid as Kenzie's or Kala's. They'd all grown up speaking it as often as they did English.

Kala frowned. "I thought Gabby's Russian was terrible. Didn't Sosa say that?"

Kenzie nodded. "She did."

Sophy shrugged. "It's not great but they do go into Russian when they obviously don't want us to understand. Sometimes French, but Sosa constantly points out how much she hates it."

"What's your take on them?" She trusted Vivi's instincts.

"One of them is lying. They don't fit right. I know that sounds weird and everyone reacts differently to trauma, but something is off between them. I'll figure it out," Vivi said with confidence. "We're taking them to buy some clothes tomorrow, and we're going to make it a whole girls day and see if we can learn anything else."

"They have zero net profile I can find, but I'm not done yet." Sophy might be working as some kind of assistant to her uncle, but she had absolutely followed in her momma's footsteps. She was a phenomenal hacker. "And it was Damon and Penny who asked us to figure out the newbies. He's worried your mom and dad are soft when it comes to this. Ariel is planning on having sessions with them, and she's excellent at what she does so Damon and Penny feel comfortable with her profile, but they wanted some more insider info. I'm going to pull out the black card tomorrow. That makes me lots of friends."

It made a lot of people try to take advantage of her.

"I know you're working for the Brits, but I would love a report on anything you find," Kala said before sitting back down at her station and picking up her brush. "Now can we get to the questions I've been waiting to ask for hours and hours."

Oh, there was no question what was about to come out of her sister's mouth. "You can't kill Ben."

"Why would we kill Ben?" Sophy asked.

Vivi sighed like she was disappointed, like she'd hoped she hadn't been right. "He was kind of cold when he first came in. He's probably struggling with the whole you're twins thing. Have you always worked together well?"

"No, and we finally talked. Well, he had me talk." She stared at herself in the mirror. She was on some sort of precipice. Whatever happened next would change her life for the good or the worse, and she wasn't sure how she would bet this would go. "It was good. He's just unsure about how to handle his role as my Dom."

"Is he?" Kala asked. "Because I did not see a Dom this afternoon. I saw a sulky boy."

She wanted to argue, but she'd kind of thought the same. "He made up for it."

"I don't see how. Oh, I'm sure he blew your mind in bed, but you know that's for him, too," Kala began. "He's the kind of guy who definitely thinks he can control you through sex."

And Kenzie shut down entirely. Kala was talking about how Cooper would never do that to her and how TJ worships the ground Lou walks on and Kenzie should demand better.

A weird numbness settled over her as she brushed her hair and finished her makeup. Kala always did this with her boyfriends. They weren't good enough. Not smart enough or strong enough. They were all assholes who didn't fit because they hadn't grown up together. Kala wouldn't admit that. She would say things like Matt was a dick face because he watched a lot of sports. Leo was wrong for her because he didn't understand foreign policy.

TJ didn't understand foreign policy either, but he was perfect for Lou.

Kenzie's friends were dumb, too, and Kala was pretty bang-on when it came to those, but it still hurt. Or didn't anymore. She'd thought things would change once her sister was happy. Kala had everything she could want. The perfect husband. The best best friend. Parents who thought about her all the time because she was special.

Kenz was the one who didn't need as much watching, as much care.

"Are you even listening to me?" Kala asked.

Kenzie stood, pushing back her chair. "Sure. I've once again picked an entirely unsuitable person to bring into our group. He's an asshole who can't even forgive a hard-core betrayal overnight. I should probably kill him and accept the fact that I'm destined to be alone with my dogs."

Kala didn't seem to get the sarcasm in her tone, which was weird since it was her main language. "You'll be happier with them than you will be with that asshole. He ignored you and you let it happen."

She couldn't do this with her. It had been a horrible couple of weeks, and she hadn't had a Cooper to go home to at night. She didn't have a Lou who would sit by her side. She'd had sisters, but they were married and moving on with their lives and she was happy for them. But she wasn't going to listen to this. "I get it. You're the main character and I'm the dipshit sister. You know, how about you go back to your happy marriage and all your friends and I won't bother you anymore. Maybe you're the one I need to be more professional with. Now, I'm going to play with the asshole who will inevitably break my heart, but don't think you'll get a second of grief from me. I won't cry in front of you or ask you to listen. You can sit in self-satisfaction knowing you beat me again."

Her sister's eyes had gone wide, and for once she looked genuinely shocked. "What are you talking about?"

She couldn't. She couldn't have this fight with her right now. Her skin felt too tight.

Between the morning with cold Ben, the afternoon with warm Ben, the further proof how entangled he was with Huisman, and now she realized how long she'd been fighting her sister over this and it was a storm inside her. One that she was supposed to drown in pop songs and overly dramatic gestures because that was who she was. Simple. Easy to deal with. A little dumb. She was her twin's opposite, and everyone took Kala seriously.

She knew her sister loved her. There was no question about that. But then Kala didn't really like her very much.

"It doesn't matter. I'll see you at the meeting tomorrow. Have a good night, Mistress Kala," she said.

Kala moved into her space. "You need to change into fet wear. I'll help you and you can explain this hissy fit to me."

"Hey," Vivi began. "Maybe you should back off."

But that was just it. When Kala got mad it was always serious.

When Kala was hurt the world stopped because everyone worried she could do some damage. When Kenzie cried, she would get over it. It was teen girl stuff or young adult stuff, and she would get hugs and promises it would get better while Kala got therapy and long discussions about life and her place in it.

Kenzie worried she was starting to see her place.

"Viv, I love you, but this is between me and my sister," Kala was saying. "She's got to get into that damn corset she wears, and she can't do it on her own."

Oh, but there was another option. Kenzie pulled the T-shirt she wore over her head and tossed it aside before pushing her jeans off her hips. She wasn't wearing underwear. She turned and shook out her magenta hair, checking herself in the mirror. She looked hard and beautiful and cold.

Maybe that was what she needed to be. She worried who she was without her sister, but now she asked herself if she ever truly had her in the first place. They'd been close as children, but when Tasha had come along, she'd taken on the role of Kala's adviser. Then Lou had become her best friend, and now Cooper had her whole heart. The only thing that bound them together was the job they'd longed for, and now that was over.

At least it felt like it was ending and she needed to figure out who she was because she was worried the Agency wouldn't want a single Ms. Magenta. Hadn't she always been the one they tolerated so they could have their dream operative?

"I think I'll skip the clothes," Kenzie said. The one place she'd always felt powerful was the dungeon floor. "I won't need them."

"Please tell me we're not going into angry queen mode," Kala said with a sigh.

Kenzie got into her sister's space, not giving a damn that she wasn't wearing a stitch. "I'm not angry, Sister. I'm just done."

She noticed Lou walking in, but it didn't matter.

She walked out and like Sosa before her, she didn't look back.

Chapter Eleven

Ben stood outside the locker rooms feeling oddly comfortable in leathers when Cooper McKay walked out.

The American wore leathers similar to his, but the wide smile on his face was different. He held out a hand. "Hey, my man. How did your afternoon go?"

He shook the man's hand. It was odd to be friendly with him since for so long Cooper had been the man between Ben and what he wanted. Except he hadn't ever been that. It had all been an act. That made it awkward, too. The trouble was this man was important to Kenzie.

They all were, and he was kind of pissed at her family.

"We had a nice rest. I know the plane was comfy but Kenzie didn't sleep well, so she needed that nap before tonight." She hadn't slept on the plane because she'd worried he was cold to her.

How could he explain that he had to be cold or he would be over-the-top hot? She was the only thing in the world he was passionate about, and he wasn't sure he liked it.

He wasn't sure she wouldn't be one more thing Manny took from him in the brutalist way.

Cooper stepped back. "I'm glad to hear it. I got the feeling Kenz was going to be a handful, but she seemed nice and sweet at dinner. I was surprised. She can be way dramatic."

He was sure Cooper meant it as masculine bonding. "And your wife can be violent. Kenzie is fine. She's exactly the right amount of dramatic."

Cooper stopped and his brows rose. "Hey, I didn't mean anything by it."

He was sure Cooper was a good guy and that all of this was a dynamic that played out with people who'd known each other since they were babies. But he hadn't. He was an outsider, and that meant he saw things the rest of them didn't. "I'm sure you didn't. I'm sure you all tease Kenzie for being too much and think it's okay because she laughs along. I actually took some advice from the big guy. You know, the one who hates me. He said I don't know her. I know whoever the hell Kara represented, but I don't know Kenz. I'm fixing that. I spent the afternoon learning about her childhood and what it was like to grow up in her family. Now I'm figuring out how to be a good Dom. Not an overall good Dom. *Her* good Dom. Don't fucking call her overdramatic where I can hear it. Am I clear?"

Cooper nodded, and there was a certain look of respect in his eyes. "Understood. You're the first one of her boyfriends I've met who wasn't willing to joke about her…quirks. They're adorable, by the way. I've always considered her a sister, and she's one of my favorites. We joke around all the time."

"I think she feels the ridicule more than you know."

Cooper seemed startled. "There's no ridicule. I tease her but I love her."

"I don't think that's how she experiences it." One of the things he'd gotten from this afternoon was that Kenzie often felt left out of a world that seemed to revolve around her siblings. She hadn't said it in so many words, but he'd been able to read between the lines. Tasha was adopted. Kala had a brain that worked differently, and she struggled to fit in. Seth was a handful, and Travis was the baby. And Kenzie was a ball of sunshine so no one worried about her. "I think she feels like she's in her siblings' shadows. She was the happy one so she was also the forgettable one."

"No one forgot Kenzie. And Kala went through a lot," Cooper began. "The world wasn't made for her."

This had been going through his head for hours. While she'd slept he'd tried to really see her. As she was now. As she'd been then. Some things only added up when he plugged her twin into the equation. "The world wasn't made for Kala so Kenzie gave up her world to make her twin comfortable. That woman in there should have been a cheerleader, prom queen, student body president. She should have a whole yearbook full of her, and yet she dimmed herself so her sister never felt like she was outshining her."

Cooper's jaw tightened. "Kala never asked for that."

Ben wasn't backing down. He signed a contract with Kenzie earlier. It was a basic contract, but protection was in there. On both sides. He meant to honor his. Even if what he was protecting her from was her family. "She didn't have to. Kenzie loves her so she sacrifices, and I would bet she never would complain."

"It sounds like she's been complaining to you," Cooper countered. "Don't think Kala hasn't sacrificed plenty for her twin. There is nothing in the world my wife wants more than for her sister to be happy."

"Just not with me." Oh, he'd thought a lot about this since the moment Kala had walked into that bedroom in Nepal and he'd been forced to confront the fact that he'd been an idiot.

Cooper seemed to try to calm himself. "She doesn't hate you. Look, there's some kind of misunderstanding here. I know Kala has a tough exterior, but she wants her sister to get what she desires."

"Is that why she tried to get me to hate Kara on every level?" He knew he hadn't imagined it. "Do you think Kenzie didn't properly communicate how she felt about me? Or do you think Kala believed I was nothing more than another one of her sister's mistakes? I get it. Kenz had a lot of boyfriends. Couldn't find one who stuck. I wonder if that was Kenzie's fault or her sister's."

It bugged him. The whole dynamic he'd witnessed earlier rankled. Everyone deferred to Kala. It wasn't a malicious thing, merely the dynamic they'd never quite broken from childhood.

"She would never willingly hurt her sister."

Ben knew Cooper wasn't going to see it the way he did, but it was worth a try. "But she thinks she's smarter than her sister. We talk about all the times she was a heinous bitch to me like it was some kind of sitcom running joke. I was in love with a woman who cared so little for me she left me to die."

Cooper huffed like Ben was the overdramatic one now. "She didn't think you were going to die."

"She didn't care." He'd been there. He'd seen the look in her eyes. It had taken months to get back to where he could work with her.

Of course, then they sent in Kenzie and he was panting after her again, thinking there was something deeply wrong with him.

He'd had fucking therapy sessions about it.

Cooper's head shook. "You don't understand her. She didn't mean anything by it. She's not good with physical affection from people she's not close to, so it was her way of keeping you at arm's length."

Of course her husband would come up with the best explanation he could. "I was there. I know exactly how she made me feel and I'm still struggling with it because when I look at Kenzie, I can't help but see Kala's face sometimes. Looking at me like I'm a bug and she can't wait to step on me."

Cooper looked like someone had punched him in the gut. "Fuck. We apparently need to sit down. I'm going to go get my wife and we'll clear this up."

He wasn't going to have some kind of therapy session. "No need. It's been made plain to me that we're not going to get along. All I'm asking is don't walk up to me like I'm your friend and we can joke about how silly and childish my woman is. If you can't say kind things about her, keep your damn mouth shut."

He was well aware it would be far smarter to play nice with Kenzie's relatives, but he couldn't right now. He wasn't thinking about the mission. He'd spent hours holding her and listening to her and watching her sleep. When he'd been with her, her head on his chest, her arms around him, he hadn't thought about that other Kara. Even though they'd had sex it might have been the only time since he'd discovered her secret that there was no anger in him directed at her.

But there was some anger *for* her. He wasn't sure any of them saw how they marginalized Kenzie, but he wasn't going to do it, and he wasn't going to joke about it.

"Hi, Ben." Lou rushed by, her bag over her shoulder. "I'll be right out, babe."

TJ strolled up, an indulgent look on his face. "Sorry, she got caught up working with Lucy on the op. They found some stuff about deliveries or something and now Lucy and Sami are heading to Northern France to do surveillance."

"I thought none of us were going for a few days." Ben didn't like plans changing. He didn't want to get stuck with Oliver. He might kill the fucker.

"Like I said there was some kind of shipment. Apparently Lucy's been tracking equipment that could be used in producing the anthrax variation, and one of the addresses matched a property on the list from Nepal. They want to check it out. They haven't left if you want to go with them."

Hell yeah, he wanted to go with them.

Hey, Kenz, I know we're in a delicate place but fuck playing. I want to work.

Somehow he didn't think that would go well for him.

She needed this in a way he was only now starting to understand. In a club she could shed all the weight she carried on a daily basis. She could shine all she liked because she kept it there. She could unleash the part of her that longed to be the center of things, the part she sacrificed because she loved her family.

If she loved him, would she mold herself around him? Would she choose him? He would make her the center of his world, his reason for existing. He could give her that. He didn't have a family. She had too much family. Could they be enough?

"Hey, we need to talk because Ben is under the mistaken impression that Kala hates him," Cooper was saying to TJ.

TJ chuckled. "I don't know if that's mistaken."

They started to argue but the door Lou had walked through opened and Kenzie walked out.

Completely naked.

Her hair was down, curling around her shoulders, which were back as she walked with careful pride. Her eyes were on him, no one else, and he could feel the heat from where he stood. It threatened to burn him up.

But there was also a coldness to her. Like she was half expecting him to reject her, and she would handle it like the queen she was and move on to the next Dom.

He felt his jaw drop and then the most compelling need to cover her the fuck up. He kind of wanted to tackle her and wrap her up in long skirts and turtlenecks.

"Oh, shit," TJ said, his face falling. "Ben, if she's doing this it's because something hurt her."

"Damn it." Cooper ran a hand through his hair as Kenzie brazenly walked toward them. "Something's going on. I need to talk to Kala."

He'd picked out her fet wear from what she'd brought. He'd been clear what he wanted from her.

Was she being clear about what she needed from him?

"Well, hello, gorgeous," a deep voice said. "Kenz, you are looking supremely sexy this evening."

Oliver. Ben watched Kenzie's lips turn up as though the compliment did something for her.

She was feeling vulnerable, and her beauty was one thing she was confident in. Or maybe it was her skin she was comfortable in. Maybe without clothes she wasn't playing any part. She was Kenzie not Kala, because Kala would never walk through a club naked.

She needed this, needed him to play his part as her Dom because this was a place where she could toss off those clothes and be perfectly safe. Her chin was up like she was daring him to act on his impulses. To prove he was one more man who was going to put her in a cage and not let her shine the way she wanted.

He hadn't grown up in the lifestyle, but he'd learned some of its tenets. There was a challenging look in her eyes, and he needed to soften her up. He wouldn't do it by punching Oliver. He would do it by proving he could be what she needed. "Oliver, my sub is the single most beautiful woman in this club. I don't mind you looking. She's a fucking work of art. But we should talk about what happens if you touch."

Kenzie stood before him, and he could sense some of her tension go when he said the words. She was still brittle, and it was obvious all the work he'd done on her when they'd cuddled and talked was gone.

So he would use his other skills to get his sub where he wanted her to be.

Purring and content and thinking about him.

"Absolutely not. I would never misbehave on a dungeon floor. I know this is my father's club, but I'm in charge when he's not around, and it might surprise you but I'm a stickler for rules. You have a contract in place?" Oliver asked.

He reached out a hand because she seemed so alone. She took it and squeezed as though letting him know she appreciated the contact.

She was such a physically affectionate woman. She needed touch and attention and praise, and in exchange she would be his entirely.

At least that's how it felt.

"I sent it to the club's email, and I left a copy with your father." Ben didn't take his eyes off Kenzie. "I also booked a privacy room. I talked to one of the monitors and he explained everything would be laid out for us."

"Then I wish you the best of nights." Oliver stared toward the locker room as the door came open and Kala strode out, followed by Lou. "You should probably run because trouble is on the way."

He realized TJ and Cooper had been whispering, and they moved in now.

"I think we should go to the lounge and talk this through," Cooper announced. "There seems to have been some miscommunication, and I want to nip that in the bud."

"Kenz, why don't I get you a robe and a glass of wine and we can sit down and talk about what's going on," TJ offered.

"Kenzie, don't be ridiculous. You're not going to say that shit to me and then walk away and play with this asshole," Kala said, folding her arms over her chest and staring at him like she could intimidate him into backing down.

Lou hovered in the background, waiting like she wasn't sure she should change because Kala had decided they would spend their night in a different way.

Like they were in charge of Kenzie. She was his. He'd signed the contract. It was time he let them know who was in charge of Kenzie Taggart now.

"Ben, come on. We'll let you sit in," Cooper suggested.

"Or he can go do whatever he does," Kala returned. Her tone softened slightly. "Kenz, come on. We need to talk. I'll buy you a drink, but please put on some clothes."

And she was back to stiff.

"Mistress Kala, do you intend to enter my dungeon floor in street clothes?" Oliver asked in a surprisingly intimidating voice. "Because right now Kenzie is in full compliance with The Garden's rules, but you are not."

"Oliver, I'm trying to talk to my sister not top a sub," Kala replied through clenched teeth. "This is a family thing."

If he let them, they would take her away and shove him out and she would always be the fifth wheel in their happy family.

"And this is a Dom thing." Ben leaned over and scooped Kenzie up. "When she wants to talk to you, she'll talk to you. Until then, she's mine. Don't interrupt us."

"I told you this was a bad idea." A pretty young woman stood behind Lou. He thought she'd been introduced briefly. Vivian.

"Hey, I wasn't done," Kala began as Ben turned away.

"You are unless you want me to cancel your rights here," Oliver announced. "He has a contract with her. She has not indicated she wants to void that contract, so I assure you, Mistress Kala, that if you don't back off, we're going to have a problem, and we will not need to call in the parents to settle it. I'll have you hauled right out of here and you can spend the rest of your time in London in your flat."

"Oliver." He hadn't met the other young woman. She looked like she could be related to Kenzie. She had darker hair, but it was there in the set of her chin and those gorgeous eyes.

Oliver held out a hand. "No, Sophy. It's the first time I've seen Kenz select what I feel is a proper top for her, and I won't fuck that up."

Someone said something else, but it didn't matter. Ben walked toward the privacy rooms.

It was time to be the Dom she needed.

* * * *

Kenzie sank to her knees when Ben set her on the floor.

Head down, hands on her thighs, eyes on the floor as her hair flowed around her giving her a little space from the world. This was a position she knew well and felt comfortable in.

What had she been thinking? She took the moment to breathe. Had she really done that? Walked out naked? She knew everyone in the world thought she was some kind of confident boss babe, but she'd been running on pure adrenaline. She knew Ben could be a jealous ass. It was kind of hot. It wasn't modern of her, but she accepted the fact that watching Ben sort of manhandle Oliver because he dared to flirt with her did something for her. But it also pointed out that Ben had some work to do being comfortable in his role, and walking out naked might have sparked something other than desire.

So why was she poking his soft spots so early on?

Because her ground suddenly felt shaky beneath her feet.

She didn't fight with her sister. Never. Not about anything important. Oh, they squabbled over TV shows and toys when they were kids, but not since her sister came back from being kidnapped at the age of fifteen. She'd been delicate in a way only Kala could be, and they never normalized. Tonight was the first time she'd told her sister off in years.

It felt good and bad. She loved her sister but their relationship was in flux, and there seemed to be no way to talk about it without seeming like some pathetic hanger on.

But Ben made her feel something else.

"Kenzie, are you all right?" His boots came into view as she stared down at the floor.

The privacy rooms at The Garden were way nicer than the ones at The Hideout, though they were working on it. This particular one was large with a spanking bench and a St. Andrew's Cross on the wall. There was a bed in the back and a wall full of floggers and whips and rope. He could use those on her and she would float for a while and not think about the storm waiting for her outside this room.

She took a breath. This man had given her something lovely, and he wouldn't want a sulky sub. She would likely hold on to that moment when he picked her up and whisked her away forever. She lifted her head and gave him her serenest smile. "Yes, Sir. I'm good."

He stared down at her, his eyes studying her carefully. "I doubt that, but I think we should work this out in another way. Although I should ask. Do you want to talk to your sister?"

Now that it was over, she wished she'd sucked it up and took it like always. It wasn't anything abnormal. Kala wasn't a silver-linings girl and never had been. She didn't want some big rift between them. Life was already opening those chasms. "Not now. I'll apologize tomorrow. Or later tonight."

Kala wouldn't want to fight with her either. A simple apology would reset them.

"What do you need to apologize for?"

Shouldn't he want to get to the sex? The last thing she expected was that he would want to talk about what happened between her and her sister. He kind of hated her sister, and she didn't want to deal with it tonight. She didn't want to think right now. But he'd asked her a direct question, and she was supposed to obey him in this setting unless she chose to end the session.

She didn't want to end the session.

"I was a little dramatic with my sister earlier," she explained. "It's fine. Nothing to worry about."

His gaze hardened. "I don't like that word when it comes to you. You don't create drama. You simply don't turn away from it. So that means Kala said something and started a fight. I have to wonder if your fight wasn't about me."

Was it? "My sister has never appreciated my taste in men. Even when they were boys. It's nothing against you, but I think my sister would be happier if I fell for someone in our circle. She has trouble trusting people outside of it. It won't affect us. We'll just play separately."

He seemed to consider that for a moment. "So the woman who spends all her time with her family thinks not being able to be around her sister won't affect us? Or are you thinking we'll keep it to the club? That wasn't my plan, by the way."

"You have a plan?" As far as she knew he was going with the flow.

"I have wants and needs, and neither of them are about limiting my time with you. You do not need to apologize. If I'm correct, she started saying shit and you finally couldn't handle it anymore. But you weren't properly dressed and she would have followed you because she's relentless. Your choices were dealing with her, leaving, or throwing off your clothes and walking out because nudity is allowed on the dungeon floor but street clothes are not. You were magnificent. I like your drama, Kenzie. It makes me feel alive. You make me feel alive."

Damn him. She wanted to forget everything and concentrate on her body, but he was making that impossible. All his coldness was gone, and she could never resist warm Ben. Warm Ben felt like home. "You make me feel alive, too. Ben, don't worry about Kala. I won't let her come between us. Honestly, I don't think we'll be working together for much longer. At least not the way we have up until now."

Yeah, she was starting to think that was part of this awful restlessness she was experiencing. The world was changing, and she had no idea where she would land. Her parents had come back to the

Agency to watch over Kala. Oh, they'd included Kenzie in it, but she knew they worried about her twin far more.

Would they retire now? They deserved it.

Tasha was talking babies. She wouldn't want to roam the world anymore. Cooper and Kala talked about taking over McKay-Taggart since they were legally McKay and Taggart.

"Why would you say that?" Ben asked. "We've had no indication anything is changing."

"She can't go into the field the way she used to. Not after what happened with Huisman. Her heart…" It was hard to talk about it. She hadn't been able to be there the first time. Ben had. She'd been hiding. The second time, at least they'd let her stay close. She hadn't gone into the house where that asshole had held her twin and cousin, but she'd been on the ground. And at the hospital.

How many times had she nearly lost her sisters? She could still remember sitting in Tasha's hospital room when she was in a coma. She and Kala had held hands and cried. Well, she'd cried. Kala had been her stoic self, but she'd been there for Kenzie.

"So you take over the construct. No one will know," Ben said.

"I'm not sure if the team will stay together now that Kala's on the bench." Kala seemed oddly at peace with it. She would have sworn her sister lived for her job, but Kala was happily running logistics with Cooper and helping Lou and being the voice in Kenzie's ear. "I think our handlers were always more interested in her."

"I doubt that." His hand found her head. "Have I told you what my dick did the minute you walked out of that locker room?"

This was way better. She smiled up at him and felt her nipples tighten because he was looking at them and there was no doubt he liked what he saw. His cock was pressing against his leathers. She wanted her mouth around him, wanted to spend these hours serving this man while he did the same for her.

This was their time.

"I don't know, Sir. Tell me."

He chuckled, the sound deeply sexy to her ears. "Well, let's just say that all the blood in my body went straight there. You arc so fuck-able, Kenz. And you are an excellent operative. I know we're in this space and you want to sink into the submissive part of yourself, but I need to make that clear. You are great in the field. You're patient and you don't do harm that doesn't need to be done. I would let you watch my back any time, and I wouldn't with your sister. If they close down the team because she can't go in the field anymore, they're idiots."

Every word felt like a stroke of his hand. Soothing, but at the same time it made her restless.

He continued on. "Then I wanted to kill that Brit again."

"He's seen me naked many times. I've got a pretty strong streak of exhibitionist in me. We've never played. He's too close to me."

A growl came out of Ben's throat, but he seemed to move past it. "How did you find someone to play with at The Hideout? It feels like you know everyone there the way you do Cooper."

She had to hope that he'd taken his training seriously. "I've played with Cooper before. Not in a way that you would think of as sexual."

"He spanked you when you needed it?"

She winced. "Ew. Nothing so intimate. He's genuinely like my brother. Well, maybe like my cousin since I would die before I would let my brothers on the same dungeon floor with me. We have protocols. I would never want Cooper's hands on my skin. He's used a flogger on me before, but I kind of transitioned over to Gabe when it was clear it bothered my sister."

Not that she admitted it.

"Gabriel Lodge? Oldest child of billionaire Julian Lodge?"

Of course he had more than simple jealousy. She took a long breath because this might not go the way she wanted it to. "Yes. That Gabriel Lodge."

She'd introduced them the one time Ben had been at The Hideout. To her parents' horror, she'd joined the conference room debrief in fet wear since she was in a club. It didn't fool anyone. She wanted Ben to see her, to think she was pretty. Sexy. She wanted a chance to show him her world wasn't all betrayal and CIA teams wrecking the fun since his only experience with clubs at that point had been when her team kidnapped him.

"I don't want you playing with him." His mouth was turned down but his hand still stroked her hair. "I'm sorry, Kenz. I'm struggling with a couple of things. I know you won't believe me but I'm not normally jealous. I'm a casual boyfriend, but I can't do it with you."

"And the rich girl shit?"

"Oh, did you skip the no cursing part of our contract? That's ten."

"Don't threaten me with a good time, motherfucker," she replied with a smile.

"Brat. Get up. Let's move this to the bench. It's clear you need some discipline."

He hauled her up. She wasn't used to being manhandled by anyone. She wasn't exactly a lightweight. She was fit but she wasn't tiny. She worked hard to put muscle on her body, and her curves never went away. So the fact that Ben picked her up like she weighed nothing sent a thrill through her.

The games she could play with this man. He was the alpha werewolf and she the lovely but mysterious omega who needed protection, and he knew exactly what he wanted in return. She was the maid and he was the billionaire who suddenly desperately needed a fake bride, but shouldn't they look like they slept together?

He flipped her and then eased her on the prepared spanking bench, reaching to move her breasts so they dangled.

"Have I ever told you I fantasize about fucking your tits? I hold them together and move my dick between them. It's surrounded by all that softness and warmth, and you let me. You accept it. You like it when I squeeze your little nipples and go all rough. You love it when I come all over your chest and rub it in like I can leave a mark on your body."

She felt her pussy clench at the thought. "I think we can make that happen, Sir."

His fingers traced down the length of her spine, warmth flooding her system. Anticipation. She had no idea how long she had with this man. She wanted forever, but she wasn't going to get that from him. She would get hurried moments, nights when their worlds connected.

If Huisman didn't kill him.

"How many Doms have you had?" Ben asked, and she heard his footsteps on the hardwoods.

She tilted her head. One wall was mirrored, and she could see him moving toward the desk in the bedroom portion of the room. She was sure that desk had seen many a sexual act. Now it was where someone had placed Ben's kit. "Like played with? Probably more than I should admit. Slept with? Not many. I know the spy thing seems like a great way to have an enormous amount of sex, but it's mostly sitting places and watching for people while eating snack foods I'll work off later on in the gym. Or when I'm running from people who are trying to kill me. I don't regret that Swiss cake roll when I'm racing through the streets of Prague trying to make sure a Chinese agent doesn't gut me."

He laughed and moved back into her space. "I once ran at least five miles with a gunshot wound in my bicep to get away from two dudes working for an arms dealer. They were up to date on all the ways to take a man down," he said. "And I didn't even get snack cakes."

"That's where you're going wrong."

"And I wasn't asking about who you've played with or who you've slept with. Who have you signed a contract with?"

She almost didn't want to tell him. It made her feel too vulnerable. "No one. I have a contract with The Hideout, and everyone knows my rules. When I need a session, I usually ask Gabe and whoever his switch of the week is. Sometimes Doms who work at Top come in and I play with some of them. I'm not a nun, Ben. I've had D/s sex. It's what works for me."

She felt his hand on her ass, cupping it as though testing the flesh he found there.

"So you've never had a full-time Dom?"

"Is that what you are?" It was what she wanted, but she didn't see how it could work. Not really. Although they did work together a lot, and if she was Kara then she could request his backup or he could request hers. Their countries had some awkward times together the last decade, but they were working to repair the issues.

"As long as we're together, yes. Like you said, it's what works for you. I would have told you I could take it or leave it, but I want that contract with you. I want you bound up. I think it'll be far easier to deal with your family if I have that contract," he admitted. "But mostly I want it because I want to look at it and see your signature. The one that lets me know you trust me to do this."

The smack was heard before she felt it. The sound cracked through the room, and Kenzie felt the air whoosh out of her lungs. He hadn't warmed her up.

She liked it that way. She'd even told him once. She'd been flirting with him, talking about D/s. It was her way of putting all the flags on the table and letting him decide which ones were red.

She lost the purity of the pain later. Later it was something comforting, but these first few moments were like a shock of cold water.

Like the times when she was a kid and she would jump into the lake long before it was warm. She would leap and for a moment her whole body felt like a live wire, and then she would jump out and the sun warmed her and she felt open.

The sensation was both shocking and weirdly arousing. It was a jolt to her system, and she got to decide how to react to it.

Her nipples tightened, and she let herself relax. "Again."

"Oh, you think you control this, sub?" Ben asked, his voice going to a lower tone that made her pussy tighten again. "I have a contract that says you don't, and I have things I want to do. Do I need to tie you down? Or can you be still?"

"It depends on what you have planned." She didn't always enjoy being tied down. She would need to work her way into it, but she was excellent at staying still.

Another crack and she could swear her eyes damn near crossed. It had been so long since she'd had a Dom who was willing to go hard with her. The guys at The Hideout always treated her like she was made of glass even after she talked to them.

They were afraid of her family seeing the welts and bruises.

The trouble was she wanted them.

"I'm going to do whatever I want." Every word out of Ben's mouth felt like a wicked promise. "Your body is mine. This ass and pussy are mine. Your tits are mine." He reached out and dragged her arm up, kissing her fingers before sucking them into his mouth. "This is mine. So is this."

He leaned over and put his mouth on the side of her neck and bit down.

She nearly came off the bench. He'd meant that bite and he'd done it well. Not enough to break the skin, but the mark would be there for days. She would feel it and remember this time with him and…

"You can't do that," she said suddenly, remembering. She could hide it with her hair. Except she often had to put it up or it could be a weapon against her in a fight. "Shit. You can't mark me like…"

He stopped and pulled back, his hands coming up. "I'm sorry. You said you like biting. I won't do it again. I'll help you up."

What happened? She took a long breath because that had been a response she no longer needed. She'd forgotten. For a second she'd forgotten she didn't have to be careful anymore. She sat up, reaching for his hands. He'd paled. "Ben, I'm the one who's sorry. I wasn't thinking. For years I've had to worry about marks on my body, especially where someone could see."

"Because you and Kala were Kara, and Kara had to always look the same. It was why you had the same hair and wore the same clothes?" he asked quietly. "Kenzie, I want to ask about the scar on your back. Can I touch you?"

She gripped his hand. The last thing this man needed was more guilt. She laid back down, hoping they could get through this quickly because he'd done nothing to her except give her hope this session would be different. "Of course. Ben, I'm sorry. It's something I'm having to let go of. I had to be careful before."

"You weren't even allowed to play the way you liked," he murmured, and his fingertips traced the scar right under her shoulder blade.

She did not want to explain how she got that one, so she went with history. "I got that in a knife fight."

"The one in Lyon? You chased the target down an alley and he had a knife."

Oh, those words felt like a trap. She'd known Kala had run into Ben since they'd all been after the same intelligence. But she'd sworn she lost him. "Did you read that in a report?"

"Are we still playing, Kenzie?"

That felt like a trap, but she wasn't sure she wanted out. "Of course we are."

"Did you get that in Lyon?"

She had. Just not in an alley. "Yes."

He spanked her again, but this time he didn't stop. He counted. One and two and three and four. The pain flashed through her, and she realized that he knew she lied. Not technically since she had been in Lyon when Kala carefully shoved the knife into her and then sewed her up after a couple shots of vodka.

He got to thirty when he stopped and stepped back. "I watched Kara fight. More than that I had an interaction with her. She lied to me and sent me off on a wild-goose chase that only ended when I saw her following the target. It wasn't you. I damn near gave myself up that day because I watched him stab you, but McKay showed up. It was the only reason I didn't show myself."

She wasn't going to lie to him. Not again. "It's in a place you can see. I wear a lot of strapless gowns. It would be on all the dossiers foreign agencies keep on us. You know one of the records they keep is on an agent's scars and tattoos. And before you get pissed at my parents you should know this was a protocol Kala and I put in. My father lost his shit every time we did it, and my mother threatened to quit. I called her bluff."

She'd known her mom wouldn't be able to sit on the sidelines. Though she had been more and more since Colton was born. Her mom wanted to be a happy grandma and spend time with her husband and their dogs and have some peace, but she followed her daughters around the world, constantly worried they would die playing this game.

"Every time she got wounded, you let them cut you up so you would have the same scars?"

Well, it hadn't been all one sided. She'd done her own damage. "I made her do it. She didn't want to, but we did it for the good of the mission, and don't think she didn't take a couple of my scars, too. I know you think it's crazy, but we were building something epic."

"And now you are fucking not because I can't take this, Kenz," he announced.

"She got a burn on her calf from the fire she was in when Huisman took her to Virginia. I tried to get a picture of it so I could replicate it and she promised to murder me if I ever did it again." That was when she knew it was over. The career they dreamed of.

"That's the first thing Kala and I have ever agreed on." He took a long breath. "I understand that you were trying something new, but baby, you can't do this to yourself anymore. It's not just the scars, it's everything. If you couldn't have a fun night without worrying about your sister, this is not worth it. Have you ever played the way you need to?"

"I've played a lot, Ben."

"But not the way you wanted to." He leaned over, and she felt warmth on her shoulder. And then pain when he bit her. Again, it was controlled, and the thrill of sensation went through her. She fucking loved this. Her whole body was alive and awake and aware. "I'm not as experienced as I should be, but I swear we'll work this out. For tonight, you tell me if I go too far."

He bit his way down her body, little nips that wouldn't even leave marks, but they lit up her skin. They made her gasp, hands curling around the bench. Normally she would be completely still, like this whole thing was a massage. Good for her body, so she accepted it all.

Now she realized she didn't squirm because she didn't get super aroused during a session. Not in years. Never like this.

Desire coiled through her, and she was ready to beg when he finally made it down to her ankles. He nipped her there and stepped between her spread legs.

She felt vulnerable, and she never did. She always knew she could take whatever Dom was servicing her, but this didn't feel like some cold exchange. This wasn't service. It was possession.

Her ass ached as he pressed her cheeks apart. "How familiar are you with anal, Kenzie?"

Fuck. "I've never had anal sex. Honestly, I've probably had less sex than you imagine. My father is serious about honey pots."

A smack cracked through the air and then the delicious pain scorched through her. He did not hold back. She wasn't some porcelain doll to him.

"Let it all go now, baby. Let go of the stress. Let go of the job. Your one goal right now is to let me take you somewhere only the two of us can go. You take everything I give you, including this plug because I'm going to take that sweet asshole of yours. And, baby, you should be grateful I only brought regular lube. If we'd had this conversation before, it would be ginger lube and you would feel the burn. It might be tomorrow. I might plug your ass before we go to the meeting, and I assure you I will do worse if you bring up your dad again while I'm staring at your asshole."

He didn't understand how open her parents were about sex. She'd discovered a person's ability to talk about sex was a lot like how they handled blood. The sight for some sent them fainting dead away, but some people could eat a hearty meal while watching an operation.

Ben would need time to adjust since from what she could tell it wasn't like his parents had him babysit his younger siblings so they could spend time at their sex club. And that was sad for him.

She wasn't going into that tonight because he seemed serious about the whole lube situation, and it wasn't like they were in a place where he couldn't walk outside and ask for some exotic lube and not have twelve tops offer up some.

"Nothing to say? Excellent. You know I like this side of you, you glorious masochist. I like being the one who gives you what you need. And I think you need this."

She gasped as she felt something hard against her asshole. His finger. He rimmed her and then she felt the lube. Somehow he'd warmed it, or she wouldn't put it past Ollie to have a warmer of some kind in here since the fucker loved his luxuries.

She shivered as that finger dove deep, lubing her up and stretching her.

Never. She'd never let a Dom do this to her. There was something too intimate about it, but it felt right with him. Everything was right with him.

She gritted her teeth as she felt the hard edge of the plug. Still. She was always in motion, and here it was right and good to be still, to let him do what he wanted, to sink into a part of her soul that had always been hers. Now she found a person to share it with.

He worked the plug in, fucking her with it and lighting her up with sensation after sensation. Then he settled the plug deep inside.

"Damn, that's pretty. I like discovering this with you. It makes me feel like this can work. Don't lose the plug," he commanded before he picked her up and started for the bed.

She clenched down because that sucker was slippery.

She found herself flat on her back with him inside her before she could take another breath. It didn't matter. She was so wet she could easily handle his cock. That gorgeous monster filled her, stretching her, the plug making her tight.

He felt good. He gripped her like he worried he could lose her, but she wasn't going anywhere. This was what she'd wanted. To belong to him. To have him belong to her.

"Hold on to me. I want your mark on me, too," he said, looking down on her as he thrust inside again. He was so big above her, so strong. Her dream lover, and he was saying everything she wanted to hear.

She might be submissive when it came to sex, but she wanted the world to know he was hers and they should back off.

She let her nails find his back, something primal taking over. Pure pleasure swamped her as she watched Ben's whole body tighten. He worked over her, never taking his eyes off her. The connection felt like it went soul deep.

"You feel so fucking good. Nothing ever felt this good," he said between clenched teeth.

Because they had been made for each other. They were meant to be together.

She didn't say it because he wasn't ready for those words. Despite the afternoon and this evening, she knew he was still thinking, still wondering if she was playing him.

But that didn't matter in this moment. In this moment, they were connected and together and everything was right in the world. For now. She held on, giving him everything. The world seemed to explode in the best way possible, and then Ben was stiffening over her and she felt him come. She tightened her arms around him.

He let himself fall on her, giving her every ounce of his weight.

She took it, loving the way he felt on top of her.

He rubbed his cheek against hers. "I like being your Dom, baby. I think we're going to play a lot. You know I always want to get through a mission, but we could settle in here for a while. And you're with me. You stay with me in my room. No staying with Lucy."

She wouldn't want to now. As long as he wasn't cold, she would stay with him even without promises of forever.

"Baby, did you keep the plug?" He whispered the question in her ear.

She had not. It was impossible to keep the damn thing in when she was wrapping her legs around her man and holding on for dear life. "Uhm, no."

His head came up and he was heartbreakingly handsome with his hair tumbling over his forehead and a grin on his face. He looked younger and happier than he normally did. "Then we have to start all over again. After I clean us up."

He winked and Kenzie knew she was in for a wild night.

Deep in the night Kenzie was sleeping, having a lovely dream, when she awakened to the sound of a gun being primed.

"What the hell?" Ben was on his feet.

"Dude, do not kill us," a familiar voice said. "I told you this was a bad idea. He's not TJ."

She was groggy, but she knew Cooper's voice.

"Well, what am I supposed to do?" Her sister was here. "She's not sleeping with TJ, which would be weird. She's made her choice and I have to deal with it. At least that's what Vivi said."

Then she felt the bed next to her sink as someone crawled on.

Kenzie yawned but didn't move. "What did Vivi say?"

"She said I'm being a meanie and kind of a bitch, but not in those words. She used very scholarly words, and there was some stuff about being emotionally dependent, but I don't care about that. Babe, I'm going to need a blanket because little sis is almost surely naked and while I love her, that's weird," Kala said and Kenzie felt an arm go around her waist as her twin spooned against her, their bodies separated by the thick blanket since she was in fact naked. A shudder went through Kala's body and she whispered. "I can't sleep."

Tears pierced her eyes, and she squeezed her sister's hand. This was something they'd done in childhood. They'd shared a room almost all of their lives, their twin beds on opposite sides. When one was scared, the other would climb in. When Tash joined them they sometimes made a big pallet and slept like puppies in a pile, the sweetness of sleep bonding them as sisters.

Later, Kala would turn to Lou for this comfort.

She hadn't realized how much she'd missed this until now. "Did Lou lock you out?"

"Seriously, dude, you can't shoot me," Cooper was saying. "I know you're the new guy, but this is something you should get used to."

"I don't see why I can't shoot you. You literally broke into my room," Ben pointed out. "What is this?"

"Lou isn't the one I hurt," Kala whispered. "I love her but she's not my twin. Kenz, I'm not completely sure what I did. I can be arrogant and selfish and say things that feel like truth to me but it's hurtful to others, but I love you so much. I want to make it right."

"Be nice to Ben," Kenzie replied and held her sister's hand. "That's all I ask."

She didn't want her sister to change. She loved Kala the way she was but she wanted Ben to have a shot at blending in with her family and friends. She wanted to feel like everyone welcomed him like they had Dare. She didn't need them to love him like they did Cooper. Coop had been part of their family for a long time, but Dare was doing well.

Dare and her dad got along great.

She was almost certain part of the reason Dare had been willing to forgive Tasha had been her family. He'd wanted so much to not be on his own, to have people he could count on. She didn't know a single human being who could use a nosy, helpful family more than Ben Parker.

She had to prove to him that he was worth more than his guilt, was more important than any vengeance.

Kala groaned. "Fine. I'll be nice. Scoot over. Coop doesn't have any room."

"I'm sorry. What the hell is happening?" Ben asked. "Cooper doesn't need any room. Cooper is supposed to have his own room."

"He's got a nice package," Kala said with a chuckle. "Very well made, and he keeps a nice grooming routine. I can see where that would be appealing. There. I said a nice thing. About your boyfriend's dick. It's handling the cold quite well."

"Could you put on a robe or something?" Cooper asked. "Also, where's the… Ah, found the blanket. Scoot over."

Kenzie yawned and propped herself up on one elbow. There was a thin shaft of moonlight coming from the window and it illuminated her boyfriend's hot bod and the gun he held. "Babe, this is something we do from time to time when one of us needs comfort."

"Uhm, she has a husband," Ben pointed out.

"Yes, that's why I'm here. Look, man, have you ever dated a twin? Because it gets weird and I've learned to go with it." Cooper settled in. "They didn't talk earlier and Kala gave up her play session for what I think amounted to a therapy session with Vivi and Sophy. She can't sleep unless she knows Kenzie is okay. We don't have to talk about it now, but she needs the connection. Kenzie is half her freaking soul and we will never understand their bond, but we can honor it. Also, is there an extra pillow?"

Ben set the gun down and picked up one of the pillows he'd tossed off the bed earlier because Penny apparently loved pillows. He fast balled it Cooper's way. "I would like everyone to acknowledge that this is weird."

"It's weird," they all said at the same time.

Ben settled in, crawling under the covers again. "And we all sleep together?"

"It gets fun when one of them needs to go to the bathroom," Cooper complained. "Because they do not want to be on the outside even though they have tiny bladders."

"We made a deal. If we're getting murdered in bed, you go first, babe," Kala said through a yawn. "Did you have fun tonight?"

"Yes." Kenzie felt a smile go across her face even as the world felt soft again and sleep called. Ben turned on his side. "And I have the marks to prove it."

She expected her sister to gag and that was okay.

Instead, she rested her head against Kenzie's. "I'm so glad to hear that. I want to see them tomorrow."

Likely so she could assess Ben's performance, but hopefully she would be nice about it since they were a new couple.

"You could put on PJs," Cooper said quietly.

"You can't see it but I'm flipping you off, McKay," Ben murmured. "You crawl into my bed, you deal with all of me. Also, I will be fucking my sub in the morning and if this is the way we're playing it, I won't care that you're here."

"We'll be gone by then," Cooper promised.

"I don't know, babe. I could give tips," Kala offered.

Kenzie snorted and elbowed her twin. "You will not. Go to sleep. We have to work tomorrow."

"I'm so glad you finally got to play," Kala said quietly. "The one good thing that's come from that fucker Huisman is my sister finally getting to be herself fully and completely."

It was enough. More than enough.

Kenzie went to sleep hoping the next few days would go well.

Chapter Twelve

Week One

"Kenzie, I do not need to see that…place where bugs obviously bit you," her father managed to choke out as she entered the conference room.

She was pretty sure she glowed. It was amazing what having truly filthy sex with the man of her dreams could do for a girl. She might have selected this slouchy sweater to show off the superhot bite marks she had. "It wasn't bugs, Dad. It was Ben." She moved to the coffeepot. "Do you need some coffee? Did you get breakfast? Tell me you didn't order a full English. Dad, you are supposed to be watching your cholesterol."

"I do not eat any breakfast that comes with beans," her father announced. "The coffee just finished brewing, so yes, I will take a cup and don't worry about me eating breakfast. I'll never be hungry again. Are you and Kala okay?"

Oh, they were getting serious fast. She grabbed two mugs and filled them. Black for her dad. A splash of creamer and two sugars for her. "You still get all the best gossip. Were they betting on whether Kala and I would have fight club?"

Her father's brows rose as he took the mug. "It got that bad?"

"Not really." She felt so much better about her sister right now. Kala had snuck out in the early morning hours, but not before she'd thanked Ben for letting her stay. Actually thanked him. With words and not with just not killing him, as was Kala's traditional gratitude offering. "She's wrapping her head around the idea of Ben hanging around."

"Is he?" her dad asked. "Hanging around? We've got a lot of sites to investigate. We could be here for a couple of weeks. He might miss… I'm trying to figure out what he could miss in Canada. There has to be something."

"Poutine. Tim Horton's. The smell of true freedom." Ben was suddenly striding into the room, dressed in his gym clothes. After their morning play session, which had ended up with him kissing all her boo boos before fucking her senseless, he'd gone off to work out while she'd spent the morning making herself pretty. And staring at the places where Ben left his mark. She felt beautiful with those marks and the ache in her ass from his hand and later a paddle. "Hey, baby. Is there any left?"

She pulled down a third mug. A little cream, one sugar for him. She remembered everything.

He didn't even question it as he took the mug. He gave her a smile that told her he remembered last night, too.

"What the fuck is the smell of freedom? America is the smell of freedom," her father insisted. "We invented freedom."

"I know something from America that smells good," Ben said with a low, sexy tone. He got into her space, rubbing against her from behind. His hands went to her hips and he nuzzled her neck. "Hey, gorgeous. Your father sounds irritable this morning. Is his sciatica hurting?"

Oh, he was going to play things that way? He would discover her dad dealt with sarcasm and teasing way better than performative respect. "I think it's his knees."

Her dad stood up. "It's my stomach from having to watch all of this. Could you keep this whole thing to the club, please? We don't need this kind of distraction."

Ben took a long breath like he was taking in her scent and then kissed the top of her head and took his coffee mug before turning to her dad. “Somehow I think you’ll get used to it. And sit back down, Mr. Lemon, because we have new intel. Manny’s on the move. According to Joseph, he’s in Taiwan. Also, we’ve got some intel that puts another assassin in Dallas.”

Her dad sighed and sat back down. “All right. Let’s hear it. Also, it’s both, okay. You two wait until you’re old and your body starts getting back at you for all those times you tortured it for the job.”

The door swung open and her mom strode in, a tablet in her hand. “Ian…”

He held out a hand. “Ben’s already working on it. Did Drake send us an update?”

Her mom nodded and found herself sitting on her dad’s lap. Kala and Cooper walked in seconds later followed by Lou and TJ and a happily chatting Tim.

Ben took her hand, and when she was going to sit next to him, he pulled her onto his lap.

Her dad groaned but her mom gave her a thumbs-up.

Ben kissed her cheek and started his briefing.

* * * *

Ben frowned as he watched Kenzie in the kitchenette their flat contained. Apparently at some point in time almost all of the flats here at The Garden had been actual residences for the operatives. Robert and Ariel had started their family here. Nick Markovic and his wife Hayley had done the same before they bought their place in Kensington. Damon and Penny had lived here many years before retreating most of the time to their country house.

If this was what it was like back then, he had no idea how they got anything done.

“Bro, you want a beer?” Cooper asked from the living room.

“Are you asking me if I want one of my own beers?” Ben was still feeling out this whole family thing.

“I think he’s asking if he can have one,” TJ corrected. “You know, if you are. Also, Kenz, whatever you’re cooking smells amazing.”

Kenzie looked at her cousin and winked his way. “I’m trying a recipe for cheese puffs. And dinner is pulled pork. Ben’s never had mine before.”

TJ made some satisfied sounds and might have started drooling. "I've missed your pulled pork. Kenzie mostly cooks when she's happy. When she's sad she bakes. Not that I would want her unhappy, but if you want to have like the tiniest fight with her, I could use some cookies. She makes these apple cider cookies that I dream about at night."

"Is there a reason they're not in their own flats?" Ben asked since he hadn't had a moment alone with her all day. They'd been in conferences with her parents and the Knights. They'd had a virtual meeting with Lucy and Sami. They'd been watching a remote villa Manny owned in France, but the shipment they were concerned with hadn't shown up yet.

He and Kenzie had already done a day trip to Scotland where Disrupt had a compound. They'd managed to set up surveillance and were monitoring the situation. Next week they were heading to Italy to do the same thing.

He wanted to be in Taiwan, but they'd sent an MI6 team because Manny shouldn't have ever met them. He wouldn't know them by sight, and they might be able to keep eyes on him that way. He hadn't spent much time with the other members of Damon's team, but he trusted them.

Besides, he was starting to wonder if he wanted to put Kenz in Manny's way. He would have to figure out a way to gently leave her behind when the time came.

He'd started all of this to see if there was any way it could work. He wasn't going to lie to himself now and say he was investigating her. The only thing about that woman he was investigating was her gorgeous body and that wickedly absurd brain of hers. She amused him. She confused him. She made him want something he hadn't in a long time. A normal life. A life where they lived together and had friends over to watch ball games and she cooked and he cleaned up.

Pretty much like now except he was being a dick because they were her family. He didn't have any family. He had Tim.

He missed Dare.

"I might have a surprise coming," she said with that mysterious smile she got on her face from time to time. The one that made his heart clench and pray she was exactly who she said she was.

She was his fucking favorite person, and it had taken exactly five days of living with her to know he wanted this. Wanted to bicker with her father and watch her around her sisters and friends. Wanted to be the one she went home with. He wanted her damn dog here so he could get in good with Bud Two.

This tiny flat felt more like home than his own back in Toronto, and it was all about her.

There was a knock, and he sighed before kissing the top of her head. "I'm sure that's your dad come to tell me what a dumbass I am."

"It's how you know he loves you," she called out.

He stopped at the fridge and pulled three beers, handing them to TJ and Cooper before moving to the door.

"Thanks, man," TJ said, popping the top. "Hey, what do you know about the Blue Jays' new pitcher?"

No one asked him about sports. He was the dude who worked twenty-four seven, and now he realized with the exception of Dare, he hadn't had a male friendship that didn't revolve around work in…years. After what happened with Deanna, he'd pulled in on himself. He hadn't wanted to bring in anyone who Manny could hurt.

TJ and Cooper could handle themselves.

Was Kenzie offering him way more than her beautiful body? Was she offering him a whole circle he could be part of if he opened himself a bit?

It couldn't hurt to sit and drink beer and talk about the baseball game it had taken Tim a couple of hours to manage to get on their satellite. It helped to have a dude who knew how to cut into national television feeds. Tim sat beside TJ, but he was happy with his soda.

Kala and Lou were playing some card game in the dining area.

It was comfy. It was warm. It was one of those random Saturdays most people enjoyed. One where he didn't work, simply had fun with the people around him. It was still awkward with Cooper and TJ, but he was getting to where he didn't not like the time he spent with them. He was still the new guy, which was why he wished Dare was here since he'd been through all of this before.

He opened the door and stood there for a moment because he wasn't a man used to having the universe send him the things he wanted.

Dare stood in the doorway, Tash by his side. They looked relaxed and tan.

"Hey," Dare said, holding a hand out. "You didn't think we would let you have all the fun, did you?"

Dare. His friend. Ben hadn't realized how much he'd wanted to talk to him.

"I'm here for the drama," Tasha announced.

He frowned Tasha's way. "We don't use that word around Kenz."

Her smile amped up mightily. "Then things are going great." She moved past him. "Hey, Kenz, why are we neglecting drama now? I thought we loved drama."

Tasha walked in and Kenzie leaned out like she'd expected they were coming. "Cooper said some mean shit about me and my drama and Ben took offense because he's my dream Dom and he knew I would want him to valiantly defend me."

"I was not being mean," Cooper contested.

"He's not actually capable of being mean." Kala strode forward and hugged her sister. "How was the flight?"

"Good, and even better since I smell pulled pork," Tasha said, hugging her back. "Are we doing sandwiches or tacos?"

"Tacos and nachos," Kenzie replied. She looked soft and sweet in her yoga pants and T-shirt that hid all the marks he'd put on her.

His girl liked when he went wild on her.

He'd never gone wild on anyone before. Only her. Only ever her.

"Oh, man, I know that look," Dare said.

Dare. He could talk to Dare. He felt something weird. Something infinitely warm and satisfying.

He thought it might be joy.

He hugged Dare, who chuckled and did the whole manly hug thing.

"I'm glad you're here." The man had cut his honeymoon short, and Ben was pretty sure it was because Kenzie had asked them to. Because she'd known he needed support.

He stepped back, letting the wave of emotion ease his soul.

It was time to stop being suspicious. Time to accept that maybe he was in a good place.

"Come on in. These two know nothing about baseball," he said with a grin.

Cooper straightened up and looked slightly offended. "Dude, I played all through high school."

Dare put a hand on Ben's shoulder. "And this man was scouted by every team on the East Coast. Let a couple of Canucks teach you something about America's game."

Ben shut the door as TJ started talking shit and Kenzie was dancing around the kitchen with her unique energy and the game went on. Ben joined them and for the first time felt like maybe, just maybe, he belonged here.

Week Two

"Yes, that's Claire." Sosa stared down at the picture. "She is okay?"

"No one is ever okay," Gabby replied, staying back.

Kenzie watched them. She was actually getting to the point where she could handle Sosa. Gabby was easier, but she was also far more distant. They were working with Ariel and Penny and Kenzie's mom to get down as much about their organization as they could remember, which was a lot.

If they could trust them.

"She's in police custody right now, but we're working to get her out," Kenzie explained, trying to handle the situation with delicacy.

"She's a terrible assassin." Kala didn't understand the meaning of the word.

Kenz sent her twin a what-the-hell look since they'd already talked about how to handle this.

Kala shrugged. "They caught her at our house. She didn't even know Dad wasn't there, and if the dogs weren't in Colorado, she probably would have killed them."

Sosa's eyes went wide. "No. No. Claire would never kill poor puppy. Only humans. We are not monsters."

Gabby nodded. "Humans are terrible. Dogs are good. So are cats."

"Claire is allergic to cats so she might…" Sosa allowed with a shrug. "I mean she is assassin. We're not known for being kind."

"She would not," Gabby argued. "She would get some medications and keep cat. I already told her when we kill all the people who harm us, we're getting cat and living in the forest."

"I have thought about that myself," Kala agreed. "I called it my bog witch era, but I was getting goats."

Kenzie stared down at the picture. The girl couldn't be more than twenty-one or twenty-two. She had the same haunted look she saw in Gabby and Sosa's eyes when they weren't shoving bravado around to cover up how vulnerable they felt. Sometimes they were like kids, excited about exploring the world around them. Other times they shut down like they knew it would all go to hell and there was no reason to pretend otherwise.

Ben could be like that. Especially the first week. Before Tasha and Dare joined them, Ben was wary about everything but playing with her. Then the Dom came out and there was no hesitation.

But last night the club had been open to the OGs and the younger set had put together a movie night and Ben had laughed and joked with the guys. He'd given Cooper shit and made sure TJ had an extra sandwich. He sat with Tim and Dare and talked about Canadian things like ice hockey and whatever curling was.

He's fitting in nicely, her sister had told her.

He'd even had dinner with her dad and only told him twice that he would murder him in a dark alley one day but he probably wouldn't even know who was killing him because the dementia would have taken hold.

Her dad thought that was hilarious and went on about Ben's hair.

It was good hair. Strong, thick hair. That hair wasn't going anywhere soon, but it didn't matter because she loved more than his full, luxurious head of hair. Her dad thought that all men's hair should be either buzz cut or super long so it went into a queue. Not a ponytail. Which Ben pointed out since her dad's hair was slightly below his shoulders at this point. He'd asked her dad how he liked his man bun.

They were getting along well.

So why did something feel off?

"I like goats," Sosa said, still staring at her friend's mug shot.

"They are used in witchcraft," Gabby complained.

"Good. I would like to be learning the witchcrafts." Sosa was unperturbed. "I would like to curse people and send horrors their way. It would be fun hobby."

"Yeah, it would be," Kala said with a wistful sigh.

Sosa looked to Kenzie. "They will kill her in jail. They have to know something is wrong by now."

"They think we're all dead." Gabby sat back in her seat. According to Vivi, Gabby hadn't been sleeping. She wasn't taking to the new life the way Sosa was, but it could be a lot of factors.

Including the one where she couldn't trust that she would survive and that life could be good.

Kenzie's life felt really good right now.

They worked well together. They'd been to a compound in the Scottish countryside and recently had spent three days watching a tiny apartment in Amsterdam. Everything went well and when other guys hit on her, Ben stayed cool and calm except for the one who put a hand on her.

They had ridiculously hot sex that night.

She was starting to see how they could work together. They'd gotten excellent intel out of the occupants of that apartment. All it had taken was watching them for a couple of days.

The woman worked for Disrupt Europe and probably had no idea she was facilitating terrorism, but she had led them to the accountant who almost certainly did. It was all about getting the right data. Huisman was in hiding and they needed to figure out where he was, but it seemed buried in piles and piles of red tape. His foundation was connected to a multinational conglomerate with more arms than they could count.

This was the real, rough work of espionage. Digging into the data, trying to find the clues they needed to pinpoint where Huisman would be.

"I will miss Claire. She was good friend." Sosa sat back like the younger woman's fate had already been decided.

"She's going to get out later today, and we'll help her disappear," Kenzie explained. "It might take a day or two, but she'll be here soon. We'll even send a bodyguard with her."

Sosa sniffled. "Sorry. She is scared we are going to be found. They won't let us live. And our other friend is there."

Kala stared at her, blue eyes assessing. "I'm surprised they keep sending you in. It's almost like you're being used to test our boundaries. How many missions have you completed?"

"Many." Sosa's shoulders straightened. "So many, I cannot be counting."

Kenzie doubted that. Oh, she had no question the young woman was good with a sniper rifle, but she didn't know hand to hand at all. She was catching on quickly, but it made Kenzie wonder.

Were they assassins or Trojan horses and they were the dumbass Trojans who let them in?

"But you don't have the names?" Kala asked. She'd been going between being their fun big sister who brought them beer and watched music videos with them to their interrogator.

It did seem to keep the girls on their toes.

"We were given photos, and our handlers knew all the proper informations," Sosa said defensively.

She'd mentioned this before. "So you have handlers. Do you know their names?"

"I am to call them Mister or Missus. They change often," Sosa replied.

"When we were younger, they traveled with us and pretended to be our mom or father." Gabby seemed utterly forlorn.

Vivi had been working with them under the guise of being their guide. Ariel was having therapy sessions with them but thought they were still hiding something.

"But you didn't have a handler for this job?" Kenzie asked.

"They say we're trustworthy now." Gabby's chin came up with something akin to pride. "We even get some money and a nice hotel room. That I will never see again because you catch me."

"Sorry about not letting you kill my father," Kenzie said with a long sigh. "I'm sure your life was way better before."

She shrugged. "I like the city. Dallas is nice. I've been a few times." She glanced down at her watch. "I'm going to get ready for my session with the doctor."

Sosa stood as well. "I'll talk to her. She's worried about Claire."

They walked out, and Kala's brows rose. "She's been to Dallas before? I thought they weren't allowed out of Europe. From what I've pieced together they've worked strictly in the Schengen Zone."

That was Kenzie's belief, too. The Schengen Zone was a group of countries that agreed to forgo internal border checks so movement could happen freely among the countries. Passports weren't necessary when moving around the zone, and no one would question young women traveling with their parents.

But if Gabby had been to Dallas, then that wasn't the case.

Kala hissed suddenly.

Kenz didn't have to turn around to know who had entered the room. "Hey, Lucy. How was France?"

"It was good." She rolled her eyes as she walked past Kala, who was making the sign of the cross. Her sister got distinctly more religious whenever Lucy was in the room. "I think I've identified a couple of patterns. I also think I found the house where Sosa and Gabby were kept. It's a big-ass compound in the countryside. I couldn't get close to it. It's incredibly well guarded."

Kala sat up, all professional now. "Can we connect Huisman?"

"Not yet, but I will." Lucy sounded determined. "Something's going down. I think he's getting desperate. This whole assassination thing proves it."

But Kenzie wasn't sure. Sometimes Huisman's "desperate" was all an act.

She had to wait to see who was starring in this part of the play.

* * * *

Ben watched as Tim's whole face lit up. He grabbed his laptop and started for the door.

"I'll catch you later," Tim said, following after the young woman who'd walked by the doorway.

Cooper looked up from his computer. "Was that Gabby? Uh, does he know what she does for a living?"

Lou sat at the desk across from Cooper. They'd taken over this part of the building. It had been explained that once a group of men had used this lower floor as their offices. Robert often came in and told them stories of the men he called the Lost Boys. "I think it's sweet."

Ben was on Cooper's side in this small disagreement. "I think it's dangerous. We still don't know why they're here. I know Sosa had a big reaction to seeing a picture of Manny, but that could be an act."

"Which is why we're watching them carefully," Cooper assured him. "And apparently Tim is watching them even more carefully. I noticed him hanging out with them both a couple of nights this week. I thought they were being friendly. You know something we don't?"

He knew Tim pretty much fell for every woman they met, but he was awkward around them. "I think it's safe to say he's making his move. I hope Gabby doesn't kill him."

"I still think it's sweet," Lou said before diving back into whatever she was working on.

Ben sat back, staring at the board they'd made weeks ago. Tracking Manny's movements around the globe. Trying to pinpoint where he would strike next.

Or he could think about the scene he was going to perform with the most gorgeous girl in the world. That seemed like a much nicer way to spend the afternoon.

When had he become this guy? He was a workaholic. It wasn't like he hadn't dated while he worked, but he never let a woman take up space in his head when he wasn't with her.

Kenzie had built a mansion there, and his brain was twenty-four seven Kenzie Taggart.

"Hey, babe. You want to ditch work and go see a movie?" Kala walked in and planted herself right on her husband's lap. She glanced over Ben's way. "Hello, Benjamin. I hope you are having a good day."

Ah, the Peace Accords were still in place. Although Kala's politeness often scared him. "I hope you are having a good day as well."

Lou snorted and shut her laptop. "All this love is making me hungry."

Cooper had an arm around his wife's waist. "Well, that's going to make TJ happy. What do you say we hit up that fish and chips place you love and take the crew out for the evening while the olds play. If we drink enough, we might not notice your dad railing your mom in public when we get back."

Such a weird world he found himself in. But he wouldn't go back. Not for anything.

"You know I'm thrilled my parents play at Sanctum and I never, ever enter that club," Lou announced. "Is there a reason we haven't gone to Ollie's club? I think we made an excellent decision when we opened The Hideout."

Kala's lips curled up. "I've heard Damon wouldn't front Ollie the money for his club and they don't have a couple of handy billionaires around to cover the costs. So Ollie's club is a pit of despair. Vivi's words, not mine."

A sharp huff came from the doorway. "I will be having a talk with

Vivian. How dare she impugn my beautiful club?"

"It's a dump," Sami said, walking behind him. It looked like the whole gang was here. They'd been spread out, investigating the properties they'd found during the Nepal mission, but it looked like they were all at base for the next couple of nights. "But it's our dump."

Ollie wore a suit even though he'd been around the office all day. He frowned in that rich-boy male-model way of his. "Well, I didn't have an inheritance to buy a whole building in Chelsea with. My parents decided to stay alive, and that apparently means I'm on my own."

Sami snorted. "I'm telling them you said that."

Ollie's eyes went wide. "Don't you dare. I was only joking, and Dad's loaning me money for reconstruction of the second floor. How was I to know that tiny hole in the roof would lead to a deluge?"

"For fuck's sake," Lucy said as she strode in. Though she didn't look Kala's way, she seemed to know instinctively where she was and held up her middle finger. "You should know because I told you, and I also told you I could fix it. My father is big on fixing things himself. I started learning home improvement at a young age. I can also build furniture."

"Yes, evil furniture," Kala said.

"It's not evil." His whole fucking world walked in. Kenzie was in jeans and a sweater that contrasted with that gorgeous hair. She looked soft and sweet and so fuckable it made his cock ache. He'd had her twice a day for almost three weeks, and he was fairly certain no amount of time or familiarity would make him want her less. "You know the dining room table you've sat at for years that I told you I found at a garage sale?"

Oh, he loved it when she got that evil glint in her eyes.

Kala sat up. "She did not build it."

Lucy flashed her a grin that held all the arrogance in the world. "Shipped it to her for her birthday. Which is also yours and proof that the universe does indeed make mistakes."

Kala sighed. "Damn it. That's the solidest table. You can't get that shit at a furniture store. It's because of her deal with the devil. The table at our place sucks. It can't even handle the weight of two people."

Kenzie dropped herself right on his lap. Like she belonged there. Which she did. She looked at him seriously. "Is she being nice to you?"

"She wished me a good day like we're back in the Gilded Age and met up in the park before going about our days amongst the common people," he admitted.

"You're welcome, Mr. Parker," Kala said and wrinkled her nose. "I almost called him sir. But like little s Sir. Not big s. I caught myself. That would have been gross. Also, just because Ollie's club is a dump is no reason to stay away when we have to share. The price of admission is catching sight of my dad's ass. Now I'm thinking about that table. I almost declared fight club over it."

Oh, they were not doing fight club. He started to say something but Kenzie stopped him, looking to Lucy.

Lucy sighed. "I had my dad do it. I thought about putting a curse on it that would make her lady bits itch for years, but my sister wouldn't let me. She said curses should be saved for the truly evil people of the world and then they put it to a vote on whether Kala was evil. I lost. Stupid democracy."

"I commissioned a table from Lucy a couple of weeks ago since I saw what Cooper was planning to buy. Let me say it was not built for two tops to go at it on," Kenzie offered.

"Dad totally knows how to make a bang table," Lucy admitted. "Let me tell you, there are closets in my house no kid should wander into. You should be grateful you were raised in a place where your dad had a club and could keep all the weird stuff in a locker or something."

Lou stood, glancing down at her phone. "TJ's in the lobby. I told him we might be going out for dinner and he's ready. I mean, he's always ready. And we can see the new rom com."

Lucy and Kala both groaned at the same time.

And then looked embarrassed by it. From what he could tell, they either didn't realize they were kind of the same person or they did and it bugged them. Either way, it was infinitely amusing.

Lucy's eyes narrowed. "I love rom coms. Thanks for the suggestion, Lou."

Kala practically growled. "You don't love them more than I do. I love them all."

Kenzie leaned in. "We totally planned this earlier today. Lucy and Kala would have wanted to go see either some overly analytical treatise on the working class or an action film where some dude avenges his dog. This was my and Lou's compromise. Tash said it wouldn't work."

Ah, but his Kenz could perform miracles when she wanted to. "Awesome." A rom com would put his baby in a good mood, and he was surprised at how much of his thought process was starting to be taken over with making Kenzie smile. "Let's do this. Should we invite Tim? If we invite him, we probably end up taking the assassin twins with us."

Only the slightest tightening of her jaw gave away the fact that she was disturbed by that bit of news. "They're getting along?"

Kala stood. "Then we should absolutely invite them."

Lucy nodded. "I'll go get them. Meet you upstairs in five."

Kala agreed without complaining, making the sign of the cross, or initiating an exorcism.

Something was wrong.

But then Kenzie kissed him and he didn't care.

Life was as perfect as it could be.

Week Three

"I should be there. If we have absolute certainty that Huisman is on the ground in Taipei, Tim and I should be there," Ben argued.

Her dad sighed. "I've told you why. He knows you. He doesn't know the MI6 team. I made the call to send them in because Joseph feels better working with MI6 than sending in another CIA team. They're watching him. Honestly, Huisman isn't the one we should be looking for. We need to find the bombmakers."

Over the last few weeks a pattern had emerged. Kenzie had been monitoring a bunch of syndicates and other criminal organizations who would link to freelancers. She and Lucy had IDed four bombmakers.

Three of them were now dead, their bodies dumped in countries they did not reside in.

"We need to be looking for a man named Alen Grul. He's a former biochemistry engineering professor from Bucharest. His work was specifically in how bombs are made." She couldn't tell that he had any criminal ties like the other three, but he had done some work for Disrupt on the dangers of using explosives to the environment. "As far as I can tell, he went missing two days ago."

"Then he's likely in Taipei, and we should be there on the ground,"

Ben argued.

"I seriously doubt he's building the bombs in Taiwan," Damon added. "We've got a shipment of something necessary to build bombs arriving at the Scottish compound in two days. Lucy is going up to watch it. From what we've discovered, he's got everything he needs to build the bombs there."

"Everything except the right person to do it," Lucy agreed. "Zach's taking his mom camping for a few weeks. Devi's with them. There are a couple of off-the-grid places in that part of Colorado. They can hide for weeks. Keeping Shannon Reed out of Huisman's hands is our most important duty right now."

"Henry's staying in Bliss for a few months," her father explained. "He's watching over my sons, and he'll be there if Zach and Devi need anything. Theo and Erin are hanging out, too."

"So we're stuck here?" Ben's whole body was tight.

She reached under the table and put a hand on his thigh.

Ben took a long breath. "I'm sorry. I'm getting anxious. He's been too quiet. I don't like it. My every instinct tells me he's planning something and we're walking right into the trap."

She was feeling that way, too, but putting Ben directly in the line of fire wasn't going to help. "Which is why we keep a low profile. I worry that one way or another, he's going to try to drag you into this. He'll want you to witness his final act."

"It's not his final act," her father disagreed, "but I do think he'll want Ben to participate. I know he still wants his hands on Kala again. So we stay safe. Well, as safe as we can be with a trio of kid assassins who might or might not be playing us."

"They're all capable of it." Ariel sat at the opposite end of the table, her eyes moving back to Ben as though she needed to study him. "Claire is worse than Sosa, a bit better than Gabby. I've had the doctor prescribe her sleep medication since from what I can tell she doesn't get more than an hour or two here and there. I think she was more physically abused than the other two."

Claire had joined them after being sprung from Dallas County Jail. She was quieter than the other two, though she'd seemed deeply happy to see them again.

She wasn't enjoying therapy, though, and she'd heard them all discussing Gabby's growing "relationship" with Tim.

It was a bad idea, but she also knew what forbidden fruit could do.

Ben assured her Tim was solid and it was nothing more than a crush.

She hoped he was right.

"For now we're keeping them close," Damon announced and closed the folder in his hand. "All right, you have your assignments for the week. We'll be back here in the morning. Be safe out there."

"Out where?" Ben complained since they were staying close to the club this week.

She turned her hand over, offering it to him. He was getting anxious.

Still, he took it and seemed to calm.

The last few weeks had been sheer perfection. They could do this. Even if they had to be long distance for a while. They could work together. Be together.

She was in love with him.

And she would show him tonight.

Chapter Thirteen

Kenzie watched as Ben strode out of the locker room. This afternoon's showdown with her dad had been rough, but they'd had dinner earlier and all seemed well.

Now he walked out with Dare, a smile on his face.

"He looks happy," Tasha said, adjusting her corset.

Kala was already on the dungeon floor. She and Cooper had found a play partner in one of Ollie's closest friends. He was a big-time barrister during the day. Pain slut at night. They loved topping a sub together and then would retire to a privacy room to go at it hard.

She had prepped their privacy room earlier today. Her man needed some relaxation time, and she needed him. For all the joy of the last few weeks, there was still tension hanging over them. Huisman was being quiet, but that simply meant he was planning something. Something big, and she was almost certain it would have to do with the three young women they were watching over.

She hoped the traitor didn't turn out to be Tim. She wasn't sure Ben could handle it if Tim turned out to be Huisman's insider. She was sure he had one.

"I think he is. I think Ben's spent the last few years of his life trusting no one except his team members, and he's figuring out how nice it is to have a friend group." Kenzie gave him a smile, and her whole body tightened with anticipation as he went from friendly smile for Dare to his eyes heating as he looked her over. He would find out that a friend group rapidly became a family group.

She was certain he would pick her when the time came. When Huisman dropped whatever bomb he was planning, Ben would pick her. Like she'd picked Ben when Huisman tried to make them believe he was working with him.

During their last mission, Huisman had planted several rumors that Ben was working with him and had been the entire time. He'd said it to Zach, but Lou recorded the incident. They'd analyzed it and she'd been Ben's biggest supporter. In the end, they all saw through Huisman's lies.

But Huisman would try again and she would find a way to protect the man she loved.

"He's fitting in well," Tasha said with a satisfied smile. "I think this is actually going to work out. And I caught him smiling at one of Dad's truly horrible jokes."

The good news was with the exception of Ben's objections the other day, he and her father seemed to be getting along. She didn't worry about her mom. Her mom got along with everyone.

"Hey, baby." Ben reached for her hand, dragging her close and kissing her forehead with a tenderness that made her ache. "Are you ready? All the olds are safe in their beds. It's our night to play."

They weren't. Her mom and dad were out on the town with Damon and Penny and the so not old Robert and Ariel and Nick and Hayley Markovic.

"I'm ready." She'd never been more ready.

The Garden was beautiful, but she wanted to be back in Dallas. At The Hideout. Their club. She loved her team but she missed Brianna and Devi and Daisy, and she so missed Bud Two. She wanted to settle in with Ben, and this felt like a holiday. Not the work part but the part where they were floating, enjoying the time they had and not pushing real boundaries.

Except the sexual ones. They'd pushed those, and she was going to crash through at least one tonight.

She took his hand and let him lead her into a fantasy world.

An hour later, she felt her whole body light with anticipation as Ben closed the door to the privacy room.

They'd spent their time on the dungeon floor watching some heavy scenes, Ben's hands on her waist as he leaned in and whispered the sexiest things in her ear.

The only thing that marred the experience was the cell phone in his pocket, but they'd all agreed to lift the no cell phones on the dungeon floor rule while the mission was ongoing. She wasn't carrying, but then her handlers could come running into the dungeon if they needed to, and Ben's was back in Toronto.

Still, it was his choice because Joseph could call her father.

He needed it, and she wasn't going to complain. It was put in silent mode, and in the weeks they'd been playing he hadn't answered it once. It was there because he struggled to let go of control when it came to Huisman.

Everything else was pretty fucking perfect.

She dropped to her knees, spreading them wide and letting her head fall forward. She offered him the greatest gift she could give him in this sacred space. Her submission.

"I will never get used to how I feel when I see you like this." His boots came into view, and his hand came out to touch her head. "You are the most gorgeous woman I've ever known. Seeing you like this, knowing you're willing to do this for me, brings me peace."

It was as close as he'd gotten to *I love you*. Ben could be shut down emotionally. He often followed her cues, and she was going to give him a big one tonight. She was shoving away all her doubt and worry. It had no place in this room. This room was their temple where they worshipped each other, where they became whole.

"I find peace with you, Sir."

He was silent for a moment. "Do you think we could move forward, Kenzie? Could you call me Master? In our contract we said we would revisit the title in a week or two and see how you felt about it."

She would have called him Master the first night, but she realized she was too bright eyed sometimes and Ben was the one who felt like he needed to earn his title. A deep wave of satisfaction curled inside her, and she brought her head up so she could see his gorgeous face. "Yes, Master. I would like that very much."

The smile on his face warmed her.

He gripped her hand and helped her to stand. Since that first night, they'd explored and played, and she'd spent a lot of time on a St. Andrew's Cross and that spanking bench, though he liked to spank her anywhere, really. When she got particularly saucy in a meeting, he would pull her into a room afterward and slap her ass silly before turning her over and sliding her on his cock. He'd fucked her up against the door to the conference room once after a healthy argument about Huisman. He didn't appreciate her careful—he called it slow—investigation, and she thought his get-in-there approach was reckless.

But neither of them cared after a good long fuck.

She was ready for another.

"How are you tonight?" He asked the question he always did before they started a formal session.

"I'm perfectly green, Master."

"Even after that meeting? I know your father is annoyed."

Her head shook. "We are not allowed to talk about my parents in here. No parents at all."

His lips curled up slightly. "Well, we won't talk about mine when yours are so much more interesting. I'm supposed to go fishing when this is done. I think your father might try to drown me. He doesn't think Canadians can swim."

Her father was a menace. "He would never desecrate his precious lake house with a murder. He would just bury you there, so I think you're safe."

"I do not want to ask." He stepped back. "Strip for me."

He liked to watch her get naked. Oh, he would rip her clothes off when need came over him, but he loved to stand back and watch as she carefully revealed everything that belonged to him.

She worked the fastenings of her corset, the one her cousin designed so she could unbind herself with one hand. She carefully took off her shoes and then pushed her thong over her hips. All the while she watched as Ben's leathers tented with his erection.

She loved his cock. She loved sucking it and playing with it, and she went wild when he used it on her.

He made her drunk with love and lust.

"I'm ready for you, Master."

His eyes heated. "Not yet you aren't. But you will be."

He eased her to the bed, placing her the way he wanted. On her back, knees bent and her ass nearly hanging off. He spread her wide. "Stay there. Don't move or we'll have punishment."

She could be a good girl when she wanted to be, and she always wanted to be his good girl.

"Let me tie you up." It was a command, but she could tell him no.

She was comfortable with him now. "Yes, Master."

She let her arms float over her head. The bed was fully equipped with restraints. He wrapped the rope around her wrists, lovingly binding her, and then kissed his way down her body. He ended up dropping to his knees between her legs, his mouth hovering over her pussy as her body pulsed with desire.

The man had the most talented tongue. He could make such a feast of her.

"Kenzie, baby, you know what I'm going to do tonight."

She knew. She'd worn carefully selected plugs for weeks. And had the best time complaining about it in the morning conferences. At first Ben was kind of shocked that she would mention it in front of…everyone…but now he simply grinned and went with it and talked about lube in a way that made her dad talk a lot about vomiting. Naturally Coop and TJ joined in, and Tristan started sending group texts about best practices when it came to anal sex. He was working at Langley in DC, but he proved he could cause trouble even with an ocean between them.

"You're going to take my ass," she whispered, loving how vulnerable she felt. It was good to have a place where she could be vulnerable and open and let this part of her flow. The part only Benjamin Parker ever got to see.

A shudder went through him, and he seemed to have to control himself. "Yes. I'm going to take your ass, baby. It's mine. The way you're mine."

She was perfectly fine with that as long as he was hers.

Ben pulled his vest off and laid it over the tray she prepared. It was not only a way to honor and serve her Dom, but also to control the kind of lube used. It was kind of nice that Ben was willing to leave that work to her. She could control the scene in some small way.

She closed her eyes and prepared for a truly delicious evening. He would eat her pussy and bring her to orgasm four or five times before he gently took her ass. She'd planned it out to perfection.

The crackling sound and then distinct smell of ozone let her know something had gone awry.

She looked up, but he wasn't in her line of sight. She could see the carefully prepared tray, but it didn't look like he'd started to use it for anything but a place to lay his leather vest. "Ben? I didn't ask for a violet wand."

He came into view, his face alight with pure joy. She had never seen him so open and happy. "I know, babe. But see, it's been pointed out to me that I'm a lazy Dom. Asking my sub to do all the work for our scenes. Now I might have explained to your sister that you enjoy preparing the scene."

Oh, shit. Her twin was causing trouble. "Kala is giving you hell. It's fine, Ben. You're right. I do enjoy it. I like making sure everything is ready for you, Master."

He smoothed back her hair with the hand that wasn't holding the violet wand. The wand that was right there, and she had no idea what setting it was on. She had no idea how good he was with a violet wand. "Oh, sweetie, if Kala talked to me about how I top my sub, I would start a fight club and we might finally be able to work on our issues. I'm not joking. We have discussed that. We think a couple of hours of punching the shit out of each other might help our relationship, and I happen to know how hard she can punch. You know, now that I think about it, I should have known the difference between you because of your fighting style. She's way meaner than you."

She was a little offended. "I can be mean in a fight, but I didn't want to fight you. And no, there is no fight club."

He leaned over slightly and touched the violet wand to her left nipple.

And she damn near came off the bed. It wasn't like the sucker was on a higher setting. It had been a flutter over her skin, but it was enough. "Ben."

He sighed as though he'd done something deeply satisfying. "It wasn't Kala. It was Tash, and she pointed out that you like to top from the bottom and you might like to put it as service when it's your way of ensuring you know what happens. Well, I would be a bad top to allow this to continue."

He touched the wand to her right nipple, the sensation sizzling across her skin. Kenzie gasped and held on to the restraints her asshole

Master had placed her in knowing she would think he was going to eat her pussy. Liar.

It was kind of sexy.

"Tash might have pointed out that it's not submission if you're in control of everything." Another sizzle along her skin. He was on the side of the bed, but his stupid long arms and ridiculously tall body treated the queen-size bed like it was a twin. He didn't have to struggle to reach her. "You're in control of one thing tonight, Kenzie. Whether or not you say yes, but you're not going to say no to me. I'm going to torture this gorgeous body. I'm going to put my mark all over you, baby, and you're going to do nothing but ask me for more."

The trouble was, he was right. She would never say no to this man.

Even as he started to trace a line of fire down her body.

"I like the violet wand. Don't you, baby? I can torture the hell out of you at this setting and not leave a mark."

Kenzie whimpered. She wasn't sure if she was whimpering about the fire that skittered over her skin or the idea that he wouldn't mark her. She loved it. Loved the bite marks and where he sucked her skin it bloomed like a little tattoo, proof of how primal he could be when it came to her.

"But don't worry." He moved to the end of the bed, taking one of her legs in his hand and settling it on his shoulder. He turned his head slightly and gave her calf a hard nip. "I know how much you like a bite."

She let out a strangled scream because the pain flared and then became heat pooling between her thighs. Ben nibbled his way down her leg even as that fucking wand found her nipples again.

He was killing her. He didn't let up. Between the sharp nips to her skin and the electricity lighting up her nipples, she couldn't breathe, couldn't think past the next sensation. Time seemed to bend on itself as Ben worked her over thoroughly.

When he touched her pussy with that fucking wand, her back bowed as she came. She was thankful for the restraints because she needed something to hold onto. Pleasure swamped her senses as she gritted her teeth and rode the wave.

Ben was smiling when he placed the wand on the tray she'd prepared and he seemed intent on not using. "You're so wet, baby. It's a fucking beautiful sight." He dropped to his knees and before she'd had a chance to catch her breath, his tongue dove deep, mouth covering her pussy with a heat that threatened to singe her soul.

This was what she'd been waiting for. She felt possessed by him, loved by him. Tonight they connected on a level she'd never felt before.

"Turn me over," she whispered. It would be easier for him.

He stared down at her. "And miss looking at your face? No, Kenzie. This is going to be my way. All the way." He released her, unbinding her with a practiced hand, and then he eased a pillow under her lower back, opening her further to him. "And I want to feel your hands on me."

She was more than ready when she felt his fingers rimming her asshole, rubbing the lube in. Her breath caught because he wasn't going to use a plug this time.

Her body softened in submission. This was what she'd dreamed of since the moment she'd understood what sex was. She wanted this communion with the man she loved, with the man she could build a life with.

He was here now. With her. And there was no going back.

She gasped as he loomed over her, and she felt that big dick start to breach her.

Pressure but no pain. She bit her bottom lip as he gently worked his way in, little thrusts back and forth, opening her up in short passes.

And then he was inside her. She forced herself to breathe. She was too full. He was too big. She clutched him, letting her nails sink into his skin because she knew he liked to have her mark on him, too.

"You feel so good. I hope you like this because I can't believe how good this is." His jaw was tight, his face a mask of pure desire.

He was the most beautiful thing she'd ever seen. She tilted her pelvis up, taking him deeper.

Then he pulled back, his cock stroking her in a way she'd never felt before. Kenzie cried out, her whole body in tune with his, every nerve ending lighting with pleasure.

She felt their connection like she could feel the pleasure coming from his own body. He fucked her with ruthless precision, his hands on her hips, holding her still while he took and gave and connected them.

It seemed endless, this place she found with him. Endless and over far too soon since her body was already primed for pleasure. The orgasm felt cataclysmic.

Ben's hands clenched around her as he came, filling her with warmth and life, and he was smiling as he fell down on the bed beside her.

He chuckled and helped her move up on the bed. "Give me a second and I'll get you under those covers."

"I love you so much." The words were out of her mouth before she could think to call them back.

Ben went still, and she felt him tense.

Well, she'd known he probably wasn't ready.

His cell phone buzzed in the now-awkward silence, and Ben rolled off the bed like it was an oven that would burn him. He went to the bathroom, and she heard the sink turn on. The cell kept buzzing.

Kenzie knew her perfect night was over.

* * * *

She'd said she loved him.

Ben left the bathroom after cleaning up. He walked over and picked up his cell, looking at the phone in his hand like it was a life jacket someone had thrown to him. Because those three words from her hit him like a bomb exploding.

His body buzzed with the pleasure she'd given him. Everything. She'd given him everything, including three words he wasn't sure he could say back.

He wasn't sure he was capable of loving anyone. He wasn't sure it was safe for him to love anyone. Anyone he loved, Manny would come after, and it could put Kenzie and her twin in serious danger.

He cared about her. More than anything in the world. But love. He didn't like the word.

"Are you going to answer that?" All the sweet passion was out of Kenzie's tone. Her face had gone a careful blank, and she was reaching for her robe.

He'd absolutely seen her like this before. When she was unsure, she could put up a hell of a front.

No. He shouldn't answer. He should talk this out with her. He slid his phone back on the side table. "Kenzie, I care about you."

Her lips turned up, and if he didn't know better, he would think she was fine. But her eyes lacked the sparkle they always had when she looked at him.

He'd never realized how good it felt when she looked at him like he was the sun in the sky.

"Good. I care about you, too," she replied, her voice carefully controlled. "I'm going to head to the locker room and get dressed."

"I thought we were meeting Kala and Cooper for drinks."

"I think I'm going to make it an early night." She chuckled, though it was all performative. He knew the sound of her laughter, and this was tinged with bitterness. "I think sitting on anything that's not a bag of something frozen would be a mistake."

"Did I hurt you?" He thought he'd been careful. He'd insisted on preparation. Should he have taken longer?

When he tried to reach for her, she turned away. "I'm fine. I'm sore but fine. It's been a long week. I think I'll get some sleep."

Fuck. He'd fucked it all up. His phone went quiet. All the intimacy of moments before now felt awkward, and he had to find a way to save this. "Kenzie, those words are kind of loaded for me."

She pulled the robe around her body and gathered her corset and thong. "Of course they are. I'm sorry. I got carried away. I won't say them again if they bother you."

She wouldn't. Kenzie was a giving woman, but he got the feeling she was one of those women who gave and gave and gave until she was done. She wouldn't beg for his love. She'd shown him. She'd told him. It was up to him to accept it or not.

He grabbed his leathers, ignoring his cell for the moment. This was a conversation they needed to have. He wished they weren't having it now. Wished he'd handled this in a way that left them cuddled up in bed. "Baby, I'm fucking this up. I need you to understand how much it means to me that you care about me. If you want to call it love, I'll get used to the words. I'll figure out a way to say them."

Her head shook, and he would bet money she was fighting back tears. "I don't want you to give me words you don't mean. But I would like to know where you see this going if we're not in love."

Not in love. He didn't actually like the sound of that, but there was a part of him whispering. His parents "loved" him until he was inconvenient. Deanna "loved" him until she found someone who could give her more. Manny was supposed to be his best friend. How many times had Manny said he "loved" him like a brother?

His brain buzzed with warning alarms.

This was a woman who read romance novels like they were her lifeline. She talked about epic love and swooned over weddings. He would lose her over this. Why hadn't he fucking said the words? They didn't have to mean anything. Hell, he didn't like rom coms and yet he sat there and watched them to make her happy. She had zero interest in what she called sportsball, but she laid with her head in his lap while she read a book and he watched the Blue Jays play so he could stroke her hair and have her close. Couldn't he say a couple of dumb words?

She took a long breath and put a hand on his arm. "It's okay. We don't have to talk about it now. We're just having fun."

Not what he'd told her. He gripped her wrist, unwilling to let her walk out. Not like this. He needed to get her back in bed. He was good in bed. Fucking terrible at this. "We agreed we were serious. When we met that day at Top, we agreed we would give this thing a try. Are you threatening to leave me over a few words? I didn't once say we were just having fun."

"And when this mission is over?" Kenzie asked, and now the tears filled her eyes. Her blue eyes that kicked him in the gut every time he looked at her.

The cell buzzed. A text. He ignored it. If it was Joseph, he could talk to Tim. "I don't know. We both go back to work and see each other when we can. We work together a lot."

"We work together when it comes to Huisman," she said. "If we take down Huisman, I think you'll find there's not a lot of work for us to do. What if I decided to work less? With my sister moving into a supervisory position, I was thinking it might be time to look at the private sector. Maybe it's time to open an office in Toronto. My dad always wanted one in New York, but this could be better."

Kenzie in Toronto? He liked the idea, but what would they do? What would he do? He'd joined CSIS to take down Manny. What would he do when the job was done? Would the job ever be done? Could he marry Kenzie and have kids, because that woman would probably want kids. He didn't have anything to offer kids. He couldn't bring his family into it because he would never trust them again. He could still hear his father telling him to look them up once he'd solved the problem and maybe they could talk then.

He would never speak with them again, much less introduce them to children he loved so they could fuck them over, too.

Why was she pushing this? He wasn't ready for any of this. "I think you should hold off on making decisions like that. You like the job too much. We can work things out. We'll be good."

If they weren't living together, they wouldn't have to deal with the whole kids and marriage thing. He could still be her Dom. They could meet up and play and spend long weekends together. He wasn't sure he would be a good husband. She deserved a good husband. She deserved the kind of life her parents had, and he wasn't sure he could give that to her. Certainly not until they handled Emmanuel Huisman.

She pulled away, and this time he let her. "All right, Ben. I'm going to clean up and I'm going to stay with Lucy tonight. I need to think."

So she was going to punish him. A hint of bitterness crept through his fear. This suddenly felt like manipulation. "So the princess doesn't get the words she wants and I get cut out."

Her eyes narrowed. "Ben, I'm emotional. I'm trying to keep it together, and I've attempted to avoid this conversation several times now because I don't want to say something I don't mean. If you had let me have a couple of minutes, I might have been able to pull myself together."

"So now I'm not reacting the way you want." He knew the words she was saying made sense, but he was getting a restless feeling. This was where everything fell apart. He hadn't danced to her…

Fuck. He'd hurt her, and he was making it worse. She was literally asking him for a couple of minutes to process the fact that she'd told the man she loved that she loved him and he was never going to return the words.

He backed up. "I'm sorry, Kenzie. I'm acting like an ass because I'm terrified of losing you. Baby, can we get dressed and go back to our flat and talk about this? Please?"

"I need time," she replied, tears rolling down her cheeks.

She looked so young and hurt, and he'd put that expression on her face.

Another text came through. Damn it. Joseph wouldn't keep calling unless it was necessary. He didn't know what else to say so he picked up the cell.

Unknown number.

The room went cold.

Kenzie seemed to sense something had gone wrong. Something else.

Pick up the phone, Benjamin. You won't like how I express my dissatisfaction that I'm being ignored.

"Is it him?" Kenzie asked, her voice suddenly tense. "I'll go let Dad and Damon know."

"Don't." He knew the protocols. No one was supposed to talk directly to Manny, but he'd always known he wouldn't follow that rule. "This is between me and him."

He stared at the phone like it was a snake waiting to strike. It would ring and he would answer, and maybe this time he could figure out how to take the fucker down. His heart rate ticked up in a way it only did when facing the fucking monster in his life.

"Ben, you need to destroy the cell and I'll get you another," Kenzie insisted. "You can't give him a chance to get into your head. This is what he does. He causes chaos. The only way to stop it is to not play this game with him."

The cell rang. She didn't understand Manny. Not the way he did. If he didn't answer, then he wouldn't know what was coming his way. Manny would do something and it would be his fault.

"Ben, I am asking you to give me the phone. If you care about me, don't answer that phone."

Another manipulation. He slid his finger across the screen. "Hello."

He turned and heard Kenzie walk to the bathroom. And lock the door behind her. She either didn't get what was happening or she was trying to control him. Either way, he had to answer that phone.

A deep chuckle came over the line. "Did I interrupt something, Benjamin? How is London treating you?"

Well, he should have known. He turned and looked at the door that separated him from Kenzie. "What do you want, Manny?"

"One would think you don't like me."

He wasn't taking that bait today. He remained silent. Big Tag was right about a couple of things, and one of them was that Ben let Manny get his goat. Although the big bastard had said something like Huisman gets your goat and impregnates him in front of you so then you have baby goats and then he takes those too.

Kenzie's dad had a way with words.

He wasn't using words on Manny right now. Silence would have to do.

"All right, you're not in a talkative mood. Tell me, are the girls with you?" Manny asked.

"I'm alone." He might actually be if Kenzie was that pissed at him. He would make it up to her. He would go directly to her dad after he was done and then they could sit down and talk. "I don't know where the women of the team are."

"I was talking about the assassins I sent to kill Mr. Taggart. They didn't seem to do a good job," Manny said over the line. "I'll have to punish them accordingly."

A cold chill went up his spine. "So you are involved in trafficking little girls."

Another chuckle. Manny was endlessly amused with the horrors around him. "There's no such thing as a little girl. They're all born venomous, and you should know. Benjamin, how many times do you have to learn this lesson? I assure you those girls, as you call them, have committed more atrocities than you can imagine and they are part of my army, though they believe I'm just a client. Actually, it was my grandfather who set up the network. Apparently the medical profession didn't pay much in the beginning, but he did meet some poor people in the old country who didn't mind selling their useless daughters. Now I want my naughty girls back."

Ben remembered how Sosa reacted to Manny's photograph, and his stomach threatened to revolt. "So now you rape children."

"Benjamin, I wouldn't touch a woman for anything other than procreation." His disgust was plain in his tone. "You're the one with that sad bourgeois notion that you need a female in order to be a man. I assure you they're easy to hire, and maids and cooks won't expect you to dance to their tunes. And if they do, you can kill them and bury them in the garden. Have you wondered why the roses bloom so beautifully at my home in Montreal?"

Every word from his mouth turned Ben's stomach. He was glad Kenzie was locked in the bathroom because he wouldn't want her to overhear this. The menace in his voice felt like it could come over the line and crawl into his veins, poisoning him. Still, it was all data. All information he could take to her father. She would forgive him when he got the intel they needed to bring Manny down.

And then what? He'd practically told her he didn't want her to live with him. Why the fuck had he said that? Because he couldn't imagine her being happy with him long term? Because she was sunshine, and everything he loved seemed to turn to ash?

"Excellent. You're a murderer. We already knew that."

"Is it murder or simply taking out the trash?" Manny asked.

"And we all know you've had at least one girlfriend. Have you considered that the reason you can't get a girl is because you're a walking, talking piece of shit? The only way you could get one in bed is to pay her."

"Is that what I did with Deanna? You know the funny thing is she didn't want to have an affair with me. She loved you. Which was why when I explained to her if she didn't fuck me, you would have a terrible accident and your career would be over. She was so proud of how you threw a ball around."

His heart clenched. "You threatened her?"

"I blackmailed her. It was fun. Not the sex. That was a simple task. You see for a man like you, having your precious woman violated by a stronger man is devastating, and I wanted to devastate you. I didn't expect for you to actually survive that accident."

He forced himself to stand there, to not punch something. "Yes, that was clear. What do you want, Manny? I'm not going to discuss the past."

"Because you think Deanna is in the past."

The words stopped him. He heard the bathroom door open and Kenzie walked out, the robe carefully pulled around her and her hair in a long braid. She'd washed the makeup off her face and there was no expression there as she started to gather what she needed. "What is that supposed to mean?"

"It means you shouldn't always believe your eyes, my friend. Haven't you learned how women can lie and lie? Didn't your girlfriend teach you that?"

"Don't talk about Maggie." He used the name he'd called her before he knew her real one.

Kenzie's middle finger came up, though she didn't look back at him. She was too busy picking up her shoes.

He hoped that was for Manny.

"Maggie? You're still calling her that? I rather thought you and the boring one had finally given in to your forbidden passion," Manny replied.

Kenzie started for the door. He was about to follow her when the weight of Manny's words hit him.

The boring one. Like there was more than one. "What do you mean?"

A low huff came over the line. "Benjamin, please tell me you're not sleeping with her and you still don't know about her twin. Did she even tell you her real name? Women. This is what I was talking about. Her name is Kenzie Taggart. Unless you're sleeping with the interesting one. I don't know that I like that idea. I'm going to be honest. I find Kala Taggart infinitely intriguing. I've started to wonder if there isn't a woman out there for me. Her."

He felt sick. "You know. How long?"

"From the beginning." He paused like he hadn't expected this. "Did they not tell you? It wasn't in those reports they send you? I've known since they came into our game. It was amusing watching you fumble and get confused because you couldn't tell them apart, but I never expected them to take it this far."

"No. If you know, you know, but they didn't know you knew." The words sounded dumb and confusing. Like the situation he found himself in.

She wouldn't have done this to him. Not Kenzie. She wouldn't have let him follow her around like a fool for Manny's amusement. She wouldn't.

"I assure you they know everything. We've talked about it. Did you not understand that I have a relationship with them? Or perhaps we've been working together all along. Anyway, they know I have no interest in their precious sunshine girl. She's not, you know. She's ordinary. Her sister is the extraordinary one. She's a woman who doesn't lie. Well, except to you."

The world felt colder as he stood there in the room where he'd made love to her. Love. There was that stupid word.

"I can sense that you have some work to do, my friend. I'll let you get to it. But I have a task for you, and I think you'll be intrigued. I'll send you a video tomorrow and let you know where we can meet and discuss the situation. Good night, Benjamin."

The line went dead, and Ben's world practically went red.

He needed to breathe. Needed to figure out what had actually happened.

And yet his rage took control.

He strode out the door ready to confront the latest woman who betrayed him.

Chapter Fourteen

Kenzie walked toward the dungeon, trying her hardest to stop crying. She'd gone into the bathroom so he wouldn't see her sob. She'd managed to clean up, wash her face, and calm down. She'd worried he would be waiting for her, but she should have known. He was with the man who formed the center of his life. Huisman. She should have known nothing would matter when he had Huisman's attention. Certainly not an inconvenient lay.

Ben might not give a shit that she was upset, but there would be plenty of people who did. It wasn't even midnight. The scenes would be going, the club would be hopping, and the last thing she wanted was a bunch of people trying to figure out what had gone wrong.

Her. She'd gone wrong.

She'd mistaken lust and comfort for love.

She might never forget how his expression had gone from wonder and satisfaction to that blank look the minute the words *I love you* were out of her mouth.

She wanted to be home. If this was her club, she could get dressed and be home with a bottle of sauv blanc in one hand and the other arm wrapped around Bud Two in less than twenty minutes. She would cry and send Ben some nasty breakup texts and come up with a plan to pretend like he didn't mean anything to her.

She couldn't do that now. The minute she asked Lucy if she could bunk down with her, everyone would know how poorly she'd chosen again. Poor Kenzie. Couldn't keep a man. Kept "falling" and all she had to show for it was a bruised heart while everyone around her was happily settling down.

Well, too fucking bad because she didn't have some fated mate like Cooper or TJ waiting in the wings. Hell, Tris got two damn soul mates. Daisy "The Curse" O'Donnell had found true love despite being constantly in the middle of a hurricane. Zach had lied to everyone and hidden his true mission, but did that stop him from finding love with her cousin? Nope.

Tasha had lied to Dare and they were happily married.

It was only her. Only the one who spent her whole stupid life hoping and praying she would find that magical love that would make her feel whole.

She stopped at the edge of the hall. The Garden's privacy rooms were separated from the rest of the dungeon by a set of opaque glass doors that slid open when the right code was used.

She wiped her eyes and stuffed her thong in the pocket of her robe. There wasn't much she could do with the shoes or corset. Normally she would have taken a shower and redressed for the "after" party. They'd taken to meeting with Kala and Cooper and Dare and Tash after play was done. Sometimes Lou and TJ would join and they would sit around talking and having some wine and snacks.

She'd thought he was fitting in, and maybe he was. Maybe he liked having friends more than he liked having a girlfriend. Or he needed them to get to the one person in the world who truly mattered to Ben Parker.

Damn it. She had to get it together. Deep breath. Smile like nothing's wrong. She could do this.

She put in the code that allowed the door to slide open. Before she walked through, the door to the closest privacy room came open and she could have sworn she had a brief glimpse of one of the assassin girls before she slammed the door closed again.

Tim was staying down here.

And she would have to deal with that, too. Her parents were going to be thrilled to end their night with yet another meeting, but she wasn't going to sleep on it. Her handlers had to know Huisman contacted Ben and that Tim was getting in deep with a group of women they weren't sure about yet.

And they would know she'd fucked up again. Poor Kenzie, with her head in the clouds.

She heard the doors hiss closed behind her.

"Hey, what's going on?" Lucy was sitting in the dungeon monitor chair. She looked adorable in a miniskirt and corset and thigh-high boots that made her legs look a mile long. She must have taken over for the big beefy Dom who'd been there when she'd entered with Ben. She had a book in her hand. It would either be a treatise on equity in political access or a manual on how to blow the shit out of something or a really filthy romance. "Where's Ben?"

She was going to tell her parents about Huisman, but she didn't have to out him to everyone. "He's cleaning up. Hey, is it okay if I stay with you tonight? I'm afraid Ben and I need a break."

One brow arched over Lucy's dark eyes. "What did he do?"

Yep. She wasn't getting out of this easy. "Can we talk about it later?"

Lucy's jaw went tight but she nodded. "Yeah. First we should talk about the fact that two of those girls are in Tim's room, and I can't monitor them in there. They showed up with a pizza and a six pack of beer and said Tim invited them down to play board games. Which they could do in the living spaces upstairs and be far more comfortable."

"But those spaces are monitored by CCTV." Her deepest instincts were firing off. Something was going on, and they needed to figure it out.

"That's what I'm saying," Lucy admitted. "I'll bug the room when he's working tomorrow, but Tim's not dumb. I worry he'll check and then we have to explain."

Or they wouldn't because they were working on opposite sides.

She didn't need this tonight. "I've got to talk to my parents anyway. Do we know if they're back?"

Lucy nodded. "I tracked them coming back an hour ago. Damon and Penny, too. I think Rob and Ari went back to their place, and so did Nick and Hayley. I don't understand it. I like it here. Communal living makes sense."

She was sure it did. To Lucy, who'd basically grown up in a commune known as Bliss. "I'll handle it."

Lucy reached out, putting a hand on her arm. "Hey, are you okay and how much wine should I steal from the bar?"

Kenzie sniffled. "Maybe one. For me."

Lucy pulled her in for a hug. "Two then. It's going to be okay, sweetie. My mom's going through a witch phase. We can curse him so his dick falls off."

Somehow she didn't see Nell Flanders working dark magic. She would work to manifest world peace or something.

"Kenzie Taggart," a familiar voice called out.

She turned and Ben was there wearing nothing but the leathers he'd dragged on during their fight. Or rather the first part of their fight, since it looked like he was up for round two.

Her gut twisted when she saw his face and realized Huisman's work had been superlative tonight because Ben was angry. Volcanically angry.

She needed to get them someplace quiet or he was going to cause a scene, and he would hate himself when he could think again. "Let's go back to the privacy room. You need your boots and vest."

"Fuck the boots, Kenzie." He towered over her, getting into her space and using his height for full intimidation.

"Uh, you're not going anywhere with him," Lucy said. "And I think you should back off, Parker."

He ignored her, staring down at Kenzie. "I bet you would love to get me alone again. Isn't that what you do? You get me alone and suddenly I'm doing whatever you want."

She was confused. Their sexual encounters—she wouldn't call it making love again—were dominated by him. He brought her enormous pleasure, but she served him in those sessions. "Ben, I'm sorry for what I said. I didn't realize those words would be such a trigger for you. I won't say them again. I told you I need some space."

"I don't give a damn about the *I love you*, Kenzie. I see it for what it is. That's what you have a problem with. You figured out you can't manipulate me with words. So you want to get me in private so you can manipulate me with your pussy. Well, sweetheart, I've had that and I can get better."

Lucy moved closer now, and her whole body was primed for a fight. "Back off now, Parker. I think she's trying to spare you. If you don't then I'll go get backup, and I don't think that will go well for you."

Those words from Ben had been like a kick in the gut. She felt hollowed out. Never once had she attempted to manipulate him. She handled him at times because he was stubborn and could be his own worst enemy, but never once had she thought he would view *her* as the enemy.

But then she was sure Huisman had done some serious damage. He'd tried it with her team, tried to split them up, but it hadn't worked. It looked like he'd found an easier target. But then she loved Ben and he didn't love her.

"Stay out of it," Ben barked.

Lucy strode away. Kenzie blinked back tears because she was certain who Lucy would go straight to, and it was everything she was trying to avoid. She reached out and put a hand on Ben's arm. "Please, let's go somewhere and talk about this."

He pulled his arm back, jerking it away like she was poison. "I didn't give you permission to touch me, sub, and I told you I'm not going to be alone with you so you can work your magic on me. I understand that it's worked well in the past, but I see you clearly now."

Wasn't this her nightmare? That Ben would turn on her because Huisman told him to, and the truth was Huisman was always more important than she was. She'd always known if she went into a relationship with Ben, Huisman would be there, too. But she'd been sure her love could overcome his hate. That's what love did. It conquered. It won.

Except he didn't want her love. He didn't even believe in it, and he couldn't possibly feel the same way if he was saying the things he was saying.

She wasn't doing this with him. It was time to retreat and build up her defenses. Hell, maybe it was time to request another assignment. If she convinced her team to pull out and allow Ben to work with another Agency team, would Huisman leave them alone? "Write up whatever story Huisman told you and present it to my team. They can decide if I'm a whore they want to throw away or not, but I'm not doing this with you."

She tried to turn but he reached out and gripped her arm again.

She was covered in his marks, every one of them a gift she'd accepted with glee because she was proud to have the whole world know she belonged to this man, that she'd finally found her one. Not this time. He gripped her tight enough that it would bruise, and she would look at it and feel how much he hated her.

She might not be able to play that way again.

"I'm not some asshole you get to order around, princess," he growled.

There it was again. The derision. She was a princess. She was entitled. It was time to call it. Time of death eleven forty-eight. She twisted her arm, ignoring the pain even as she reached up with her free hand and popped him right on the nose. Ben cursed and let go.

"What the fuck, Kenzie?" He put a hand on his nose.

"Oh, I would like to know the answer to that question," a familiar voice said.

Awesome. Her twin was here. She turned and saw that Kala wasn't alone. Cooper was with her, and TJ, too.

Kenzie let the sleeve of her robe fall down to cover the red marks on her wrist. She didn't want some big scene that everyone would call dramatic. "Nothing. Benjamin and I have decided to part ways."

"Why?" The question came out of Kala's mouth directed at Kenzie, though her eyes were on Ben.

"It doesn't matter." Work. She could change Kala's focus with work. "He's had a call from Huisman. We need to meet in the conference room so he can fill us in."

"Or I can leave since I'm obviously not needed here unless I'm playing your idiot stud." Ben massaged his nose, but it didn't look like she'd broken it. She'd pulled her punch.

Oh, Huisman had done spectacular work this time. "You don't have to worry about that anymore, Ben. I get it. I was fun for a while, but the great Emmanuel Huisman has spoken and now I'm a whore who's using you. Or is it worse? Am I after more than your hot bod? Am I distracting you for him? He's trying to kill my father, but I'm probably working with him because that's what women do, right?"

The words seemed to hit Ben as he briefly lost his angry expression. But it was okay because he'd obviously rationalized it all. "Or your father's in on it, too. Wouldn't that be perfect?"

"Dude, you think way too much of yourself," Kala said, looking from Kenzie to Ben as if she wasn't sure if she should comfort her sister or pull Ben's balls off his body.

Cooper looked her way. "Can I trust you not to kill him?"

"I think Lucifer is right and he's going to do more damage than I ever could," Kala replied with absolutely no humor.

So that was where Lucy had gone. Well, it had to be awful for Lucy to call in Kala, but it looked like a day for everything to break down, including the fabric of the universe since Lucy stood way closer to her twin than she normally would.

"Oh, I disagree. I think we could do a lot of damage," Lucy countered.

The last thing she needed was those two deciding they could actually work together. "It's fine. Kala, you were right all along. He doesn't love me. He doesn't even like me. I was a means to an end, but we have to work together. I'm going to change and I'll meet you up in the conference room. Leave Tim out of it."

"I'm not leaving the only person I can trust out of it," Ben shot back.

"I'll go get the parents. Lucy, can you inform Ollie our play time is getting cut short?" Cooper was calm and collected. Like he'd always known it would end like this since it was how Kenzie's relationships seemed to go. "Also, inform him that Ben has injured a submissive in anger and he shouldn't be allowed on the dungeon floor again."

"What are you talking about? She punched me," Ben complained.

Kala moved in and gripped Kenzie's arm, way more gently than Ben had, but the sleeve fell back and there was a clear imprint of his hand on her wrist. "He's talking about this. You weren't playing with her. You were trying to hurt her, and that is not allowed in this club. Consider your rights here stripped. You can leave the dungeon floor, Master Ben. Also, you don't get that title anymore."

"Could you back off, please?" She didn't need her twin's rage. She needed to be alone. She needed to mourn him. Or at least mourn the him she'd thought he was.

Ben had gone a pasty white as his eyes found her wrist. "I didn't mean to do that. I needed to talk to her."

TJ stood at Kenzie's other side. Cooper had left to inform her parents that the world had blown up. "Yeah, that's why she said you touched her in anger. Man, I get something happened, but that's not right."

"I didn't mean to hurt her. Kenzie, let me look at it." Ben started toward her.

TJ stepped in between them. "No. Cooper can look at her when he gets back. He's had some training. He'll decide if we need to call a doctor. I have no idea what happened, but you two need some space."

"I know what happened," Lucy said. "Huisman called and Ben picked up like the good boy he is."

Kala's eyes flared. "He did what?"

The words seemed to remind Ben that he was the injured party here. He straightened up. "Yes, Manny called me and I answered because I know what happens when I don't. He laid some hard truths out for me."

Kenzie felt infinitely tired. She covered her wrist again. "You can tell us all the horrible things we've done in conference. That way you don't have to do it twice. Or you can write it up before you head back to Toronto."

A low huff came from Ben. "Ah, now I'm getting kicked out."

"Why the hell would you want to hang around with the whore who's leading you astray?" She was getting sick of Ben's crap.

Kala's head shook as she considered Ben. "What are you talking about? You're listening to Huisman? About what? You're supposed to hate Huisman. We went through this months ago when that fucker told us you were working with him. Kenzie is the one who convinced us you would never. Now you're having long phone conversations with the man?"

"He told you I was working with him?" Ben asked, his eyes going hard.

Kenzie didn't care. She wanted to get this over with. "It doesn't matter."

"When we were in Nepal, Huisman had some interesting thoughts about you," TJ pointed out. "He told Zach you were working with him. According to him, you were the reason they found us in Liverpool. Kenzie shut that down quickly because she knows he lies."

"I would never work with that sociopath," Ben said.

"But I would." Kenzie knew the answer to that question. She'd known it would all go bad the minute he answered that call. He would believe Huisman because he desperately needed their game to continue.

She wanted out now. She'd thought she could save him.

You can't save someone. You can only love them enough that they want to save themselves, but sweet girl, sometimes it doesn't work and you have to know when it's time to save yourself.

She could hear her mom's words. She should have listened better. Her dad was all about the condom, but her mom was about protecting her heart.

"Did you or did you not know that Manny was aware the two of you were twins?" Ben asked the question like he already knew the answer.

What the hell? "Of course I knew."

He nodded like she'd made his point. "You told him. Did you do it in Australia? How long has he known while you lied to me?"

Kenzie was so fucking confused. "Ben, have you read the files my father sent to your handler? He sent everything to you after Nepal."

"Of course," he replied. "Not that I can trust a word in those files since your whole family lies."

Kala seemed to deflate. She moved in and put an arm around her sister, letting her know she was going to be what Kenzie needed her to be. "Dude, Huisman's been watching our family since before we joined the Agency. Did you read that part? Because I know my mom and dad made sure your agency knew."

Ben went still as though trying to figure out what he was missing. "Manny blames your father for his father's death."

Even though her father hadn't been there that day and it hadn't been one of his men who'd shot the elder Huisman. "Yes, and Huisman's grandfather kept a file on us from then on. When we joined the Agency and they erased Kala and me, Huisman had the files from before. Of course he knew. His family has been watching mine since we were children."

He didn't move, as though he needed time to process information he should have already known.

"Wait, all of this is about Ben being pissy that Huisman knew you two were twins?" TJ asked, sounding confused. "But you sent him the intel as soon as you brought him in."

"It didn't say Huisman knew," Ben argued, his hands in fists at his sides.

"Logic states that he knows if he's been watching us since before we were redacted from life," Kala said with a sigh. "Seriously. Did you even read the file? Should I tell you the moon is out or would you know that because it's nighttime?"

"It's not about that." She had lost him, and this turn of events wouldn't solve the problem. "He can't ever forgive me for lying to him, and beyond that he won't ever trust another woman because the one he really loved chose Manny over him and then she died and he couldn't beat Manny and win her back."

"I didn't love her," he said between gritted teeth.

"Okay." She wasn't going to argue with him. "I'm going to get dressed. Do what you want, Ben."

Her heart was a dull thing in her chest.

She loved him. She wasn't sure why right that second. It had felt like fate, like an invisible string tethered them together, but she could get some psychic scissors and clip that right away.

"Kenzie," Ben called out.

But she walked away, her sister at her side.

It was done.

* * * *

She wouldn't look at him. Kenzie sat in a chair pretty much as far away as she could.

How could she think this was about Deanna? She genuinely thought he was still in love with a dead woman? A dead woman who'd betrayed him.

It was ridiculous, but then she wasn't wrong about the fact that it was his fault he hadn't figured out Manny was smarter than him once again. One would think he would learn.

If Kenzie wasn't lying, then he'd ripped her apart, and the thought made him sick to his stomach.

He needed to talk to her. He'd been an ass, but she was also right that he might not be over the fact that she'd lied to him.

"What did you do?" Tim whispered the question.

Fucked everything up. That was what he'd done. On every level since when Big Tag had sent him a message that the team was meeting and wanted to speak with him alone, he'd gone and gotten Tim.

Who had Claire and Gabby in his "room." Oh, it looked innocent enough, but he understood one of the things they wanted to talk about was Tim. But by that point he couldn't come up with another excuse for barging in, and Tim was here.

So that was why they wanted to talk to him alone, and he'd fucked that up, too.

"I took a call Kenzie didn't think I should." She'd changed into an oversized sweater and jeans. The sweater's arms came down past her wrists, covering the spot where he'd left his most ruthless, harmful mark.

Had she put some ice on it? Taken some anti-inflammatories? She wouldn't let him take care of her. Her sisters were already forming a protective wall around her. Now he wouldn't be allowed back in the dungeon she loved. He was probably about to get his ass kicked out of The Garden altogether.

Kenzie was here along with her sisters, Lou, their husbands, Samantha, and Oliver. The parents hadn't made it in yet.

Oliver had been plain. He was no longer a Dom in his eyes. He was banished from the dungeon floor.

The court was protecting their princess.

No one protected him.

Except her, you massive ass. She tried to spare you all of this, but you wanted to call her out publicly. You wanted to humiliate her, and turns out you only made yourself look like an idiot.

I love you, Ben.

He was never going to hear those words again.

Tim seemed to think about that before quietly replying. He didn't need to be told who had been on the other end of the line. "We're not supposed to answer his calls. What lies did he tell this time?"

Tim sat beside him at the opposite end of the table to the Americans and Brits. He'd mentioned they could move closer but had seemed to realize something had gone wrong.

"He didn't tell lies. He gave me the truth. He's known about Kenzie and Kala all along. He's known for years. Now that I know I can see how he's been taunting me about it," Ben whispered. Tim would back him up.

Tim's head tilted and reminded him of how Kenzie's dog looked when he was confused. "Uhm, yeah. That's not some big revelation. You read the files, right? It was clear that Manny knew the family before they were an Agency team."

Embarrassment flashed through him. He wasn't sure why he hadn't made that connection. It was in the way Big Tag had written it up. He'd talked about his family but hadn't explicitly mentioned the twins.

Of course he was a fucking intelligence officer who was supposed to be able to read between the lines. It was clear in that report.

He wished she would look at him.

What the hell had he done? How could he undo it? Did he even want to?

Now that his rage died down, he could see how calmly and fairly she'd tried to handle the situation. She'd tried to spare him that scene in the dungeon, but no, he'd plowed through because he'd known he was right and she was…

He hadn't meant to call her a whore. Didn't even think the word about her, and yet he could see he'd described her that way.

He felt hollowed out, and he definitely felt the distance between him and this team he'd become a part of over the last few weeks.

They wouldn't have anything to do with him now.

The door flew open and Big Tag walked in with his wife. The head of the table had been left for him. Since he was the king.

Ben would never be a king. There would be no younger people who looked up to him. He wouldn't have a group of found family around him. He would be alone because he was never going to get over what happened to him. Kenzie might be right about that, but she was wrong about Deanna.

"Parker, what the fuck did I tell you about answering the devil when he calls?" Big Tag was still standing, his massive frame dominating the room.

Kala held up a hand. "I know. You hang up on that bitch, block her, and then you sage your phone."

Lucy sent Kala her middle finger.

"Kala." Charlotte Taggart sank into her chair and looked toward her daughters. They sat in a line. Tasha and Kenzie and Kala. Her sisters were protecting her.

They were protecting her from him.

"Sorry." Kala actually looked embarrassed. "I forgot I'm working with evil to bring down a bigger evil. I apologize, Lucy."

"I hate you so much," Lucy said under her breath.

"I'm waiting." Big Tag's eyes never left him.

What had it been like to have this man as a father? His own had been absent most of the time. So had his mother. They'd been working, and he'd figured out pretty early on he'd been a mistake and they'd never wanted kids. They kept him due to pressure from his maternal grandmother, who had died when he was young. His father had never sat him down and given him a lecture until he'd been forced into witness protection. That wasn't really a lecture, though. It had been more of a confession. He'd never wanted him, cursed the day he was born, hoped to never see him again. "You told me not to, but you don't understand what he can do when I ignore him."

"I know what he can do when you give him all your attention." With a low growl Tag sat down by his wife. "Damon and Penny are already in bed. I'll brief them in the morning. Ben, what happened? Or do you want to talk to Joseph first? He should still be awake."

"Already done." It hadn't taken long since he hadn't mentioned what he'd been doing when Manny called or the clusterfuck that happened after. He would have to deal with that in the morning because he was pretty sure he was going to get his ass kicked back to Canada. "I wrote up the briefing while I was in the locker room. It's already been sent to you, so there's no real reason to have this meeting."

He needed to talk to Kenzie. He'd said some things he shouldn't have, but even though he was dumb and hadn't made a connection he should have, this was still her fault. She'd distracted him with sex and thought he'd never figure it out.

"You're right. There's no reason to have this meeting with anyone but you and me." He glanced his wife's way. She stood.

"Hey, sweetie, come on. I've already got you moved into Lucy's room." Charlotte reached for her daughter's hand.

He couldn't let that happen. If she walked out that door, he might not see her again. He stood and used language these people would understand. "No. I need to talk to my sub."

Kala's eyes flared. "She's not your sub."

"You don't have rights in this club or any of our clubs, mate," Oliver said. "And if you don't want to get kicked to the curb and spend the rest of the night in the Tube station, I suggest you sit down."

"Normally I would say my brother is talking out of turn, but I'm pretty sure Father will agree," Sami said with a shake of her head. She stood. "I'll reassign Kenzie's tasks. Lucy and I are planning to go back to France and see if we can figure out a way into the chateau where Sosa lived. She can come along. Will Ben be leaving us?"

"Undecided." Tag reached out a hand and drew Kenzie in, whispering something to her.

She straightened up. "I'm fine. Just another of my missteps."

Was that what he was? Another mistake she'd made? Another man who wasn't worthy of all her sweetness and light?

"Kenzie," he said, putting his will into that one word.

She didn't turn, merely stopped at the doorway. He noticed every woman in the room was going with her while all the guys stayed where they were.

Shit. He might really get his ass kicked.

"This isn't over." He would take a beating if he had to, but he and Kenzie would talk because she wasn't innocent in this. He might be stupid, but Manny liked to point out inconvenient truths. Why bother lying when the truth was so awful?

She walked out, a solemn line of females following her. Supporting her.

And he was left with the males of the pack. Dare once told him Charlotte likened her family and friends to a pack of wolves. Dangerous but loyal and loving. Was the pack about to protect one of their own?

Tim held up a hand. "Uhm, Mr. Taggart, sir, I would like to point out that I was not around when Dr. Huisman called and I'm working on figuring out how he got the number since Ben has a phone I personally programmed. I'll talk to Lou and see if we can figure it out."

"No, you weren't." Taggart's tone was flat and icy. "You were holed up with two underaged girls."

Tim's eyes went wide. "They aren't. I mean…they told me they're twenty-three. That's not underaged. Shit. Is that underaged in Europe? Is it like the opposite of beer? Here you can drink legally at eighteen. But maybe they don't like sex." Tim went beet red. "Not that we had sex. We have not. We were playing Uno and eating pizza. I know the room is for sex and stuff, but I was just having friendship."

"Did you wear a condom?" Big Tag asked, every word frosty.

Tim's head shook. "No. I mean yes. I mean I didn't need to because I wasn't having a three way. I was getting my ass handed to me, and I think they cheat. But the point is I didn't need a condom. I need an antacid because they over-sauced those pies. They are not sitting well."

"You may go," Taggart commanded.

Tim frowned. "Uh, I thought this was an important meeting."

"It is. I'm going to talk to your friend. Do you want me to lump you in with him?" Taggart's words were a grumbly threat.

"No."

But an effective one. Did he want Tim to watch these men tell him he wasn't good enough for their princess? "You should go."

Tim hesitated.

Ben turned his way. "It's fine. I'm fine."

Tim stood up. "I seriously doubt that. Are you sure? They look mad."

He'd hurt Kenzie. He hadn't meant to. Not physically. Hell, he hadn't meant to hurt her heart. He hadn't meant for any of this to happen, but he was the dumbass who fell for everything. Who thought just once he might find a family that wouldn't leave him. "I'll be fine, but we might need another place to stay for the night."

"No one's kicking you out," Taggart said.

But he might want to leave. He watched as Tim walked away. When the door closed, he sat up straighter, all those judgmental eyes on him. "Mr. Taggart, I would appreciate the opportunity to speak with your daughter. I owe her an apology."

"For what?"

Shit. He'd hoped the man already knew. "I gripped her wrist too hard."

"That sometimes happens when you play. I assure you Kenzie isn't going to blame you for that."

"We weren't playing. We were arguing, and I did not mean to hurt her," he admitted.

Taggart sat back, his gaze glacial. Those blue eyes could go cold so fast. "Let me see if I can get the timing right. You fucked my daughter. She says something that disturbs you. Then while she's scrambling to try to make you feel better about rejecting her, your boyfriend calls."

So he did know and this was torture. "That's insulting, Ian. You know what he's done to me."

"Which is why you probably shouldn't take his fucking calls." Taggart took a long breath and seemed to calm down. "I'm sorry. I promised Kenz I wouldn't rip you up, but it's hard. She's my daughter."

"Which is probably why you shouldn't send her out to spy and potentially get killed." Ben couldn't help it.

Taggart's eyes rolled. "Come back when you have a stubborn, brave daughter and we'll talk."

He wouldn't have a daughter. Not one who would someday dye her hair pink like her mom had. Not a daughter or a son. "We both know that's not happening for me."

Cooper's blank expression softened slightly. "Why would you say that? Unless you don't want kids."

"Which is a perfectly reasonable thing to do," Ollie said and then put up a hand as though defending himself. "Not me, of course. I have a family name to uphold. I shall marry someday and have at least one of those little nippers."

"I don't think Ben doesn't want kids." TJ was studying him carefully. He was the calmest of them all, the one most likely to say "hey guys, we probably shouldn't kill him." "I think Ben doesn't think he'll live long enough to have them."

"Yeah, he's got a death wish," Taggart said with a long-suffering sigh. "Can any of my daughters find a man without a fucking shit ton of trauma?" He then seemed to remember Cooper was sitting right there. "Sorry, buddy. You really are the dream."

Cooper snorted. "I think the dream is Lou and TJ. They've managed to make it through everything without racking up the trauma. But Parker over there came to us with it. I don't even think he understands why he does the things he does."

"Of course I understand. I do it to save the planet from what Manny would do to it. I do it to spare the people around me the future he wants." Frustration was starting to well.

"And you're the only one who can do it." It wasn't a question out of Taggart's mouth, and there was suddenly sympathy in his tone.

Not that it would help, but he found himself explaining. "It's a game to him, and I have to play it."

"Why?" Taggart asked but not unkindly. "Why does it have to be you?"

"Because he hates me. Why am I getting this from you? You know damn well Manny can hold a grudge for no reason. You weren't even in the country but he blames you for his father's death."

"And I wouldn't answer a call from him if I didn't have to," Taggart replied.

"That's the point. If I don't answer him, he'll make me."

Taggart sat back and took a long breath before looking to Cooper and nodding as though he was agreeing with something the younger man had previously said.

Cooper seemed to take that as some kind of unspoken order. He stood and nodded TJ's way. TJ stood and sent Oliver a look.

Oliver shrugged. "I don't want to leave. I want to watch Uncle destroy him. I think it'll be amusing. I have no idea why the women left. All the drama is in here. Although I supposed Kenz is probably revving them all up."

Ben stood. "You take that fucking back."

Oliver snorted and didn't seem intimidated at all. "Well, this is sort of Disneyland for her. You know how dramatic she can be."

He launched himself at the Brit.

It felt good when Oliver cursed and punched him back. Oh, so good. Yeah. This was what he needed. Violence. He couldn't kill Manny, but he could take this fucker out.

Oliver's handsome face was hard as he shoved Ben back. "You want to fight someone your size? Hurting little girls isn't cutting it anymore?"

"For fuck's sake," Big Tag huffed.

Ben got Oliver with an uppercut to the gut, but out of the corner of his vision he saw Coop and TJ shaking their heads like this was some kind of boyish altercation.

"I didn't mean to hurt her. I do mean to hurt you, asshole." Ben punched out again but Oliver kicked and Ben found himself on the floor of the conference room, the air whooshing from his lungs.

Oliver's lips curled up in a snarl as he started to launch himself toward Ben. The Brit didn't play fair, and that was good. Because Ben didn't either. The fucker was trying to pin him down? He brought his foot up in time to catch Ollie in his junk.

A low groan huffed through the room as the MI6 operative cupped himself and rolled over on the floor as if to protect himself even more.

Ben flipped himself up and started to reach for his opponent.

"Nope, you're done. Believe me, man, I understand the impulse. I've beaten that asshole, too." TJ was shorter than Ben, but he was built like a linebacker and had all the training.

Oliver groaned and managed to get his ass up. "I wasn't flirting. I admit I was flirting with Lou that day a bit, but it was all for…" He grinned even as he winced. "That's a lie. Louisa is such a pretty thing, and it wasn't like you were engaged at the time."

"Or you could kill him and I could help you bury the body." TJ's hand came off his arm.

Cooper stepped between them, his hands up. "No. We're leaving. Ben, listen to Big Tag. I know he's a sarcastic asshole but he's solid even when he doesn't particularly like you. And Ollie, I'm going to tell Kenz you called her a little girl."

Oliver paled. "Coop, don't. That is not what I was saying."

"Don't call her dramatic again," Ben said between clenched teeth.

"I will not." Oliver frowned his way. "You're a very unpleasant individual. Have you considered therapy?"

The men strode out—well, Cooper and TJ strode. Oliver kind of waddled since his dick was probably still shoved into his body cavity. It was satisfying.

And then he was alone with Kenzie's father.

"I don't think he'll be the one continuing the Knight line." Tag sat back with a weary sigh. "Lucky for Damon he's still got Archie. He's the normal one, you know. Smart kid. Never left academia. What are you not telling me, Ben?"

So much. "Manny said a bunch of shit about my old girlfriend, and he's sending me something tomorrow. I put that in the report. Not the stuff about Deanna. That was just him…"

Fuck. He hated it when everyone was right.

"Say it," Tag encouraged.

"He was baiting me." Every muscle hurt. And his hand. Oliver had a surprisingly strong jaw. Guess that stiff upper lip stuff was real.

"Yes, and you took it and let it fester. What did he say about Kenzie? You conveniently left it out of the briefing."

His report had been short and to the point. Manny called. He said he was sending something tomorrow. That was it. But he was certain Big Tag had already gotten other reports. "I'm sure Cooper and TJ and Kala told you exactly what was said."

"They seem to think this is all about the fact that Huisman knew Kala and Kenzie are twins," Big Tag summed things up simply.

"According to my snarkiest daughter, your panties are in a wad because you can't read a debrief. Harsh, but maybe true. He's been tracking me and my family for years. Yes, he knew, and he let me know he knew way back in Sydney."

"So after I told you what a danger to the world he was, you still allowed him to have knowledge that I didn't have?"

"I did." Kenzie's father stared at him. "I also told my daughters not to tell you because guess what, Ben? I didn't know you, and Huisman is good at covering his tracks. So, no, I did not tell the operative I'd just met the main secret of my fucking life. Nor did I tell you after you offered to sacrifice Louisa to prove to me that you were right. Nor did I tell you any of the times we were working together because I didn't trust you until recently."

Ben's jaw locked, and his response came out between clenched teeth. "Understood."

Tag sighed as Ben sat back down. The silence stretched between them.

"You hurt her," Tag said.

Ben felt his heart twist. "I didn't mean to."

"But you did. I'm not talking about the physical, although we need to be honest enough to know that is possible, too. Ben, you can't deal with the problem until you acknowledge there is one."

He knew what was coming next. "Is this your famous lecture? The one you give all the suitors? Dare told me about his."

"I had a discussion with Dare because I thought he was truly the best man for Tasha."

"And I'm not good for Kenzie?"

"Are you?"

The question threatened his calm exterior. He wished he was still punching the shit out of Oliver. Was he good for her? Good for a woman who so deeply desired to be loved?

Or she was playing a game and knew how stupid he was. Knew he would fall for it time and time again.

"No." He was toxic. "I'm not good for her at all."

Taggart nodded as though that was the right answer. "Excellent. And you wanted her to hurt. You wanted to tear her apart for what you believe she did to you."

"In the heat of the moment, maybe. I was angry."

"You were afraid," Taggart countered.

Ben rolled his eyes. "I'm not fucking afraid of Kenzie."

"And we're taking two steps back."

"I don't think Kenzie's going to kill me."

"No, but she could break you," Taggart countered. "She could break you in a way Deanna Fisher never did. I know this part, Ben. The most frightening thing in the world is to figure out you're nothing more than a dumb asshole like the rest of us. When the right woman comes along, we want to reject her because it couldn't possibly work out. See, this is where Kenz has it better than you. She's been through some guys, but none of them ever truly touched her heart, so it was easy for her to walk away. None of them knew what she really wanted."

"To be taken seriously. To be seen as Kenzie and not just a part of her twin."

Taggart sighed and leaned forward. "And that is why you're so close. I like the fact that you call us all out. It's easy to tease Kenz because she seems so solid. Kala's always had a difficult time fitting into the world."

"Why?" Ben asked. "Her sisters altered their worlds so she would fit in. I haven't met your sons, but I would bet they're the same. I would bet Kala got the majority of the attention."

A laugh huffed from Taggart, but there was nothing amusing about the sound. "Don't critique my parenting. Not until you've had a kid who's on the spectrum. I'm going to be honest. I wouldn't be surprised to find Kenzie was, too. Hers comes out looking shiny and adorable so it's easy to overlook, but it's there. I've heard what you said. She should have been a prom queen. I know that sounds good, but I question it. Having her twin made her think about things beyond herself. I know I talk about Kala like she's completely mine and Kenz is completely her mom's, but the truth is our kids are always a combination of their parents and something that's uniquely them. Kenzie could have been the golden girl, but she chose to be a sister. She chose to love the people around her more than she loved herself."

That sounded like Kenzie. Like how when she was ripped apart, she hadn't turned it on him. She'd sucked it up and tried to spare him embarrassment. She'd tried to make their fight private, but he'd wanted to tear her down publicly. He'd wanted everyone to see who she was. Even though they all loved her.

Who the fuck was he? Did he want to be this asshole who dragged his girl?

"Ben, I like that you won't let anyone call her dramatic even though she is."

That got his back up. "Don't fucking say that."

Tag's lips curled. "Does it help that I like drama? Kenzie feels things deeply. It was odd to have the two of them. Tasha was so normal. She had normal relationships, and honestly, not that many. Kala has never looked at anyone but Cooper in a romantic fashion. But Kenzie." He sighed, and his head shook like he was thinking about trying times. "She fell in love once a week, and it was over the top and usually ended in screaming and crying and vowing to never love again. Then Monday rolled around and the cute guy in her math class smiled her way."

Bitterness welled inside him. "So you're saying I'm the flavor of the week."

"I'm saying the young woman who sat here with her face as blank as a doll's wasn't going through the end of a crush. I'm saying that since the moment she met you she hasn't taken a boyfriend or a Dom. Oh, she's played from what I can tell, and I try not to be able to tell. It's been a long dry spell for a woman who likes to drink, if you know what I mean. I wonder if you can say the same."

"Are you asking me if I remained pure while your daughters twisted me every way they could and Manny laughed behind my back? Hell, he laughed to my front. He pretty much told me, but I was too stupid to hear it."

Big Tag sighed again and stood. "All right, then. I'll talk to Joseph in the morning and we'll figure out how to handle this. Personally, I think we should separate the teams and confer only through handlers from now on."

He'd known it would be this way. "With you keeping the Brits, of course. So what you're really saying is Tim and I aren't welcome anymore."

"Or I could bench my girls. That actually might be better. Send Kala and Coop into the woods with Zach and Devi, and the rest of my family can stay in Bliss. I'll stay here at The Garden with Lou and TJ, and Sami and Oliver can take the lead on my side. If I do that, you and Tim can stay."

"Or we can be the professionals we are and do the job."

A brow rose over icy eyes. "Professional? Ben, you're the one who disobeyed a direct order and will do it every single time because the truth of the matter is you need him. You need Huisman."

They kept saying it, but it didn't make it truth. "I fucking hate him."

Tag nodded in agreement. "Yes, and that's the flip side of love, but they're equally powerful and Kenzie's right. I worried she might be in a love triangle with the memory of your ex-girlfriend. She told me it wasn't Deanna. It's always been Huisman."

He felt his hands fist again and tried to get control of his rage. "I'm sick of hearing this. It's a manipulation so you can take control of the op."

"Make no mistake. I am in control, and you're on thin ice." He started for the door. "I expect you to send me anything Huisman sends to you. You step out of line one more time and I'll pull my whole team, and not just my girls. I know Tim is smart, but Lou runs circles around him, and Sami and Oliver know Europe better than anyone. So think about your next move. And I expect you to be civil. I probably can't get Kenzie out of here for a couple of days."

"I'm not getting the lecture?" Ben asked. "I thought you would either beat the shit out of me or tell me all the ways I should get therapy for my anger issues. I was certain you would tell me all the things I need to do before I'm even vaguely acceptable as your daughter's true love."

Tag looked back, and there was a sadness on his face. "You might be, but my daughter is smart. Sometimes love is not enough to save the people we care about. Love starts with ourselves. I know that sounds all new agey and Whitney Houston, but it's true. The baseline of our love has to start with ourselves, has to begin with accepting the surprisingly hard-to-deal-with fact that we are worthy of love and happiness. You aren't there, and I don't think you will be. The good news is, unlike her sister, she'll move on. She'll cry for a couple of weeks and miss you, and maybe she'll miss you for the rest of her life, but soon she'll find herself at her club and some well-meaning Dom will look at her and know how good his life could be if he had that beautiful soul to take care of. And she'll say it's nothing more than sex. She'll tell everyone she's got to get back on the horse, but he'll be good to her. He'll show up for the little things. He'll make sure she has coffee in the morning and someone to watch TV with at night, even if he's not interested in the show. He'll sit and let her lay on his lap, and he'll enjoy it because she's enjoying it. One day she'll find her heart is soft again and he's filling it. She'll figure out the big grand gestures mean nothing in the face of the comfort of everyday life. Somewhere in the days they share and the nights they cuddle close and get through whatever life throws them, you'll become a memory. One more brick in the path that led her to real love. She'll have her wedding day with her family around her, welcoming her chosen husband. She'll have a collaring night with her club family, and it will be every bit as emotional as her wedding because it's another part of herself being loved and accepted. Somewhere down the line they'll have kids and they'll raise them and grow old wrapped in my daughter's unique and loving energy. And it will begin because she will love herself enough to not stay with a man who cannot love her back."

Every word felt like a dagger. This was not what Dare had talked about. What Cooper had warned him was coming. There was supposed to be a ton of dad advice and calling him son, which he would reject because he wasn't this man's son. The truth of the matter was he wasn't anyone's son.

"Stay away from her and we'll be fine. I'll have her out of this in a couple of days and once this op is done, I'll make certain we don't come into your orbit again," Tag promised. "You can work however you like, and one day you'll find that bullet with your name on it and you and Huisman can be together again. You know she never doubted you. Huisman tried his best, but he couldn't get her to turn on you. I guess he then remembered who the weak link was. Good luck, Ben."

He stood there as the door closed, and Ben wondered if it hadn't closed forever.

Chapter Fifteen

Kenzie stared at the screen in front of her. She'd said good-bye to Lucy that morning as she and Sami headed back to France. She'd thought about going with them, but her mother had let her in on Dad's plan and she'd reluctantly agreed that taking a sabbatical was for the best.

Removing herself from the equation would let her father handle things in whatever way he felt served the mission. It also took her twin out of harm's way.

They'd sat up with her last night, obviously expecting her to cry and wail her pain like she normally would. She would hang with her girls and say everything she needed to say, and they would hype her up so she could move forward and find the right one.

"You heard me, Gabe." Her twin walked into the office in the basement, but she paced toward the front of the big space, so Kala hadn't seen her. Probably thought she was still in bed since her usual routine after a breakup was to lie around for a week or so crying and listening to sad songs, and then on the seventh or eighth day she would rise like a phoenix, put on her sluttiest clothes, declare she was ready to live again, and that looking hot as fuck was the best revenge. "I want a top-tier Dom. What do you mean what does that mean? Do you not understand words? Why would the fact that it's three in the morning affect your ability to speak English? We both know you're awake."

Kenzie sat back and watched Kala pace. Why was she looking for a Dom? It must be some weird project she had going because the last person in the world who would cheat on her spouse was Kala. Cooper was it for her.

Like Ben seemed to be for her.

It was different this time. The ache felt more…permanent.

Somehow she hadn't cried as much. Like if she cried, she might get him out of her system and he would be gone.

This. This was why she wasn't going to fight her parents. They were going to discuss the situation with Drake and Taylor Radcliffe, but her parents were fairly certain they would be okay with it. She'd placed her father in a position where he had to ask his boss to change plans because his dumbass daughter slept with another operative and now needed space.

Kala sighed, still pacing. She was dressed for a workout in yoga pants and a tank top that showed off toned muscles. "I want a Dom who is looking for something permanent, not a fuck boy. I'm talking someone late-twenties to mid-thirties with a solid career and enough self-worth that he wouldn't ever let a sociopath dictate his life."

Fuck. Now Kenzie sat up because her twin was obviously talking about her.

"I don't know. Buy one if you have to." Kala huffed, the sound she made when she was impatient. "Don't tell me that's not possible. You are Julian Lodge's son, and when that man farts a million dollars falls out of his ass."

It wouldn't work. She'd finally decided that she would need time to deal with this, and getting into another relationship wouldn't solve things. She needed to be with herself for a while. Besides, they had no idea how long they would be in Bliss. Was Kala planning on having this stud she was trying to get Gabe to buy shipped to Colorado?

She might go into the woods with them. It would be okay. Sure, she would be the fifth wheel, but she could hang with Zach's mom and stare at the stars and breathe clean air and figure out what her future looked like without Ben Parker.

"Yes, you can use that on your Christmas cards this year. Find me that Dom." Kala hung up and then sighed when she caught sight of

Kenzie. "Hey. I didn't think you would be up."

Her sister knew how she handled a breakup. However, she'd never had one like this. One where she ached and she knew she always would.

But she kept it quiet, unwilling to voice her pain for fear that it would be seen as more Kenzie drama.

"I wanted to get some research work done for Lucy before we leave." She turned her attention back to the screen. She was searching through property records, trying to dig up when that chateau changed hands.

Kala walked over and stood by her desk. "Are you okay?"

Kenzie took a long breath and sat back. "I'm okay. I'm sad, but everyone was right."

"Kenz, this isn't about right or wrong. This is about you and the fact that you loved him." Kala leaned over, as though she needed to be close so her twin could feel her will. "You loved him. This isn't like the rest. You had crushes and fell into relationships because you were lonely and liked the guy. I understand this is different. You loved him with all your heart. You genuinely thought Ben Parker was it. I'm so sorry he wasn't worthy of you."

Tears sparked, but Kenzie sniffled and tried to hold them back. "Thank you. I appreciate that."

"Are you sure you don't want to talk to him?" Kala asked.

"What good would it do? Also, if you think I should talk to him, why are you trying to import a top for me?" Kenzie returned with a snort. "When did Gabe get into that business?"

Kala sighed and moved to the chair next to her. "You're going to need sessions."

"I'm going to be in the woods. I think that will be my session."

Kala's brows rose. "I thought you were staying with Nell and Henry."

"I'd rather go with you," she said quietly. Watching Lucy's mom and dad would remind her of what she wasn't going to get in the future. No one to grow old with. She was left with the memory of what she'd thought she had. That was the hardest part. Acknowledging that only her feelings had been real.

"Then we'll enjoy the woods." Kala reached out and held her hand as the door opened and Lou walked in, carrying her laptop.

"Hey, guys," Lou said with a bright smile. "Kala, I was hoping I could catch you. I need someone to put on the nanite suit. I've got some stuff I've been working on, and I need a test subject. I think I've figured out how to easily split them up. I've been worried ever since that time Kenz got caught in that strip club and couldn't find her clothes and had to wear Coop's shirt when we ran through the streets of Bucharest. If one of us was wearing the nanite suit, we could transfer some and she would have been fully covered."

Fun night. They'd been monitoring an arms dealer who liked strip clubs, and whoops, Kenzie got made and had to run in pasties and a thong. It would be nice to have had some clothes. "Ooo, can you also find a way for them to form warm boots? Europe is cold, and cobblestones are rough on a girls' toes, if you know what I mean."

Lou frowned. "Yeah, anything hard is tough. Trust me. Your father has tried to convince the little suckers to form bulletproof vests, but we're not there yet."

"Where do you want me?" Kala asked her bestie, willing to spend a couple of hours indulging the mad scientist. Kala liked it when Lou went all technical on her.

"Locker room is probably best." Lou grabbed a file folder. "The Internet is good in there, and no one will need to bleach their eyes if I mistakenly have the nanites fall off your body." She grinned suddenly, an inventor on the verge of a breakthrough. "Actually, that's kind of what I'm trying to do. To get them to separate but in a super-controlled manner. It's exciting."

She'd worn that experimental suit the day she and Ben had first made…first had sex. Maybe that day was where it had all gone wrong.

"Come with us," Kala offered, joining Lou at the door. "It's going to be dead down here because everyone's out of the building but the Canadians. Ollie's at his club dealing with contractors. Sami and Lucifer are on their way to France, and Coop and TJ are getting ready for us to move out. The 'rents are at MI6 headquarters meeting with the big boss. You'll end up hanging with Tim if you're not careful. Or worse. Sosa might show up and ask an infernal amount of questions."

"Don't worry about Tim," Lou said. "He's sick. I asked if he wanted in on the experiment, but apparently he ate something he shouldn't have last night, and let me tell you, you do not want to walk into his bathroom."

She was suddenly glad she hadn't tried the pizza. "I'm good here. I think I could use the quiet. I want to finish this before we have to leave. Not a lot of Internet in the woods."

"And that's why we like it." Kala gave her a wink. "Lou and I will drag you to lunch. I want some fish and chips before we go."

It would be nice. She would sit by the Thames and have a pint and some fish and chips and simply be.

That was what she needed to work on. Being. She sometimes found it hard to sit with her own feelings. It was easier to turn the world into a soap opera, but this time it was serious, and she wouldn't move on if she didn't deal with the hollowness she felt.

She didn't have to have any plan beyond taking some time. In the past she would throw herself into anything else to distract her, but her feelings for Ben deserved time and attention.

"Are you willing to talk to me this morning or are you planning on pretending I don't exist?"

She steeled herself because Ben was in the doorway. He looked worse for the wear. Tired. She wanted to run to him and stroke his hair and make him get back in bed. She would cuddle him while he slept.

He wasn't hers to take care of.

She plastered what she hoped was a steady smile on her face. "It's fine. What do you need? I'm finishing up the property reports. I'll send them to you and the team this afternoon."

"I'm not talking about the op, Kenzie." His eyes were on her, and despite his obvious state of weariness, there was a predatory gleam to them.

Her whole body responded, but she wasn't giving in now. "I think we should keep this professional. I'm willing to talk to you about anything having to do with the mission."

"Except you're running away from the mission."

"Well, it's not my mission, is it?" Kenzie mused. "It's yours. I'm a distraction. When I'm gone, you'll be able to one hundred percent focus on Huisman."

He frowned. "I'm getting sick of your family trying to turn this into some kind of romance between me and Manny. It's cruel when you think about it."

She didn't want to argue with him. She was tired, too, and had so many miles to go before she slept. "Then it's a good thing you don't have to worry about my cruelty again. Ben, I'll be gone in a day or two. Can you leave me alone? I don't want a scene. I don't want a fight. I want to do my job and leave with some dignity."

He was quiet for a moment. "And you said you loved me. Well, it's good to know I was right about that."

She stood and picked up her laptop. Lucy's room had killer Internet and a lock. She would use both. "Yes, it's good you know what a lying whore I am."

She started to move past him, but he reached out and grabbed her wrist.

The one with all the bruises. She winced, and the laptop slipped from her hand.

Ben let her go like she was made of fire. "I'm sorry. I forgot."

So some of his bravado was performative. That made her feel somewhat better. At least he wasn't a complete jerk. "It's fine. It's not that bad, but I would appreciate it if you would stop grabbing me."

She started for the door.

"Kenzie, please talk to me. I don't know what I did. I understand that I didn't handle you saying those words well."

She bit back a sigh. "It's okay. I'll be okay and so will you."

"If you love me, how can you walk away? Make me understand it."

Was he really this dumb? She asked the question mentally and answered it the same way. Yes. He was male and hadn't figured out that feelings should be handled with something more than a gun or a bottle of Scotch. It was hard sometimes to date because her family was so open to talking, hell-bent on ending the idea that their sons didn't deserve the same examined lives their daughters did. That they couldn't feel sorrow, only rage. That anger and lust were the only acceptable emotions for a man to feel.

She turned. "Okay. I love you. I think I always will. I've pretty much loved you from the moment I saw you. It was one of those fate things."

His eyes narrowed on her. "Then I would think you would want to fight for me."

"I already did that," she replied. "I fought through my job and my family. I thought about leaving all of them for you. I was serious about moving to Toronto and figuring out how to be your wife. But you don't want that."

"I think we can't dream about the future until this mission is done." It was clear he was choosing every word carefully.

"And if Huisman is alive and kicking ten years down the line?"

"I'll still be waiting to take him out," Ben announced.

"I can't live like that. The funny thing is if you'd asked me to marry you a couple of months back, I would have done it. I would have married you and followed you and done everything you wanted me to do. But the truth of the matter is you've always seen this thing between us as temporary. There's a reason you reacted poorly to me saying I love you. You don't want a wife. You don't want a long-term girlfriend. It's fun right now to have someone to sleep with, but you're waiting for him to call and start the game again."

"Or I could be trying to keep you out of the game altogether," he countered.

She wasn't sure they needed to have this talk. It all seemed set. "Then you should be happy I'm leaving."

He took a long breath and then nodded as though finally figuring out what he wanted to say. "I told you I care about you. I care about you in a way I don't think I ever have before. Kenzie, you're not some convenient lay. You're…you're the reason I wake up in the morning."

If only she was. "I'm not. He is. You might not want him to be, and I know you don't love him, but you need to see that he's the center of your world."

"Because he's stalked me since I was a child. Because in his twisted brain we're connected."

"So shut off the connection. Let my dad deal with this. Hell, let my sister do it. I know she's not going into the field, but when we find him, she's an excellent sniper." A bit of hope bubbled up. That optimistic side of hers unwilling to completely let go. If he was here and asking, he might see reason.

"And when he kills her, you'll blame me."

And they were back to Huisman. Manny the Great Evil. He Who Cannot Be Stopped by anyone but Ben. He would put it in a million different ways, but this fight was the center of his world, and it would color everything he did. She could see that now. There was very little space for anything but Ben's hate and fear. And she couldn't blame him for anything but trying to keep her. "When you take him down, what will you do with your life?"

"Have one," he said, frustration evident. He ran his hands over his already tousled hair. "I don't know. I'll finally get to not watch my back all the time."

"That's why you have friends. To watch your back while you have a life," she said quietly.

"My friends get killed."

"Who? Besides Deanna? Dare's somewhere in this building living his best life. Tim is apparently either puking or doing the other thing. So who has Huisman hurt because you liked them too much?"

"Your sister. He thought…" Ben frowned. "Well, he knew who she was, but he was well aware I didn't know. So he hurt Kala to hurt me."

And now she had to question his professional analysis. "Ben, he hurt Kala because she offended him. By being our father's daughter. By being a woman. I was going to say a strong woman, but I think he hates all of us. No matter who we are. I think in a weird way, he's attracted to her strength, and that makes him want to break her."

"He wants to hurt me," Ben insisted.

Her heart ached because she understood. He'd lost so much, spent years of his life hunting this man, and the thought that it wasn't all about him was… She couldn't imagine. "All right, Ben. He wants to hurt you. Well, when we're gone he won't be able to use us that way."

A long moment of silence filled the air, and she was ready to walk away when he finally spoke again, the words sounding tortured. "I don't fucking want to lose you."

"You never truly had me."

"It felt like I did. It felt like I was becoming part of all of it."

"But you don't want to be." That was the hardest acknowledgment of all.

"Of course I do. Do you honestly think I don't want a family? That I don't want to be able to wrap my arms around you and hold you tight? Fuck it. If I say the words, will you come back to me?"

"You wouldn't mean them." She'd thought about nothing else all night. "Ben, I'm not the woman for you. I wish I was. You can't conceive of how much I wish I was the woman who made you want to heal yourself, but I'm not."

"Killing Manny will heal me and then we can be together. I'll say the words."

"No, you'll kill Manny and then be left with an aching void. You'll have to figure out who you are without him defining your life. I know you're going to hate me saying this, but therapy helps."

"I don't need fucking therapy," he said, his hands in fists before he seemed to realize what he was doing. He took a deep breath, as though forcing himself to calm down. "Kenzie, I'm not crazy."

"It's not about being crazy." If he didn't even understand that, he wasn't close to getting to the heart of the problem. "It's about talking through your feelings. They're complex."

"There is nothing complex about how I feel about Huisman. I hate him. It's quite simple." There was a darkness in his eyes that frightened her. Not that he would physically harm her. Despite the bruises on her wrist, she wasn't afraid of Ben Parker.

She was afraid for him. But he didn't want to hear that.

"I was talking about your feelings for me." He'd gone straight to Huisman because when it came to feelings, his old friend seemed to get the lion's share.

His face fell. "They're not complex either. Baby, I want you. I want you so much I sometimes can't think of anything else. I've told you I'll give you everything you want. I'll say all the I love yous and I'll give you grand gestures and make your life a damn rom com if you'll wait for me to figure this whole thing out."

"Because all I want is the grand gestures, right?" She'd been such an idiot to think he'd really seen her, really known her. "I want life to be like a movie so I don't ever have to do any hard work or tax my brain."

"I didn't say that." The words came out in a soft tone, no hint of offense. "I know how smart you are. I know how hard you work. I'm struggling here, Kenz. I'm trying to give you what you need."

"Did you think I worked for Huisman?"

"No." He said it with a sigh. "I didn't mean most of what I said last night. I was angry and Manny spun me up. Then I felt ashamed because everyone is right. I should have put that together. I'm still upset about it. But I know you're not working with him. I'm sorry. I will try to keep my temper from now on."

He was so close. It wouldn't work without therapy. He might learn to shove the anger down, but it would be there. Waiting to explode. She was about to explain that to him when his cell buzzed.

He pulled it out and his jaw went tight.

Huisman.

Her gut twisted. “Don’t answer it.”

“He’s not calling. It’s a text.” His fingers moved across the screen. “Naturally. I have to deal with this.”

Panic flared. “You have to call Joseph or wait for my dad. I’ll call him now.”

He walked out, not giving her a backward glance.

* * * *

If you want to know the truth, come to Café Orleans. There’s a laptop with all the information you need to find out about what truly happened that day.

Kenzie called out after him. He knew what she would want and knew she wouldn’t listen to him.

He briefly thought about taking her as backup but discarded the idea. He would never put her in Huisman’s way if he had the choice. Never. Tim. He needed Tim.

That day. That day. It flooded his brain, tuning out everything else.

He strode down the hall, trying not to think about the attachment that came through.

It was impossible. The “photograph” Manny sent was burned in his brain now. The one that sent him back to “that day.” The one where his world fell apart.

He’d stood there after the doctor declared Deanna dead, and Manny had chuckled and shown himself truly for the first time.

It’s better this way, Benjamin. She wasn’t worthy of either of us, and now you can concentrate on something more intellectual than tossing a ball around. Now you can come with me and change the world.

He’d punched Manny right then and there and told him to never contact him again.

You’ll regret this, Benjamin. You’re the only friend I have in the world. Do you really want to be my enemy?

Deanna Fisher.

There was no question it was her, and she stood beside Manny, older than he remembered. She had a scar on her arm from the accident, but other than that she looked good for a dead woman.

Tim. Tim would be able to tell if that picture was a fake. He would run it through all his software and tell Ben that it was an AI fake and here were all the reasons why.

Deanna wasn't alive. He'd gone to her funeral.

Her closed-casket funeral.

His heart raced, brain throbbing. He heard Kenzie on her phone. Calling in the cavalry, he was sure.

He would be out of the building before they managed to catch him. He knew that café. It was bustling and right down the street. Smart of Manny to pick a place that was always full. He was sure Manny would try something, but it would be hard in a place so public.

There was a certain amount of safety that came with being surrounded by millions of people.

He stalked through the club level of the building, trying not to think about how at home he'd felt here once. He'd been becoming someone new here, someone happier and more settled. Someone who had a place in a family that didn't only involve work. This evening when the space transformed into a sensual dreamland, he would be barred from entering.

He couldn't think about that now. He had to concentrate on the mission. The mission was everything.

"Are you okay?" a quiet voice asked. Gabby. She was walking out of the hall that housed the privacy rooms. She was still in pajama bottoms and a tank top she'd gotten when Vivi and Sophy took them to an H&M. "Are you sick like Tim? He and Sosa are violently ill. Like terrible. I do not think they will eat again."

Something about what she'd said sparked in his head, but he couldn't think about it now. "I need his technical skills."

He pushed through anyway and was greeted with Tim looking shaky and pale.

His cell buzzed again.

If you're not here in fifteen minutes, the laptop will disappear.

Damn it. He should let it. He should put this in Big Tag's hands and march into those Colorado woods with Kenzie and just be with her until this was over. If he did that, he might be able to save his relationship with her.

Deanna wasn't alive.

The doctors had told him she died on the operating table.

The doctor in the hospital that likely had affiliations with the Huisman Foundation.

He wouldn't. He couldn't. Not for all these years. He knew Manny. If he'd been hiding Deanna, he would have taunted him by now. He would have used it.

"I'm pretty sure I'm dying," Tim said, his voice hoarse.

"I need you to look at something for me. Huisman sent me a picture I'm certain is fake, but I need you to verify," Ben said and frowned. He was being an asshole. Tim looked real rough. "Do you need a doctor?"

"Cooper already looked me over. He's a medic. No fever. Just food poisoning. Those girls must have cast-iron stomachs," Tim said and paled. "Uh, you should ask Lou. She's down here working with Kala on her nanite project. I have to…"

He ran for the bathroom.

Ben's time was running out. "I'll handle it and come back and help you. Don't die, man. I'll run out and get some electrolytes. Hang tight."

He would have to go without verification.

He turned and ran straight into Gabby, sending his cell to the floor. It hit the carpet and bounced but didn't break because Tim knew how to protect their tech.

"Sorry," Gabby said, dropping to her knees. She reached for the cell. "I was worried about…"

He knelt down and realized something was wrong. Her hand started to shake. Was she getting sick, too? "Are you all right?"

"This," she said, showing him the screen. The picture of Huisman and Deanna was there. "Where did you get this? Who sent it to you?"

A chill crept up his spine. She looked a little like Sosa had when she'd first seen a picture of Huisman. "Do you know that woman?"

Gabby handed the cell to him, her face a mask of disgust. "She's the madam. She runs the chateau. She runs it for him. I think she is his lover."

Ben felt his gut take a deep dive. She wouldn't. Deanna had been many things but cruel wasn't one of them. She'd been ambitious and naïve, but she…wouldn't. She wouldn't hurt anyone, much less innocent girls. This was a trick. He had to prove it. This was one more way to fuck with his head. If Deanna was alive, would Kenzie even believe him that he didn't know?

This was how he would put a wall between him and Kenz. And her team. Manny wanted him alone and vulnerable, and that was when he would strike.

He could fix this. He needed that laptop. Whatever was on it Tim could prove it was false. And maybe this would be exactly what they needed to prove several of Manny's crimes. This was a mistake on his part. Manny was so fucking arrogant.

He was halfway to the lobby when Lou ran up next to him.

"Hey, I heard something's going on. Gabby said you need Tim to verify some file for you." Lou had her laptop in hand. "I was going up to Kala's room to grab some clothes since the test went a little too well. It's okay. I adjusted and it should work now, but she told me the nanites bit her and she doesn't trust them. I tried to explain that was impossible. Ben, where are you going?"

He strode out the door, hoping no one had taken his access code to get back in. He had to risk it because he knew something bad would happen if he didn't get to that laptop.

He would take it and let Lou and Tim go over it with a fine-tooth comb. He was halfway down the block when he realized Lou had followed him.

"Ben, you're not supposed to be walking around London alone." Lou had left her laptop behind and jogged to catch up to him. "You need to take someone with you. Like Coop or TJ."

Damn it, now he had to worry about Lou because neither of those people were around this morning, so he had to do this alone. "Get back in The Garden."

His time was running out. There was another text, but he ignored it. He was certain it was another of Manny's countdowns. He loved to put Ben on a timer and watch him run himself ragged, but this time Ben would find a way to make him pay.

"You can't be out here alone. What's going on?" Lou was surprisingly fast. He had a good foot on her and she was matching him.

He stopped in the middle of the sidewalk. It was a spectacularly sunny day in a city that didn't have a lot of those. There were people everywhere. Tourists and people going to work and running errands. They were in one of the biggest cities in the world with an excellent CCTV network. Lou was brilliant, and why was he freaking out? Not even Manny would be able to pull off a kidnapping in the middle of a London street. But his time was ticking down. He turned the cell to her, offering her the picture. "I need you to prove that's a fake."

Her eyes went wide as she studied the photo, moving out of the way as a group of schoolkids ambled by, their harried teachers trying to keep them together. "This looks like…"

"Deanna. Yes. My dead fiancée. According to Gabby, she's also the woman who tortured and trained them. Which I find highly suspect since that woman had never fired a gun. But it's fake because she's dead."

Lou bit her bottom lip. "I don't know. I need to run it through a couple of programs."

"Good. You can do it when I get back." He turned and started walking. "He left a laptop for me at the café up ahead. I'll get it and be back soon."

"You can't simply pick it up and run with it," Lou insisted, her boots sounding against the pavement. "You have no idea what's on it. It could have a locator or hell, it could have a detonator."

He knew she was speaking truth, but it didn't matter. His brain was concentrating on one thing—his mission. He had to get that laptop. It was all that mattered now. He would take it somewhere else. He would get a hotel room or…he could take it straight to MI6.

Yes. That was what he would do. That would please both his need to have all the evidence he could gather and Kenzie. He found himself nodding even as he took back his cell and started jogging toward the café. "Call Big Tag and tell him I'll come in. He's at headquarters right now."

She kept up with him again. This time full-out running beside him. "I'm pretty sure Kenz is doing that right now, and Kala will likely come after us."

Then he better get moving. "She needs to stay inside the club. You need to stay inside the club. Damn it, Lou, you would be a valuable hostage. I don't know if you know this but you're quite smart, and he's talked about forcing you to work for him before."

"I'm not leaving you alone," Lou insisted with sheer determination.

Up ahead he saw the café. It was normal. People walked in and out. The dining room looked to be bustling. "What do you think you'll be able to do, Lou? We're not going to test the laptop in there," he said, approaching the door. "I'll grab it and we can test it later."

Did she think he was an idiot? That he was going to sit down and order a latte and wait for Manny to pull something shady?

He was an idiot. This was stupid, but he couldn't stop it now. He had to know.

"Yes, we are. I can at least tell if it's going to explode." She said the words loudly and then winced. "This is not smart. We should call the authorities in."

No way. That would lead to terrible outcomes. No one could predict what Manny would do if his will wasn't done. He only knew it would be horrible and it would likely happen to someone he cared about.

It would happen to her.

He was well aware his heart rate was high. Adrenaline pumped through his system as he looked around the small café. There was no hostess station. This was a place to get pastries and coffee and sandwiches for lunch. The seating was first come, first serve.

"It's there," Lou said, pointing to the back of the café, in the leftmost corner. There was a small bistro table with a laptop sitting open.

He moved to it, ready to pick it up and run. He looked at Lou. "Get back to The Garden. Now. I'll call when it's safe. It's a public café. What's he going to do?"

"It's a public café owned by a friendly syndicate," a smooth voice said. "Thanks for bringing my prize. At least one of the bitches can do their job."

Manny. He stood in the kitchen doorway, and he had an entourage. No one in the café even looked up.

He turned and Lou was in a large man's arms, her whole body limp. They drugged her.

Fuck. This had never been about him. This had been about getting Lou out of her hidey-hole. It was a gamble, but Manny was willing to take them.

Gabby said Sosa was sick like Tim, but he happened to know Sosa didn't eat that pizza. She hadn't been in Tim's room that night at all. She'd been working, and he'd even heard her talk about skipping the pizza in favor of a turkey sandwich.

Fuck, he'd been played, and it was going to cost him everything this time.

"Don't harm her. She's important," Manny ordered. "Get her in the car. You can rough this one up all you like. He'll enjoy it. My Benjamin is quite a masochist, as you'll find. And a bit of a fool, though I always forgive him for it."

Ben tamped down his panic, though it was easy to see not a single patron in the café was going to help. They were all ignoring the fight for life and death happening in their midst. Lou. He had to get Lou out of here. Kenzie would never forgive him if he got Lou killed. She had to be his priority.

He let his training take over. He kicked out, catching the guy nearest him in the gut.

Out of the corner of his eye he saw the man closest to Manny pull a gun, but Manny put up a hand.

"No, let him play. He's going to have to deal with so much heartache. Let him get some of his anger out now."

Ben continued to fight, punching out and trying to make his way to Lou, but there were so many of them. A massive man got up from the table across from him and joined in.

"Benjamin, did you like the photo?" Manny asked. "She can't wait to see you again. I told her she could play with you when I'm done."

Pain flared through him. He was surrounded and being attacked from all sides. Only the fact that they were strictly using their fists saved him. Though he felt a rib crack as he was shoved down on one of the tables. He fought back but they had hands on him now, dragging him to the ground and holding him there.

He was useless. Pathetic. He couldn't save himself.

This…this was how he died. This was what Ian had been talking about. It wasn't a bullet, but it would kill him all the same. He put himself here even when he'd known it was likely a trick. He'd convinced himself he was smarter, that he could win this game. He'd been running headlong to this point, desperate for something in his life to change even if that change was death.

Manny stood over him, a syringe in his hand.

But he didn't want it now. He didn't want this. He wanted her. He wanted to make different choices, to decide to be more than Manny's partner in a twisted game.

He should have given in, should have accepted whatever she was willing to give him. Should have been her boyfriend, her Dom, her husband. What a life that would have been. It flashed through him, what they could have had.

All gone now.

The only way he was ever going to win this game was to walk away and refuse to play at all.

"Well, *mon frère*, it looks like we're moving into endgame, you and I." He chuckled and looked genuinely amused. "We'll see how your girlfriend likes the gift I'm sending her. And while I'm thrilled to have the surprisingly gifted Ms. Ward on the team, I want Kala under my roof again. I'll see if taking her best friend brings her back where she belongs. It's going to be so much fun. Consider this our family reunion."

Ben fought until the end, until the needle pierced his skin and darkness began to encroach. He felt himself lifting, the men carrying him, following the one who had taken Lou out the back.

His last thought as the drugs took over was for Kenzie to forgive him.

Chapter Sixteen

Kenzie's hands were shaking as she stared at the security cam footage of Ben racing out of The Garden, with Lou following behind him.

It had been twenty minutes. She hadn't even realized anything was wrong until she got that video.

Kala stormed in. "They're gone, and apparently that fucking café is a syndicate front. Not one friendly to Dusan and our cousins. I didn't go in. It's a trap. I did manage to pull their CCTV footage, and the fucker carries Lou out himself and winks at the camera."

"And Ben?"

"I didn't see him. I'm sorry." Kala's jaw was tight, her eyes filled with unshed tears. "I'm sure they have him, too, but he wanted me to see Lou. Kenz…"

"It's the girls." Her stomach was in knots, but she couldn't fall apart now. "At least one of them, probably all three of them. I checked our inner CCTVs and saw Gabby walking in and out of the dungeon at all the right times. I've put us in lockdown in case they decide to try to slip away. The question now is does she know we know."

Kenzie had quietly put the whole place in lockdown. The Garden's security was excellent. Only a few people in the world knew how to get around it. She'd watched Gabby and Claire on the CCTVs. They'd been in the hallway, and now they were in their room. Sosa hadn't been seen this morning.

Naturally, they'd pulled it all on a day when there was no one in The Garden. They'd planned it carefully and taken extreme advantage of her mom. This had been a calculated plan to use Charlotte Taggart's past against them all. Even though they'd been on guard, Huisman had proven he was a serious game player.

"One of them will know what's happening." Kala sniffed, banishing her tears. She would be terrified for Lou, but she knew it wasn't the time to panic either. "I've put in a call to Mom. They're on their way. Do we think Tim is in on this?"

She didn't think so, but she couldn't discount it. "As far as I can tell, he's still downstairs, but I haven't studied the security cams. I checked to make sure the girls were in their room, but I can't do the same with Tim. Are we the last ones left in the building?"

"Tash and Dare went to breakfast. Vivi and Sophy are out for the morning on a restock run for the breakroom. Ariel and Robert are at a school thing. I texted Tash to stay away for a few hours while we deal with them," Kala said with quiet determination.

"He needs her." She had to give her sister all the hope she could. She had no idea what Kala would do if Lou was killed. The guilt would eat her alive. She had convinced Lou to leave her cushy university job to come with them.

Kala nodded tightly. "She can't help recreate the bombs if he hurts her too badly." Her hand went to her chest as though she could feel the damage that fucker had done to her. "Although he can cause pain that doesn't kill."

She stood up and wrapped her arms around her twin. "We'll get her back. I promise."

Kenzie meant it. Fully and wholeheartedly. She would get Lou back. And she would leave her sister out of it. It was Ben who got Lou caught. He hadn't listened to reason or logic. He'd done what he always did. When Huisman called, he'd answered.

"We will," Kala said with a sniffle and steadying breath. "All right, Mom and Dad and the Knights are on their way back. They've already informed MI6 what happened. I take it her tracker is off-line? Did he figure it out?"

Lou's big brain had invented a new system for tracking, but they'd always known Huisman would find a way around it.

She'd already tried pulling Lou's tracker. She didn't have access to Ben's, but his organization used older ones. She knew she would find nothing when it came to him. "Her signal dropped off at the café sixteen minutes ago. I'm sure Huisman knew Lou had outsmarted him after Virginia. We knew he would counter it before too long." The man had half the tech world in his pocket through the Disrupt organization. "From what I can tell the signal dropped off when he put her in the car."

"So he's using the car as a fucking Faraday cage?" Kala asked.

It was a scenario they'd discussed. If Huisman couldn't figure out how to find and disrupt the trackers Lou had invented, he could go old school, though it would be difficult. A Faraday cage was a structure—large or small—that stopped electromagnetic radiation, including light waves, microwaves, ultraviolet rays, certain sound waves including AM/FM radio, and blocked all Internet. It would be hard, but if the vehicle was large enough, they could have one to transport Lou in. Maybe even the trunk. She was sure if he'd planned it this carefully, he would have a way to get her into another cage without the signal going out.

Lucky for her, she knew where to start looking. And if she was right, she would get further instructions in the next hour or so. Well, "Kala" would.

Which was why she'd stolen her sister's phone, replacing it with her own.

It hadn't been long, but she already knew what she had to do, already had plans in motion because this would be quick. Huisman wouldn't want to wait.

She just had to figure out how to let her team know where she was.

"I think I'm never eating again." Tim walked in looking way worse for the wear.

Kala had a gun trained on him in no time.

"Whoa." Tim's hands came up. "Hey, I'm sorry. I know the bathroom is haunted now, but I'll clean it up as soon as I have some strength back. Where's Ben? He said he had something he wanted me to look at."

"Ben is with your friend Huisman and they have Lou," Kala said, her arm not moving at all. "And I suspect you had something to do with it."

If possible, Tim paled further. "What? What happened? I told him I would look at it. Or that he could ask Lou. I think it was a photograph. He was upset."

"Yes. You told him to take Lou along. I find it interesting that you've rallied all of the sudden," Kala said in a deeply predatory way.

Tim seemed to understand he was in danger. "Kala, I didn't know he was going anywhere. He came down and I… Damn it." He looked panicked for a moment and then ran to the nearest trash can and dropped to his knees, throwing up.

"We need to interrogate Gabby." Kenzie checked her SIG. "We always knew they could be a Trojan horse."

"It's a poison," a low voice said. Sosa stood in the doorway. "Not food poisoning. Real poison. It's tasteless, odorless. I've got some immunity to it since we were trained in this fashion. He needs doctor. Gabby and Claire are trapped in the room, but it won't take them long to get out. I destroy the secret phone they have, but they'll find a way. When they try to get out, they'll know their game is up."

"Their game?" Kala asked.

"The game we were sent here to play," Sosa admitted. She looked like a shrunken version of herself.

How could they believe her? Except she looked as sick as Tim. "Why?"

"Why did they do it or why do I turn on them? It all comes down to same thing. It comes down to him. Huisman. He's monster, and when he plans this, I decide this is how we get out. It is first time we ever have such freedoms. I think I will wait until Gabby and Claire are 'caught' and then we will run. Then I talk to your parents and think maybe we will not have to. But Gabby… I thought she was listening to your mother. I thought Charlotte was getting through to her, but it was all act. She believes if she delivers everything he wants, he will elevate her. I know better, but she talk to Claire. They poison me last night and Tim. Huisman wants the smart one."

"And you didn't bother to tell us?" Kala didn't seem to know where to point that gun anymore.

"I wanted more time." Sosa sounded exhausted, as though all the weight of years of torture were on her now. "To sway them. They are like sisters to me. At least that was how it feels. Felt. I have no one now. It doesn't matter what happens to me, but Tim did not betray you.

He needs doctor. I have written down how they make the poison. It might help. It's not a quick kill. There's still time. They were eating with him so he gets a lower dose since they can easily handle it. Our training was cruel but effective."

"And you?"

Sosa managed to shrug. "I'm only alive because I ate half. I save other half. It's a habit they should remember from our childhoods. I eat half and save the rest in case they choose not to feed us. They have gotten greedy. I never forget. Given how I feel, they gave me much," she said, a hand over her stomach.

Could they believe her? Or was this another trick? If Tim was working with them, it was a good way to hide his connections and keep him on the inside.

Of course, if she believed the video Huisman sent to her supposedly private cell phone, then it was Ben and not Tim who betrayed them all.

For Deanna. Who was alive. But was she?

Kenzie had questions.

How much lying had Sosa done? First, they needed a damn doctor, and they couldn't leave until someone was here to make sure the rest of the fuckers didn't get out.

The security system beeped once and then cut out. Kala moved to the monitor.

"Is it Mom and Dad?" Kenzie asked. They would be with Damon, who would absolutely be able to get through the lockdown. She was sure his senior agents would know how, and Oliver, too. She'd shot him a text to get his ass back to base, but it would be a half hour before he made it through traffic.

"Better." Kala kept her weapon at her side. "Tris is here, and he's not alone. Asshole didn't lose a step. He doesn't have that passcode, but he was a warm knife through cold butter."

Tris. He would be able to tell her if that video was real.

Kenzie started out the door, but she could already hear Tris calling for them. "We're in the basement."

It wasn't long before Tris was walking in. He'd easily gotten through the security system, and Kala was right. He hadn't come alone. He'd brought his partners with him. Carys and Aidan strode in behind him. The doctors. Aidan specialized in trauma and Carys in obstetrics, but they could handle this.

"I got here as fast as I could," Tris announced, not seeming to notice the dude hunched over the trash can or the half-dead assassin slumped in the chair usually used by Cooper. "Gabby is a plant. I have proof."

"No shit, Sherlock." Kala gestured around the room. "She's locked in for now, but she's already poisoned these two."

Aidan was on one knee, a hand on Tim's back while Carys had noticed Sosa.

"This is a pharmacological effect," Carys said, examining Sosa's eyes. "She's almost surely been poisoned. We need to get her to the hospital. She says she knows the formulary."

"This one, too, and he's in worse shape." Aidan frowned up at his partner. "I told you to text them but no, you had to have your cinematic moment."

"I called Uncle Ian this morning and he said everything was fine." Tris ran a hand through his hair, pink staining his cheeks. "I told him I had some intel I was bringing him. He didn't demand it or anything. Damn it. I'm sorry. I wanted to verify my findings with Lou before I did anything. Where is she?"

"With Huisman." Kala said every word cold. "Ben took her straight to him, and he's using something to block her tracker. Everyone's gone. They knew exactly when to strike. I've got word to Lucy and Sami. They're going to watch the chateau, but it seems so obvious."

"Obvious might be the whole point. He won't keep Lou there, but I think he might keep Ben somewhere different hoping we'll focus on the chateau. He has to know we're looking into it. Chaos. He wants chaos. It's why he sent me a video right before he took Lou." Kenzie started to explain as Carys was helping Sosa stand.

"She is right. This was his plan. I was not in on most of this," Sosa managed, standing with Carys's aid. "Gabby was the lead, and that mean the rest of us follow. What was on video?"

"A video of Ben fucking the hell out of his supposedly dead fiancée and saying some shitty things about me," she admitted.

It was a porn-worthy performance, and that alone made her question the authenticity. She knew how Ben made...had sex.

Or maybe you know how he performs when he's working a job, when the act itself is slightly distasteful because the woman he really loves is waiting for him.

She was not listening to that annoying voice. There was something wrong with that video. She just couldn't put her finger on it.

"I'll kill him and I'll make sure that bitch doesn't come back from the dead again," Kala announced. Her twin would fasten straight onto rage because it was far easier than the anxiety she had to be feeling about Lou in Huisman's clutches.

The video had been graphic. It was Ben balls deep in his ex-fiancée before some nasty pillow talk about how stupid Kenzie was and how Deanna was his only love.

He told her he loved her. He'd laid with his head on her breasts and said he loved her and always would, promised as soon as he'd taken down the dumb bitch—she assumed he was speaking of her—and her family, they could be together when Kenzie was dead and Manny's revenge was complete.

How many times had Manny watched it? Had he gotten off? Or was he jealous?

Yep, she was going to have to shut that voice down.

"TJ and Coop are here." Kala started for the door.

"We're ready to go. Hail a cab for us," Aidan said, wrapping an arm around Tim and helping him up.

Kala nodded and ran out the door.

"I'll come," Tris offered.

Aidan shook his head. "Nope. You stay and figure out how to track Lou down. Cooper can go with us if we need a guard. He can escort us, and then you can send someone else."

"I'll call Robert and Ari," Kenzie promised with a massive sigh of relief.

In moments she was alone with Tristan. She quickly brought him up to date on everything, including the video she'd received.

"I downloaded it on my laptop," she explained as Tristan sat down at the desk she'd been using. The one closest to Ben, where he could look up and wink at her or gesture for her to join him, and then he would kiss her senseless.

Tris's eyes were on the screen as he started the video. "Why not leave it on your phone?"

"Because I switched it with Kala's a few minutes ago." When

she'd hugged her sister, she'd slipped her cell in Kala's pocket and taken hers. They were on work cells for the time being, so they looked exactly the same. Same screen. Same passwords. Two different numbers, but they were programmed so they would look the same. It would take Kala time to figure out it wasn't hers.

Hopefully long enough for what Kenzie was absolutely certain was coming.

It wasn't merely Lou Huisman wanted. He wanted her sister, and she wasn't about to allow it.

Tris hit a button and the video paused. "Shit, Kenz. You watched this? Who is the woman? The time stamp is a couple of weeks ago. Right after the Nepal mission. Do we know where Ben went?"

"Supposedly back to Toronto." She was pleased with how even her voice was. She stared at that still shot. It showed Ben's back as he worked over Deanna's body, her legs wound around his waist. "Can you tell if it's a fake? I don't know what was on the picture Ben was upset about, but I know he wanted to see if it was AI."

"AI is so good now," Tris said, his hands on the keys. He pulled out his phone and connected the two systems. "I have some protocols that can tell quickly if it's AI." His eyes closed as he looked down at the screen. "Uhm, Kenz, I'm sorry. According to my software, it's likely not AI. It's not showing any markers."

Something eased in her chest as she realized what was missing.

"You're sure the time stamp is after Nepal?"

Tris nodded. "About a week."

So where the hell had the wound gone? His back was perfectly smooth. "He took a little fire on his way out of the complex. There was a lot of confusion, and some of the mercenaries were firing at anything that moved. Ben took a bullet to his left shoulder, right above the scapula." She pointed to where it should be onscreen. "It's healed now, but there's a visible scar."

Tris stared like he was trying to figure something out. "Maybe it's from earlier."

"It's a fake." She was certain now, and more certain than ever that she was going to need to find a way out of here. "He's got more advanced AI than we can imagine. Ben is an idiot who doesn't love me, but he wouldn't betray me like this, and he wouldn't work for Huisman, which is what Huisman wants me to think. This is a play. It's his go-to."

"Chaos."

Kenzie nodded. "He wants us chasing so many leads, dealing with so many problems, that we won't notice when my sister slips away and goes wherever he's going to tell her to go or he'll hurt Lou."

Tris paled. "What? Shit, that makes sense given what we know about him. You think Ben is a distraction."

Kenzie sighed and let her brain go through all the scenarios. All the ones that made sense. This was all a plot and Ben fell for it because deep down he wanted to play this game with Huisman. He needed to win, so he was open to manipulation. Kenzie wanted Huisman dead, but she didn't care who did it. She would happily go into hiding if that made things easier on whoever could take the fucker down. "I think he wants to humiliate Ben and wants him so wrapped up in trying to convince me this was all a lie that he doesn't notice Kala slipping off to meet Huisman. If I'm right, this phone will get a text with explicit instructions on how to get Lou back."

"But only if she trades herself," Tris surmised and sat back. "Kenz, he'll kill you."

Like she hadn't thought that one through. "He'll think he's already damaged me. I think he'll go easier. He won't want to kill me right away. He wants to break Lou. He'll take me to the place where he has Lou since I'll be used to get Lou to do what he wants. Pain won't break her, and honestly, he needs her sharp to do what he wants. So what's the quickest way to get her to comply?"

"Hurt someone she loves," Tris agreed. "Why wouldn't he go for… I was going to say TJ, but he's being practical. He has to know he's got one shot at this, and he wants Kala."

"TJ would go to my dad. Kala wouldn't. She wouldn't even tell me or Cooper. If she thinks she's the only way to save Lou, she'll do it no matter the cost." She knew how her twin would feel.

And that was precisely why she intended to take her place, and she couldn't think of a better partner than Tris. He wasn't afraid of Kala, and he would see the logic.

"You're going to do it." Tris stood. "You're going to walk into the lion's den for your sister's best friend."

It was more than that. "I'm doing it for all of us. Lou's my friend, too." She looked to the CCTV monitors, and Kala was wrapped around her husband. She'd held it in until Coop showed up, and now she sobbed while he held her. TJ looked lost. He was on his cell. Likely calling his parents.

She couldn't let this end in tragedy. They had their whole lives ahead of them. They were happy. That fucker didn't get to take it from them.

Not while she was on duty.

"Kenz, you can't walk in. He'll do the same thing to your tracker that he did to Lou's."

"Which is why I need another…" It hit her suddenly. Damn. Necessity really was the mother of invention. Though Lou hadn't thought of this application yet. "Lou's been working on a way to split the nanites."

"Yeah, she wanted to be able to separate them in case someone needed clothes or a blanket. She's working on a bunch of stuff with those little fuckers. I'm kind of afraid of them since they could become sentient and take over the world," Tris complained. "You're going to wear the suit? It could help. I could lock it on, and it's got some defensive utilities."

And then she would be locked in a suit, and she didn't want to think about the bathroom impossibilities. "Back when Lou was working with them as a beta project, didn't she lose a couple and figure out a way to track singles?"

"Yeah, but that was because she hadn't figured out how to keep them… Shit, you want to leave a trail of breadcrumbs, something Huisman won't recognize as a problem. He likely wouldn't even notice if we figured out a way to peel single nanites off."

Fate. That was what it felt like. "Lou solved the problem earlier. Her laptop is downstairs. I need you to reprogram the suit. She's been working with colors and fabric styles. I need all black, something that looks like I'm working."

Tris stood. "One Black Widow cosplay coming up." He sobered. "Kenzie, this is dangerous. If he figures out you're not Kala…"

She knew what could happen. It didn't matter. Huisman knew there were two of them, but they were careful. They'd spent years perfecting being each other. Kala knew how to plaster on a smile and look like the world was a party. Kenzie knew how to shut down her brightness and get serious and very sarcastic. They'd worked hard to ensure every scar matched. Every one except the burn mark on Kala's leg, but Huisman hadn't seen that and there were no medical records.

She could do this.

She had to do this.

"Your parents are going to kill me," Tris said with a sigh. "Maybe you're wrong. Maybe this isn't his plan and we need to look for them both."

She was certain. There was zero reason to send her that video.

Huisman had played Ben perfectly. He'd set Kala up perfectly, too.

She would bet he wouldn't consider her a player at all. He'd sent her the video so she would cry and rage and either walk away from Ben or find him because she wanted to hurt him.

What if she did neither? What if she changed the game altogether?

She would need to plan it carefully, and she needed Tris as her accomplice because if the rest of the team found out, they would likely do something to stop her.

She didn't want to be stopped.

She looked on the security cams, and her parents walked in the door with the Knights in tow. Her mom wrapped herself around Kala so she was surrounded by her and Cooper.

Her sister deserved a wonderful life with Cooper and Lou.

TJ deserved his happily ever after. Lou was the best. She wasn't going to die at fucking Manny Huisman's hands.

He didn't get to use her genius to his own ends. That man thought he ruled the world and that women were walking wombs who should serve men.

It was time to show him how she served him up.

On a silver platter. Or maybe one made of nanites.

"Uh, it looks like Gabby and Claire are trying to get into the air ducts," Tris pointed out. He gestured to one of the monitors.

"Tell Damon. I'm pretty sure he has a nasty surprise for anyone in his air ducts." Her dad had tried to pull a prank once and had never stopped complaining about it. She sat back at her desk as the cell pinged.

Kala's cell pinged.

Huisman was right on schedule.

It was time for the show to begin. It was a part she'd been preparing to play all her life.

Fourteen hours later, Kenzie snuck out of her room. It was fairly simple since Lucy was in France with Sami, preparing for the rescue of Ben Parker. Naturally she was supposed to be leading it, but she'd left detailed instructions for her twin, who would be surprised to find herself leading the op again. But she would do it. She would go into the field.

I know you don't like him and you think he's bad for me, but I'm asking you to save him. Play the part Huisman set for me. You know you can do it. Save my stupid, foolish heart, and I'll save the piece of yours that will die without Lou.

She'd dressed in the nanite "fabric." Tris had quickly learned Lou's protocols and had programmed a tactical suit. He'd also programmed the nanites to shed single "cells" every half hour. The nanites would simply make more and fill in the spaces so no one would notice.

Ben was in France. He was at the chateau.

"You're going in."

She winced and turned. Sosa stood there looking worse for the wear.

"I'm not to be telling. You are saving your sister," she said quietly. "He will kill you if he figures out you're not her. How did you keep her from getting his text? I assume that's how he did it. He's trying to lure goth Bratz doll out so he can have her. He's using her friend. You have to know he won't exchange you."

"I know."

"So this is suicide mission?"

"I have plans," she assured the young woman. "Are you all right?"

Sosa nodded. "I'll be weak for a while, but I know how to fight for me. They come and take Gabby and Claire away. Will they take me in the morning?"

MI6 had come this afternoon and taken Gabby and Claire. They were being questioned, and what happened to them was no longer Kenzie's worry. Sosa was another story. She did feel responsible for the kid. "No. My parents have agreed that you should stay here and work with Ariel. Her husband is an investigator. He's going to look into what happened to your parents and how you got taken."

"Your mother is… She is who I hope to be. Maybe if she survives, I can, too. I won't lie again." Sosa hugged her arms around herself as though trying to get warm.

"But you will keep your mouth shut."

Sosa nodded. "You are trying to save your sister. I would never stop you, but I would say that you should keep your eyes open. He's arrogant and makes many mistakes. He likes to call his guards his army, but they are mercenaries. They're not as careful as they should be. I hope you are safe. He loves you, you know."

That was the rub. "He doesn't. Or if he does, then he won't admit it. He can't."

She started down the hall again.

"You are good Bratz doll, Kenzie Taggart."

Kenzie wiped a tear away and walked off to meet her fate.

* * * *

Ben's fingers twisted around the bars of the cage he was being held in. He could feel the hard press of the gun Kenzie held against the back of his neck. "Do it."

It would be better than having to face what he'd lost. Her. He could hear it in the ice of her tone, the way she'd mentioned his mistress.

Manny had been hard at work. He still had no fucking idea if Deanna was alive or dead, but it was clear Manny had sent information to Kenzie that made him look bad. Look like he betrayed her in the worst possible way.

His head still ached from whatever drugs Manny used on him. He couldn't see straight, couldn't think properly. All that mattered was her.

He knew that now. He'd been a complete idiot. She was the most important thing in his world.

"Do it, Kenz. Do it and get the hell out of here. He wants to hurt you. He thinks hurting you will bring Kala out into the open," he said. "He's probably watching us right now."

She was silent for a moment. "Did you enjoy fucking your mistress? Or do we call her a girlfriend? Fiancée? You take a long time getting to the ceremony, Parker."

He went still.

Was that Kenzie? Kenzie would never call him Parker.

What game were they playing now? Despite how upset his stomach was, he forced himself to turn. In the moonlight, he saw her standing over him. Avenging angel. Beautiful and cold and not his girl.

He held his hands up. "I haven't seen Deanna since the day she died."

Manny was likely watching. If Kala wanted him to believe she was Kenzie, then he wasn't going to wreck her play. Kenzie would be somewhere in this building, likely doing a far more dangerous job.

"I have a video that states otherwise," Kala said, her voice dead calm.

That was when Kala was at her most dangerous.

Video?

"Whatever he sent you, it's a lie."

She wore all black, her hair tied back and a black cap on to help her blend into the night. She stared down at him, not a hint of real expression on her face. "I watched you fuck her and talk about what a moron I am for believing you would care about me. Tell me where she is, Ben. I would like to have a word."

He was going to throw up. What the hell had Manny done?

"I listened every time you told her you loved her. It makes sense now why you wouldn't tell me," she said quietly, every word a condemnation. "I listened to you tell her how you'll kill me when the time is right and I'm no longer useful."

"Kala," a deep voice said. "I didn't tell you to torture him. We took out the cameras. The place is empty, but I think it's supposed to be. Tris, turn the lights on."

The lights came on and Ben had to blink.

"Step back." Ian Taggart was dressed like his daughter. Tactical pants, black shirt. He'd pulled up his balaclava and looked predatory as he pressed something against the cell door. "It doesn't make much of a mess, but you can never tell. Fire in the hole."

Ben scrambled away, expecting an explosion, but there was a small poof and the door swung open.

"Mr. Taggart, I…" Ben began.

Cooper strode in, dropping to one knee and holding up a small flashlight. "Hey, look here. Do you know what he gave you?"

"You didn't have to be so harsh," Taggart was complaining. "You know she wouldn't want you to."

"Well, if she wanted to handle it differently, she would be here doing her job and she would have let me do mine," Kala complained.

Kenzie hadn't wanted to come get him. He suffered through Coop's basic exam, telling him it was some kind of sedative and he had no idea where he was or how long he'd been gone.

"You've been gone for almost twenty hours." Cooper was a cool professional, taking his pulse. "You're in France. We believe this is where they kept Sosa and the others. It looks like they cleared out. Sami saw them bringing someone in and then we found the message from Huisman."

Something about Gabby. Yes. He remembered now. "Gabby said Sosa was sick, too, but she didn't eat the pizza. I think…"

"You shouldn't think," Kala said with no small amount of venom. "Gabby and Claire were plants, and they're now MI6's problem. Tim and Sosa were poisoned. Like really poisoned. By assassins, who tend to know how to poison a person."

"Hey, we talked about this," Cooper admonished.

"Yeah, I'm supposed to be fine because my sister wants this complete asshole to feel good about himself. He ran off. He knew the protocols and he still ran off like a puppy being called by his master," Kala accused. "He got Lou kidnapped, and god only knows what's happening to her now."

"She's not here." TJ strode in. "The place is deserted."

A new face was with him. Tristan Dean-Miles. He'd met the man before, but it had been a while. "He planned this out. It's his way of letting us know whatever we discover about him, he can get out of it. Sami and Lucy are going through what look like the offices, but I think he bricked everything before he left. We also found the tunnels they used to get everyone out under Sami's watch. She saw nothing out of the ordinary until they brought Ben in. Huisman wasn't sighted at all."

"Because he never meant to be here. Ben was the distraction," Taggart said and touched his ear where Ben was sure a comm was. "We have the target. Tell our doc he'll need to look him over, but Coop thinks he's good to come back to base. No. No sign of her, but then we knew that would happen."

Cooper stood and reached for his wife's hand. "Come on. Let's get back to base and try to figure out where to look next."

"Lou?" They were talking about Lou. He'd gotten Lou caught. His anger was at a low simmer since guilt seemed to be taking up all the space. And anxiety. What had Kenzie seen? What had she believed?

Was that the reason she wasn't here?

He needed to see her, to let her know he wasn't going to allow a few fucking words to keep them apart. Who was to say this feeling he had for her wasn't love? It was definitely commitment and passion and companionship and affection. She made him think about the future in a way he hadn't in years.

"Lou's somewhere being tortured because of you, asshole," Kala spat.

Her husband wrapped her up in his big arms. He whispered in her ear, and she seemed to calm.

"It wasn't his fault." TJ was perfectly stoic. He had a hand on the P90 he wore on his chest like he needed the comfort of it being there. "We talked about this. Huisman set us up. Tris pulled the CCTV cams around the building. You know he told her to go back."

"Yeah, and I know she wouldn't let him go alone because she's a good human being who knew how dangerous it was for him to be out there. She wouldn't let anyone go alone," Kala said in a calmer tone. "Which is why idiot here should have known something was up. Tim was poisoned, you know. He almost died. And all because Huisman knows which strings to pull with you."

"Hey, he did a good job with all of us," Taggart reminded her. "After all, he knew which of mine and your mom's strings to pull."

"We never trusted them," Kala argued. "We always had eyes on them."

"And yet they managed to set us up perfectly," TJ replied. "Even down to knowing Sosa was going to break and trying to kill her, too. Lou did what she was always going to do. She helped. Now we have to pray Kenz knows what she's doing."

"He won't hurt her. Not while he needs her." Ben managed to get to his feet. The world still felt woozy. "He wants her to make the bombs for him. I need to talk to Kenzie." The whole thing had been a play to get Lou. He'd understood it at the time, but it crashed over him again. How useless and pathetic he was. How Manny manipulated him and got him to throw away the best parts of his life. He looked to Kenzie's father. "Mr. Taggart, I didn't sleep with Deanna. I haven't seen her since she died. Well, I thought she died."

He still wasn't sure what was going on.

"We know, Ben," Taggart said.

"The video is AI." Tristan moved in. "It took me a while because it is incredibly advanced AI. Like nothing I've ever seen. My dad had a program that was similar, but this is light years ahead."

"She doesn't think I cheated on her?" Ben's head was still whirling. "I wouldn't. I couldn't. I know I acted like an ass."

"She knew before Tris verified it," Kala replied. "She knew when she watched it. She told me there was zero way it was real. Damn it, she knew everything and I treated her like dealing with her boyfriend was an annoyance because Lou is in danger."

"I'll find Lou." He was fairly certain they wouldn't believe him, but he would do it. He would visit Tim and make sure his friend was all right and then he would do whatever it took to find Lou and bring her home. He would sacrifice himself if he had to.

"You've been recalled to Toronto," Taggart said, his voice grave. "Tomorrow. Tim should be strong enough to leave the hospital. I spoke with Joseph and CSIS is recalling you."

"I quit." Nothing mattered but getting Lou back and making it all up to the woman he…to the woman he loved. "I can help you."

A brow rose over Taggart's icy eyes. "From what I can tell you're the reason I'm down two members of my team, so I will withhold judgment on whether or not you can help us. Trust me, Ben. If I thought I could trade you for Lou or Kenz, I would." He touched his ear again. "We're coming out. Let French intelligence know it's all theirs now, and thank them profusely for their quick aid."

He stood there as everyone started to move, his mind processing what Taggart had said. "What do you mean? He's got Lou. He's going to try to use Lou to get Kala. You should be prepared for him to send her a private message. He'll do it only to her because he knows she'll turn herself in if it means Lou gets to live. He's lying. He won't trade Lou for anyone, but he'll take Kala if he gets the chance."

"Yeah, she figured that out." Kala frowned, holding her husband's hand like she desperately needed the support. "This whole thing was to throw us off and make it easy to miss it when I slipped away for my meeting with Huisman. He sent instructions and everything. But in the chaos of dealing with what happened yesterday, the team would be planning the mission to save you, led by my sister, who would obviously want revenge on her cheating, betraying boyfriend."

Every word felt like a cut, but he would deal with it because she was scared. And angry. "I'm glad you saw through it. The act was for Manny? He was probably watching up until the moment you took the cams down. Let him think it worked. I'll act out the next time he calls. I'll tell him how he ruined my relationship with Kenzie."

"You fucking moron," Kala spat.

"Ben, Kenzie figured it out," Taggart said with a grimness that sent a chill down Ben's spine. "She knew what would happen shortly after she received the video. She didn't fall for it at all, but she did make plans. She changed phones with her sister so when Huisman called, she was the one who answered. She was the one who offered herself up to save Lou. She told him she was Kala and that she would do whatever it took to save her best friend."

For a second he could have sworn his vision dimmed, and he couldn't make the words make sense.

Kenzie had offered herself up?

"He'll hurt her." The words sounded dumb on his tongue. "He wants to hurt Kala. He'll kill Kenzie if he figures it out."

"She's excellent at pretending to be her sister. I know I don't like to admit it, but when they decide to go all out, I can't tell them apart," Taggart admitted. "But he will hurt her. I don't even know if she's made it to the meet spot since she didn't leave me a handy note."

Kala's hand swiped at her eyes, but she remained steady. "I let you read it. She didn't tell me anything else. I don't even know how she shut her tracker off. There wasn't any blood that I could see, and we don't have anything at The Garden that would disrupt the signal. She wore Lou's suit. The nanite project. It can fuck with our trackers. Lou's working on the problem."

Kenzie was gone. Kenzie had walked out of her perfectly safe hidey-hole and into whatever Manny had planned for her sister.

He was going to be sick. He could hear Manny talk about how Kala might give him strong sons.

What the hell was she already going through? "How long?"

"She left six hours ago." TJ looked like his light had dimmed. He was always sunny, but his fear for Lou weighed on him. "We were supposed to be resting, getting ready for this op. As soon as she knew we were all occupied, she slipped out. She even managed to override the security system."

"She's a multi-talented girl," her twin said. "Now we have to hope her research helps us figure out where the hell she is. She was doing a deep dive on all of Huisman's properties. I know she had some ideas about where he was trying to build the bombs. I have to think Huisman would take Lou there, and that's where he would want me, too."

Kenzie was gone.

She'd walked out because she'd known her sister wouldn't want to live without Lou. Because her cousin loved Lou. Because she would desperately want to keep all those happy ever afters alive. Since her own hadn't worked out. She was out there alone, and she didn't know he loved her. She thought he didn't, thought that he would always pick Huisman first.

She thought she was the expendable one. The one who could sacrifice for her family because she would be the least missed.

This was it. This ache in his heart and body and mind was love, and he'd been scared of it. Scared that if he loved her, he would lose her. Scared that if he loved her, she would end up hating him.

This was the punishment Manny had doled out, and he'd done it because he was jealous. He was jealous that his grandfather told him to be more like Ben. He was jealous as hell that Ben wouldn't be his sidekick or some shit. It didn't matter. He'd allowed Manny to win. He'd wanted to be the center of Ben's world, and he didn't care if that was a positive thing or an evil thing.

"We need to move out," Taggart announced. He stared Ben's way. "The only reason we're here is Kenzie asked us to save you. She sacrificed herself for Lou and Kala and TJ and for you. I'm only willing to bring you back with us because I know she would want me to, and I'm going to honor my daughter. I should ship you back to Toronto right now."

"I won't go." He forced himself to stand tall when all he wanted to do was beg. "If you won't let me help, I'll try to find her on my own. I won't allow anything to stop me. I was an idiot. I love your daughter. She is the most important thing in the world to me. I will find her and then we're going to hide and I will let you deal with Manny. I'll go wherever she needs me to go, be whatever she needs me to be."

Taggart looked to Kala, and the two seemed to have a silent discussion.

Kala shrugged. "If we don't know where he is, he could cause trouble."

Taggart moved, his motion causing everyone to jump to action. TJ and Cooper headed out, Kala following.

Tristan had a tablet in his hand, his eyes studying it carefully.

Ben took the moment. "Mr. Taggart, I'm so sorry. I can't begin to apologize. Kenzie was right about everything, and if she'll let me, I'll do what it takes to get better."

Taggart's head shook. "It can't be strictly about her. She doesn't allow or disallow your healing process. You realize you've been in an abusive relationship for years, right? I know your masculinity is threatened by that fact, but you can't move on to anything healthy until you acknowledge and accept that it happened."

He'd been battered emotionally by a master.

He didn't want to think that he was being held back by toxic masculinity. He was far more evolved than that. And yet it was there. The rage at the thought he was in a "relationship" with Manny. But how else would he explain it? The turmoil he felt proved Taggart's point. "I hate him. I want so very, very much to not care. I want to not think about him. I want a life with Kenzie and a home. I'm tired, and I didn't know it until I met her."

"You can forgive her for lying to you?" Taggart asked.

Somewhere in that cage he'd been held in a weight had lifted.

She hadn't required proof to believe him, to change the course of her life for a man who couldn't love her. Who did love her.

"I forgive her wholly and unreservedly, and if I get the chance, I'll prove it to her," Ben promised.

Taggart sighed. "Then you're ready for the talk. But I need to explain to you that if this is all performative bullshit, I'll bury you."

"Understood." He felt changed already. Lighter than before.

He'd been alone because he wouldn't let anyone in. But he'd meant what he said. Kenzie was his priority, and he would leave Manny Huisman to Ian Taggart. He would trust this man to take care of the situation.

"Then we should get back to The Garden. I've got a plane waiting. We caught Kenzie on CCTV at a private airport outside of London. Tris is working on figuring out what plane she took and where it went," Taggart explained.

"Uhm, Tris isn't doing any of that." Tristan held up his tablet. "Tris has been following the trail of breadcrumbs our princess has been leaving behind. She's in Bulgaria. The location hasn't changed in six hours, so I think that's her final destination. I connected her location to an old castle purchased by one of the Huisman Foundations' many companies. I have her."

"Breadcrumbs?" Taggart asked.

"Nanites," Tris corrected. "Lou was working on this project, and Kenzie figured out how to drop them in single units…"

"Which would then send out their location, but only if you're looking for it." Taggart's head shook. "Kenzie planned this. She knew her sister's heart can't handle another of Huisman's sessions and so she found a way to get us Lou's location. And she brought you in."

Tris winced. "She did, but she asked me to keep quiet until I had the final location. Which I now do and yes, I know I'm going to get my ass kicked."

Taggart walked right up to Tris and hugged him. "I think you'll find a lot of forgiveness if we get our people out, Nephew."

"I know I should have stopped her, but she's right. This is our best bet," Tris whispered.

"Then let's go get her." Taggart stepped back, a light in his eyes. "And she's grounded. Forever."

Tristan moved in behind Taggart as they started out of the cell. "I don't think you get to do that now. I hope my parents can't do that anymore. You know shrink wrapping a person gives you time to think. My dad's an expert."

Ben followed, desperate to get to her, to save her, to be with her.

Chapter Seventeen

Kenzie shivered in the cold stone cell she found herself in. She was finally in a castle. A princess in need of rescue.

Yeah. Her fairy tale kind of sucked.

Bulgaria. She was pretty sure that was where she was given the distance and the language she'd heard being spoken at the private airfield. Not that the pilot would tell her, and there hadn't been a nice flight attendant who gave her champagne. Nope. She'd had three guards and was lucky they hadn't tried anything. This was where her trail would end since she'd been forced to change into a hospital gown when they'd arrived at this cold, stony, seemingly rundown castle. She'd been careful about it, treating the jumpsuit made from some of the most technologically advanced material in the world like it was nothing more than polyester and Lycra. If they looked closely they would likely figure it out, but she had to take the chance.

She was taking a lot of chances today. Including the one where her fucker of a kidnapper had other things to do with his time.

She was being held in the part of the structure that looked like a rundown castle. She'd had a glimpse of the lower floors and realized they resembled the compound in Nepal. A door had come open, and she'd caught sight of stark white walls with strong lab vibes. The man was into white and seemed to want a world that looked sanitized. Which was odd for a man who also loved chaos.

She'd been here for hours. Which when one was facing torment and torture was a plus, but she hadn't seen Lou. She needed to put eyes on her. She needed to know that this hadn't been for nothing.

Her heart felt twisted at the thought of Lou fighting so hard he killed her. *Please let her be fine. Let her be alive.* Lou was smart. She would know how to slow down the process. She would play things right and wait to be rescued. Lou would know they would never leave her behind.

She took a deep breath and prayed.

Let Tristan have found her trail. He would give it some time before announcing what they'd done. They'd agreed they wanted to be sure she was at the final destination before racing to a spot where she might only be held for a brief time.

But it was over. She didn't have access to her breadcrumbs anymore. She was on her own if they moved her again.

Where was Ben now? She knew he'd been taken to France. Had her team gotten him out yet? They should have reached the chateau and extracted him…maybe yesterday. Had Ben figured out Kala was playing a role? Or did he hate her for tricking him again?

She felt heavy. Weighed down. She wondered if she always would now that it was over between them. A door had closed, and it wouldn't open again.

Would he miss her if she died? It was a pitiful thing to think, but she was here, waiting, and her brain was going to a hundred different places, none of them good. She thought about dying and how it would be okay because she didn't have much of a future. Would he love her if she died and it was suddenly simple? A martyr was always easier to love than a living, breathing, fallible person.

The camera placed in the corner of the room reminded her to keep her expression as closed and cold as possible. Kenzie Taggart might long to weep and mourn her lost love, but Kala was just pissed.

The waiting was probably part of the torture.

The one thing she was trying not to think about was pain.

If Huisman wanted to continue his experiments on her sister, she would know what made her twin—her tough-as-nails twin—scream and cry and wish for death. What had damaged her heart.

It felt oddly right to potentially go out this way, taking pain that was meant for her twin sister. They'd shared everything else. Clothes and secrets. A face and a life. For so long they'd shared their scars.

Kenzie's breath caught as the cell door opened and that fucker strode in like this was an ordinary meeting.

He actually smiled at her.

Asshole.

"I want to see Lou." She didn't move from her seat. She kept up the casual anger that often seemed to be her sister's trademark.

"Such a rude girl. Well, I couldn't hope that you would come for me." Huisman was dressed in a suit and flanked by two burly guards loaded with weapons.

Weapons she could get off them if she had a chance. She saw the scene play out in her head. Attack the first guard, take the semi-automatic off his right hip while she kicked out and caught the second guard in the solar plexus, pushing back against the wall. She would shoot Huisman first and then take the guards out if she had to. The door was on a key card system with no biometrics, but that didn't mean the rest of the building didn't have them. She would have to keep his body close in case she needed a fingerprint or retinal scan. She was absolutely certain this was when her twin would gleefully take the body parts she would need and leave the rest behind, but one thing she did not share with her sister was a love of blood. Nope. She preferred cleanliness, thank you very much.

The problem was she hadn't seen Lou yet. Kenzie wasn't even sure she was here. If Lou wasn't here… Well, if she wasn't here, then it was all for nothing.

"I want to see Lou."

Huisman's eyes narrowed on her. "I'd like to talk first. Did your sister find Benjamin?"

"I don't know. I don't care." She frowned. "And I suspect you already know. You're a pervert who likes to watch." She gestured to the camera. "I doubt you didn't have them on your boyfriend."

He chuckled, a low, oddly charming sound, but then the devil likely needed to be charming from time to time. "Oh, I assure you there's never been anything sexual between me and Benjamin. I am far more evolved than that. I find sexual relations distasteful, though it is obviously necessary to continue my line. A man's name living on after his death is imperative. A fact I've been considering lately."

She intended to end his cursed line. "Is that why you run a brothel? To continue your line? It's pretty wild."

"Ah, which one talked?" Huisman asked, though there was no shock in his tone. "Well, I knew one of them would. I suspect it's Sosa. Troubled girl. Always causing problems, but she was a risk I was willing to take."

"Why? Why not simply assassinate my father? Having thought about it, it's obvious Sosa's real job was to infiltrate my family. Were they strictly there to cause the problems you needed to kidnap Lou?"

He paced like a professor in front of a crowd of eager students. "That was the main plan. You see the key to life is knowing the weaknesses of the people around you. Your mother, like all women, has many weaknesses. Your father only has one, but it's a large one."

"My mother."

"Proof that the great Ian Taggart is a pathetic male bowing to women's weaknesses. I knew your mother's childhood would make her sympathetic to a young woman raised in similar circumstances," Huisman continued. "I offered my problem up to the board at the chateau and they suggested a psy-op on your family. We sent Sosa in first."

Now she was catching on. "She was the most expendable. The one you trust the least. But she was also the one you thought my mother would connect with since she's a Russian girl abused and forced into a life she didn't want. Yes, my mother would risk a lot to help a girl like that."

"It didn't hurt that the girls would drop hints and get your parents curious. They were willing to risk a lot for intel. I'm sure your father thinks it's smarter to keep your enemies close. I knew Sosa would turn the first time she had the opportunity. She was weak. So I ensured that Gabby and Claire—good soldiers who know their place—had everything they would need to take care of the situation when the time came. Sosa was a problem child. Always asking questions and getting the rest of the girls riled up. We won't miss her."

She hadn't expected empathy from him. She wondered if he thought Sosa was dead. Tris had gone in and cleared all the hospital records for her and Tim. She certainly wasn't going to tell him, and Gabby and Claire believed they'd succeeded on all levels with the exception of getting away. "Well, you did have her taken from her home and tortured so she would kill people for you."

One slim shoulder shrugged. "Young girls make the best spies and thieves and assassins. It's because the world rightly ignores them except for their obvious uses."

"And when they're no longer young women?"

"Then their usefulness is over and they are no longer needed at the chateau. Naturally there's no way to leave the group once you're in. It's how they've stayed a secret for so many years."

She was sure they didn't get to retire to the country. The longer she kept him talking the more time Tris had to find her. And the longer she put off the eventual pain she would go through this evening. She was curious at how the group had adapted over the years. "Do you have any hackers?"

"Oh, of course. More than you would imagine. The world right now is nothing but technology, so yes, hackers are trained at the chateau as well. Their clients require money and information, and that is best acquired these days online. Personally, I think they should get out of the sex business, but they cling to their traditions. I'm told the threat of being moved to the other side keeps the girls in line."

She would take as much information as she could. If there was something she'd learned about this man, it was that he didn't mind talking when he thought he had the upper hand. He believed she would never leave here so he was willing to discuss all of his fabulous plans. "I would bet a lot that you also have some incredibly powerful artificial intelligence. Or did you really kidnap Ben's fiancée right off the surgical table and keep her hidden for years?"

"I wondered if you would suspect. I thought I would try it out. It's brand new, and I think you'll be surprised at who coded the base. My people have perfected it. An AI that so perfectly creates the way this one does could change our perception of reality. It could simply change reality altogether. What does anything mean if we can't agree on something so basic as what is real and what is not real? So my question is are you real?" He moved closer but still kept some distance. Like she was a dangerous animal. "How can I be sure you're Kala Taggart?"

She rolled her eyes. "Because I'm not crying and begging you to save my friend. My sister is overly dramatic. She wouldn't even listen to me when I said that sex tape was probably AI garbage. I couldn't break it because you have the one person on my team who could likely figure it out. So, despite the fact that Lou is worth ten Ben Parkers, she only cared about rescuing him. So she could try to kill him. She only thinks about her own damn feelings. It was easy to get out of The Garden because everyone was paying attention to Kenzie. It was a whole scene, but I suspect you anticipated that."

"I do like a touch of chaos," Huisman admitted. "She does seem to be a bit on the unstable side. Unlike you, from what I can tell she's a bit of a slut."

Like that was the worst thing she could be called. Or original. "My sister has had a lot of boyfriends. She always thinks she's in love and makes mountains out of molehills, but Ben has been a pain in my ass since the day she laid eyes on him."

"He's a traditionally attractive man. Very masculine. Women are attracted to Benjamin because of their biological needs."

She'd been attracted to him because of that pull she'd felt. And then she'd gotten to know him, and when he wasn't thinking about Huisman, he was sweet and they fit together like puzzle pieces finally falling into place. She forced the thoughts out of her head because the last thing she needed was to go soft and have Huisman asking more questions. "My sister is addicted to drama. She gets bored when the world is too peaceful, so she lapped this new development up like a cat with cream. So tell me—did she arrive like an avenging angel? She sure as fuck was more interested in dealing with her dumbass lover than saving the woman who's been our friend for most of our lives."

"She was intriguing in her rage. I was surprised she didn't cry. I honestly expected more tears."

Fuck. Her sister was supposed to play for the camera, to let Huisman think his plans all worked. She'd hoped for a full-on *Real Housewives of Spyworld* scene. "She's a damn spy. You think she can't turn the waterworks off when she wants to? I assure you she's an excellent actress, and she wouldn't want to give Ben another second of her tears. My question is what are you going to do when my sister kills him?"

There was the first crack in his armor. A slight tic of his jaw. So he was lying about being concerned about Ben, but she'd known that. She'd made a thorough study of the man who seemed to always come between her and the man she loved.

Ben was his obsession, the center of his twisted universe. Yes, he wanted to burn the world down, but he damn straight wanted Ben at his side while he did it.

"She won't kill him. She's too in love with him. Or rather she believes herself to be. A woman's love is a useless, selfish thing, but she won't be able to murder him." He took a long breath, as though letting the tension go. His mask slipped back into place.

But she'd figured out how to shake him. It was time to stand and get her Academy Award. "Did you watch? Was it a tender reunion because when I left, Kenzie seemed unhinged. I love my sister. I've never seen her so angry. She thought she found the one, and I don't know if her heart can take a betrayal like this. I think she could do something she'll regret, and my father won't stop her. My father will do the deed himself if he thinks he can get away with it."

Huisman went still, his eyes reminding her of a snake about to bite. "He wouldn't."

Well, she'd known this would be painful. She wasn't about to start playing it safe now. "If my father thought Ben Parker betrayed my sister? That he has someone on the side he's sleeping with? He saw the video you sent. It won't take much to convince my father to take out his more violent impulses. Did you leave anyone for him to fight? Or was Ben offered up like a sacrificial lamb?"

"You don't know what you're talking about." He edged closer to her.

If she managed to break his neck, would the guards fight or run?

"You think you know my family, but I don't understand your logic, Emmanuel. I'm going to call you that from now on. Or maybe Manny. Isn't that what Ben calls you? Manny, explain to me how you can reconcile the idea that my father is a brutal killer willing to protect his men at any cost, including your father's life. Which he didn't do, by the way."

"We will have to agree to disagree on that. Your father is ruthless. I actually admire him a bit. He would have been a good addition to my team if he wasn't so intransigent."

"Reconcile that man with the one you hope he is today. The one who doesn't hurt your bestie. My father is ruthless, and he loves his children." She felt her heart rate tick up every inch he moved in. The need to fight was almost too strong to ignore, but she still didn't know where Lou was. He could have protocols in place when it came to her. "My father would do anything for us, but he's always thought Kenzie was a bit of a changeling. Don't get me wrong. Kenz can do the hard stuff, but she's soft inside. She's the sweet one, the one who so desperately needs everyone to love her. It can be pathetic at times. So my father has always protected her, and now you've given him an excuse to take out the biggest threat of all."

It was close enough to the truth. Her father would never kill Ben in a way that anyone could find out. She also knew her father would question the validity of that tape. She made it plain that it wasn't real and they had to take care of Ben and find out if his girlfriend had been a captive all these years.

"He would not."

She allowed her lips to curl slightly, trying to capture a particular expression of Kala's. The smug smirk she used when dealing with assholes. "They took out the cameras. You should have expected that. Did you think without Lou we couldn't take out a couple of security cams? You don't know what happened. You saw the beginning but not the end."

"I know they left the grounds in the early morning hours," Huisman admitted. "I am sure they had Benjamin with them since he wasn't found there. Your father called French intelligence, so we'll have to move the operation. But that's for the best since I also assume your father handed over the girls to MI6."

Not all of them, but she wasn't going to out Sosa. If he thought she was dead from the poison, then that was probably a good thing. "I don't care what happens to them, but I suspect you'll be worried about your bestie. Do you wonder how many parts he's in now? Bet you didn't count on that."

A cracking sound split the air a second before the pain bloomed across her face. He'd meant that slap. It snapped her head back and split her lip, but she didn't care. She was Kala now. Kala never minded some blood. She smiled. "I wish I'd been there. I would love to have been the one to do it, to watch the light in his eyes die."

She thought he would hit her again, but he took a step back, his gaze going dark.

"Well, at least I'm no longer worried I might have the wrong twin. You should hope Benjamin isn't in pieces. I'm the only one allowed to hurt him. The women of your team don't know their places. You should expect more of that if you continue to behave like an animal."

Sure. She was the animal. She wiped her hand across her lip, coming back with blood. "Maybe you can trade Lou for Ben's parts."

"It's good that you understand you're not going to be traded. Now that I have you here, I won't let you go again." He stepped away and straightened his suit. He glanced back at the guards. "Bring her in."

The door opened again and two more guards were there and had hands on Lou.

Kenzie could breathe again. Lou was here. She was alive.

But she obviously hadn't been complying. She had a black eye and her lip was busted up. There was a brace around her left wrist. What the hell had they done to her? Kenzie's brain went to a thousand dark places. Lou had been alone here with a bunch of fucking mercenaries. What scars couldn't she see? The minute the guards let go of her, she ran to Kenzie, throwing her arms around her and holding her tight.

Kenz could feel tears on her neck as Lou squeezed so hard.

"What did you do?" Lou asked.

She breathed her in. They'd been friends for long enough that now they were family. Lou was closer to Kala, but she'd always been there for Kenzie, too. "What I had to. Tell me how they hurt you."

"She wasn't raped." Huisman's eyes rolled as if that was so boring a punishment he wouldn't dream of it. "I told you I need her. She attempted to escape, and my men brought her back. It's her fault because she fought them. I assure you I didn't want her arm injured, and I know how easy it is to mentally break a woman. I need her working, not sitting around crying about a little sex."

"He's not lying," Lou whispered. "I did try to escape."

"And now you will have reasons to focus on your work," Huisman said. "Take her back."

Lou was dragged from her arms, tears streaking down her face.

Kenzie kept her own expression blank, though she was caught between anger and terror. "She'll do what you need her to do."

Lou's eyes went wide. "Kala…"

"She will," Huisman agreed. "And she'll do it quickly. You will be taken to the lab. We should continue our experiments. I didn't get to look at your heart after our last session. I'm intrigued to find out how it handled my drugs."

He nodded, and the other guards took Kenzie by the arms.

She wanted to fight but Lou was right there with guns trained on her. "I'll be all right."

Lou's head shook, and she looked to Huisman. "I told you. I don't know how Shannon did it."

"You're a smart girl. Or at least that's what everyone tells me. Kala will be having sessions with me. I can only focus on her when I'm not working on my main project," Huisman explained as though it was all a normal academic process to torture someone for science. "So how often and long our sessions are depends on you, Ms. Ward."

"You can't do this to her. She could die after what you already put her through," Lou pleaded, terror plain in her eyes.

Because Lou thought she was Kala, and that might scare her into doing something she didn't have to. Kenzie could handle the pain. She feared it, but she didn't fear anything more than losing her family.

"I'll be okay. It's like Mrs. Stapleton's class in high school. I hated it so much, but I survived," she said. "It's as boring as that was, but somehow I came through it."

Lou stopped for the briefest moment.

Kenzie took that class for Kala while Kala took her chemistry class. They would exchange clothes in the locker rooms after lunch. Lou knew it. Lou's eyes closed, tears dripping, and when she opened them again Kenzie saw the knowledge there. The knowledge that she had time. That someone was coming. That their team wouldn't let them down.

And then she was back on. "This isn't some fucking lecture, Kala. It's not boring. It's pain. He wants to kill you."

"Nah. I think he wants to play with my insides to see if I'm worthy to carry his demon spawn. He might not have offered up rape as part of your torture, but it's on the menu for me." She wasn't stupid. He was a walking pile of misogyny and therefore would reduce any woman he found intriguing to a walking womb. Although she probably wouldn't be walking. He would ensure she couldn't fight.

That was why she had her family.

They dragged Lou out and she was left with Huisman and a bunch of guards surrounding her.

"I'm glad we understand each other, Kala Taggart." Huisman came in close. He ran his fingers down her cheek as though tracing the red marks his own hand had left. "I'm going to enjoy the next few hours, and you should understand that I recorded all of this and I'm going to send it to your sister. I think she'll love to hear how you speak of her."

Oh, he loved to cause pain. If she'd heard her sister talking about her that way... Well, she would know her sister was playing a role. It was there, actually. Now that she was at her bottom, facing something truly terrible, she knew nothing would shake her sister's love. Or her parents' or her friends'. She was blessed beyond measure with love. She just wished she'd been the one for Ben, but it was time to move on. "It won't surprise her."

"Well, let's see if I can surprise you. Take her to my lab."

Kenzie kept her mouth closed as they hauled her away. She figured she would need the energy to scream.

* * * *

Ben looked to Big Tag. "Come on, the sun's down. Can we move now?"

It had been a vicious form of torture to sit in the forest outside of the castle waiting for the right time to move in. Hours. Four, to be exact. Four hours and twenty-two minutes he'd been sitting in this van while the rest of the team did recon.

He wasn't allowed to leave the van because apparently he was a puppy who liked to lose his leash, and Big Tag wanted a disciplined pack today.

His future father-in-law was weird.

He kind of loved him.

Ben, it wasn't your fault what Huisman did. It certainly wasn't your fault that he targeted your parents, and your father's reaction was something he needs to examine himself. But how you react is yours. You talk like Manny forces you to do things, but you have choices. It's time to accept that and find a way out, and you're not going to do that by ignoring the situation.

Therapy. Big Tag wanted him in therapy, and Ben was starting to think that he wasn't wrong. He would do it for Kenzie because she mattered. Because she was where his loyalty lay now. Kenzie and her family. If he wanted to fit in, he could sit in a room and talk about his feelings for a couple of weeks. He could do it.

Or he could do it because he didn't want to live this way anymore. He could do it because he wanted to be better for her and himself and the people around him.

Big Tag turned his way. "I'm waiting for shift change. If it's anything like his Nepal operation, it should be in fifteen. That's why I had you change into tactical gear."

The van was borrowed from a man Tag worked with from time to time. He was State Intelligence Agency, and he'd opened a lot of doors for them. SIA was on the ground, though further back, and they would provide logistics and backup if they needed it, but only after they'd extracted Kenzie and Lou.

It was tight but built for remote work. He was in the first van, the one that had the satellite connection. He'd been studying Kenzie's work. She'd actually pointed to this property as one for them to re-search.

"But I want the go-ahead from TJ and Cooper first," Big Tag continued.

Charlotte moved in behind him, putting a hand on Ben's shoulder. "I know how scared you are. I am, too, but we have to do this right and we have to be clear on our mission priorities."

"She means she wants everyone to know who's doing what." Kala had been a peach. Well, if a peach felt like a walking grenade and someone had pulled her pin.

He knew what she was saying, but it might help to say it again. "I only care about Kenzie and Lou. I'm only going to interact with Manny if it means sparing her more pain. If I can trade myself for either one, I will."

"And that's why I want to bench you," Tag admitted.

"Ian, we talked about this. If you bench him, he'll do something even more dangerous," Charlotte said.

"Or I can tranq him and ship his ass back to Canada," Kala offered.

"Don't start again." Tasha had helped him work through all of Kenzie's research, which pointed to this castle being an excellent place for him to launch his plans. She'd been at the airport with her mother and Sami and Lucy when they'd been ready to go.

He'd found out Oliver was pissed to be left behind, but his sister had told him those were the breaks and she'd brief him later.

Sami and Lucy were in a Jeep on the other side of the castle, and

Tris, Cooper, and TJ were in a third vehicle, so they had a triangulated outlook on the eerie-looking castle.

"I'm not going to freak out, and I'm not going to martyr myself." He stood, closing the lid to the laptop. "But according to Kenzie's own research, there were several shipments that match the chemicals we believe are in both the drugs and support the bombs he's building. Obviously we can't track the anthrax, but he has everything else he needs. He's got the drugs he used to damn near kill Kala. He's had her for hours."

"Yes, but Tris already found a way to cut into their feed," Kala replied. "Besides, we know she was talking shit only a couple of hours ago. He says Huisman didn't show up until right before we received that video of her. I think it's safe to say he hasn't figured out he has the wrong twin yet. He sent it to hurt Kenzie, not realizing Kenzie was talking about herself, and we're going to have a chat, my sister and I."

"It could be AI like the video of me and Deanna." Who he'd discovered was absolutely dead. Another of Manny's tricks. He'd talked to his handler, and Tim had done some work from his hospital bed at The Garden. After they'd been stabilized, both Tim and Sosa had been quietly brought back to The Garden via a set of tunnels Knight used from time to time. Tim had verified that Deanna's body was in a grave.

Ben didn't like to think how they'd done that, and so quickly.

Kala's head shook. "Nope, that was my sister and that was Lou, and at the end Lou knew it was Kenzie so she'll hold up on making those bombs. Hell, if I know my bestie, she's planning some shit. And TJ had to see her with her face all fucked up and he stayed calm. His only focus is killing everyone who stands between him and Lou. I want to believe that's yours as well."

The things Kenzie said about herself. "She doesn't believe it, right? She knows everyone loves her."

"Well, some of us say it. Others say they don't. I think she knows exactly who loves her and who thinks she's good in bed," Kala replied.

Charlotte sighed. "It's more complex than that, and you know it."

But was it? "I have a hard time with that word, but you should know I'm going to say it because I'm not going to be afraid anymore. I'm going to put in the work I need to in order to give Kenzie everything she needs. I'm not going to freak out and go off script unless I absolutely have to."

"Our versions of necessity are two different things," Kala countered.

"Hey, I'm not the only one who needs to handle how I feel about Kenzie. If that tape wasn't fake, then I worry that's what she believes everyone else thinks about her. She's not overly dramatic. She feels things more sharply than the rest of us," Ben argued.

"Do you think I don't know that?" Kala got in his face. "Do you think I'm not going over every single time I ever joked about it? Every time I accused her of fading like a fairy princess? She's in there and I know what she's going through, so trust me, I understand that she was talking about us. I love my sister, and I'm going to be better to her."

"I love your sister, and I'm going to be better to her, too." Ben wasn't going to back down. Kala was the hard case, and he had to make her believe him.

She stared for a moment before handing him a rifle. "I'll kill you myself if you hurt her again."

"I love it when my family hugs it out," Big Tag said and he stood. The van was way too small with two large men and two tall women in it. "Ben, you memorize the place? Tris will be working from the comms van, but I want you to have good knowledge of what we're walking into."

"We're going in via the delivery door, which is on the west side of the building. Tristan will take out the security cameras, but it won't take Manny long to figure it out. We go in and then split up. We believe Kenzie is going to be held in the lower levels." Kenzie had done a lot of research, including discovering that the castle had undergone extensive renovations. She'd managed to track down the company who'd done it and gotten the schematics. It was very industrial. They believed this was where Manny would do his medical research and make his bombs. "Lou should be down there, too, but we're not sure which wing is for technical research and which is for medical, so we'll have to take a chance. Manny's residence seems to be on the top floor, and like Nepal, it's got some serious security around it. He'll try to get there. There's a helo on top of the building, but the only way to access it is through Manny's apartment or climbing up, which is how Lucy will ensure the fucker can't fly."

Tag reached for a handheld radio. "Lucy, how's the climb?"

The radio crackled. "Easy peasy. Lou's C-4 is in place, so blow this sucker when you will. Although we might want to think about how it's going to affect the environment…"

Tag shut the radio off. "She's excellent at her job, but her mother has infected her with a deep desire to save the planet. We're working on it. Everyone should be ready for that fucker to have the place wired with explosives. I don't think he'll blow them before he knows he has a path to the helo, but he could do it early. Be careful. Our prime mission is our people. And it's go time. Charlie, baby, are you ready? You're with me. Kala, don't kill him."

Well, this was going to be fun.

Ben entered third, Kala at his back and Big Tag at his front. His heart pounded, but he took a long breath as they moved across the loading dock. He had a comm in one ear and could hear Tristan's and Tasha's calm instructions.

"Lucy is almost on the ground. Sami's meeting her, and they will be causing some chaos in the east wing. The shift change is on, and I expect a good portion of them will head that way. You have roughly three minutes before the new guard takes his first round if he doesn't run off to see what's going on. I don't think these guys are particularly well trained, but there are a lot of them. Wait. I have movement. Stay put," Tasha said.

Big Tag stopped at the end of the last dock, a wall separating them from the five or six guards who were huddled around what looked like the office portion of the loading dock. There was a computer system and a desk where the men were signing in or out, depending on their schedules.

It was good to know Manny kept all the proper records for his evil empire.

It was taking too long. He needed to get to Kenzie.

This was why the military guys were way better at this. They'd been trained to wait and not go strictly on their guts. His was telling him that Kenzie was in trouble, that she needed him, and all he wanted to do was run screaming for her.

What had she already been through? What had Manny done to her? It didn't matter because he would do everything he could to help her heal. He just wanted her alive. He would deal with everything else.

He was going to trust. It was a start. He was going to trust one person, and that person was Ian Taggart. He was going to trust Ian and not allow himself to panic, not allow himself to give in to the need to meet Manny so they could finish this.

He didn't want to finish because he now knew what he would be finishing was his life, and that wasn't acceptable anymore.

He'd spent years working toward a point—defeating Manny—and not seeing anything beyond that moment.

He wanted a future now. A future with her.

Kenzie needed him. He saw her in a way no one else did. They were meant to be, and he wasn't going to fight it one more second. He was going with it, and if his heart got broken then at least he'd fucking used it, given it to a woman who was more than worthy.

"Oh, we have a friend. Looks like Zach made his flight," Tasha said. "He's coming in with Cooper and TJ. Unit two, you have a go."

"Zach, welcome home," Big Tag said.

"Happy to be here, sir. You should know Henry Flanders is taking care of everyone we have in Bliss, and he's monitoring the situation," Zach said over the line.

From what he'd learned Henry Flanders was Big Tag's mentor and Lucy's father. "How did Zach get here so fast?"

Taggart kept his voice down, his eyes on the door about forty feet away. "He asked me to call him when I thought it was going down. I called the minute Lou was taken. He's been making his way here for two days. I wouldn't leave him behind, and he won't leave Lou."

The ground beneath them shook slightly.

"That'll be Lucifer," Kala said quietly. "She was going to blow two of the vehicles. I tried to get her to take down that weird wall thing, but I got a lecture on pre-Christian European architecture and why we shouldn't explode it. See, that's her real evil superpower. The power to bore me."

He heard a whooshing sound as the door came open and then booted feet on the concrete floors.

"All right. You lost four of seven," Tasha informed them. "And they left the laptop on. So if someone would like to murder a couple of assholes and take a look, that would be great. We need key cards. Tris is having some trouble with the interior security system, and that's where we're sure they're keeping Lou and Kenz."

"I'll take the laptop. Tim's taught me a lot." Ben looked to Kala. "Don't let them kill me."

Her eyes rolled. "Like I would. I want to do it."

She was going to be such a fun in-law.

There it was. The future. He was thinking about it more and more now, and without fear. He thought about marrying Kenzie and starting a life with her.

He wasn't sure how they would do it, the logistics and all, but they would work it out because they were end game.

Tag nodded his way and then looked to his wife. "You got a spot, Charlie baby?"

She gestured to the stairs behind them. "I'll take out the guy on patrol. Kala can get the two by the desk, and then I'll have a perch for anyone who comes in. We'll meet back here for extraction."

"Mom, they're not watching. You can take the perch on the west side without too much trouble." Tasha proved she'd worked with her parents and knew exactly what her mom would do. "I'll move the van in once we get this party started. Tris says he's got eyes on the lab and we need to move. Kenzie is in a medical lab. It's the fourth door on the left. He says it's bad, so Coop, you might want to make your way."

"Does he have eyes on Huisman?" Ben asked. He wasn't going to call him Manny anymore. Manny had been the dude who was his friend. He might never have really existed, but Ben wasn't going to argue that now. Huisman was a target. Nothing more.

"He's in the medical wing. Lou's got three guards on her. She's in a lab working with some dangerous shit, from what Tris can tell," Tasha replied. "No weapons should be fired in that space, and now Tris is worried about oxygen tanks. He's got Kenzie on one."

"Is she awake?" Ben forced the question out of his mouth.

A pause and then a quiet reply from Tasha. "She is aware of what's happening to her."

Then he felt it. A hand on his shoulder. It wasn't Big Tag. It was Kala.

He was still for a moment, letting the emotion between them settle, and then he turned. "Let's get her out of here."

Kala nodded. "Let's do this thing."

The moment her mother was in place, Kala took off and Ben followed, ready to get his girl.

Chapter Eighteen

Kenzie was dying.

She was fairly certain of it. In a lot of ways, death was welcome. The pain was… She'd thought she was tough, but this was fire in her veins. Unrelenting waves of pain, and there was nothing she could do because the devil had paralyzed her.

"You remember this, right?" he'd said as he stood beside her bed. There was a "nurse" helping him. A young woman with hollow eyes. She'd placed the IV while guards held Kenzie down, though she hadn't struggled at the time because it seemed such a useless thing to do. "You're quite brave. I appreciate that in a female. When the time comes, I won't disgrace either of us with animal rutting. I'll do it like the civilized men do. I'll harvest your eggs and then find a broodmare to carry our sons."

She should have fought, would fight if she ever got off this table because dignity be damned, this was hell.

Not being able to move was part of the horror. She was aware, her eyes wide open, but she couldn't scream now, couldn't do anything but endure.

And the worst? Huisman was still fucking here hours and hours later. He sat just out of her view, which was straight up staring at a gray ceiling.

Not how she thought she would go out.

The cycle ended, and she could breathe for a moment.

How long had this one been?

"Milena, I need a printout of her vitals for the last hour." Huisman's face appeared in her line of sight. He stood there with his clipboard and glasses perched on his nose. He wore a white coat like he was a big-boy doctor. "She's surprisingly steady from what I can tell. I expected heart damage from previous sessions."

Shit. She wanted to spout shit, but she couldn't talk yet. This was the second go-around, but she was already learning the schedule. The drug would leave her system and then the paralytic would take another five minutes or so. Maybe longer, since this was the second time.

She tried moving her left hand. She managed to rub her thumb and forefinger.

Breathe. Survive. That was all that was left now.

"I should have done a baseline EKG, but I was overly eager to get back to our fun." Huisman gave her a grin like they were playmates.

She wished she could spit in his face, but her mouth was dry and nothing seemed to work anymore.

What had Kala told her? She and her sister had gone over everything she could remember about her time with Huisman. It was a ritual they'd done for the last few years when something important happened. In case one had to take over the role, it was necessary to try to remember every detail so throwbacks could occur. He was faltering, wondering if he had it wrong, and she didn't want to know what happened if Huisman figured out she wasn't his favored egg donor.

Though her eggs were fine, thank you very much. She was pretty sure their eggs were similar, though Kala's were coated with an extra veneer of sarcasm. Maybe that would help since any kid of this man's was going to go through some things.

Yes, she remembered. Kala had been able to do one thing.

She concentrated hard and forced her middle finger up.

He chuckled. "Yes, I believe that was your response last time. Your heart is a remarkable thing, Kala Taggart. You can handle pain in a way I didn't imagine. I would have expected you to have at least one cardiac episode. I even tweaked the drugs so they would damage your heart muscle less. Can't have you dying on me before I get what I need." He frowned, and a look of distaste came over his face. He reached down and moved her gown back, exposing her clavicle. "I suppose your husband gave you those. He's an animal, you know."

Her bruises. The bite marks where Ben set his teeth on her and sent a thrill across her skin.

A flash of him moved over her brain. Ben's gorgeous face smiling down at her when he thrust up and joined them together.

And then she heard him saying he couldn't love her.

She wished they'd had a shot, a real shot.

Her teeth chattered, and she realized she could talk again, though her mouth was so dry. Her body felt heavy, but she wasn't giving in. "I thought you liked 'em submissive, asshole."

"Interesting take," he allowed. "Though I don't think we're viewing it in the same light. I suppose you're right and if the male in your life is pleased by harming you, it's your job to give this to him. I simply don't understand the impulse."

"Are you fucking kidding me?" Every word felt forced and jagged coming from her mouth.

He shrugged. "Oh, this is all for science. Sacrifices must be made. Like your father sacrificed mine."

"Like a moron named Levi Green killed your father to save his own hide." She shook her head. "You're delusional."

He took a readout from the sad-looking nurse/slave. "And you are incredibly strong."

Well, that's what happened when she shared her heart with the right person. She hadn't moved for hours, and she couldn't imagine they'd shipped her suit out, so unless they'd managed to destroy it, her parents had to know she was in Bulgaria. If they'd taken half a minute to look at her research, they would know where to start the hunt.

"Is she like Sosa and the others? Did you steal her off the streets so you wouldn't have to pay her by the hour and offer health care? Do evil organizations have health care? That would be weird."

"She was trained at the chateau. I purchased her when she was… fourteen or so. She was trained to be a technical aid. I certainly wouldn't call her a nurse. She's adequate at following directions and taking notes. Probably because she knows what happens when she fails." He kept his eyes on the reports the youngish woman had brought. "I have one like her in all the medical testing zones I keep.

Don't think you can talk to her. She is well trained. She only speaks when required. She lives here, and if she wants to keep her tongue, she'll remain silent and loyal."

Kenzie managed to look at the young woman, who had closed her eyes as though remembering something terrible. "You threatened to take her tongue?"

"Only if she causes me trouble," Huisman replied, and shook his head. "Well, it looks like I'll have to try harder to get these numbers up. We'll double the dose this time and perhaps give her a little longer. I want a full workup on her overnight. She'll sleep down here after the last session."

There was the whooshing sound of the door opening, and she heard a guard's voice. He said something in French. Something about the girl in the lab and that he should come and see.

"Bring her to me," Huisman said, and walked out of her line of sight.

When Kenzie had been brought in, she'd tried to study this place as much as she could. He walked toward the bank of computers and lab equipment.

"Get a blood sample and give her another dose of the paralytic. Can't have her moving too much, can we?" His voice sounded like he was roughly thirty or forty feet away.

She was starting to get control of her hand again. Tears sparked. She couldn't do this. She couldn't lose it, but this was… This had brought her tough-as-nails sister to cry and scream and beg for death, and she would be here longer. What was happening to her heart? Were the muscles already weakening? How long before the heart attack? Her sister had a heart attack.

She was going to die here.

She wanted to see Ben, but he was an illusion. He never loved her. She was incidental to him, a way to pass time and make his job easier. That was kind of her whole life, though, wasn't it? Relegated to the backup role. Her sister was the better operative. Her brothers were more talented. Tasha was the leader. She was…background.

It hurt so much. So fucking much, but her brain seemed to want to torture her, too.

Why did it have to be him?

She felt something cold in her hand. She wasn't tied down. As

Huisman had said, he didn't need things like ropes and cuffs to hold a woman down. He could do it with the power of his mind, or rather his research. He'd done the same to Kala and laughed when the paralytic wore off while she was still under influence of the drug. Kala had dislocated joints and nearly broken bones when that happened.

So at least she wouldn't do that.

Milena put a hand over hers, the warmth feeling odd. When Kenzie looked up, Milena's eyes were serious on her. She squeezed Kenzie's hand, and that was the moment Kenz realized she'd place something small in her palm. Like a pencil.

Or a scalpel.

"These numbers are intriguing," Huisman was saying.

Kenzie was able to move her head slightly so she could see the hypodermic needle in the nurse's hand as she prepared to push the medication. Milena looked down and winked.

Fuck. Something was happening.

Milena pushed the needle in, her eyes darting over to Huisman. She leaned down and whispered. "Sosa says take him out."

It hadn't been a paralytic. She didn't feel the wash of ice in her veins that accompanied her losing the ability to move. No, this was something that countered it. Suddenly Kenzie could close her hand around the scalpel.

Sosa. They'd underestimated her. Gabby might have broken the sisterhood Sosa tried to form, but it was obvious this one wouldn't. Sosa had been trying to save them all for years. She hadn't given up. She'd quietly built family from nothing.

This Bratz doll wasn't about to let her down.

But she had to wait for the right time.

The door came open, and Kenzie forced herself to stay still and not turn her head to see what was coming her way.

"I want to see her," Lou was saying as the door opened again.

If she tilted her head slightly, she could see what was happening through the mirror on top of one of his torture machines. Lou was carrying what looked like a remote control or something. There were two guards with her.

She liked those odds much better.

"She's fine," Huisman said with a deep frown. "According to these reports it's almost as though we never spent any time together at all. Do you know something I don't?"

She needed a couple more minutes. She could wiggle her toes, but she would be unsteady. Deep breath. See it in her head. Visualize the fight. Don't panic.

"I know you've nearly killed her before. I'm sorry she recovered too much for you." Lou sounded annoyed, playing her role perfectly.

Just a few more minutes.

While Huisman was concentrating on Lou, Milena eased the IV out of her arm.

"What is that?" Huisman asked.

"It's done," Lou said. "At least the prototype is."

She had to lay there looking at the stupid concrete ceiling, keeping her breath steady, her body still. It was hard because she wasn't known for stillness. She was the one in constant motion, touching on everything and everyone, while Kala sat back and took in the whole picture. It was how they worked, but she could do this. She wasn't alone.

Sosa had sent her a lifeline and Lou was here, and her parents wouldn't let her down.

"This is the detonator?" Huisman was asking. "I thought you would use an app or something. This seems old school."

Lou always used her phone if she could.

"These bombs are unique and require a handheld system," Lou explained. "Now obviously they haven't been tested, but I'm sure it will work. I put together a…"

Lou said a bunch of technical things. It didn't even sound like English. Then Huisman said technical words, and then Lou said something about the trigger mechanism.

She didn't like this part. Her twin was better at patiently listening to the most boring things. Like couldn't they throw a murder or something in there?

Her leg twitched slightly.

Kenzie forced it still.

She needed him closer.

"Yes, that does seem like it would work, but we can't be sure until we try it out. I'll schedule it for Monday," he said like it was nothing more than a normal test run and not something that would likely kill hundreds of people and crash an economy. "Until I'm sure it's right, you'll remain my guest and so will she."

"You told me you would let her go if I did this for you," Lou argued.

"I lied. Take her away," he ordered.

That was when she felt it. The ground shook subtly, like an explosion had happened but a distance away.

Her parents were here.

"What the hell was that?" Huisman asked and started barking orders to his guards.

They would blow something up and distract the guards while they infiltrated the castle.

But Huisman knew the place far better than they did, and he would likely have more than one escape plan in place.

She needed to try to take his ass out here and now.

The door closed and Huisman loomed over her. "I suspect we'll have to put our plans on pause, Kala."

There he was. His smug face stared down at her.

She smiled. "Name's Kenzie, buddy, and Sosa says hi."

She brought her arm up, burying the scalpel in the crook of his neck. Blood spurted, not in the insane amount she'd hoped for since she'd tried to clip his jugular. Well, her hands were shaking.

She needed another weapon. She would use her body as one, but it was kind of busted at the moment. Years of strength training and martial arts classes and she didn't even get her Bruce Lee moment. Nope. She barely managed to get to her feet with Milena's help.

"We need to go," Milena said quietly as Huisman held his neck with one hand and pulled a gun with the other.

His first shot grazed her arm, but Milena managed to get them to the door.

She needed to kill that man.

But she needed to live more.

The door slid shut behind them.

There were guards running through the halls, obviously confused. One of them stopped Milena, saying something in a language Kenzie didn't understand. Milena was quiet, her eyes submissively down as she explained.

Could she get his gun? Why did her hands have to shake so much? She needed to be stronger than this.

"I tell him the doctor wants me to take you back to your room," she explained as they started down the hall.

"Stop them!" Huisman shouted behind them. "Stop those bitches."

They probably would have if the gunfire hadn't started.

Textbook Ian Taggart. Distract. Cause confusion. Use it to take out everyone in your path.

Unfortunately, she had to find Lou.

Milena pulled her into another of the labs. "We should hide."

She squeezed the younger woman's hand. "Do. Hide in here, but I have to get to my friend. Where would they take her?"

"She was working in lab four. It's a mechanical lab. She's been sleeping in there, too. That is where they will go. You should stay," Milena implored.

Kenzie shook her head. "Can't, but you stay here and keep your head down. If you see a big blond dude, he's one of the good guys."

And then Kenzie was off. She slipped back into the hallway, steadier on her feet this time.

She wished she had those damn nanites now since she was trying to save the world in a hospital gown. Her ass was on full damn display as she raced across the hall. There was no sign of Huisman now. He'd likely retreated to deal with the hole in his neck. Or to get Lou.

She had to get Lou first. He would have a plan, and if he got out of here with Lou, it would all be for naught.

Kenzie was nearly thrown to the ground when the castle walls shook again. Someone was having fun with explosives.

And smoke grenades. The hall filled with gray smoke, threatening to choke her, but she clung to the wall, forcing her way through even as guards ran past her.

Up ahead she heard volleys of gunfire and shouts. Where was the lab? Was it the last one on the left?

Her chest ached. A sharp pain that had her putting her hand there, trying to calm down.

And then it felt like time slowed. The smoke cleared and the most beautiful man in the world stepped into her line of sight.

Ben. Ben was here. He was big and glorious and alive and here.

She could kind of hear music. Oh, she knew it was all in her head, but it swelled and the world went soft and cinematic.

He shouted something, but it didn't matter because he was here.

And so was her sister.

"Hey, dumbass. Where's Lou?" Kala offered up a warning volley of gunfire that sent the remaining guards running.

"We think she's in lab four," Kenzie managed to get out.

"You got her?" Kala asked.

Ben nodded and pulled a SIG from his belt, handing it to Kenzie. He touched his earpiece. "TJ, she's in lab four. Kala is en route. I've got the package and I'm heading to the extraction point."

She knew what he would truly want. "Huisman is back there. I injured him, and I think he's in the med lab. He was bleeding but it wasn't fatal."

Ben simply leaned over and picked her up. "Watch our back, baby."

He started walking.

She saw TJ rush by as Ben turned right and started for what she suspected was the loading dock.

Damn. TJ had taken out a lot of guards. He'd torn through them and didn't look like he had a scratch.

"Huisman is back there," Kenzie shouted.

"Your sister can handle him." Her father was suddenly jogging by. "Tris busted the security system, so all the doors are unlocked."

Cooper was somewhere in there, too. She heard him shouting orders.

"There's a friendly in one of the labs. A girl who helped me."

Her dad waved to let her know he would take care of it.

"Ben, he's back there and he's wounded," Kenzie explained.

"I don't care. I came here for you." Ben kept moving.

He didn't miss a step when Kenzie aimed and fired at the guard who was about to take them out.

"Ben, he's here. I don't want to be the reason you miss this chance. I can walk." She could crawl, maybe.

"Not a chance," Ben replied. "On our left."

Kenzie took that guy out with a head shot. "Ben…"

"Kenzie, I love you. I'm not leaving you."

All around her everything was chaos, but those words cut through it all. "You don't have to say it."

"I love you. Baby, I promise I will do a deep grovel when we get out of this. Trust me. I know what is expected, and I've signed off on the plan. Kala and Tash gave me explicit instructions, including dates and timelines, and I'm pretty sure I signed some legal paperwork we will have to deal with later. I am going to be the best groveler, but if maybe you could…"

"I love you, too, Ben." She wouldn't make him grovel. Much. Right now all that mattered was that he was here and he was choosing her.

He smiled down at her. "Besides, letting your sister kill Manny buys me so many points. So many." He stopped suddenly. "Kenzie, I'm putting you down. I need you to run."

The door in front of them slid open and Dr. Huisman stood there with the detonator and two large guards at his back, rifles trained on Kenzie and Ben.

There would be nowhere to run to.

"I wouldn't move if I were you," Huisman commanded. His normally pristine lab coat was covered in blood, and she was sure most of it was his.

Ben pushed her behind his back. "Manny, I only came for her. Let us out and I swear you won't see us ever again."

"What fun would that be?" Huisman's lips curled up in a snarl. "Your bitch whore nearly cost me my life, and I will deal with her. I think I will deal with you as well this time. Don't expect your friends to help you. I left them with a gift. They'll be trying to save Louisa. They will fail."

Kenzie's heart threatened to seize. "What did you do?"

A guard was at their back, shoving them forward, closer to Huisman, though he kept a careful distance. They were through the threshold when he answered.

"I gave her a dose of what I gave you. A large one. She was screaming when I left. I didn't bother to give her the paralytic, so it was fun to watch her jerk and break some bones."

She hated this man. He was right about one thing, though. It would give him a hell of a distraction since everyone would need to help hold Lou down and pray she made it through.

She had to hope Tris and Tash were still watching. Her father would have left her mother in a sniper position, protecting the evacuation site. If they could get there, her mom would take them all out before they could consider doing anything.

But she wasn't sure how far away that was or whether Huisman would have the same exit strategy.

She suspected he would have a helo somewhere. It was how he liked to roll.

She tucked her hand into Ben's, threading their fingers together. They'd almost made it out.

"Take their guns," Huisman ordered.

She squeezed his hand. It might be better to go out in a fight than to let him take them away. If he had them both, he would torture them in ways she couldn't imagine. Except she had a really creative mind and so she could, and death might be preferable.

"Stay calm," Ben said quietly.

He handed over his P90 and they took Kenzie's SIG.

"I should have done this sooner," Huisman said. "I've enjoyed this game of ours, Benjamin, but it's time for you to face some consequences."

Ben turned away from Huisman, cupping her face with both hands. "Kenzie, I love you. Do whatever it takes to survive."

"I'm talking to you, Benjamin." Huisman sounded awfully annoyed.

Ben leaned over, placing his forehead on hers. "You are everything, Kenzie Taggart. You are worth it all. Worth the pain. Worth the fear. Your love is the bedrock of my existence, and I'm so sorry to drag you into this."

Tears pierced her eyes, and she was so happy Kala had the foresight to get him to sign that non-legally binding document because she wouldn't make him grovel at all after those words. Those beautiful words. But she did enjoy a good grovel.

If they survived…

She moved into his space. "I wouldn't change a thing. I would always want to be here with you. No matter what."

Come what may, and what was coming was likely an enormous amount of pain.

Her heart hurt, an actual ache in her chest.

"Benjamin," Huisman shouted.

Ben simply held her, hugging her tight.

"You ignore me for your whore?" Huisman was starting to sound unhinged. "This is your problem. You cannot see what is good for you. You have a small mind."

"I'm pretty sure you have a small penis. And don't you dare call my daughter a whore," a familiar voice said.

That was when her father opened fire.

Ben immediately moved, hauling her down. He covered her body with his. "Keep your head down, baby. Let your dad and Zach do their work."

Zach was here?

She heard the sound of doors closing and saw that while her dad and Zach had taken out all the guards, Manny had managed to get the door closed.

And they were on the wrong side. They were locked in with the madman.

"Huisman, let my kids go and I won't have you murdered while you flee," her father said.

Ben wouldn't move. If anything, he shifted so she was completely covered. Like he was ready to take all the bullets that were coming their way.

Huisman was oddly quiet for a moment and then sounded somber. "I think I'm finally caught, Mr. Taggart. Rather like my father. But my father wasn't as smart as I am. If this is the end for me, it's the same for you. And you can thank your little freak Louisa for this. I primed the bomb before I left her. It should be more than enough to blow this whole place sky high and scorch the earth around us. Your precious daughters all gone."

She heard something smash against the door. Likely her father's fists.

"Don't. Don't you fucking dare," he screamed, though the heavy doors muffled the sound.

Someone took a couple of shots at the door, but it was definitely bulletproof.

Her father wouldn't make it in time.

"I wish you had been a better friend, Benjamin. I blame you. If I had never met you perhaps my life would have been easier," Huisman was saying.

"Stay still, Kenz," Ben whispered. "It'll be over soon. I love you so much."

It would be over soon. For all of them.

She would miss her brothers, miss Seth's concerts and lazy

Sundays with Travis and Colton. She would miss Colton growing up, but they would be okay. They would know how much she loved them.

"Good-bye, Benjamin. Remember you brought this on yourself," Huisman intoned.

Ben tensed over her, and the world seemed to explode around them. She heard the sickening sound of squishy things hitting the floor.

And then the door opened again.

How? What?

"Ben, you got some asshole on your back there," her dad was saying.

"And I'm pretty sure he's in your hair, too." Zach sounded close. "Lou might have gone overboard with the C-4."

She was confused. Ben moved off her.

"I'm so sorry, baby. I knew what Lou did. Tristan told me, but I didn't have any way to tell you." He held a hand out to help her up.

At least his front wasn't covered in evil doctor.

"Lou wired the detonator to blow," her dad explained. "Tris watched her on the security cams and figured out what she was doing. She modified the C-4 she was given through the process she developed. She wasn't building Shannon's bombs. She was building her own."

"My mom's going to be so proud of her," Zach said with a grin. "Lucky for you Ben's a big bastard or you would have… Kenzie, are you alright?"

"Hey, you went pale," her father said.

Her chest was too tight. Far too tight, and they were surrounded by blood and a fine pink mist that was probably Huisman.

She couldn't breathe.

Her father touched his earpiece. "I need Cooper down here now, and Lucy I'm going to need you to undo whatever you did to that helo because we're going to need it. Kenzie's having a heart attack."

Was she? It was odd because she'd thought it was just emotion.

Pain shot down her arm.

Nope. Probably a heart attack. Asshole might still get her.

Her vision dimmed and Ben caught her, hauling her against his chest.

They started moving, but her last sight was of his gorgeous face.

He would survive, and so would her family.

It was enough.

* * * *

"Dude, you got to get covered in the blood of your enemy. Do you know how often I dream of that? You're welcome."

Ben looked up from his spot at Kenzie's bedside. She was being monitored, but her heart seemed to have come through.

Her heart was such a mighty thing.

Kala stood at the end of the bed, dressed in her usual uniform of black on black on black, while Tristan was unusually casual in sweats and a T-shirt, his hair rumpled like he'd recently rolled out of bed.

"Shouldn't it be Lou I'm thanking? I don't think you rewired that detonator to explode," Ben pointed out.

Tris shook his head. "Yeah, Kala's good at a lot of things, but hiding a tiny, powerful bomb inside a detonator that then detonates itself is pure Lou."

Kenzie's hand squeezed his as her eyes opened. "She's jealous you got to see it. How is Lou?"

Oh, every time she woke up, he breathed a sigh of relief. They had their chance now, and he wasn't about to waste it.

Kala seemed to sober. "She's in the room next door, and she's going to be fine. Thanks to Milena. She heard what happened and snuck in while we were trying desperately to figure out what to do. They trained that kid well. She told me the doctor always had a counter drug in case he needed it. Lou broke her leg when she was in the throes of it, though."

"How is TJ?" Kenzie asked.

TJ hadn't left either. He and Ben had taken turns getting coffee and snacks so one of them was around. Watching over their women. Their hearts.

He had one again, and it was full.

"He slept on the floor by her bed because he didn't want to risk touching her leg, but he wouldn't let go of her hand," Kala said with a hint of a smile. "Slept like that all night and can't figure out why he's got cramps in his hand now. Dumbass. Also, he's hangry. Like super hangry. I can't help it that we're in the ass end of nowhere Eastern Europe and there's no street vendors to dole out hot dogs. Lou is up now and asking about her nanite project. Do you know where they put the suit? I'm sending Lucifer in to get it."

Lucy and Sami had been instrumental in getting them to the hospital, and Lucy proved she was good with logistics as she found a small hotel a block from the hospital. Not that he'd stayed there. He wouldn't leave her side for more than a few moments.

He could have lost her.

He was never leaving her side again.

"There's a room at the front of the lab wing where they had me change. I think it's in one of the lockers," Kenzie explained.

Tris pulled his cell. "I'll let them know. The Brits are all out at the site."

Kala nodded. "Oliver showed up last night. He's pissed, by the way. He and Sami have been arguing for hours about him being left behind, so she gave him the fun job of dealing with Bulgarian intelligence. I'm pretty sure he already slept with the liaison they assigned to us. He's so gross."

He'd seen the attaché. She was lovely, but no one moved him any more except one pink-haired, gorgeous girl. "I think he called it supporting good political relationships, and as we haven't had to deal with the local authorities, I'm going to thank Oliver's dick."

"He should call it spreading syphilis," Kenzie quipped.

Kala ignored her. "Mom and Dad are on their way up. They've already called back to base, and we've got a shit ton of paperwork to do, but it looks like we're going to be able to take down Disrupt now. Tris already found a ton of intel."

"I got the fucker's personal system," Tris admitted. "The one he kept off the Internet. I'm worried about some of the projects he refers to in there. We might have cut off the head, but there's more work to be done."

Kenzie yawned and sat up straighter in bed. "Hey, I never got the explanation of how you figured out Gabby was still working with Huisman."

"He did?" Ben stood. She was awake now, and they'd told him she was stable. "Scoot."

She smiled up at him as she made a place next to her. "That's what he said, but you were all knocked out and on your way here when he showed up. I bet the Agency is going to yell at us for the last-minute plane tickets."

Ben slipped off his shoes and climbed into bed with her, wrapping an arm around her shoulders as she curled around him. She fit so perfectly.

"Like I would fly commercial," Tris said with a sigh. "I took the small jet. My dad didn't even complain once I found the footage."

"And I'm pretty sure Zach used one of the billionaire's jets," Kala explained.

"What footage?" If he let Kala continue, she would go into a ton of stories about how weird the town of Bliss, Colorado, was, and he wanted to know what Tris had found.

Kala stepped back as though giving the floor to Tris.

He pulled his cell phone and started typing on it. "So I put Gabby, Sosa, and Claire through my dad's facial recognition program. The one he's been tweaking. Chelsea's been working on it, too."

Kenzie's Aunt Chelsea was legendary in the intelligence industry. She'd once been the all-powerful Broker, but now she worked for her own company. They often did projects for friendly intelligence agencies, and while they were careful with their intellectual property, they would never turn down a request from the Agency team. "Were you trying to figure out their real identities? I thought Lucy said it was clear the group erased the girls they brought in."

"I wasn't doing it for that purpose, though you should know I've got an AI working on that," Tris explained. "I need it to study their bone structure so we can get a good picture of what they would have looked like as children. But I wanted to see if their faces were in any of the systems. And I got a shock. Because she was in our system."

Kenzie shifted so she could see Tris. "Our system? The Agency's?"

Tris's head shook, and he offered her his phone. "No. Miles, Dean, Weston, and Murdoch. In our security system's archives. This is from a consultation that happened over a year ago."

Ben watched the screen Kenzie held. There was an older gentleman in a suit walking into the lush offices of MDWM. The receptionist greeted him and the young woman he had with him. He recognized Gabby, but she was dressed younger, her hair in pigtails. She looked like she was eleven or twelve when he was fairly certain at that time she was at least nineteen.

"I lose her when they go back to Dad's office. The man she's with is David Gatton, a businessman from Paris," Tris continued.

"What was the consultation about?" Ben asked.

"He was looking for his missing wife. Gabby was introduced as his daughter." Kala took up Ben's seat. "I've looked through all the files they have. Which isn't a lot since two days later Gatton had them drop the case."

"He didn't even ask for his hefty retainer back," Tristan explained. "So we don't have cameras in the individual offices. Since everyone's married and somehow still horny, that's understandable. But I caught sight of Gabby wandering. Probably looking for the bathroom, but she disappears down the hall where the servers are kept. She's gone for at least fifteen minutes."

"But that room would be locked," Kenzie pointed out.

"And yet I believe she got through." Tris looked grim as he took his phone back. "I believe there was never a missing wife. That meeting was taken to get Gabby in the building, in that room."

Kenzie shook her head. "But Gabby's specialty was stealing. She didn't know the technical things. I could believe she could follow simple instructions, but getting into your dad's servers wouldn't be simple."

"Sosa admitted they lied about their specialties." Kala crossed one leg over the other, showing off the combat boots she wore. "It was something Huisman told them to do. Gabby was their hacker, and apparently an excellent one since she got around everything your dad and my aunt had. The question is, what did they take?"

It sent a shiver down his spine.

But that was a problem for another day. And he had them. He had all the days with her.

"I'm hungry," Kenzie said. "I know they don't have hot dogs, but Mom said something about the café having those fried dough things."

He kissed the top of her head and slid off the bed. This wasn't even close to his groveling, though Kala had pointed out that being Kenzie's servant was all part of the contract. But this was part of being hers. "It's called *tulumbichk*, and I will get you that and some tea."

The door came open and his future in-laws walked in with smiles and flowers.

Charlotte and Tasha immediately went to Kenzie's side.

Ian waited back as Ben approached the door. "She okay?"

"She's great. The doctors told us she's recovering well. I don't think the damage is as extensive as what Kala went through, but I've got it on our calendar to pick a cardiologist in Dallas," Ben explained. "I'll make sure she goes."

"Good, because she often forgets about herself," Ian replied.

"I won't let her." He was planning on being everything Kenzie needed him to be. Her partner. Her top. Her husband. "And I've already talked to Joseph. I'm quitting. I'm moving to Dallas and I'll be happy to consult, but the truth is I'm not a spy. I was Captain Ahab and my white whale has been defeated by one of the smartest women I've ever met. So I'm going to need a job."

Ian frowned. "And that is my problem?"

"Ian," Charlotte said.

"Dad," the twins managed to say in stereo.

"Dad, how can he grovel if he's in Canada?" Kala asked. "I've got a ten-page document detailing all the ways he has to serve this family. He's going to learn how to make lemon tarts. I have a class set up with Marley Brighton."

"He can start in the bodyguard unit." Ian moved to join his wife. "And those tarts better be good. Damn kids always have their hands out."

Kenzie grinned his way as she was surrounded by her family.

His family. They were going to be his.

"Love you, baby," he said. "And I'll get TJ a sandwich and drop it off."

The words were easier now that he understood what they meant to her. Love for Kenzie was everything. Love was in the grand gestures and the small ones. She lived and breathed her love. It was in her every movement, every gesture.

He stared at her for a moment, just taking her in.

Ian kissed his daughter's forehead and then joined Ben again. "You do the other thing?"

His future father-in-law had his own requests, though it wasn't groveling. Quite the opposite. The task Ian Taggart asked him to complete was all about taking himself seriously. About understanding himself. About loving himself so he could completely love Kenzie. "I've got an appointment with Dr. Rycroft, and I'm going to take my training classes over again at Sanctum."

"You're ready." Ian put a hand on his shoulder. "I'm proud of you, son."

Damn. Dare told him it would be this way. "Thank you. For everything."

For his kindness. For his tough love. He had the feeling he would learn a lot about being a good father from this man.

For raising the person he loved most in this world.

For welcoming him into the best family he could possibly belong to.

"Let's get these people fed, son. TJ is turning into a goblin." Ian held the door open. "I'm serious about that. He's got this crap coming out of his face."

His future father-in-law was a trip. "I think he hasn't had a chance to shave. I don't think he's turning into a mythical creature."

"Then you haven't had to smell the kid," Ian said as he walked out into the hallway.

Ben turned back and Kenzie was smiling at him.

He winked her way and followed her dad.

For the first time in years, he had a future.

Epilogue

Dallas TX
Many years later

Charlotte Taggart loved that the kids club was full again. She couldn't help but smile, watching her grandkids run around and swing from places they shouldn't swing from and remembering how they were all the products of the amazing love her kids had managed to find.

Well, Colton had been the product of a spectacularly awful relationship, but it all worked out in the end and now Colton had the best mom and a couple of adorable younger siblings.

They were all happy.

"She's talking about redecorating my office," a familiar, deeply grumpy voice said behind her right before she felt big hands on her hips and a kiss to her ear.

Oh, how she loved this man. "It's not your office anymore. It's hers, and you know she's going to have opinions."

"Tasha's not changing yours," Ian pointed out.

She turned and put her hands on his broad shoulders. "She'll be sneaky about it. She'll keep it the same for a couple of months and then you just watch. She'll have it painted that sky blue she loves so much and she'll get a bigger desk, and I'm so happy to give it to her."

His lips curled up slightly. "Kala will probably paint the whole thing black."

"Which is why Tash and Cooper handle the clients. You sure you want to do this?"

"Retire?" her husband asked. "Are you asking me if I want to stop working so I can spend my golden years playing with my dogs, napping, letting my grandkids treat me like a jungle gym, and seeing the world with my gorgeous wife and our best friends? You bet I do."

McKay-Taggart was under new management. Which was a bit like the old management as there was a McKay and a Taggart in the manager's offices. It was a family company in a way it hadn't been when they started it. Oh, they were found family, and that had been everything. They'd been people out in the world looking for something to believe in, and they found it not truly in a business. They found it in each other.

Tasha was taking over Charlotte's role dealing with the office and handling most of the client relationships. Cooper and Kala were taking over the company. Dare had been in charge of sales for years. Seth was happily making his music with his family, and Travis was settled.

Kenzie wouldn't ever truly settle down. Not when she could roam the world having adventures with her gorgeous husband.

"Hey, we have cake." Speak of the devil and she appeared. Kenzie shook her head. "Please tell me you're not planning some intimate time before you go. If you are, I suggest Kala's office. She's already had it mystically cleansed. She'll be super pissed if she has to call Lucy again because she doesn't know any shaman who can cleanse a space of what she calls geriatric sex magic. Her words, not mine."

Her husband's hand was suddenly in hers. "Oh, we're doing something truly nasty on her desk."

She chuckled but held her place. "Babe, we need to leave in about twenty minutes. Did you forget the flight to Miami? Alex and Eve will be surprised to go on our ridiculously expensive cruise all alone."

Her bags were packed, and they had two weeks of sun and sand and all the lemon tarts her hubby could eat. They had a suite with a private balcony and no reports or responsibilities at all.

It was going to be glorious.

Her husband frowned.

Kenzie gave her dad a side hug. "It's okay, Dad. You'll be up here all the time. You can sneak in. I'll get you a key."

Ian snorted and hugged her. "Will you now? And when is that? I thought you and Ben were going on assignment. You know he's been the shittiest employee. The only one who's as bad as you. Half the time you two are off on some classified mission, and I'm paying all the bills."

"Uh, that's my job now." Kala was in what she liked to call her big-girl uniform. Since she'd left the Agency and taken over the company, she started wearing the corporate equivalent of tactical wear. Black slacks, a crisp shirt, and some kind of blazer. But her hair…was still a glorious pink. Like her twin's. "And they're both fired. I don't think we should keep paying for Agency upkeep."

"Like you can fire me." Kenzie obviously wasn't worried. "You like going with me every now and then. We just got a call, and we're supposed to hop over to Macao to catch an international arms dealer at a celebrity poker event. I can get a contractor rate."

Kala frowned. "Damn it. Cady has the league championship game next week. Maybe I could send Coop and take Zach with me. Devi won't mind."

"Oh, they will all mind. You're stuck. You decided to have kids," her husband pointed out. "Your sister was smart."

Kenzie grinned. "We're happy being everyone's auntie and uncle for now. Who also travel the globe solving international security issues. Now we need to get to that cake because TJ is hovering, and he's not the only one."

"Little Boomer can only be held off for so long," Kala said with a sigh. "I'm still not sure how that kid came out with none of Lou's genes. He's all TJ. Hey, Alex, do not use that as a weapon." Kala sighed. "And that one is too much like me."

She ran into the kids club to save the day, her twin following along because it looked like Tash and Dare's youngest was going to try her hand at climbing the bookshelves.

Charlotte leaned against her husband, so grateful for all the years they'd had and those that were left to come.

"We did good, baby," Ian whispered.

"Hey, let's get some cake and get this party started." Alex McKay was dressed for the trip. He already had a Cuban shirt on and casual slacks. "If we hang around too long, they'll try to put us back to work, and that's the last thing I want."

Eve was beside him. "Yes, Ben already asked if I would give him some advice on how to approach the new bad guy he and Kenz are hunting. I told him to call my daughter. That's her job now. Mine is to find the best beach in St. John's. And we need to talk about Christmas. Avery wants to do a Christmas market cruise. Theo and Erin are in, but I've had to promise Boomer the best buffet because you know he gets seasick."

Ian took her hand in his and started for the conference room where their retirement party was set up. "That's because Serena moneybags had us on a small yacht. The big cruise ship you can barely feel it. And I don't think he's allowed on a yacht anymore. No chef will feed him. I've never seen a grown man cry like that."

"Only because you didn't see the poor stewardess who tried to unpack Erin's bags. You would think she'd never seen a gun before," Eve said.

They were going to be menaces. And it would be the best time.

They had done good. So good.

"Are you ready?" Ian asked, opening the door.

Ready to spend her golden years with the man of her dreams? Ready to live out some more fantasies with him? Ready to watch her children and grandchildren thrive?

"I am." She tilted her chin up and was rewarded with a kiss.

She was ready for all of it.

* * * *

Vivian McKay and the London crew will return in Big Girls Don't Spy, coming September 22, 2026.

Author's Note

I'm often asked by generous readers how they can help get the word out about a book they enjoyed. There are so many ways to help an author you like. Leave a review. If your e-reader allows you to lend a book to a friend, please share it. Go to Goodreads and connect with others. Recommend the books you love because stories are meant to be shared. Thank you so much for reading this book and for supporting all the authors you love!

Big Girls Don't Spy

Masters and Mercenaries: Global Domination
By Lexi Blake
Coming September 22, 2026

Vivian McKay loved her life in the States, but she's finding a freedom in London she can't deny. She's studying and working with a mentor at McKay-Taggart and Knight. It's exciting and fills something inside her, especially the covert ops work with MI6. She's learning the art of espionage and intelligence work but from the safe confines of a comfy desk.

Until a mission goes wrong and she finds herself in the middle of a dangerous game she has no idea how to play.

Malcolm Mays spent a lot of time getting shot at in various parts of the world as a member of British Special Forces. After being forced to retire due to injuries, he signs on at McKay-Taggart and Knight. It's a job for now while he finds a way to get back to where he belongs. He'll make some money, heal and decide on how to spend the rest of his life. What he didn't count on was meeting Vivian. She's too young for him. Not merely in age but in experience. And yet he can't stop thinking about her.

When Vivian's life is threatened, Malcolm finds himself at a crossroads that could lead to happiness or the greatest danger he's ever encountered.

About Lexi Blake

New York Times bestselling author Lexi Blake lives in North Texas with her husband and three kids. Since starting her publishing journey in 2010, she's sold over three million copies of her books. She began writing at a young age, concentrating on plays and journalism. It wasn't until she started writing romance that she found success. She likes to find humor in the strangest places and believes in happy endings.

Connect with Lexi online:

Facebook: Lexi Blake
Twitter: authorlexiblake
Website: www.LexiBlake.net
Instagram: authorlexiblake/

Sign up for Lexi's free newsletter.

www.ingramcontent.com/pod-product-compliance
Lightning Source LLC
LaVergne TN
LVHW041105080826
845145LV00007B/1692